Alex unscrewed the tip of the umbrella with delicate fingers. Today's task called for something fast-acting. Alex had selected hydrocyanic acid—cyanide. Alex positioned the tiny pellet with great care. There were certain mistakes it didn't do to make.

"How about restaurants?" Emma Fronczek said as Alex emerged from the bathroom. "Does the trip cover my meals?"

"Oh, yes," Alex said, standing behind Emma and jabbing her lightly between the shoulder blades with the tip of the umbrella.

Emma said nothing. She merely snapped upward, every muscle in her body tensed, bending her nearly backward in her chair. Then she fell forward, hard, on the coffee table, making a bit more noise than Alex cared for.

The old woman slid off the table to the floor, scattering magazines about the worn carpeting and rolling over on her back as she hit. Her eyes bulged lightly, and her mouth worked for a few seconds as her face turned a vivid pink.

Alex stood over Emma Fronczek, watching her closely. The old woman was dead in less than ten seconds, staring sightlessly at Alex, her mouth torn open in a silent scream of horror . . .

ACTION ADVENTURE

SILENT WARRIORS (1675, $3.95)
by Richard P. Henrick
The Red Star, Russia's newest, most technologically advanced submarine, outclasses anything in the U.S. fleet. But when the captain opens his sealed orders 24 hours early, he's staggered to read that he's to spearhead a massive nuclear first strike against the Americans!

THE PHOENIX ODYSSEY (1789, $3.95)
by Richard P. Henrick
All communications to the USS *Phoenix* suddenly and mysteriously vanish. Even the urgent message from the president cancelling the War Alert is not received. In six short hours the *Phoenix* will unleash its nuclear arsenal against the Russian mainland.

COUNTERFORCE (2013, $3.95)
Richard P. Henrick
In the silent deep, the chase is on to save a world from destruction. A single Russian Sub moves on a silent and sinister course for American shores. The men aboard the U.S.S. *Triton* must search for and destroy the Soviet killer Sub as an unsuspecting world races for the apocalypse.

EAGLE DOWN (1644, $3.75)
by William Mason
To western eyes, the Russian Bear appears to be in hibernation — but half a world away, a plot is unfolding that will unleash its awesome, deadly power. When the Russian Bear rises up, God help the Eagle.

DAGGER (1399, $3.50)
by William Mason
The President needs his help, but the CIA wants him dead. And for Dagger — war hero, survival expert, ladies man and mercenary extraordinaire — it will be a game played for keeps.

Available wherever paperbacks are sold, or order direct from the Publisher. Send cover price plus 50¢ per copy for mailing and handling to Zebra Books, Dept. 2379, 475 Park Avenue South, New York, N.Y. 10016. Residents of New York, New Jersey and Pennsylvania must include sales tax. DO NOT SEND CASH.

DANIEL LYNCH

DEATHLY PALE

ZEBRA BOOKS
KENSINGTON PUBLISHING CORP.

Also by Daniel Lynch:

Deadly Ernest
A Killing Frost

ZEBRA BOOKS

are published by

Kensington Publishing Corp.
475 Park Avenue South
New York, NY 10016

Copyright © 1988 by Daniel Lynch

First printing: June, 1988

Printed in the United States of America

To Judd, who had the idea

Before the beginning

"Please come up here, young lady," the substitute said.

Alma rolled her eyes. Just what she needed.

"Yes, ma'am," she said, going up to the desk.

"You're Miss Pale, I presume," the substitute said.

"Just like Dr. Livingston," Alma said.

"What?"

"I didn't say anything," Alma told her.

"Yes, you did."

Alma shook her head. "I didn't say a word."

The substitute was a wrinkled woman who could have been anywhere between forty and sixty. Alma couldn't judge age when people got that old.

"Are you being smart with me?" the substitute demanded.

"No, ma'am," Alma said. "I just thought of something I saw in an old movie. I didn't mean to say it out loud."

The substitute's eyes narrowed. She didn't know whether she was being had or not. Not that it made

7

much difference. Alma knew they'd been gunning for her.

"You report to detention after school," the substitute said.

"Yes, ma'am," Alma said, going back to her desk to start the school day. It was hardly an auspicious beginning. By day's end, however, things had grown measurably worse.

First, Alma came bopping into home room conspicuously late, which had become something of a habit with her. She'd overslept; it had been as simple as that. She'd just stayed up late the night before, watching Johnny Carson interview Joe Namath, the new quarterback for the New York Jets. Alma hadn't made up her mind about Johnny Carson. He'd only had the "Tonight Show" a few years, and while it might conceivably be true that he wasn't a patch on Jack Paar's ass, as Al liked to say, Alma couldn't remember Jack Paar well enough to make a reasoned judgment on the matter. Al might be right, but Alma didn't much care—didn't much care about Jack Paar or Al's opinion on that or any other topic.

Joe Namath was a different matter. Alma had made up her mind about Joe Namath, and she certainly would have cared about his opinion. He was gorgeous. And he was the toast of New York. Anything that pleased New York pleased Alma, too. After graduation, no matter what Al said, she was going to go to New York. She was going to become a star on Broadway.

If Julie Andrews could do it, so could Alma Pale. She knew she couldn't sing as well as Julie Andrews, but she knew also that she was prettier, even at seventeen. And she knew how much pretty counted. Alma had figured out about the time she was ten or so that pretty women had power that, in all but the most extreme cases, made up for talent. If they had the brains and guts to use it, that was. From looking at her mother's old pictures, Alma could tell that the woman had been pretty enough. But she hadn't known how to use it, and it hadn't done her any good as a result.

Alma could barely remember her mother, but she was reasonably sure that her mother's problem had been that she simply hadn't been too bright. That wasn't Alma's problem. Her problems were Al and St. Cloud, Minnesota, more or less in that order.

Alma's mother had married a man named Freddie Pale, from New Bedford, Massachusetts. Alma wasn't entirely clear on why Freddie Pale had come to Minnesota, but she knew that he'd stayed just long enough to get Alma's mother pregnant. Then he'd gone and gotten himself killed in Korea just after Alma was born. Alma's mother had bounded back. She'd married Al Swenson, who was a positive creep. A few years after that, with no particular warning, Alma's mother had awakened one morning and decided that she wasn't really married to Al Swenson at all, that she'd really married Johnny Desmond, the singer. When it became clear that nobody was about to talk her out of that particular vision of reality, Al had reacted with his usual brand of compassion. He'd slapped her into a state mental hospital, where she'd lost her looks along with her mind and eventually lost her life, too. They'd said she'd slipped in the shower

9

and cracked her head. Al had never believed it.

"One of those other nuts got her," Al said constantly. "Don't you doubt it."

Alma didn't doubt it, but it didn't much matter now. Besides, it wasn't going to happen to Alma. She wasn't going to hang around here long enough after graduation to let anything like that happen to her. Or anything like Al, either. Alma was extraordinarily pretty—she had her father's sultry Portuguese features and her mother's Swedish red-blond hair and light coloring—and she sang well enough. She could dance fairly well, too, and Julie Andrews couldn't dance a step. If she could, Alma had never seen it on television.

Last year, Alma had starred in the junior class production of *My Fair Lady,* and the woman who worked part time reviewing local theater for the *St. Cloud Times* had written that Alma Pale had been as good in that role as Julie Andrews had been on Broadway. And the reviewer had seen Julie in it live a few years before, as she had pointed out several times in the review.

That had been enough for Alma.

Before the junior play, she hadn't known what she was going to do after graduation. She wasn't going to work for Al, flipping burgers at his hot dog stand in scenic downtown St. Cloud, which was his plan. That much she had known. But she hadn't known precisely what she would do, what steps she could take to create the special life she'd vaguely planned for herself. She'd thought about becoming a model, knowing even as she pondered it that she was too tall, too busty and a touch too earthy in appearance to pull it off. The play had changed that—the play and the applause and the good

10

review and the attention it had all brought her. The play had iced it for Alma. She now knew what she was going to do and what she was going to become and where she was going to become it.

The "Tonight Show" came live out of New York, and for that reason alone Alma liked to watch it even if Johnny Carson wasn't a patch on Jack Paar's ass, which she personally doubted. Al was probably as full of shit on that as he was on so many other topics. And if she was late for school once in a while, so what? Alma didn't even need her diploma to become an actress on Broadway. She was just going through the motions now in school. She wasn't even sure why she bothered.

Alma had been forced to wait until the very end of the show before they brought out Namath, but it had been worth it. Namath had not only been cute, he'd been funny. He'd even gotten out of his chair to throw Carson a pass, which the slim, dark-haired host had dropped. It had been worth staying up for, even if she had yawned through the past half hour.

Then Alma had gone off to bed, thinking about what life would be like in New York after she graduated high school in a few more months, and she'd drifted off to sleep dreaming of applause and of somebody handing her roses during curtain calls.

And, of course, she'd slept right through the alarm. She'd missed the bus and run all the way to school, but she'd ended up with detention anyway, given her spotty attendance record. Detention in the cafeteria was where she was when the word came in about the shooting. A secretary from the main office came in and whispered in the ear of the teacher assigned to detention that week.

11

"Could I have your attention, please?" the detention teacher called out. He was a chubby, crew-cut man in his forties who taught wood shop and was shaped like a Bartlett pear.

Sixteen teenaged heads popped up, Alma's among them. She looked up from her copy of *Hawaii,* a huge new paperback novel she'd been struggling to read for months.

"The Rev. Martin Luther King, Jr., has been shot by an assassin in Memphis," the teacher said. "He's supposed to be in very critical condition. We'll keep you posted."

The news came as something of a surprise to Alma, although not as great a surprise as it would have if she hadn't been able to remember the time John F. Kennedy had been shot five years earlier. That, too, had taken place on a Friday, just like this one, only Alma had been in junior high school at the time, more worried about training bras than political murders. She remembered thinking, though: Who would do something like that? Who would have the guts to do something like that?

She'd been horrified at the Kennedy murder. Alma had liked Kennedy—at least as much as a twelve-year-old kid could like any politician. But she'd been awed that somebody could actually pull off something like that—actually killing a president. Martin Luther King meant little to her. In St. Cloud, Negroes were little more than a rumor, and he had never touched her in any way. It wasn't as though he was president or anything. He was just somebody you saw on the news every once in a while. But he was famous, and he was somebody important and somebody had managed to kill him, just like that guy—what's his name—had killed Kennedy.

It was all a little staggering to Alma, and she thought about it as she walked home through the center of town—past Al's tiny luncheonette that served downtown businessmen and merchants, past the row of stores that lined Main Street, past the Rialto Theater where *Bonnie and Clyde* was playing. When she got home Al was watching TV in the living room, a can of Bud in his hand and his big gut hanging over his pants. He was still in his white uniform, the one he always wore when he worked behind the counter. He was watching Walter Cronkite.

"They shot the head nigger," he told her. "You hear about that?"

Alma dropped her books on the kitchen table. "I heard in school."

"The guy who did it ought to get a medal," Al said. "They ought to put up a statue in his honor. How come you're getting home late? Where you been, anyway?"

"Detention."

Al turned in his chair. He was no more than ten feet away. There wasn't much room in the trailer. The whole thing wasn't more than fifty feet long and about twelve feet wide. The living room, where Al was sitting watching TV, and the kitchen, where Alma was digging through the refrigerator, were actually one big room. That, two small bedrooms and a surprisingly good-sized bath made up the entire structure, which sat in a trailer camp on the southern outskirts of St. Cloud, which Alma was fairly sure was the armpit of the globe.

"Detention what for?" he demanded.

Alma gazed up from the open refrigerator door and

gave him a bored look. "What do you care?"

"You're my daughter, that's what I care."

"Ha!" Alma said. Then she added, "I'm your stepdaughter, Al. You married my mother, but that doesn't make me your daughter."

Al frowned. That was always a worrisome sign. Alma knew he'd shut down the hot dog stand about three, as was his habit, and then come home to watch TV and drink beer, which was his great talent in life. When he frowned like that, it usually meant he'd drunk too much beer, and when he drank too much beer Al tended to get one of two ways: He got filled with fatherly authority or he got something worse. For a while, until a few years back, Alma hadn't been sure which she detested more. An incident during her sophomore year had helped her choose, but the truth was that neither mood did much for her.

"Don't worry about it," she told him, softening her tone. "I'll get some supper for you as soon as I change my clothes."

Al stood up. He was not a terribly big man, no more than a bloated middleweight, really. Al was only an inch or so taller than Alma, who was taller than she liked, and at one-eighty-five he was only sixty pounds heavier, and a good thirty pounds of that was in his gut. Still, he was nobody for her to fool with. Alma knew what he was capable of. She saw him rise and turned to go down the narrow hallway to her room.

"You stop right there," Al ordered.

Alma didn't like the sound of that. She kept on going—more slowly, to be sure—and she tried to loosen him up with a disarming quip.

"You sound like you've got a gun, Al," she said.

14

"I have got a goddamn gun," he said, his voice booming after her. "I got a goddamn gun in the top drawer of my dresser that I could blast your head off with, you smartass little bitch."

Alma made her room and closed the door behind her. She leaned against it and let loose a ragged sigh. He did have a gun, too, she knew. It was an unregistered .32-cal. Beretta automatic that had belonged to Alma's mother, before her mother had gone nuts. Alma had no idea where her mother had gotten it, and she had had—until just this past moment, when he had told her—only the vaguest idea of where Al kept it.

Handy information, Alma thought.

She changed her clothes slowly, waiting for him to calm down as he rooted around the other end of the trailer, mumbling to himself. Alma knew that if she could stay in here long enough, she probably could get out of making him dinner, because he'd be too drunk to eat by then.

Once in her shorts and a St. Cloud College sweatshirt she'd stolen from another girl in gym the year before, she flopped down on her narrow bed and dug through her pile of beauty magazines. She leaned back, listened to her stepfather open the refrigerator for another beer, and flipped slowly through the pages of *Glamour* magazine. She settled in on a story and pictorial spread on Miss America, winding down to the last months of her reign. Alma studied the color photos of Jane Anne Jayroe, Miss America, with great care. Then she shook her head.

Shit, Alma thought, I'm prettier than she is.

CHAPTER 1

In a way, Richie Wertowski was to blame.

Richie wasn't the only one to blame, to be sure. But it started with him, and none of it would ever have happened if Richie hadn't been such a jerk, which was his gift.

Being a jerk, Richie kicked off everything by chug-a-lugging five cans of Coors in less than one minute. This feat was prompted by a two-dollar bet and was accomplished during Richie's lunch break. He was pleased with his prowess, and the two bucks went for two more Coors, just for show. Consequently, when he got back to work, Richie was a little shaky.

He was more than a little shaky, actually. If the truth be told, Richie Wertowski was half in the bag. And, since lunch had consisted of nothing more than the aforementioned beers, a bacon cheeseburger and some particularly greasy fries, Richie's stomach began doing the hanky panky roughly forty minutes after he got back to his job at Bishko Pontiac, where he had worked ever since getting out of the U.S. Air Force seven years earlier. He was working on a yellow Sunbird coupe with a bum power steering system. Pulling the whole power steering unit was no picnic for starters, and the task became immeasurably less pleasant when Richie's stomach unexpectedly said, "Well, enough of this," and emptied itself into the engine compartment.

Richie was sent home by a furious service manager, who then called Ellen Berger and apologized profusely as he told her that her car wouldn't be ready until sometime tomorrow.

Which was how Ellen ended up riding with Arthur Rubin the following morning. She was catching a lift to her classes at Drexel Institute of Technology. If it hadn't been for Richie Wertowski and his jerky bet, she wouldn't have been caught dead with Arthur Rubin, who was renowned by his peers as one of the great nerds of the western world.

As if to prove this, Arthur pulled up in front of her house in Elkins Park in his brand-new Chrysler LeBaron GTS Turbo coupe with the computerized dashboard. He didn't get out of the car and go to the door, even though he was a few minutes early. Instead, he blasted on the horn. Arthur was into his cool mode that morning. Let her come to him; that was his plan. He wanted desperately to perform all manner of unnatural acts on Ellen Berger—would have given ten years of his life for the privilege, in fact—but Arthur's method of attracting women was to go into his cool mode, which went a long way toward explaining why he'd had only four dates in the preceding twelve months, each with a different woman who was not interested in an encore performance.

Ellen's father, reading the *Inquirer* and sipping tea in

the kitchen, heard the horn and frowned. He got up wearily went to the bottom of the stairs.

"Ellen," he called out. "Your ride's here."

"He's early," she called back. "I'm coming."

Ellen bounded down the stairs moments later, all flying black hair and bright brown eyes and so lovely that her father's heart almost broke when he saw her. He always thought of her as a child. When he dreamed good dreams, he tended to dream of her as a child. And every morning for years now, when he first saw her, he was startled to view this woman, with her woman's body and her intense, adult expression. All so fast, it had gone. So soon she would be gone too, out on her own, a big engineer, and he would be left with *bupkes*. No, worse. He would be left with *makkes*. Nothing, he would have. Only his nice memories.

But they would have to do when Ellen left. The nice memories he would settle for. Perhaps they would help him forget the other memories, the ones that still— after all these years—sometimes brought him to horrified wakefulness in his darkened bedroom upstairs, screaming in horror and disbelief.

She kissed him. "See you tonight."

"I won't be home tonight," he told her. "A banquet. I told you."

"I forgot."

He frowned. "Forgot. So, she forgot."

"You never forgot anything, Papa?" Ellen asked him, gathering her books.

"Nothing," he told her solemnly.

Ellen stuck out her tongue at him. "Love you," she said, scurrying out the door.

He looked after her going down the walk.

19

"Love you, too," he whispered, knowing she would receive the thought if not the words.

In the car, as he pulled out of the driveway, Arthur Rubin said, "You look nice this morning."

"Thank you," Ellen told him, wishing she had her own car back from the dealership. Arthur Rubin, of all people. A creep. A *schlump,* her father would call him. And so early in the morning, too.

Arthur Rubin had been pestering Ellen since the beginning of the semester. He was a tall young man, hopelessly awkward, the *schleppy* son of a banker and the victim of a particularly cruel case of zits that made his round, red face look vaguely like underdone pepperoni pizza. Arthur's idea of a good time seemed to consist of doing complex computations with his Apple II and detailing his adventures in voluminous detail to whoever would listen, which was usually nobody. His only virtue was that he lived precisely three blocks away and, like Ellen, had an 8:30 class on Mondays, Wednesdays, and Fridays. They were, thank God, different classes.

"How do you like the car?" he asked her.

Ellen, still half asleep, hadn't noticed. She looked around her and suddenly realized she wasn't in the Toyota Arthur usually drove. Instead, she was sitting on a plush, blue bucket seat, and the dashboard was blinking at her like the display screen of a video game.

"Nice," she said. "When did you get it?"

Arthur smiled. "Over the weekend. It turned a hundred miles just as I pulled in the driveway."

"Turbo?"

Arthur eyed her suspiciously. "What do you know about turbos?"

20

"I am a mechanical engineering major, Arthur," Ellen said.

Arthur nodded. "Yeah. I forgot."

Ellen frowned. "A Chrysler turbo, right?"

"Yeah, right."

Ellen leaned back in her seat. "Let's see now . . . A Chrysler turbo. Two-point-two litres, four cylinders, a hundred and forty-six horses with the turbocharger, right?"

Arthur eyed her suspiciously. "You got the owner's manual memorized or something?"

Ellen smiled slightly. Her expression was gloriously evil. "Girls shouldn't know about cars? Is that your point, Arthur?"

"No . . ."

"But we shouldn't, should we?"

"All right," he said. "How do you know the numbers?"

She shrugged carelessly. "It's part of a research paper I'm doing on engineering in the American auto industry."

"Want to see what it can do?" he said.

Just what she needed, Ellen thought. "Not really."

Arthur looked over at her. He was in his cool mode, after all. "Come on."

"Don't be so childish, please," Ellen said airily.

"Watch this," Arthur Rubin said to Ellen Berger.

He put the pedal to the floor.

A turbocharger is not a new device. It was developed more than a century ago to improve the performance of internal combustion engines. It works on a simple principle. The turbocharger sucks outside air into the engine to increase fuel ignition and thereby engine

21

power. A turbocharger takes a small engine and makes it behave like a big engine. In the case of Arthur Rubin's new car, the turbocharger prompted the engine to roar like a lion and—a fraction of a second later—to propel the small, sleek auto forward as though it had been launched by NASA.

Arthur's new Chrysler LeBaron GTS Turbo Coupe was equipped with a special handling package. It had special springs and shock absorbers and anti-sway bars front and rear. Unfortunately, it also had Arthur Rubin at the wheel. Not quite two blocks away, with the car going just under ninety miles per hour as Ellen Berger screamed in protest, a Ford Escort backed out of a driveway. Arthur's turbo-powered Chrysler slammed into it with a deafening crunch of metal and plastic, prompting an explosion of the Escort's gas tank. For several minutes, while neighbors peered out their windows in wonder, both cars burned freely, the oily smoke and flowery flames leaving permanent scars on the pavement. The thirty-two-year-old woman in the Escort had died instantly from the impact of the crash. Since the collision had pinned both of them behind the dashboard and the turbo-charged engine had lodged against their shattered legs, the deaths of Arthur Rubin and Ellen Berger occurred soon after.

Which, when you think about it, was an incident that never would have taken place if Richie Wertowski hadn't been such a jerk.

CHAPTER 2

Beverly Kavanaugh frowned with indecision.

"What do you recommend?" she asked finally.

Murphy said, "There's only one thing to have here on Fridays. I always get the bouillabaisse, with shrimp cocktail for starters. They don't have the bouillabaisse any other day. And you have to have it at lunch. By dinnertime, all the good chunks of lobster and crab are gone, and it's mostly broth. Good broth, though."

Beverly snapped her menu shut. "Make that two," she told the waiter.

"Fine choice, ma'am," the waiter said, and scurried off.

Actually, the waiter didn't have to travel far. The kitchen at Old Original Bookbinders was right off the small, richly paneled dining room—the place where the regulars sat while the tourists occupied the big dining rooms on either side. Along one wall of the small room was an ornate old bar. Hanging over the booths were portraits of American presidents—hence the room's name, the Presidents' Room. Each table was covered with a crisp red cloth, in the center of which rested a container of fiery horseradish and a thick glass container of hard oyster crackers the size of golf balls.

Murphy reached out and took a cracker. He bit it in half, swallowing one and then topping the other with a huge dab of horseradish before popping it into his mouth after the first.

Beverly made a face. "Doesn't that stuff burn your mouth?"

"This Commie booze protects mucous membrane," Murphy announced, washing down the cracker and horseradish with a drink that was mostly vodka but also contained enough tomato juice and blazing spices to pass muster as a Bloody Mary. Murphy drank Bloody Marys only here, in his favorite restaurant, and then only on Fridays with bouillabaisse. He had a natural affinity for bourbon on all other occasions—sometimes even at breakfast, if his mood was right.

"So," he said as four giant shrimp arrived in cocktail sauce, "how are you doing?"

Beverly Kavanaugh shook her head wearily and began to eat. "You don't want to know."

Beverly was a tall, pretty, big-boned blond woman who had turned thirty-six at precisely 10:18 that morning. Two days earlier, when she had called Murphy and suggested lunch he had insisted that they wait until Friday, so he could buy and make the meal a birthday present. He had gotten her nothing the year before. Of course, she had no longer worked for him at that point. She had been in the secretarial pool at the district attorney's office, and Murphy had been down the street trying to make ends meet. This year Murphy was somewhat more flush. Besides, he could always

24

write off the lunch on his income tax form. With Murphy, sentimentality was limited to clearly defined boundaries.

"That bad, eh?" he said, smiling through his moustache and lighting his twenty-first Camel of the day. "I thought you told me once that you'd voted for Fletcher."

"I did. My mistake."

"Yours and a quarter million other people's. It's amazing what a good barber and a decent dentist can do for *putzes* in politics."

"Did you vote for him?"

"I never vote for any of them," Murphy told her. "It only encourages them."

Beverly Kavanaugh smiled. Murphy had always managed to make her do that. "You don't vote ever," she asked, "not even for president?"

He shook his head, the thick gray hair mussing slightly as he did. "I think the last guy I bothered to vote for was Frank Rizzo, when he got elected mayor the second time. As I look back on it, he probably wasn't much of a mayor—assuming anybody could be—but he was terrific theater. Besides, he'd been a cop for twenty-eight years, and I was a cop at the time, so for him I made an exception."

"Do you like being a lawyer?" Beverly asked him.

Murphy sat back and pondered the question. He folded his hands over his ample belly and drew thoughtfully on his Camel. "Like it better than what? That's the question. Do I like it better than I liked being a detective lieutenant? Most of the time, I guess. The work is duller, but it's safer, and I was getting a little too creaky to keep on busting kids a third my age. You can get hurt that way."

"You got hurt practicing law," she pointed out.

Murphy shrugged. "That wouldn't have happened if I hadn't been a cop first. Rhino Frost would never have bothered Frank Murphy the lawyer if Frank Murphy the cop hadn't sent him up all those years before. Anyway, all I got was banged up a little. And as much as I hate the newspaper and TV people, I've got to admit that all the publicity ended up helping my law practice. If you want the truth, I was just about starving when that little incident took place. Now it seems to be going okay. Better than being the honorable Fletcher Lake's chief investigator, anyway. Christ, anything is better than that was."

Beverly sipped her white wine. "You seemed to be having a fairly good time up until near the end there."

"Well," Murphy said, polishing off the Bloody Mary and motioning for another one, "that's because I spiked my morning coffee. It was the only way I could stand that job. Passing the bar at nearly forty-five and going into private practice was scary, but the thought of working for Fletcher until retirement scared me more."

"You ought to run for DA, Frank," Beverly said seriously. "You'd make a good prosecutor."

Murphy laughed aloud. "Toddman is the guy who ought to run. I'm not the politician type."

"You're honest."

"That's what I said. You better eat up. The bouillabaisse is on its way."

Beverly sat back in her chair. "I'm not hungry. I have too many things on my mind to put much on my stomach."

Murphy leaned forward. This woman had been

more than his secretary in the DA's office. She'd been his friend. During the period immediately after Murphy's wife had thrown him out and driven him into a deep, dark funk, Beverly had always cheered him when he came to work at a job he'd found increasingly oppressive. She'd always had a smile, a joke, a juicy piece of gossip. Beverly had always done her best to perk him up. She'd even covered for him on the two occasions when he'd come back from lunch conspicuously drunk. Murphy's drinking had been different during that period—a darker, more dangerous enterprise than it was now, when it was merely Olympian in magnitude. Murphy felt he owed Beverly Kavanaugh.

"Is there anything I can do to help?" he asked.

"I don't know," she said, shaking her head. "I'm looking for some advice, I suppose. That's why I called you. You always seemed to be full of advice for people, Frank."

"Yeah," he said. "Bad examples seem to specialize in giving advice. So, what kind of advice are you after?"

The waiter brought the bouillabaisse. Murphy laced his liberally with sherry and piled a mountain of oyster crackers into the concoction. He loved this stuff. If it wasn't better than sex, it was at least somewhat more dependable.

"Brian and I split up last year," Beverly said, "just after you left the DA's office."

"I didn't know that. I'm sorry to hear it."

"So was I. He just came home from work one night with a separation agreement and said he wanted me to sign it. At first I was shocked. Then I got mad. I said, 'You son of a bitch. You want out of this marriage. Fine.'"

Murphy frowned. "And you signed it?"

"I signed it."

Murphy sat back and sighed. "Beverly, you work in an office full of assistant district attorneys. It didn't occur to you to get any legal advice first? You could have shown the agreement to Toddman, at least, and gotten his thoughts on it before you signed anything."

"Paul's too busy for me to bother the first assistant DA with something personal like this. And I've seen enough legal documents to make sense out of it."

Murphy lit another Camel. "How badly are you hurting?"

"For money? I'm not. The terms were very good. Brian does very, very well. And he was giving me a good share of it for maintenance. I was just so damn mad that I signed it and told him to get the hell out. That's what he wanted, and at that point it's what I wanted, too. I still do, actually. The marriage is over, Frank. Brian has never been what anybody might regard as a paragon of marital virtue, not since the first few years. I wasn't born blind. It hurt me a lot at first, but then after Judy was born I decided to just let it go as long as he didn't embarrass me. And he didn't. We've been married sixteen years, and he was always discreet about his women. Frankly, after a while I didn't much care—just as long as Judy didn't get hurt. Well, this hurt her. And now what he has in mind will hurt her more."

Murphy ate and smoked while he listened. "Which is what?"

"He told me last month that he wants a divorce. He wants to remarry. Judy is beside herself. You know we've got her in a private school out in Devon. Early on, it became clear that she was too high-strung for

28

public school. Since Brian moved out, she's been boarding there. I thought it would be better than having her spend her nights in a house where her father was so conspicuously no longer in residence. Judy was so obviously affected when this business about the final decree and the remarriage came up that the principal asked a psychologist to talk to her. He said she's so worked up about this that he's afraid she might harm herself. You know, with all this business over teenage suicide . . . well, it just scares the hell out of me. Judy's always been so emotional. And she just idolizes Brian. She's wild about him, no matter what he does."

"So you don't want the divorce to go through?"

She shook her head. "I don't care about the divorce. But I do care about the new marriage. Judy's used to the idea now that we aren't really married anymore. A final decree won't make that much difference. But if he gets married again, that's a different matter entirely. Judy seems to be clinging to this hopeless dream that Brian and I will get back together again, and a new marriage will shatter that fantasy in a big hurry. It'll get shattered anyway, eventually, but I want that to happen when she's older and more emotionally stable. I'm really terrified of what she'll do if Brian goes through with this."

"Have you told any of this to Brian?" Murphy asked.

Beverly sighed, and her lips tightened. "He doesn't believe me. He thinks this is some desperate ploy on my part to hold on to him, which—believe me—is the furthest thing from my mind. And Judy's always on her best behavior with him. She wants so much to please him. She won't raise the topic in front of him. Basically, he just doesn't believe me. He refuses to."

"Have you talked to the woman involved?"

Beverly Kavanaugh nodded. "I tried. No luck."

"What's she like?"

Beverly smiled. It was not a pleasant smile. "Young. She might be thirty, but I don't think so. Very pretty. Big eyes. Big boobs."

"A bimbo type?"

"Oh, no. She's very bright, very smooth. She knows a good thing when she sees it. Brian has been doing very well in real estate since about the mid-seventies, ever since he put together a deal to develop an industrial park over in Pennsauken. Since then, the money has just been rolling in. The only reason I kept on working was because I like it. I could have quit years ago if I'd wanted to. Since the separation, Brian has bought a big farm out in Phoenixville. He wants to raise prize cattle. Imagine that. Brian grew up a block off Kensington and Allegheny, and now he thinks he's Ben Cartwright. He wants to be a gentleman farmer. It would be a joke if it wasn't so sad. He has delusions of grandeur."

"What's the woman's name?"

"Lynn Rice."

"How did Brian meet her?"

"She was the secretary in the real estate brokerage Brian bought the farm through. He took one look at her, and that was it. She says she's from California somewhere. She's been here around Philadelphia for a few years. Brian had her with him a few times when he picked up Judy at the school, and I met her when he brought her home once. I phoned Lynn the other night and tried to explain what's going on to her, but she wasn't buying. Here's this rich man who's gotten to that delicate stage of life—"

30

"I'm familiar with that," Murphy said.

"And she wants him and his money. That's her first goal. She'll worry about everything else—including my daughter—later. That is, if it's not too late for my daughter later."

Murphy stubbed out his Camel and finished off his bouillabaisse. Beverly hadn't touched hers, and two of her shrimp still protruded from the rim of her cocktail dish. Murphy eyed them longingly. Jesus, he loved the food here. People were starving in China, he knew.

"So," he said, "what can I do?"

"I don't know. I thought maybe you could give me some advice."

"You could contest the divorce. That would slow things down a bit."

"I've thought about that. The problem is that we've lived apart under the terms of an agreement for the past fourteen months or so. Contesting it would be pretty tough under those circumstances, wouldn't it?"

"Could be," Murphy conceded. "That's about the only thing I can think of, though."

Beverly Kavanaugh leaned across the table. "Frank, would you talk to Brian for me?"

Murphy held up his hands in helplessness. "I could talk to him. But what makes you think he'd listen to anything I'd say if he won't listen to you?"

"Brian has always had a lot of regard for you. When you finished law school at night while you were working as a detective, Brian was very impressed. He went to college nights just like you did, and he knows how tough that was. And then when you caught the Center City stomper a few years ago, and last year when all that stuff with Rhino Frost took place, Brian told me you were like some kind of movie hero. He respects you, Frank, he really does. You might be able to talk some sense into him."

Murphy thought about it. Then he said, "Look, if you think it might help, I'll talk to him. I'm sure it'll do no good at all, but—for you—I'll see what I can do."

Beverly Kavanaugh's pretty face beamed. "You're such a nice man," she said.

CHAPTER 3

After lunch, Murphy piled Beverly Kavanaugh into his huge and aging Oldsmobile Toronado and drove her back to the DA's office in city hall. After that, he piloted the great, lumbering car a few blocks down South Broad Street, moving slowly in a vain search for a parking spot on the street.

Normally, he would have walked to work that morning—as he did most mornings—and left the car in the street outside his brownstone apartment house a few blocks away. But he'd had an appearance to make that morning in Montgomery County Courthouse in suburban Norristown on behalf of a clumsy burglar and he'd had the luncheon with Beverly. So he'd used the car and now he could see a six-dollar parking bill staring him in the face. After circling the block for ten minutes, Murphy gave it up and parked in the garage next to the Fidelity Building. He took the elevator up to the small office he rented from another lawyer, Harold Warren, and found his current secretary, Esmeralda Bright, reading the *National Enquirer* at her desk. Esmeralda was a black woman in her mid-twenties so stunningly gorgeous that Murphy's heart tended to break into the mashed potato every time he saw her, unless he was profoundly preoccupied. She was married to a professional boxer, and that was sufficient incentive for Murphy to keep the relationship on a purely professional level. That and the difference in their ages. Murphy could maintain only the most detached sort of romantic interest for a woman too young to remember an event as historic as the first Cassius Clay-Sonny Liston fight.

"How can you read that crap?" he asked her.

"Phillip Michael Thomas is unhappy in his love life," she said. "I think that's important information."

"Enquiring minds want to know," Murphy agreed. "Do me a favor, get me a Brian Kavanaugh on the phone. He's at Empire Real Estate Corporation."

"Okay. There's a man waiting in the outer office to see you. His name is Berger. I made the appointment last week."

"Right," Murphy said, digging through his mail.

"And your wife called."

Murphy looked up. "Did she say about what?"

"No. Only that she wants you to get back to her."

"I'll do that first."

Murphy went into his office wondering what that was all about. His relationship with Mary Ellen was better now than it had been since years before their separation. He knew he was current with his payments. He dialed his old home phone number and caught Mary Ellen as she was going out the door.

"Patricia is coming in tonight," she said.

"I thought she was going to stay with some friend

34

over spring vacation," Murphy said. "When did all this change?"

"This morning, apparently. The friend has decided to go to Fort Lauderdale with a boy instead, so Patricia is going to spend spring break at home."

"And with a last minute decision like that, she'll be paying full tilt for air fare. Terrific."

"You're the one who got her her own credit card, Frank. Anyway, I'm tied up this weekend. Can you pick her up and keep her until Monday morning?"

Murphy was silent for a moment. "Well, you know I'd love to have her for the weekend. I'm going to have to listen to her complain about not having her own BMW like all her friends at that rich-bitch school, but I'll gladly put up with that. But I'm curious; what are your plans this weekend?"

"I have personal business," Mary Ellen said quietly.

"I see," Murphy said softly.

"Don't be childish about it, Frank. You see people. I see people. It's not as though this were a working marriage anymore. We're going to have to make this final one of these days, you know."

"I suppose. What time does she get in?"

"Her flight touches down at eight-fourteen at the U.S. Air terminal."

Murphy scribbled on a legal pad. "Flight number?"

"Seven twenty-eight."

"Got it. Have a nice time this weekend."

"Thank you," Mary Ellen said crisply. "I'll see you Monday morning."

Murphy hung up and sat there a moment, smoking and staring at the wall. He stood up, hung up the coat to his worn blue suit, grabbed his coffee cup and went

35

over to the bookcase. He moved aside his copy of *Conveyancing in Pennsylvania,* found his bottle of Jim Beam and poured himself a stiff drink. The liquor burned all the way down his throat, and he received it gratefully.

It was childish, Murphy knew. They hadn't lived together in more than two years, and he hadn't been totally without female companionship during that period. He'd even lived with a woman for several months, although there was no one in his life at the moment and had been no one since the previous summer, when he and Mary Ellen had enjoyed an unexpected fling that made it seem—for a while, at least—as though they might work out their difficulties. And now, this. The thought of Mary Ellen in bed with another man, of Mary Ellen doing with someone else what they had done together—

He swallowed the rest of the bourbon and replaced the bottle behind the law book. Murphy knew precisely how to deal with this. He wouldn't think about it. He'd try not to, anyway. He hit the intercom to Esmeralda.

"Get me that Kavanaugh guy, okay?"

Brian was on the line a moment later.

"How are you, Frank? Good to hear from you. It's been a while."

"Too long, Brian. What are you doing for lunch Monday?"

"Booked solid every day next week. Sorry. Let me check my book here for the week after next."

"Well," Murphy said, "how about breakfast tomorrow?"

"I'm out at my country place tomorrow. I've moved out of Center City, you know. I have a farm in Phoenixville."

"I can go out there," Murphy told him.

"Fine. About ten?"

"I'll be there. How do I get there."

Brian Kavanaugh gave Murphy directions, which Murphy scribbled on the legal pad. Then he hung up and hit the intercom again.

"Send in that guy who's out there," he said, his voice suddenly breaking.

"Are you all right?" Esmeralda said quickly.

"Fine, fine," Murphy responded in a hoarse voice. "Give me a minute or two, then send him in."

"Okay," Esmeralda said warily through the intercom.

Murphy lit another Camel and took several deep breaths. He thought about Patricia, now a freshman at Skidmore College in Upstate New York and the great joy of Frank Murphy's life. He thought about her as a child, how she'd grown into a stylish and elegant young woman, about the way she was going to college as opposed to the way he had gone—like a rich man's daughter instead of part-time nights. Murphy knew his old man, dead all these years, would be so proud of that. He thought about those things for a while, and when a smallish old man in an expensive suit came through his door he was fine.

Frank Murphy was just fine.

CHAPTER 4

"I know you," Murphy said slowly. "From where, that's the question."

The old man extended his hand, and Murphy took it.

"Good to see you again, Mr. Murphy," the old man said. "I'm Irving Berger."

Berger spoke with a thick European accent. And, as he spoke, it came back to Murphy. "The Caravelle," he said quietly.

Irving Berger nodded. "The Caravelle. That is correct. Your memory is very impressive."

"I remember the incident very well. How have you been all these years, Mr. Berger? I hope things are better for you."

Irving Berger smiled ruefully. "Better? Nothing gets better or worse. Things only change."

"What can I do for you?" Murphy said. This was a sad man, he knew, who had lived a sad life. Just what he needed at this particular moment.

Irving Berger sat back in his chair and produced a cigar. "May I?" he inquired.

"Please do," Murphy said, lighting another Camel. "We'd better enjoy these while we can, before the tobacco police come after us. That's coming, you know. They're like the leisure police. You get to be a certain age, and they come and make you go to Florida. That's a law now."

Berger smiled politely at the very small joke. He lit his cigar—an expensive one, Murphy noted—and drew deeply on it.

"I'm beyond the point in life where I worry about my health. In fact, that is why I am here."

A will, Murphy thought. "Your health is bad?"

"No, but I expect that soon it might be."

Murphy waited for a moment. Then Irving Berger said, "Let me come to the point. You remember me. You remember what happened."

"Yes."

"I saw his face, Mr. Murphy. I saw it very clearly. I can identify the man."

Murphy's eyes hardened. "If you saw him, why didn't you tell us then?"

"I was afraid."

"And now you're not? What's suddenly made you so brave, Mr. Berger? It's been ten years or more. You've had this on your mind for ten years and now, suddenly, you want to tell the truth? I'd have thought that you'd have wanted to do it then. It was, after all, your wife who was killed along with those two wise guys. And if you want to talk now, why come to me? I'm not on the force anymore. Go to the police. Go to the DA's office."

Irving Berger looked at the burning ash of his cigar. When he spoke, he spoke slowly. "I come to you because I feel you are a man I can trust. I felt that then,

39

so long ago, when my Sophie was murdered by that gangster. I wanted then to be a *tzaddik,* but I could not. Do you understand?"

"No," Murphy said.

"I wanted to do the right thing, to be a righteous man. But I could not. Not then."

"Why are you no longer afraid?" Murphy demanded.

"I was never afraid for me," Berger said, an edge creeping into his voice. "Look at this. Look!"

The old man pulled back his sleeve and put his arm across the desk. Murphy saw the numbers on the aged white flesh—pale now, but still visible after all these years.

"Treblinka," Berger said. "Four years, I was there. I was a boy, only. I saw them take my mother, my sisters. My sisters went to the ovens. My mother they shot. They burned her body on a barbecue, like a roast beef. They put the women on the bottom, the men on the top. The women, they burned better. No one knew why. The things I saw . . . Do you think I fear for myself after that? No, I feared for my daughter. She was a little girl. Sophie was gone. I could not bring her back. But Ellen, her I could protect. I knew what could happen. And so I did. I protected her by denying I had seen the face of her mother's murderer."

"And now?" Murphy said.

Berger was silent a long moment. Murphy thought he was groping for words, but when he spoke Murphy realized he'd been wrong. Berger had been groping for control. He managed it only because he was a man of incredible will and spirit. When the old man spoke his voice contained a depth of such deep despair that

Murphy thought he had never heard a sound so terrible.

"My Ellen is dead," Irving Berger said. "A car crash two weeks ago. She rode with this *shmendrick,* this boy she knew. They both died. We sat *shivah* for her. Then I thought a while, and now I am here. Now I can be a *tzaddik.* Now I can say what I saw."

Murphy leaned back in his swivel chair. His face was ashen behind his moustache. Finally, he said, "You should go to the DA."

Berger, fighting to control himself, shook his head. "No. You go for me. I do not trust the DA. This Mafia, they have their fingers everywhere. You go. You tell them that you have a witness to this thing so many years ago. Do not tell them who it is. Find out their reaction. Then come back to me, and we talk some more. If I am to do this thing, it must be done right. I must not fail. Sophie must rest in peace, and if I do this badly—if I am killed before I can speak in a courtroom—then all this will have been for nothing."

"I still don't understand why you came to me," Murphy said.

"Because I liked you then. You seemed like a good man. Maybe you still are a good man. You will be my lawyer. I will pay you."

"I won't take a fee for something like this," Murphy said.

"Yes. You have a living to make. You take a fee. I have the money. What am I going to do with it now, anyway? Besides, if you are my lawyer—if I pay you— then I can tell you things and no one can make you tell them."

"Lawyer-client, you mean?"

41

"Exactly."

Murphy thought about it. You could say no to a good many things in life, he supposed. But how could anybody say no to this?

"Fine," he said. "You're my client. Now, describe for me the face you saw."

Berger looked around the office. "Do you have today's newspaper here?"

"Which one."

"The *Daily News*."

Murphy hit the intercom. "Esmeralda, get me a copy of today's *Daily News* right away."

She came in a moment later, all lushness and efficiency, and dropped the paper on Murphy's desk. Berger picked it up and leafed through it as she left the office and closed the door behind her.

"Here," Berger said. "This is the man."

He turned the paper over and handed it to Murphy, tapping a photograph with his finger. Murphy studied the photo. Then he looked up.

"Mr. Berger," he said, "the first assistant DA is going to think he's died and gone to heaven."

"Major Crimes."

"Lieutenant Wilder, please."

"Who's calling?"

"Tell him it's Frank Murphy."

A moment later: "How's it hanging, my man?"

"Limp, mostly. How would you like to meet me in Toddman's office in, say, twenty minutes?"

"About what?"

"The Santamucci murders."

"The what?"

"You don't remember?" Murphy demanded. "Think, for Christ's sake."

"You mean the mob killing in that diner up in the Northeast? Shit, man. That was years ago."

"There's no statute of limitations on murder, Jim. And I've got a big break in the case."

"What kind of break?"

"An eyewitness. He can identify the killer."

"Who'd he finger?"

"Meet me in Toddman's office and find out."

"Just can't stop playing cops and robbers, can you?" Wilder chuckled.

"It's in my bloodstream."

"Then it must have liquor on its breath," Wilder said.

Paul Toddman had been born with a sad expression. As he had grown older and seen more of the seamy side of life than most, the expression had grown more pronounced. It had, in fact, become positively mournful, as though Toddman were carrying the world's burdens on his slumping shoulders. Now, in his early fifties and his face a mass of thick folds beneath dark, somewhat bulging eyes, the despairing expression was his most outstanding feature. It masked the toughest of personalities.

"So?" he said to Murphy. "What's the big fucking deal?"

The office of Philadelphia's first assistant district attorney was modest, smaller even than Murphy's sublet space down the street. Its one virtue was that it occupied an outside wall in Philadelphia's baroque city

43

hall and featured a large window that looked out over the city. Toddman had placed his battered, city-issue desk directly in front of the window so he could, at his whim, spin around in his high-backed leather swivel chair and stare out at the mass of humanity he was charged with both protecting and prosecuting, depending upon their proclivities. Today, as he was pondering a trip with his wife to Atlantic City where they would spend the weekend losing his paycheck in the casinos— Toddman's favorite form of recreation—he had his back to Murphy, staring out over East Market Street. Toddman virtually never faced into his office on Friday afternoons, instead always looking out over the city he planned to flee until Monday morning. It was a habit of his, and it irritated Murphy.

"Turn around and pay attention to us and I'll tell you," Murphy said.

Toddman swung the chair around and glared at Murphy and Wilder. "So tell," he said.

Wilder coughed slightly. He was a smallish, trim black man with too little hair on his head and a neat moustache he wore as compensation. "Do you remember Johnny Santamucci, Paul?"

Toddman nodded. "Mobster."

"Do you remember the details of his murder?"

Toddman shrugged. "He got blown away in some restaurant, didn't he? That was what? Eight years ago?"

"Not quite eleven years ago," Murphy said. "Jimmy and I were working as a team out of Major Crimes. Santamucci was the underboss of the Lucelli family at the time. Gambling was just coming into Atlantic City in a big way then, and everybody knew that the Lucellis were looking for a way to get involved. They were

44

negotiating with the national commission for a piece. The idea was that Atlantic City was to become another Vegas, an open city ruled by the national commission and with pieces handed out to the various big families from across the country. The problem was—at least this was the way we had it from our snitches—that Carlo Lucelli had always opposed the drug traffic. He'd do gambling and whores, and he had big union muscle. But he didn't like dope because the money was so big he was afraid he couldn't control his people. He was afraid he couldn't keep them from freelancing."

"Which," Wilder pointed out, "would screw up discipline within the family. Carlo was already having trouble with that. These new wise guys aren't like the old wise guys. The old guys are always talking about honor and friendship and respect and shit like that, and the new guys have got no respect for anybody."

"Like my kids," Toddman noted.

"Like everybody's kids," Murphy said. "The problem was that even though Carlo sat on the national commission and was supposedly in line for a big piece of Atlantic City—since it was in his own backyard—he was becoming increasingly viewed as a weak boss. The commission wanted the organization to control the drug trade in Philadelphia, and it didn't. Almost all of it was in the hands of black hoods working freelance. And the commission decided to twist Carlo's arm by cutting him out of the Atlantic City action. Carlo was pissed, but he wouldn't budge."

Toddman lit one of the enormous cigars he favored. Beaconsfield Rounds, they were called. Murphy thought the cigar looked like a fungo bat. "So?"

"Look, Paul," Wilder said. "Santamucci was Carlo's

right-hand man, and the rumor was that he and some of the other wise guys were planning some kind of coup. They wanted the drug money, and they sure as hell didn't want to get cut out of Atlantic City. The Atlantic City business wasn't just the money. It was pride. It would have been a national embarrassment to the Lucelli family if every other family in the country got a piece of the action there and the family that supposedly controlled the territory was frozen out."

Toddman frowned. "I remember hearing some of this stuff at the time, but not in this kind of detail. Where'd you guys get all this?"

Murphy shrugged. "Snitches."

"Bullshit," Toddman said flatly.

Wilder and Murphy exchanged glances. "All right," Murphy said. "So maybe we tapped a phone or two."

"Without court orders?" Toddman asked.

"That's why we never told the DA's office. It was all illegal evidence. You could never use it. We only did it so we could use whatever we got as a guide to find stuff that might be admissible. As it turned out, all we got were the tapes and some stuff from snitches, but we never got anything you could use against anybody."

"I really don't want to hear this," Toddman said, and not pleasantly. "I truly do not want to hear about any shit that was picked up illegally. You guys are all the same, aren't you? You know you're not supposed to pull this stuff. And where are we going with all this, anyway? It's getting late, and I've got someplace to go this weekend."

"Look," Wilder said, "that was then. All the tapes have long since been recorded over. There's not a shred of evidence that anybody ever wiretapped anybody—

with or without a court order."

Murphy smiled. "Let me guess where you're going this weekend."

"Just get on with it," Toddman said, sucking on his cigar.

"All right," Murphy said. "So you've got this bad situation, and you've got some rebellion in the ranks against Carlo. So one night Santamucci goes into this diner on Bustleton Avenue in the Northeast. This is not his usual stomping grounds. It was a place called the Caravelle—one of those big diners with a bunch of dining rooms. Santamucci is sitting in a booth near the door with a guy who turns out to be somebody named Polacho from the Genovese family up in New York. They're having coffee about one in the morning on a week night, when business is slow, and a guy comes in with a pump-action shotgun and blows them both away. And, while he's at it, the guy with the shotgun takes the time to ice the woman who runs the diner, who's over by the cash register and, presumably, gets a look at him."

"So what?" Toddman said. "This is all eleven years ago."

Murphy leaned back in his chair. "So, after all these years, an eyewitness comes into my office this morning and gives me an ironclad identification of the guy with the shotgun. And guess who? It's Tommy Lucelli."

Toddman sat quietly for a moment, his mind working. "Your witness is sure?"

"Stone positive," Murphy said.

"Will he testify in open court?"

"Can't wait."

"Holy Jumping Christ," Toddman said slowly and

almost to himself. "We might be able to nail Tommy Lucelli. Who's your witness, Frank?"

Murphy lit a Camel. "Before we get to that, let's talk a bit first. The witness is my client. I'm concerned about his welfare."

"What welfare?" Toddman said. "He's a dead man. You know it and I know it. The best that's going to happen to him is a new identity somewhere in Nebraska, for Christ's sake, and that won't last forever. Odds are they'll find him."

"He knows that. All he really cares about is staying alive long enough to testify. He wants protection, and he doesn't trust the DA's office or the police department. He wants me to take personal control of his protection, and I'll do it only if I have available to me the resources of Lieutenant Wilder, here, and maybe a couple of his people. Nobody else is to know anything about the location of my witness—and that includes Fletcher Lake. Especially Fletcher. That schmuck is sixty-forty to blab out the address during one of his weekly circle jerks with the reporters."

"I can't do that," Toddman said.

Murphy stood up. "Well then, I guess we don't have a deal."

"He's my boss, Frank. He'll insist on knowing."

"I don't give a shit what he insists on knowing. That's your problem. I do care that my witness stays alive long enough to testify, because that's what my witness cares about."

"Who's the witness?" Toddman asked again.

Murphy shook his head. "Uh-uh. Your word first."

"Look, I've got to have statements from this guy. I've got to interview him, take depositions."

"I'll take care of all that for you. I'll do it on a contract basis. Put me on the case as a consultant. I'll charge my usual hourly rate, and the city can pay me by voucher. I got used to those city checks after all those years on the municipal payroll. I just like the way the computer spits them out."

"There's no way Fletcher would go for that. It'll never happen."

Murphy said, "You might be right. On the other hand, Fletcher's an ambitious man. In the dictionary, next to the word ambitious, they've got Fletcher's picture. He'll never have a bigger case. With Carlo dead, Tommy's been the head of the whole family for a couple of years now. Any DA who nails him can count on national publicity. Maybe this'll be the case that gets Fletcher into the senate or the governor's mansion and out of your hair. And if Fletcher goes, you might get your shot at DA, Paul."

"They'd never slate me as the candidate," Toddman said, obviously thinking that they might.

"Tell you what," Murphy said. "Suppose you and me and Fletcher have lunch Monday and talk it over. I'll present the offer if it makes you nervous."

Toddman frowned deeply. "Let me think about it over the weekend. I'll call you Monday morning."

"Good idea," Murphy said. "Talk it over with Muriel. Ask her how she'd like to be the DA's wife."

Toddman frowned deeply, thought for a moment, then turned his chair back to the window. After another moment, he said, "All right, I'll think about it, Frank. Now, why don't you two clear out of here and let me get some work done before quitting time? Don't let the door hit you in the ass on the way out, okay?"

"Have a nice weekend, Paul," Murphy said as they left.

Outside, as Murphy and Wilder moved down the huge city hall corridor with rose-colored marble walls and exposed pipes crisscrossing the ceiling high above, Wilder said, "You know, I can't believe you're actually going to try to make money out of something like this. Is that what it means when you get a law degree, Frank—that you just can't resist trying to squeeze blood out of every stone you come across?"

"That's the American way," Murphy explained to his friend.

Before the beginning

Alma came awake with hands on her.

"Whuh . . ." she said, eyes opening wide in the darkness of the tiny mobile home bedroom.

She felt the body in bed with her, the moist breath swirling around the flesh of her face, the hands clutching at her breasts through her T-shirt. She could smell him next to her, the beer breath and the beer sweat. She thought she was going crazy.

"No," Alma got out, beginning to struggle.

He said nothing. He merely continued to paw her, reaching with one thick hand toward the inside of her bare thighs. He was drunk, she knew. He'd been drunk when she'd gone to bed. She felt his gut pressing against her like some kind of hot, water-filled rubber bag. She pushed at him, feeling the heat of him, the hair on his body.

Alma was a big girl, and strong, and he was very drunk. She fought free, scrambling up and backing away into the shadows from the darker blackness of the bed, where he was wallowing, reaching up for her. Alma rubbed frantically at her flesh to dispel the feel of him, of his hands on her.

"No," Alma hissed at him in the darkness. "Never again. Never."

Then she was staggering out of the room, trying to run. But there was no room in the place to run, barely room to walk. And there was nowhere to run to, either. All her clothes were back in that little room—with him. She couldn't run out into the trailer park at night in just a T-shirt. She was trapped in this tin can with him. And he would be coming for her, lurching down the hallway calling her name. Or calling her mother's name. He'd done that before.

Alma got halfway down the hall, gasping for air and dizzy, her stomach churning on her. She had known he would come at her. She had just known he would do it.

"Alma," he called out from her bedroom. She heard him stagger to his feet in there. Alma's heart pounded. She leaned against the plastic wall and ran a hand through her lush hair as her eyes narrowed to slits. The fear in her was gone now. Rage had taken its place. She had handled him just now, and she could handle him whatever he tried. Alma was older now, bigger. She remembered what he had done before.

She also remembered the Beretta.

CHAPTER 5

As the first light of day began to filter through the drapes of Murphy's bedroom, Winston Churchill II stirred.

First, he opened one watery brown eye. His gaze bounced around the room, taking in the ragged piles of discarded socks and underwear, the stray shoes, the empty Chinese food containers, the McDonald's burger wrappers, the newspapers scattered here and there, the overflowing ashtray on the night table.

Winston Churchill snorted quietly.

Then he opened the other eye, lifted his enormous head, got to his feet at the foot of the bed and yawned, revealing a set of gleaming teeth that could rip off a human hand with only passing difficulty. The big bulldog stretched his thick, short-coupled body and turned toward Murphy, who was snoring peacefully at the head of the bed. Winston's tongue lolled over his lanternlike jaw. He walked rudely over Murphy's body to his head and then dragged his sopping tongue across the stubble of his master's face.

"Ya-a-a-ghhh!" Murphy said, coming awake with a weak flailing of arms.

That task complete, the dog leaped down to the littered floor. His stub of a tail whirred like a mixmaster. Murphy sat up in the covers, ran his hands over his face and glared down at the bulldog.

"Asshole," he muttered, rubbing his eyes with the heels of his hands.

Winston panted and slobbered in greeting.

Slowly—more slowly every morning, it seemed—Murphy swung his bare feet out of the bed and onto the wood parquet floor. In his shorts and T-shirt, he sat on the edge of the bed—yawning, stretching and scratching at his private parts. In the next breath, he was lighting his first Camel of the day, drawing the pungent smoke into his lungs, feeling his heartbeat speed instantly as the blessed nicotine hit his circulatory system. He glanced at the clock. Not quite seven. He glared again at the dog.

"Fuck you," he said with more vitality.

Winston did a little dance.

"Keep cool," Murphy told him.

Murphy stood and dug around the room until he had isolated a sweatshirt, a pair of baggy chino trousers, a pair of stiff, mismatched socks, and his worn sneakers. He dressed himself while the bulldog continued his dance, punctuating it with little snorts and whines.

"All right, all right," Murphy said.

He went into the bathroom and urinated. Then he came out with his battery-powered electric razor and entered the living room. Patricia was asleep on the sofa, a cascade of hair atop a blanket-covered form. The hair was taffy-colored now, several shades lighter than it had been at semester break. The sight of the new hair color when she had stepped down from the plane the previous night had shaken Murphy. He'd never realized how much Patricia truly resembled Mary Ellen, whose own hair was only a shade or two lighter than this color, which had come out of a bottle. Murphy's own hair was silver-gray, and had been for more than a decade, since his early thirties. It had been dark once, but he couldn't remember the precise shade.

He went over to the sofa, bent down and kissed the top of his daughter's head as he gently shook her awake.

"Time to get with it," he said softly. "We've got a breakfast date."

Patricia came awake easily and quickly, a skill Murphy had never mastered. She sat up and brushed a strand of the unfamiliar hair out of her eyes.

"I'm still full of pressed duck," she said, belching in ladylike fashion.

"You'll be hungry when we get there. I'm going to take him"—Murphy gestured toward the dog—"out for a minute, and that'll give you a chance to jump in the shower."

Murphy attached the leash to the dog's choke chain and, in a moment, was following him down Schuylkill Avenue, the razor rolling over his face, chewing at his pepper and salt beard. Winston was a young dog, not yet a year old, and he moved his short legs like pistons. Murphy had to hustle to keep up, and hustling early in the day was not one of his strong points. The first Winston Churchill, whom this new animal resembled both physically and in temperament, had been well into middle age when he'd died the previous summer. That

55

bulldog had been instinctively attuned to Murphy's rhythms and moods, and he'd always maintained a more modest pace in the morning. In a few more years, Murphy suspected, this one would slow down, too. But for now he was really only a pup, and Murphy envied him his energy.

He walked the dog briskly around the block, stopping at an all-night corner deli to pick up a cup of coffee, a copy of the *Philadelphia Inquirer* and four packs of Camels to get him through the day. He leafed through the sports section on his way back home, looking for news of the Phillies in spring training. Late winter and early spring were times of torment for Murphy. He had no interest in hockey and only passing interest in basketball. Were it not for the occasional televised clash of Hispanic featherweights on Sunday afternoons and the full-contact karate matches on ESPN, he would lose his mind after football season ended. Toddman, he knew, could content himself with following the racetracks from exotic places like Santa Anita and Hialeah, but for Murphy the period between late January until the beginning of baseball season represented sports famine.

When he arrived back at the apartment, Patricia was drying her bottled hair at the kitchen table.

"Are you going to leave it like that?" he asked her. "I can't get used to that color."

"I was thinking about putting a purple stripe through it," Patricia told him. "Maybe some green along the edges."

"Forget that punk crap," Murphy said, not entirely sure she was kidding. "I didn't even get used to hippies until a little while ago."

56

Murphy showered and, as he dressed in his littered bedroom, listened to Patricia in the kitchen humming a ditty by a group called Poison, which Murphy found particularly repelling. The song was something entitled "I Want Action." Murphy hoped she wasn't getting it. He wished he could discuss the matter with Mary Ellen, but he knew that Mary Ellen figured Murphy had given up all consultation rights on Patricia's upbringing the day he'd left home.

How did we screw it all up so badly, he wondered? He had married Mary Ellen just after he got out of the navy, as she was beginning her sophomore year in college. They had met on a blind date, and Murphy had fallen in love the moment she'd smiled at him. He'd never fallen out of love with her, either, even though she had a capacity to enrage him that was unmatched in any other human being. And he her, he supposed.

Patricia had never really recovered from the breakup of her parents' marriage. She still blamed Mary Ellen, even though Murphy knew it had been both their faults. Mary Ellen's sin had been neglect, a lack of interest. She had had her daughter and her job teaching junior high English in the suburbs and Murphy had been a cop. That had meant, for starters, rotten hours and only a moderate income. Then, in his effort to better himself, he'd spent years going to college and then to law school in his off-hours, effectively ignoring his family obligations during their most crucial period. He'd also never disciplined Patricia. That task had fallen to her mother, so it wasn't surprising that when the split had occurred Murphy had emerged as the hero in his daughter's eyes and Mary Ellen the villain. It wasn't at all fair, Murphy knew, but he liked it that way. He wanted the approval and affection of Patricia more than that of any other living creature on earth. Yet he knew that Patricia harbored the dream that her parents would someday bury the hatchet, that Murphy would abandon this little Center City apartment and move back home to the brick colonial he and Mary Ellen had occupied in the city's Mount Airy section.

So did Murphy, if the truth be told. He could just imagine how Patricia would react if Murphy suddenly decided to give up that dream, to move for a final divorce decree and marry another woman who would give him some placid companionship as he grew old. He remembered badly how Patricia had reacted to his brief fling with the woman who had moved in here with him. And, in thinking about that, he could well imagine Judy Kavanaugh's response to her father's upcoming marriage. Judy was several years younger than Patricia, and nowhere as strong and independent a personality.

Patricia was one of those people who would do whatever she had to do to get through life's hardships. She was like him that way—Mary Ellen, too, actually. But a weaker kid might be capable of doing something crazy. He understood Beverly's fears. And he understood, too, Brian Kavanaugh's desire to put his failed marriage behind him once and for all.

Murphy came out of the bedroom to find Patricia playing with the dog. She had him by the ears, shaking his head, and Winston was issuing blood-curdling growls that only an intimate would recognize as affectionate.

"Ready?" Murphy said.

Patricia stood up and smiled. "Let's haul ass."

"Class," Murphy told her. "I send you to Skidmore to have you come back here and talk about hauling ass."

"You've put on so much weight lately," Patricia told him, "that you'd have to make two trips."

Murphy grinned, despite himself. "Punk kid," he said.

All the way out to Phoenixville, Murphy's Toronado guzzled gas, which was its specialty. He'd bought the car second hand, and while it had high mileage it also had all the creature comforts Murphy had come to value in his middle age. As a young man, he'd favored hot cars. His first new car, purchased nearly twenty years ago off the showroom floor, had been a lime-green Plymouth Road Runner with a hemi-head engine roughly the size of a Volkswagen bug. It had ridden like a boxcar, but it could snap back your head if you just touched the gas pedal. The Toronado had neither the zip nor the sheer muscle of that car, but it did have power seats and windows, cruise control and a first-rate tape deck. Murphy played his "Frank Sinatra's Greatest Hits" tape while Patricia made gagging sounds that were startlingly realistic.

Finally, Murphy worked up the guts to ask the question that had been bugging him since the previous afternoon. "Who did your mother go away with this weekend?"

"A guy she met at the health club. He's into bodybuilding."

"Have you met him?"

"Yes."

"And?" Murphy said.

"And what?"

59

"What's he like?"

Patricia gazed thoughtfully at the Toronado's headliner. "Well, he looks a little like Burt Reynolds, only he's taller."

"Really? What's he do for a living?"

"He owns a Jaguar dealership in Lower Merion. He drives the sharpest car. It's really neat."

"Isn't that nice?" Murphy said dryly.

"She actually went away with Sheila Wellsley."

Murphy turned and looked at his daughter. "Sheila Wellsley? Where to?"

"They went antique hunting in New Hope."

Murphy frowned. He detested Sheila Wellsley. "That's almost as bad as Burt Reynolds in the Jag."

"Not quite, though," Patricia said.

"No," Murphy admitted. "Not quite."

"Will you put on some decent music, Daddy? Please? My brain is turning to jello listening to this stuff."

"Only for you," Murphy said, hitting the button for a station that had the capacity to make him physically ill.

Murphy followed the directions to Brian Kavanaugh's farm, which turned out to be a sprawling place composed of shining white barns, fenced-in pastures, and an imposing, two-story white house set well back off the road. Murphy pulled in the driveway and had plenty of room to park beside a Ford pickup, a silver BMW 318i, and a perfectly preserved Austin Healey 3000 in gleaming British racing green. Brian Kavanaugh came out to meet them, flanked by his daughter and a burly, balding man in his mid-thirties.

"Frank," he said, taking Murphy's hand, "you remember Judy. Say hello to Mr. Murphy."

"Hello," Judy said. She was a tall, large-eyed girl of

no more than fifteen. She even looked nervous, Murphy thought.

"I haven't seen you in a while now, Judy," Murphy said. "You're growing up fast. This is my daughter, Patricia. I don't think you two have met before."

"Hi," Patricia said.

"Hi," Judy said.

Kavanaugh gestured to the man at his side. "This is Mike Webster, my farm manager."

"How do you do," Webster said, sticking out a rough hand, which Murphy took.

"Well," Kavanaugh said, "everybody hungry?"

"I think I'll pass, Mr. Kavanaugh," Webster said. "I've got some errands, and then I've got to run into town. I'll catch something to eat there."

"Fine," Kavanaugh said. "How about you girls?"

"I'm still full of pressed duck from last night," Patricia said. "We went to Chinatown."

"I'll show you the farm if you like," Judy said to Patricia.

"Go ahead," Kavanaugh told them. "Enjoy yourselves. Well, Frank, I guess it's just you and me."

"Don't worry," Murphy said. "I'll eat enough for everybody."

The kitchen was large and airy. At the stove was a strikingly pretty woman in an apron that said "Good cookin' is good lovin'."

"Frank," Kavanaugh said, "I'd like you to meet my fiancée, Lynn Rice. Honey, Frank Murphy."

"Hello," Lynn Rice said. "Sit down, please. Breakfast will be ready in a minute. Orange juice?"

"Please," Murphy said. "And coffee."

The men sat at the kitchen table for a few moments

61

while Lynn Rice prepared a mountain of buttermilk pancakes, scrambled eggs, and ham. Murphy sipped his coffee while Kavanaugh talked about the delights of owning a farm. He was a big man, a touch taller than Murphy's six feet, and a few years younger. As he'd grown older, though, he'd begun to look a little like a larger version of that Canadian actor, Alan Thicke, Murphy noted to himself. Kavanaugh's grammar and syntax were fine, but he still spoke with the flat inflection of the Philadelphia streets. He told Murphy about how he had hunted a long time for this "hay-owse," for example. You can take the streets out of the boy, Murphy reflected . . .

When the food was placed before them, it became abundantly clear that Lynn Rice had no intention of leaving the men alone to talk. She sat down with her own cup of coffee and listened intently, saying nothing as Kavanaugh carried on one of the monologues that were so much a part of his character. Murphy often thought he'd never met as intense a man as Brian Kavanaugh.

He'd rarely, too, met a woman as pretty as Lynn Rice. Her hair was dark and cut short, and she was a tiny woman—barely five feet tall. But her eyes were huge and a startling blue, and her lips—like her figure—were full, firm and appealing. Murphy could understand this. Yes, he could understand it perfectly.

Finally, Murphy said, "You've probably guessed that I'm here at somebody's request."

"Oh, sure," Kavanaugh said. "Beverly asked you to come out here and talk me out of marrying Lynn. Right?"

"Well . . ." Murphy said, a trifle uncomfortably.

62

Lynn Rice said, "Don't mind me, Mr. Murphy—"

"Please, make it Frank."

"Frank, then. Don't let my presence for this talk make you uncomfortable. We're used to this. So far we've listened to similar speeches from the principal of Judy's school. Beverly had her call Brian, but I listened in on the extension. We had a call from Beverly's mother. Beverly has made several personal appearances on the same topic. So don't be bashful. It's always entertaining to watch somebody try to break us up. It seems that everybody in the world has joined forces to keep me and Brian from getting married. Only none of it will work. Will it, Brian?"

Kavanaugh laughed and took her hand. "She's right, Frank. We're going through with this. If there was ever anything in my life that was right, this is it. But, go ahead. Give it your best shot, anyway. And eat your breakfast. Lynn's a terrific cook—among her other attributes."

Murphy frowned deeply. He didn't like Lynn Rice. There was an edge to the woman.

"Look," he said finally, "all I can say—from what you're telling me—is what's already been said to you before. This marriage at this time is a bad thing for Judy. Don't you think you ought to take that into account?"

"And how do you know that?" Kavanaugh demanded.

"How do I know what?"

"How do you know about Judy? Have you spoken to her? Have you spoken to that quack they had examine her?"

"No," Murphy admitted. "I know what Beverly told

63

me, and she's been totally reliable as long as I've known her."

"Frank," Kavanaugh said pleasantly, "Judy is fine. I've talked to her about this. She isn't wildly enthusiastic about the idea, but she'll come to accept it. She'll be fine. Beverly is overly dramatizing this for her own reasons, whether she chooses to admit it or not. It's natural, and I don't blame her. But the simple fact is that I'm not in love with her anymore. I'm in love with somebody else, and I'm going to marry her. Judy will get used to that. Beverly is the one who can't."

Murphy finished his coffee. "Okay, I've done my bit. I hope you're right. She's your daughter, and you certainly know more about the way her mind works than I do. But I hope you're right, Brian. I truly do. Look, I've got to be heading back. I appreciate the hospitality."

"Come on, Frank," Kavanaugh said. "You just got here."

"That's right," Lynn Rice said. "You haven't even earned your money yet."

Murphy leaned back in the kitchen chair and gazed evenly at Lynn Rice. Murphy had practiced that gaze. In more than two decades as a cop, he'd gotten it down pat. But Lynn Rice never flinched under it. Tough little broad, Murphy said to himself.

"Miss Rice," he said quietly, "I came here as a friend, not as a lawyer. Beverly Kavanaugh is a solid, decent woman. And Brian is a good guy."

"I know that," Lynn Rice said quickly.

"I'm sure you do. What you may not know—or may not have the capacity to grasp—is that a good many people put themselves out not because there's money in it but because they're concerned about people who mean something to them."

Kavanaugh said, "Frank, Lynn didn't mean to offend you."

"Yes, she did," Murphy said, standing up. "You take care of yourself, Brian. And do yourself a favor. Just give some thought—at least passing consideration—to how you'd feel if your daughter decided to celebrate your wedding by hanging herself from the rod in her closet."

"Frank—"

"Just a little something to ponder," Murphy said, going out the back door.

Outside, Murphy found Mike Webster loading a manure spreader into the back of the Ford truck.

"Need a hand there?" Murphy said.

Webster, groaning under the weight of the machine, said, "I'd appreciate it."

Between the two of them, they got the bulky piece of equipment into the flatbed.

"Heavy mother," Webster said. "I'm supposed to go easy on the lifting. I had my back operated on a few years back. I appreciate the help."

"No sweat," Murphy said.

"You're a lawyer, aren't you?"

"Yeah. How'd you know that?"

"I remember your picture in the *Inquirer* last summer, when that ex-con went after you and you had that big flap with him up in the Poconos. That was something."

"Something I'd rather forget, if you want the truth. The son of a bitch nearly killed me. Where are the girls?"

"Down by the creek. Judy's showing your kid the farm. Judy can use the company, believe me."

"She doesn't get along all that well with the lovely Miss Rice, I take it."

"Hates her like poison. She loves the farm, though. So do I. Being out here in the country is pretty nice."

"I like the city, myself," Murphy said. "I only leave it when I have to—like today, to visit somebody. You can get hurt in places like this. A horse can kick you. A cow can bite you. I'll take civilization."

Webster laughed. "Say," he said, "did you ever hear the story about the city guy who bought the farm?"

Murphy listened with interest. "A joke?"

"Yeah," Webster said. "This guy from the city goes to visit a friend of his who just bought a farm. They get on a tractor and the farmer starts driving. And then the guy who came to visit notices that the farmer has a wooden leg. He says, 'Hey, how'd that happen?' and the farmer says, 'Oh, it happened last year. I got it caught in a threshing machine.' They drive on a bit farther, and the farmer gestures at something and the other guy notices that he has a hook where his hand used to be. So he says, 'How'd that happen?' And the farmer says, 'I cut it off a couple of years ago cutting firewood.' So they go on a while longer, and this wind kicks up. The guy who's visiting, he notices that both his eyes are watering from the wind, but only one of the farmer's eyes are watering. So he says, 'What happened to your eye?' And the farmer says, 'Well, I was out in the field last summer and I heard a sound in the sky. When I looked up, this crow shit right in my eye.' And the guy who's visiting says, 'That sounds pretty unpleasant, but it shouldn't cost you an eye.' And the farmer says, 'It

66

will if you put your hand up in a hurry to get the bird shit out of your eye and you forget you're wearing a hook.'"

Both men laughed, and as they did the girls came into sight. Murphy motioned to Patricia and she broke into a run. Patricia had been a track athlete in high school, and she ran like a deer. He watched her glide across the pasture. If he tried to run like that, he knew, he'd drop dead after fifty feet. She was at his side in only a few seconds, with Judy bringing up the rear.

"Time to go," Murphy said.

Patricia and Judy said their good-byes. As the Toronado pulled out the driveway, Murphy said, "Have a good time?"

"Okay."

"How'd you get along with Judy?"

"Okay."

"How did she strike you?" Murphy asked his daughter.

She looked over at him. "Would you ever get married again?"

He shrugged. "I don't know. Being married to your mother probably cured me of it, if you want the truth. What would you do if I did?"

"Not what she's going to do."

"What do you mean?" Murphy asked.

"She told me that if her father marries that woman he's living with she's going to kill herself."

CHAPTER 6

That night, for reasons he couldn't conceivably explain later, Murphy dreamed of his parents.

Murphy's dreams were vivid experiences, full of bright colors, pungent smells, and crisp sounds. He always remembered them when he awakened, although he never discussed them with anybody. If anything was personal, he figured, it was your dreams. Freud would have found Murphy a barren field.

Lately, most of his dreams had fallen into specific categories. He would dream of his past life with Mary Ellen and a much younger Patricia in the brick house in Mount Airy. He would dream of being a cop again, of the snug warmth of a patrol car on a winter night, listening to the chatter over the radio and to the chatter of Wilder in the seat beside him. Less often, he dreamed of his days in the navy. Even more rare, but vastly more gratifying, were his dreams of robust sexual encounters with Ann-Margret. Those dreams always left him in a fine mood for several hours after awakening.

It had been years since he'd dreamed of his mother and father, and the experience left him profoundly shaken when he awakened. He got up and went into the kitchen, tiptoeing past the sleeping Patricia. He heated water in his microwave oven for instant coffee, smoked a cigarette and puzzled over the dream. What could have prompted that, he wondered?

The dream had revolved around his family's Sunday morning ritual of attending mass. They would leave their modest rowhouse in the city's Fishtown section and ride the trolley to the church. Murphy's mother always wore one of her best two dresses—one every other Sunday—and his father always wore his only suit, the one he had eventually been buried in. Murphy had always viewed attendance at mass as one of life's great hardships, although it had always seemed enjoyable to his sister. After mass, the Murphys would go across the street to the drugstore where Murphy and his sister would have a Coke at the soda fountain while the old man dug through the Sunday papers, as if deciding which one to buy.

He had always bought both the *Inquirer* and the late, lamented *Bulletin*, the paper the family had home-delivered during the week. Then, on the way home on the trolley, Murphy would read the *Inquirer* comics and his sister would read the *Bulletin*'s. The old man would leaf through the sports sections of each paper. By the time they got home, the sections of the competing publications were mixed into one large, ragged heap, which the old man would tuck under his arm and carry into the living room.

Strange, the things you remember, Murphy thought. Stranger still to dream about it after all these years. He went over to the sofa and awakened Patricia.

"How would you like to go to mass today?" he asked her.

"You have cancer and you're dying," she guessed.

69

"You've got twenty minutes."

They drove to mass in Murphy's Toronado, and afterward he took her to breakfast at the Harvey House across South Broad Street from Murphy's office building. Murphy ate pancakes and bacon, which weren't prepared precisely the way his mother had made them, but it was close enough to keep the illusion alive for him. Afterward, Murphy bought a Sunday newspaper and they went back to the apartment. Patricia read while Murphy phoned Beverly Kavanaugh.

"I tried to get you last night," he said, "but I didn't get an answer."

"What time?"

"Ten or so."

"I was in the tub. I heard it ring, but it really was too much trouble to get up and go get it."

"I saw Brian."

"And?"

Murphy sighed into the phone. "I didn't have much luck, Beverly. The Rice woman has him fairly well under control."

"Well, forget it, then. I guess I'll have to contest the divorce and slow everything down."

"That's about the only thing I can think of," Murphy told her.

He spent the early portion of the afternoon playing poker for matches with Patricia. Murphy was a decent poker player, but Patricia—whom he'd taught the game—was considerably better. She had a sixth sense about what the cards would be; she knew percentages, and she could read his bluffs as though she had a mirror behind him.

"This is getting humiliating," he said finally.

"Do you really play this game for money with other

70

people?" Patricia asked.

"I win most of the time, too."

"How can a stranger get into that game?" Patricia inquired.

The phone rang. Murphy folded his cards.

"You look at those and you're dead," he told his daughter as he walked over to the phone on his desk along the inside wall. "Hello."

"Mr. Murphy?"

"This is Frank Murphy."

"Mr. Murphy, this is Mike Webster. You met me yesterday at Mr. Kavanaugh's farm."

"Hello, Mike. What can I do for you?"

"I'm sorry to bother you," Webster said, "but I don't know anybody else. I need a lawyer. I need one fast."

"What for?"

"I'm under arrest down at central police headquarters. This is my phone call."

"What's the charge?"

"I don't know yet."

"Well, what did you do?"

"I didn't do nothing."

"Then why are you in custody?"

"Because they found a body in the trunk of the car I was driving. I stopped on Spring Garden Street to get some gas, and I went into the trunk to get something and—"

"Wait a minute," Murphy said. "You said they found a body. A corpse?"

"Yeah."

"Whose?"

"Miss Rice's. I really need a lawyer, Mr. Murphy."

Murphy paused for a moment before he answered. Then he said, "Yeah, I'd say so."

71

CHAPTER 7

Murphy's first call, when he got off the phone with a shaken and only moderately coherent Mike Webster, was to Manny Strobel, bail bondsman extraordinaire.

"Yeah," Strobel said, the sound of the television set blaring in the background. "I got somebody at court tonight. I'm in business, Frank, or ain't you heard?"

"Yeah, I heard. And what a nice business you're in, too. Tell me, Manny, how does somebody grow up to be a bail bondsman? When I was a kid I wanted to be a Roy Rogers."

"The hell with Roy Rogers. I wanted to be Gene Autry."

"His horse wasn't as pretty," Murphy pointed out.

"He sure as shit was," Manny Strobel said defensively. "Champion was a hell of a lot prettier than Trigger. And who's got the baseball team, huh? Who almost won the American League pennant two years running? Not Roy Rogers, I can tell you. Besides, you got no right to say snotty things about bail bondsmen. We got the same patron saint as you guys."

"Who's that?" Murphy asked.

"Saint Nicholas," Strobel told him. "He's the patron saint of lawyers and money lenders. You're a lawyer, and I'm a money lender. We got the same dead guy watching over us."

"Where'd you learn so much about saints? I thought you were Jewish."

"I am Jewish," Manny Strobel said, "but in my business you pick up a few things. You know who else he's the patron saint of? Thieves, that's who."

Murphy thought about that, then he said, "Somehow, that all seems to fit."

"You Catholics with your saints," Manny Strobel said. "Praying to dead guys. Talk about crazy. Look, you just go into the courtroom and look for a young fat guy with thick glasses. He's going bald, and he's got a face like a schmuck with zits."

"That's your guy?"

"That's my son-in-law. My daughter, she thinks he's cute. For that I sent her to Penn. Go figure. Anyway, he'll take care of you if you can talk to me about the collateral this week."

"You're a man of rare charity, Manny."

"I'm in business," Manny Strobel explained.

Murphy hung up and turned to Patricia. "It may take me a while to get you home tonight. I've got to run over to night court for a client's arraignment. I'm going to try to get him bailed out."

Patricia's eyes sparkled. "Can I come, too?"

Murphy made a face. "Night court?"

"But I love that show."

"This won't be much like TV," Murphy told her. Then he said, "Well, not all that much. You won't like

73

it. You'd be better off waiting here watching TV. I'll be back."

"Please?"

"Patricia . . ." he began.

"Please, Daddy? Puh-leeeze?"

Murphy sighed wearily. "Get your coat, then."

They drove to City Hall, where Webster was to be arraigned. Murphy, always brave, parked on the sidewalk outside next to a cop car. On the way up the elevator to the fourth-floor courtroom where night court was being held that evening, Murphy explained what he knew about the case, which wasn't much. Patricia was startled to learn the identities of both the victim and the accused.

"That guy I met at the farm actually murdered that woman you had breakfast with?" she said in shock.

"Well, he says he didn't."

"But what if he did?"

"Then he's certainly going to get yelled at," Murphy told his daughter.

"Daddy, would you still defend him if he's guilty?"

"Sure."

"How could you defend a guilty man?"

Murphy shrugged. "Maybe he's guilty, but he's not guilty of what they're going to charge him with. I know that the DA's guys will go for murder. But maybe it was manslaughter. Maybe it was self-defense. Maybe it was just an accident. That's always a possibility, too. Just because somebody's charged with something doesn't mean he's guilty of what he's charged with."

"And what if he is guilty of what he's charged with? What then?"

"Then he's still entitled to an able lawyer. Guilty

people have rights, too."

"Rationalization," Patricia charged.

"The Constitution," Murphy countered.

"That won't fly, Daddy," she said. "He may be entitled to a lawyer, but that doesn't mean you have to be his lawyer."

"That rich-bitch college has really made you a smartmouth," Murphy said, eying her in annoyance.

Patricia smiled—fetchingly, too. "It's genetic."

The elevator creaked to a halt. Outside the courtroom, Patricia announced she was going to find a ladies' room.

"It's at the end of the hall," her father told her. "If it's anything like the men's room it's got roaches you could enter in a rodeo. I'll wait for you."

Murphy stood outside the courtroom smoking a Camel until Patricia came back down the hall. Then he stubbed it out. She'd been on his back for years now about the cigarettes, but lately her disapproval had taken the form of a distasteful expression that he found particularly annoying.

"You're right," she said. "The place is filthy."

"You'd think they might do a bit better with the women's rest room," Murphy observed. "You and your mother seem to spot dirt at the level of molecules."

"Hah," Patricia said. "If dirt bothered me that much I couldn't visit you. Your place is so filthy it could support agriculture."

"It's homey," Murphy told her.

In the courtroom, Murphy seated Patricia in the rear, between a black hooker and a white bum who'd found a warm spot to spend the night. Then Murphy spotted a chubby young man in an expensive suit. He was balding and wore a quarter-inch-thick coating of Clearasil over his pitted cheeks. Clearly, this was Manny Strobel's son-in-law. A schmuck with zits, Murphy thought. It fit.

"Frank Murphy," he said, extending his hand.

"Arnold Karansky," the younger man said, studying a sheaf of papers in his hand. "Your guy is Webster?"

"That's him."

"He's up next."

As Karansky spoke, Webster was brought into the courtroom through a side door. He wore jeans and a western-style plaid shirt. His expression was tentative, and his complexion was the color of day-old buttermilk. As Webster took his place in front of the bench, Murphy walked up the aisle from the rear of the courtroom and approached the bench. The assistant DA handling the night's cases was young and clearly fresh out of law school. Murphy nodded to the public defender, another youngster who got the message and sat back to take a break.

"Murder second, Your Honor," the prosecutor told the judge, handing him a copy of the police incident report on which the arrest had been based. "And grand theft auto."

The judge, a worn, middle-aged man Murphy didn't recognize, studied the papers as Murphy took his place beside his client. Webster, a wave of relief passing over his face, started to speak, but Murphy held up a cautioning finger.

The judge looked up. "Mr. Webster, are you represented by counsel?"

"I'm his counsel, Your Honor," Murphy said. "I'm Francis P. Murphy."

"You're charged with car theft and with murder in the second degree, Mr. Webster," the judge said. "How do you plead?"

"My client pleads not guilty, Your Honor," Murphy said.

"Very well." The judge turned to the young prosecutor. "I see no evidence of any priors here."

"Nothing in this state, Your Honor," the prosecutor said. "We're still running a check with the FBI, however."

"And what's the status of that?" the judge inquired.

"It's Sunday evening, Your Honor."

The judge looked up. "By that, I take it that you have no evidence of prior criminal activity at this time?"

"Not at this particular moment, Your Honor, no."

The judge turned to Murphy. "Mr. Murphy, do you have any information on your client's current employment status?"

Murphy said, "My client is gainfully employed as the manager of a farm on the Main Line, Your Honor. It's a very responsible position."

The judge turned to Webster. "Do you have any prior criminal record, Mr. Webster?"

"No," Webster said quickly.

"I hope you have a good explanation for how that body ended up in your car."

Webster opened his mouth to speak, but Murphy broke in: "My client respectfully declines comment, Your Honor." Then Murphy shrugged. "I haven't had much time to go over all this with him yet. We just talked a bit on the phone. I do know his employer personally, however."

The judge leaned back and yawned. "The people's recommendation?"

"No bail, Your Honor. Not on the murder two charge."

The judge wiped his face with his palm. Now, Murphy thought, we'll find out what this guy's view is on civil liberties.

"Yes," the judge said. "Well, with no priors and with a solid job—and with no documented priors, Mr. Martin—I think a bail of one hundred thousand dollars would be appropriate on both charges. Can your client handle that, Mr. Murphy?"

"May we confer?"

"Please do."

Murphy took Webster away from the bench. "Have you got ten grand?"

"No."

"How much have you got?"

"I got about four in a savings account."

Murphy frowned. He had about five thousand in his legal account—most of which already had checks written against it—and another couple of thousand in personal accounts. It was enough. Manny would accept the cash in all the accounts as collateral, although Murphy had been hoping to avoid putting up his own money. That would mean he'd have to keep a careful eye on Webster to discourage him from jumping bail. Manny would go for it, though. He and Murphy went back a few years.

"We'll handle it," he told Webster. "You just keep cool." They went back to the bench. "We'll post bond with the clerk, Your Honor," Murphy said.

"Very well," the judge said. "Bail set at one hundred

78

thousand. Please see the clerk, Mr. Murphy."

The prosecutor, Martin, fumed: "Your Honor, this is a serious crime."

The judge nodded. "It certainly is, Mr. Martin. But until and unless Mr. Webster is convicted through due process of this serious crime we have no choice but to view him as an innocent man, as I'm sure you're aware. The sole questions before this court at a proceeding like this are whether the accused understands the charge against him, whether he seems a likely candidate to commit another crime if bail is granted and whether he's likely to show up for trial if we let him go. In this case, you have no evidence of any prior violations. The man has a job and roots in the community. He has the capacity to make a relatively high bail."

The young DA shook his head in muted rage. "Your Honor," he said, "there's ample precedent for detaining a defendant without bail. The Supreme Court of the United States approved it in the Salerno case just a year or so back."

The judge's eyebrows rose. "So they did, Mr. Martin. So they did. But, if my recollection is correct, Salerno was a mob boss detained on the ground that if he were freed on bail he'd simply go back to his regular business, which was operating a demonstrably unlawful enterprise. Even that position has its warts. The Eighth Amendment bars excessive bail, but it says nothing about when—if ever—bail may be denied. Moreover, Mr. Martin—and particularly in this case— it's difficult to justify the jailing of a man presumed innocent out of a fear of anticipated but still uncommitted crimes. If that's your argument in this case, you're on precarious ground."

The prosecutor shook his head and began: "But Your Honor—"

The judge silenced him with a gesture. "Holmesburg Prison is already well over capacity, Mr. Martin. The city is housing more than twelve hundred men in facilities built almost a century ago for fewer than seven hundred. And most of those enjoying city hospitality are prisoners awaiting trial. I'll deny bail to habitual criminals charged with serious crimes, and I'll deny bail to people living on the street who seem confused about what universe they're inhabiting. But I simply can't deny bail to everybody the DA wants to see locked up on general principles."

"Your Honor—"

The judge raised a hand to silence the prosecutor. "These are trying times for the criminal justice system, Mr. Martin. I'm afraid you'll have to learn to accept an occasional imperfection here and there. See the clerk, Mr. Murphy. And please be sure that your client behaves himself and shows up if this gets to trial."

"Thank you, Your Honor," Murphy said, delighted at the good fortune at getting a judge he would have cursed a few years ago.

After Arnold Karansky posted bail on Webster's behalf—shaking his head in amazement at his father-in-law's failure to insist on ten percent in cash up front as a fee—Murphy and Patricia took a shaken Webster down to the Toronado. They arrived just as a boyish cop was writing a parking ticket for it.

"Hey," Murphy said, flashing his old PBA card. "No professional courtesy left?"

The cop glanced quickly at the card and kept writing. "Expired," he said.

"I'm retired," Murphy said, glancing at the cop's name plate. "Costello. Your old man Bobby Costello?"

The young cop stopped writing and looked up. "Yeah."

"What's he doing now?"

"He's a security guard at Wanamakers."

"I went to your mother's wake," Murphy told him.

The cop tore up the ticket. "Have a nice night," he said.

"Tell your old man that Frank Murphy said he should give up the horses."

The young cop smiled. "Fat chance. You have a good night, Mr. Murphy."

The three of them got into the Toronado, Patricia in the back, Webster in the passenger seat.

"Is there anybody you don't know?" Patricia asked.

"If I don't know them, they aren't worth knowing," Murphy told her. "Well Mike, guess where you're spending the night."

"Where?"

"My place. I don't think it would be a particularly good idea for you to go back to the farm tonight."

"Why not?"

"Well, for one thing I'm not sure how Brian would feel about having you around, since you're charged with murdering his fiancée. It's possible that he might not be experiencing the warmest feelings toward you just now. Secondly, I want to spend some time talking to you."

Third, and unsaid, Murphy wanted some assurance that Webster wouldn't jump bail—at least, not on his first night out of the can.

Webster, delighted to be out of custody, simply

81

shrugged. "Whatever you say. You're the lawyer."

"Fine," Murphy said. "And now, before we do anything else, I have to take somebody home. When we drop off big ears back there, then we can talk a little."

"Just go ahead and talk," Patricia said. "Don't mind me."

Traffic on Sunday night was light. Murphy piloted the big Toronado through Center City to the Delaware Expressway and cut across the Northeast to the house in Mount Airy he had shared for so many years with his wife and daughter. Mary Ellen's aging Japanese station wagon was in the driveway. Clearly, she'd gotten home early. When they pulled in front, Webster got out of the Toronado and let Patricia out of the back seat.

"Good night," Webster said.

"Mr. Webster," Patricia said as she climbed out, "did you do what you're charged with?"

"No," Mike Webster said quietly. "I didn't do it."

Patricia studied his face for a brief moment. Her gaze was piercing. Then she smiled. "Then you'll be just fine. You've got a good lawyer. 'Night, Daddy."

"Good night, honey. Give your mother my regards."

Murphy sat in the car until Patricia was inside the house. This was a safe neighborhood, but—out of instinct and experience—he was a careful man. When Patricia closed and locked the front door behind her, Murphy put the Toronado in gear and steered back toward Center City.

"Let's hear it," Murphy said, lighting a Camel.

"Can I bum one of those first?"

Murphy gave him the pack. Webster lit a cigarette with the Toronado's lighter and sucked in the strong smoke. "I gave these up about four years ago. I was worried about my health. That's a laugh."

"Let's hear it," Murphy said again.

"All I know is this: Yesterday, a couple of hours after you left, Mr. Kavanaugh said he wanted me to take Miss Rice's car this morning and drive it down to his place at the shore."

"In Jersey?"

"Yeah. He's got a condo in Margate. I was supposed to leave it in the parking lot and catch a bus into Atlantic City. Then I was supposed to catch a bus back to Philly and take the train out to Phoenixville and catch a cab back to the farm. That's all I know. Then, after he told me that, he got into his car and drove away."

"Did you see Lynn after he left?"

"No, but I stayed away from the house. I live in a cottage back behind the big barn."

"So you don't know if she was alive when he left."

"I don't know nothing," Webster said.

"What time was all this?"

"Noon, maybe. No, more like one or one-thirty. I don't know. Early in the afternoon, anyway."

"And you didn't see her all day?"

"No."

"Did she leave with Brian?"

"Nope. He left alone. I saw that. He took the top down on that little sports car and roared out of the place."

"What was his manner like?" Murphy asked. "Did he seem sore about anything?"

"No. I don't know. He seemed like he might have had something on his mind, is all."

"Like what?"

"I don't know."

"So then what?"

"So then I took the afternoon off."

"What did you do?"

"I went over to the Feasterville Mall and bought some jeans and some underwear."

"Did you take Lynn's car?"

"I took my truck. The farm's truck, actually."

"What time did you get back?"

"Nine, maybe. I caught a movie and had something to eat. I'm not much of a cook."

"What movie?"

"*Fatal Attraction,* I think it was called. This guy has a fling with a woman, and she turns out to be nuts."

"Ah, a documentary," Murphy said. "Then what?"

"I watched 'Golden Girls' on TV and read a bit and then I went to bed. You get up early on a farm."

"And you didn't hear or see Lynn?"

"No. The lights were on in the house when I got back, though."

"They were?"

"Yeah."

"You're sure of that."

"Yeah, the lights were on."

"Okay," Murphy said. "What happened this morning?"

"This morning, I got up and went out to her car. I got in it and started off for the shore. When I got into Center City, I stopped at a gas station to get some gas. I wanted to check the oil, so I went into the trunk to get a rag and there she was. I almost shit my pants. I swear to Christ I almost did."

"Then what happened?"

Webster stubbed out the cigarette in the Toronado's ashtray. "I don't know exactly. I started yelling and carrying on. I got sort of crazy. This guy came out of the gas station. He saw the body in the trunk and called the cops, and the next thing I knew I was under arrest."

"Did you say anything to the cops?"

"Just what I said to you."

"Were you questioned?"

"Did they ask me questions, do you mean?"

Murphy nodded wearily. "Yeah, that's what I mean when I ask you if you were questioned."

"No. I mean, they asked me my name and stuff."

"Did they tell you about your rights?"

"Yeah. This cop read to me from a little card right there in the gas station. I don't remember what he said, but it was something like that."

"There's a defense out the window, Murphy thought. "Did you touch the body?"

"Yeah. I tried to pull her out, only she was all stiff, and she was heavy. I was afraid I'd pull out my back again."

Murphy glanced over at Webster. "In the middle of all that, you remembered about your back?"

Webster smiled. "You ever had a back operation?"

"No."

"You get something wrong with your back and you remember it the rest of your life, believe me."

Murphy lit another cigarette and so did Webster. The two men rode in silence for a while, Murphy's mind working as he drove. He had a lot of work to do on this one. One hell of a lot.

"I don't want you to think about jumping bail," Murphy told Webster finally.

"I wouldn't do that, Mr. Murphy."

"That's good," Murphy told him. "I'm putting up about six grand, along with your four, to keep you out of Holmesburg until trial. If you were to split on me, it would seriously piss me off. I'd have to go find you. And I would find you, Mike. Don't have any doubt about that. You wouldn't like it much when I did, either."

Webster was silent for a moment. Then he said, "You don't have to threaten me, Mr. Murphy."

"Maybe not," Murphy told him. "But I'm doing it just the same. I'm your lawyer, and I'm your friend. You play straight with me and I'll take care of you. You try to fuck me and you'll start to think of Holmesburg Prison as a resort hotel."

Back at the apartment, Murphy gave Webster a Budweiser and showed him the sofa where he would spend the night. While Webster drank his beer—and while Murphy downed a bourbon on the rocks—he checked his answering machine for messages. Toddman's voice came on.

"This is Paul," Toddman said. "Fletcher says lunch is out. He'll see you for breakfast at seven-thirty sharp at the Harvey House. You're paying."

Murphy made a mental note to set his alarm. Then he stood up and stretched.

"You need anything," he told Webster, "just let me know. Don't worry about the dog. He won't do anything unless you try to split."

"I told you before," Webster said, "I won't jump bail. You don't have to keep making threats."

Murphy smiled at him. "I'm really a very sweet guy unless there's money involved," he said.

Before the beginning

"Thank you, Miss Pale," the voice called out from the darkness beyond the footlights.

"There's more," Alma called back. "You've only seen part of it."

"That's okay," the voice called back. "That's just fine. Just leave your paperwork with the girl backstage there, and we'll be in touch if we need you."

Alma called out, "The ending is really neat, if you want to see it."

"That's okay. That'll be fine," the voice said back to her.

Alma stared into the darkness for the briefest fraction of a second, her lips drawn into a tight line. Then she walked over to the piano and gathered up her music. The pianist, a bearded fat man with his hair slicked back, said, "You did just fine, honey."

"Bullshit," Alma said to him in a low voice. He laughed.

Backstage, listening to the music as another girl did her stuff out front, she was pulling her jeans on over her leotard when the fat pianist came back to her. "What's your name again?"

She looked up, wondering what this was all about. "Alma. Alma Pale. I'm not going to change it, either. Say, if you're here, who's playing?"

"Somebody else," the fat man said. "You're not new at this, are you?"

"What do you mean?" Alma asked, zipping up and pulling on her St. Cloud College sweatshirt.

"How long you been doing this?" he persisted.

"A few years," Alma said.

"Have you gotten anything?"

"Some off-Broadway stuff."

"How long ago?"

Alma was getting annoyed. The man was about thirty, with Brooklyn heavy in his voice. He looked and sounded like a young Jackie Gleason.

"Not too long ago," she said.

He shrugged. "Look," he said, "you want to keep on with this, you go ahead. But I'll bet you ain't making enough to cover your equity dues."

"I'm not in equity," Alma admitted. "I haven't worked enough."

"So what do you do to eat?"

"Whatever," Alma said. "Lately, I've been waiting tables over on Ninth Avenue."

He made a face. "You live over there, too?"

"Yeah," she said, a hint of defiance in her tone. "So?"

The fat man lit a cigarette. "Look, sweetie," he told her. "You look good enough, and your voice ain't bad. But you can't dance good enough. I mean, you can dance better than me, but you can't dance good enough to cut it over the long haul."

"I'm working on it," Alma said defensively.

"Yeah, yeah. You're okay. But you got to be better than okay to work today. Look what's playing. Look at *Chicago*. Could you work in *Chicago?* Come on."

Alma gathered up her things. "What are you bothering me for?" she asked, knowing that what he was telling her was true and sick in the pit of her stomach over it. "You got nothing better to do than bother me?"

"Just trying to help."

"Some help," she said, starting to leave.

"You want something better than waiting tables on Ninth Avenue?" he called after her.

Alma stopped and turned. "Yeah. Like what?"

He dug in the pocket of his shirt, coming out with a card. He handed it to her.

"Ask for Ellie," the fat man said. "Tell her Carmen told you to call."

Alma studied the card. Then she looked up, her expression a sneer. "An escort service?"

The fat man shrugged again. "Hey," he told her. "Do what you want. Just trying to help out."

"Some help," Alma said.

"Yeah?" the fat man said. "You got something better going?"

Alma didn't respond. She didn't have to. He already knew the answer.

It was no.

CHAPTER 8

The second he saw Murphy coming in the door, Fletcher Lake's mood took a turn for the worse. Murphy had always that effect on him.

"There he is," Paul Toddman told his boss.

"I see him. He's late."

"He's Murphy," Toddman said, trying to make the district attorney smile and failing conspicuously. Toddman motioned toward the doorway. Murphy spotted him and started across the restaurant. He had a Camel stuck in his mouth. Fletcher won't like that, Toddman thought. The district attorney was a militant non-smoker.

"It's almost eight," Fletcher Lake said as Murphy arrived at the table.

Murphy sat down heavily. The sleep still clouded his eyes. "You must be wearing a digital watch, Fletcher. Otherwise you would have said that the little hand is on eight and the big hand is near twelve."

"Frank . . ." Toddman began wearily.

"You guys order yet?" Murphy asked.

"We were waiting for you," Toddman said.

"Isn't that sweet," Murphy responded, motioning for the waitress. When she came over, Murphy said, "Eggs Benedict, pineapple juice, and coffee. And a side of hash browns, okay?"

"Okay," the waitress said. "How about you fellas?"

"A bagel with cream cheese and coffee and orange juice," Toddman said.

"Just some fruit salad for me," Lake said, brushing away Murphy's cigarette smoke. "And a cup of tea. Murphy, could you put that out, please?"

"Just as soon as I'm finished with it."

"Say," the waitress said. "You're Fletcher Lake, aren't you?"

Lake flashed his expensive capped teeth. The woman was fairly pretty, and Lake considered pretty women something of a hobby. "Yes, I am."

"Gee, nice to meet you."

Lake extended a well-manicured hand. "Nice to meet you, too . . . Miss . . . and what's your name, again?"

"Norma."

"Nice to meet you, Norma. Do you work here full time?"

"Yeah," said Norma, a bit nonplussed at meeting her favorite politician.

"Say, Fletcher," Murphy said suddenly. "How's that secretary—what's her name—Ginnie? She ever get over that dose of clap you gave her?"

Norma's face took on an expression of sheer horror, as did Fletcher Lake's.

"Pretty mean stuff, wasn't it?" Murphy asked casually. "Wasn't it that South American strain, the kind that shrivels up your goodies?"

The moment gone forever, Norma tore off wordlessly to place their orders while Toddman wiped his face with a sweaty hand. Fletcher Lake wore the same expression he would have worn if he'd just licked a piece of public plumbing at the Trailways bus terminal.

"You never change, do you?" he said to Murphy.

Murphy stubbed out the cigarette. Then he said, "Fletcher, you never liked me and I never liked you. Because you were my boss, you were free to exhibit your dislike for me whenever the whim struck you, and I was obligated to take whatever shit you felt like dishing out. That was then, and this is now. You still have the prep school background and the Harvard law degree and I still look and talk like a cop, but I'm free and independent and I don't have to take any shit from you I don't feel like taking. And I don't feel like taking any."

Toddman made a vain attempt to restore order. "We're here to talk business—"

"I'm talking business," Murphy said. "And I'm talking it on my terms. We're two independent agents, Fletcher. You won't be giving me orders in this case. If you want my witness's testimony, it'll be on terms that I think are most favorable for keeping the witness alive. Otherwise, Tommy Lucelli can stay out of the can forever, for all I care. It's no big deal to me, believe me, I'm not the one who'd like to be governor."

Fletcher Lake leaned back in his chair. He was a well-tailored man with curly, slightly graying hair. He was lean from racquetball every morning before work and he was quick on his feet in debate even if he lacked depth. Murphy had often referred to Fletcher Lake as six feet of solid veneer, but he didn't underrate him. The man was, in Murphy's judgment, without a shred of principle and possessed a rare streak of personal vindictiveness. His only interests were women and ambition. Murphy had already tweaked him on one of those interests this morning, and he had just appealed to the other.

Lake said, "I'm not about to make any bargains until I know how good your witness is."

"Very good," Murphy said as the food arrived. He dug into the Eggs Benedict, savoring the rich, tangy hollandaise sauce. "The witness is totally reliable, totally credible and totally willing to take the stand and testify. And the witness saw Lucelli's face."

Lake sipped his tea. "Who is the witness?"

"Not yet," Murphy told him.

Lake said nothing.

"What are your terms, Frank?" Toddman demanded.

Murphy swallowed some hash browns, put down his fork and downed a healthy slug of pineapple juice. "I take personal control of protection for my witness. I'll take whatever depositions need to be taken for purposes of the arrest warrant and so forth. I guarantee to produce the witness for trial. You can prosecute the case in court. You can have all the publicity, Fletcher."

"And what's your compensation going to be?" Toddman asked.

"My regular hourly rate."

Despite himself, Fletcher Lake smiled. "That ought to be about five bucks an hour, shouldn't it, Frank? Yours isn't the most lucrative practice in town, or so I'm told."

Murphy glared at him. "My rate is one-fifty an hour."

"You're in dreamland," the district attorney said.

"That's half the hourly rate of any blue-chip firm in town. That's my bargain rate. The only reason I'm willing to take so little is because I'm such a good citizen."

"Seventy-five," Toddman said.

"What is this?" Murphy demanded. "Are we in an Armenian rug bazaar? I'm not going to negotiate the rate."

"And how many hours will we be talking about?" Lake asked casually.

"That depends on how fast you can get the trial going. I'm going to be guarding the witness twenty-four hours a day, but I'll be a good guy and charge the city for only forty hours a week."

Toddman did some quick math in his head. "You want six thousand bucks a week? You're nuts."

Murphy shrugged. "You're nuts if you don't take it. How much do you think it would cost the city to put the witness in protective custody? How much would it cost you guys to hire a contract prosecutor on top of that? I'm a bargain when you consider the size of the fish we're talking about. It's a cheap ride to the governor's mansion, Fletcher. You don't even have to give me a tip. And you won't get the witness any other way. The witness doesn't like you, Fletcher. I can't imagine why not."

"Bullshit," Toddman said in disgust. "How do we know this guy is even reliable?"

"Who said it's a guy?" Murphy said. "I never said 'he.' I said 'witness.'"

"How do we know she's reliable, then?"

"Did I say 'she'?" Murphy said. "I never said 'she.' You want to find out the witness's gender, then you've got to pay."

Fletcher Lake was quietly furious. "This is black-mail, Murphy."

Murphy smiled at the district attorney. "Blackmail is such an ugly word," he said.

"Do you really think you can shake me down? I'll have your ass in the can for extortion so fast it'll make your head spin."

"No, you won't," Murphy said quietly. "Not unless you want to focus a hell of a lot of attention on the contract prosecutors you've already got on the payroll. Your office hires contract prosecutors all the time, Fletcher. And who are they? Usually they're party hacks climbing aboard the gravy train for a few weeks, and they do zip for you. Me, I'm offering quality goods at competitive prices. And it's all perfectly legal."

"It's obstruction of justice," Lake said. "It's interference with governmental administration. It's—"

"Try it," Murphy said quietly. "You just fucking try it. If the newspapers look at your contract prosecutors, they're going to find that not one of them is from the other party. And they're going to find that with one or two exceptions they're guys who've never even represented your office at an arraignment. They sit home and watch 'Love Connection' and you send them public money because the party bosses tell you to. You want that little operation looked at, then you just try to pull something with me. You try to charge me with anything, Fletcher. I know some guys in the newspaper business, if you'll recall. And I know a few of them who know what a fourteen-karat phony you really are."

Murphy took pleasure in watching the district attorney's face turn crimson.

"And one more thing," Murphy added. "I'll want the police officer of my choice to assist me in protecting the witness—at city expense, of course."

"Let me guess who," Toddman said.

"Wilder," Murphy told him.

"Yep, I guessed."

Murphy, who had been eating throughout the conversation, swallowed the last morsels of his breakfast. He patted his lips with his napkin and lit another Camel, which—to Murphy's delight—prompted an even deeper frown from Fletcher Lake.

"Well?" Murphy said.

Toddman said nothing. Lake's lips pursed in thought. "We'll think about it," he said finally.

Murphy stood up. "Think about it until two this afternoon. After that I take my offer around the corner to the federal court house. Murdering somebody deprives them of their civil rights. Did you know that, Fletcher? That's a federal offense, and the U.S. attorney would get sexually aroused at the very thought of being able to hang something like that on Tommy Lucelli."

"You'd never shake the feds down for six grand a week," Lake said.

Murphy shrugged. "You never know. They're Republicans, too, Fletcher. Only they're real ones— not just guys who joined the GOP to get slated for office. My old man always told me that Republicans are capable of anything."

Murphy turned to go. Then he stopped and turned back to Fletcher Lake. "By the way, Fletcher, you can buy breakfast. If I go on contract, I'll throw in my food for free for the term of the case."

Murphy went out the revolving door onto South

97

Broad Street in an unusually good mood. He was full of good food, and—even better—full of satisfaction from walking up one side of Fletcher Lake and down the other. If worse came to worse, he really would go to the feds, and he'd do it for free if he had to. Still, it would be more fun—and vastly more lucrative—if he could squeeze six grand a week out of Fletcher Lake's patrician hide in the process. He whistled to himself as he crossed the street. The song was "When Irish Eyes are Smiling."

Murphy entered the Fidelity Bank Building, went up the elevator to his floor and entered his office just as Esmeralda was reaching for the phone.

"Mr. Murphy's office," she said.

Murphy liked the sound of that. For years, he'd answered his own phone, and his first words had always been something like "Major Crimes" or "Investigative Unit." As much as he missed the reliability of his city paycheck, he liked the idea of having his own professional identity—separate and distinct from the unit to which he belonged or the city he served. A secretary answering his phone with the name of his own business was tangible proof of his independence from the system of wage slavery in which he had spent much of his life. What he'd been able to do to Fletcher Lake had also been proof of the same thing, which was one of the reasons he had enjoyed it so much. Another was his deep dislike for the district attorney.

Lake had been blessed with advantages Murphy had never enjoyed. He had come from money, gone to the best schools, been blessed with good looks and had used all that to advance in politics. The problem was that aside from his arrogance and his tendency to view subordinates as human beings of inherently lesser value, Fletcher Lake wasn't terribly bright and didn't work terribly hard. He had advanced not on the basis of industry or intellectual merit but on the basis of his appearance and connections, both family and political. The Lakes of Chestnut Hill had been big contributors to both parties—kicking in to the Democrats as well as the GOP since the early fifties, when the Republicans had lost control of city government. But Fletcher Lake's old man—a politically connected lawyer himself—had more juice with the Republican party than its more prosperous counterpart, and when he had wanted his son slated for DA he had found the Republicans a better bargain.

Murphy was gray and pot-bellied. He was a slave to his bad habits. He tried desperately to keep his fingernails clean all day but never seemed to manage it, even in an office. Despite all his efforts to correct it, he still spoke with more than a touch of the flat accent that identified white, ethnic Philadelphians bred on the streets. He was, to all outward appearances, the cop he had been for so long. And yet he knew he was something else now. He was, through dint of enormous effort and an imposing intellect that probably resulted from a genetic blip, an educated man. He was as free of the power of the system as any man without an independent source of income could be. He would have liked to have been making more money, but he could get by on what his practice brought in. He had enough to pay for Patricia's ritzy education and enough left over to keep him in bourbon and Camels.

All factors considered, Murphy was pleased with himself. But he suspected that Fletcher Lake and the Fletcher Lakes of the world—those who had obtained with such ease what Murphy had been forced to scratch for his entire adult life—continued to look down on him because of where and what he had come from and because he looked and sounded the part. With most men of Lake's background and stature, Murphy usually managed to feel confident and—at long last—at ease. He respected achievement because he himself had achieved. But he did not respect Fletcher Lake's achievement, which he felt had been granted the man on the basis of factors that shouldn't count. Murphy knew that in every meaningful way—in intellect, in character, in charm and wit, in slyness and in resolve—he was a better man than Fletcher Lake, and he was baffled at why somebody with the district attorney's advantages in life still insisted on being so relentless an asshole. Most of the prep school guys Murphy knew were good guys, genuinely nice to people, probably because they'd never felt the need to be anything but. Fletcher Lake, though, seemed to have a deep-seated need to be a prick, and Murphy just couldn't figure it out.

"It's Mr. Kavanaugh for you," Esmeralda told him.

Murphy, who had been standing there almost in a trance as he pondered his hatred for Fletcher Lake, was suddenly shaken from his reverie.

"I'll take it inside," he said.

Murphy went into his private office, flipped on his Mister Coffee and picked up the phone.

"Morning, Brian."

"Where's Webster?" Brian Kavanaugh said without ceremony.

"I'm sorry about Lynn," Murphy told him.

"Not so sorry that you're not defending her killer. It's in this morning's paper."

100

"Mike says he didn't do it. I don't think he did. You know the guy. Do you think he could murder somebody?"

"I don't know," Kavanaugh said. "All I know is that Lynn's dead and the cops say Webster did it. They didn't just charge him for no reason."

"They charged him because they didn't have anybody else to charge. I know how these things work. A lot of people are charged because the department is under pressure to make arrests and they happen to be handy. As far as I know, all they have on Mike is the fact that Lynn's body was found in the trunk of the car he was driving—which, incidentally, they charged him with stealing. That leaves a lot of possibilities, Brian."

Kavanaugh said nothing. He was, quite understandably, deeply upset. Murphy could feel that over the phone line.

"Look," Murphy said. "I was going to call you this morning. I wanted to extend my deepest regrets, and I wanted to ask you what you know."

"I don't know anything. I know that somebody murdered Lynn and the cops say it was Webster. That's it."

"What do you know about Webster?" Murphy asked him.

"He was an employee of the guy I bought the farm from. He'd been there a few years. The previous owner gave him a good recommendation, so I kept him on."

"Has he seemed like a decent guy to you?"

"Yes. I wouldn't have kept him otherwise."

"Has he been a friend?"

"No, he's been an employee." Then Kavanaugh paused. "Well, yes. We've been friends in a way, I guess. We've done a lot of work together."

"Then, knowing the guy as you've known him, do you really think he's capable of murder?"

"Frank, who the hell knows what somebody else is capable of? A lot of things can happen."

"Maybe," Murphy said. "Mike told me that you told him to take Lynn's BMW down to your place at the shore yesterday morning. Is that right?"

"Yeah. After you left, Lynn and I decided to head down to the place at the shore for a few days to do some gambling and talk over what you said. I had some important paperwork to do, and if I was going to the shore I knew I'd have to do the work Saturday night and Sunday morning. So I took my car and went into Center City. When I got back to the farm yesterday afternoon the cops were there. They told me what had happened."

"I don't get it," Murphy said. "Why did Mike have to take her car to the shore if you were going back to the farm to get her?"

"We wanted to have two cars down there, and we wanted to ride down together. Lynn liked riding in the Healey with the top down."

"Where did you stay in Center City?"

"I worked until about three in the morning, then I conked out on the sofa in my office. I've got a shower and a little refrigerator there."

"Then what?"

"Then I woke up about nine-thirty or so, finished what I had to do and came back out here."

Murphy sighed. "All right. It all falls into place, I guess. Brian, I don't think Mike did it. I don't know who did—or why—but Mike strikes me as a straight guy. I've got him over at my apartment. I want to bring him out tonight and let him stay at his home. I hope you don't object to that."

Kavanaugh was silent.

"The guy needs a place to live, Brian. Part of the bail requirement is that he continues to live at the same address during all this."

"All right," Kavanaugh said finally. "Bring him out tonight."

"Thanks. We'll see you about seven-thirty or eight."

Murphy hung up and poured himself some coffee. He went out to Esmeralda's desk and went through the day's schedule. He had to take some depositions on a divorce case in the afternoon, and he had some bankruptcy papers to go over this morning, but the day appeared light. He had no appointments. He took Esmeralda's copy of the *Inquirer* and went back inside his own office.

Murphy was a compulsive newspaper reader, although he'd met damned few reporters he'd ever felt were reliable. Everything in a newspaper, he knew, was absolutely truthful and reliable—except for those items about which you had some personal knowledge. Those were invariably fucked up in some particular, large or small.

He read the brief item on Webster's arrest and release on bail, noted that his own middle initial was wrong in the story, and was halfway through Clark DeLeon's column in the B-section when Esmeralda buzzed him.

"Mr. Toddman is on the line," she said.

Murphy hit the button. "Hi, Paul. How you doing? Sure was great to see Fletcher again."

"Why do you do that to him?" Toddman demanded. "What's the point?"

"The point is that I can do it, and you'd love to. Only

103

he has you by the balls and you can't. Did he go for it?"

"You knew he would."

"It killed him, though, didn't it?" Murphy said with glee.

"He was pissed off, yes. It won't be much fun around here today."

"So, what's new?"

"Tommy Lucelli in custody, that's what's new. He's going to be picked up and charged today. We've never had him in custody once, you know. Not ever. Lucelli is a very smooth guy."

"I wouldn't know," Murphy said. "I've never met him."

"You will now. One more thing. I've got some bad news for you on another matter."

"Which is?"

"Where's your boy Michael Webster?"

"I've got him staying at my place. I'm taking him out to his own place tonight after work. What's the problem?"

"I've got to have somebody go over and take him into custody again."

"What the hell for?" Murphy demanded.

"He told the judge he has no priors."

"And . . ."

"He's got a manslaughter conviction in California from eleven years ago."

"Oh, shit," Murphy said.

"There's more."

"I can hardly wait."

"He also jumped parole. They've been looking for him for almost three years."

Murphy groaned as though he'd been kicked in the gut. "Isn't that just ducky," he said.

CHAPTER 9

As soon as he answered the phone and realized who was on the other end of the line, Richie Silver thought again about how right his mother had been all those years before.

"A doctor," she had told him in that voice of hers, the one that had sounded like ground glass. "Medical school you should go to."

"Ma," Richie had said in response, "I want to be a lawyer. I'm not interested in medicine. I'm interested in law."

His mother had sneered at him with that special sneer she had always reserved for the truly and hopelessly weak of mind. "Law, schmaw," she had said. "Doctors, they get their money from insurance companies with big computers. Nice, clean computers. Lawyers, who gives them money? *Goniffs,* that's who. Crooks give lawyers money!"

But Richie had never been any good at the hard sciences. He had always been a smart kid. He'd always gotten good grades. Organic chemistry, however, had been beyond him. And math, too. You could take these numbers—2, 4, 16, and ?—and it might take Richie maybe a year and a half to figure out that the last number in the sequence had to be whatever you got when you multiplied sixteen by itself. He could do math—algebra, geometry. He could memorize formulas. But he couldn't think in mathematical terms. His mind simply didn't work that way.

Besides, Richie had always talked better than he'd done anything else. It was a skill developed as a self-preservation mechanism from living with the old lady, who had been born with a speech pattern roughly akin to the bark of an AK-47. Richie Silver knew he had been born to practice law.

He had gone to Temple and graduated cum laude. He had gone to Temple Law and made law review. He had gone to work in the DA's office right after graduation to get courtroom experience. In his four years there, he had built a reputation for being quick on his feet in court. Quick Silver, people had called him. He had taken pride in the nickname.

Then he had gone into private practice specializing in criminal work. By his late thirties, he had made a ton of money. He had moved into a house in Lower Merion roughly six times the size of the one in which he had grown up on Rhawn Street in Northeast Philadelphia. He had a nice wife whose great skills in life were headaches at moments that might develop into sexual encounters and applying for credit cards. He had a fourteen-year-old daughter who had elevated the whine to an art form, and he had a client list that—if they gathered together in one room—would look like the cast of "The Road Warrior."

All this Richie could deal with. All this he had bargained for. Vito Caruso—that he hadn't bargained for. And that's who was on the phone.

"Hi, Vito," Richie said weakly. "How have you been?"

"Tommy needs you," Vito said in a voice that sounded like a cross between a frog belching and an auto backfire.

"Fine, fine," Richie said. "Whatever I can do."

"You can get over to the Roundhouse," Vito told him. "They just picked him up."

"What charge?"

"He'll tell you. Just move, Richie."

"Fine, fine," Richie said. "I'll be right there."

Richie Silver left his office at Fifteenth and Walnut with a frown on his face. As he picked up his Jag from the garage across the street, the frown deepened. How did I do this, he asked himself? How did I get myself mixed up with these guys?

Actually, it had begun four years ago as a favor to another lawyer. Bob Limoncelli had routinely done the legal work for the Lucelli family, which had no doubt contributed to Limoncelli's heart condition. Limoncelli had been about to go into Thomas Jefferson Medical Center for his second experience with angioplasty when he'd asked Richie, whom he'd known in the DA's office, to handle some work for the Lucellis while Limoncelli was laid up. It was work that wouldn't wait, and Limoncelli was willing to turn over to Richie every nickel of the fee to get the work done. Richie's job was to get a charge of extortion against a Lucelli soldier reduced to something more palatable, a chore he managed without difficulty. Next, he served as counsel to a Lucelli capo accused of separating an obstinate union official from several of the less crucial fingers of his left hand. Again, Richie performed admirably.

The money was good—excellent, actually—and he was only subbing for Limoncelli, who did this sort of thing for a living.

The problem arose when a Sri Lankan physician at Jefferson screwed up the angioplasty procedure and Limoncelli got so enraged that he roared and screamed at the baffled foreigner, who had never heard many of those words before and was still trying to decipher them when the red-faced Limoncelli dropped over dead right in front of him. When that happened, Richie Silver suddenly found himself the first team. And it wasn't a team he could quit.

So, for about four years now, the most lucrative portion of Richie Silver's practice—and by far the most terrifying—had been representing the Lucellis, well-known gangsters out of South Philadelphia.

At first, Richie had hoped he could keep the relationship at arm's length. He had soon learned that this simply wasn't possible. When you represented a mobster on a criminal matter and served him well, he would also call upon your services in other matters: real estate closings, wills, divorces, making legal settlements with pregnant girlfriends. Richie also found himself drawn increasingly into the social circle of the Lucelli family. Doing business with these guys meant spending time with them, going to their daughters' first communions and weddings, traveling with them to Vegas on weekends. They insisted on a relationship of that sort. They were men who placed a high premium on personal relationships, on loyalty, on friendship. It was, Richie Silver discovered, what passed for their religion.

And friends confide in one another. Richie found himself confided in to a degree that kept him awake at night. These guys took the lawyer-client relationship to new extremes of intimacy. The things they did. The things they bragged about.

At the same time, the money was very good. Very, very good, actually. Now, four years later, Richie had just picked himself up a condo in Hollywood, Florida, facing the ocean. He had another one in Vegas. He had a V-6 Jag for himself and a Seville for his wife. He had a stock portfolio that would have been the envy of a small charitable foundation. He wore eight-hundred-dollar suits and a Rolex watch. He took his wife to the islands every winter and Europe every summer. Richie had a salacious girlfriend he kept in a fairly decent split-level house he had bought for her in Runnemede, New Jersey. He had every luxury and comfort he had ever dreamed of.

All he had to do to hold onto it all was to keep these guys from getting pissed off at him for some indiscretion and tossing him into the Delaware River chained to a jukebox. Richie Silver worked very hard at preventing an event like that from taking place. Vito Caruso was Tommy Lucelli's top deputy. When he spoke, Richie listened. Vito Caruso was Richie Silver's E.F. Hutton. Vito had just informed Richie that Tommy was in police custody and that Richie's services were needed. Eager to be of assistance, Richie Silver ran every red light between the parking garage at Fifteen and Walnut and the Roundhouse, the nickname for the police administration building at Eighth

109

and Race.

He checked with the desk officer, got the information he needed, then found Tommy Lucelli in an interrogation room in the basement. A uniformed police officer guarded the door, and Richie showed the man his pass. The uniform opened the door and Richie entered. It was a small, windowless room containing a table and three worn wooden chairs. Tommy Lucelli sat in one of them, his feet on the table. He stood up as Richie Silver entered.

"That was quick," Lucelli said, smiling and extending his hand.

"I got here as soon as Vito called me," Silver said, sitting down at the table, opening his briefcase and pulling out a legal pad and a felt-tipped pen.

Lucelli sat back down. He was a darkly handsome man about Richie Silver's own age. He wore a custom-made white dress shirt with silver cuff links, and the jacket to his conservative gray suit was thrown across a chair back. His tie had been taken from him, which was customary.

"Did anybody try to question you?" Silver asked.

Lucelli shook his head. "Not until after they'd read me my rights, and then it was just routine stuff. Did I have anything I wanted to say? Did I want to make a statement about anything? No direct questions, though. They handled it all by the book, real careful. There was a guy I think was probably from the DA's office on the arrest team. He watched everything.

Silver's lips pursed. Not good. If they'd had any doubt about their evidence they'd probably have tried to get Lucelli to talk, either by trying to con him or by squeezing him, whichever seemed the more promising course of action. If they were too cocky to try even one of those tactics . . .

"They tell me I'm charged with murder two," Lucelli said. "Did you get any details?"

Richie Silver nodded. "According to the desk officer, it involves something at a diner in the Northeast ten years or so back. Two men and a woman were killed, and they're going for indictments against you in all three killings. I have the names of the victims here. I wrote them down. Take a look at this. Do you know anything about this?"

Lucelli's brow furrowed as he studied Richie Silver's scribbled notes on a yellow legal pad. He said nothing for a moment. Then he looked up and stared straight at Silver—through him, actually. His mind was working, and it wasn't a bad mind at all, Richie Silver knew. Tommy Lucelli had put in two years at Penn State before he left college to join the family business. He spoke grammatically and enjoyed reading, even if his taste did tend to run toward old Harold Robbins novels. Silver began to speak, but Lucelli merely put a finger to his lips, urging Silver back to silence. Silver immediately shut up.

"They might have this place bugged," Lucelli whispered.

"They might," Silver whispered back, "but I doubt it."

Lucelli's voice was low as he said, "I doubt it, too, but why take a chance? Give me a pen."

Silver turned the pad around and passed over the pen. Lucelli scribbled on the pad for a moment and then turned it toward his lawyer. Silver read the mobster's neat, draftsmanlike printing, a product of

Lucelli's two years of studying architecture so many years before. The message said: *I'll tell you later. They must have a witness who finally got brave. Find out who.*

Silver looked up. "That might be tough." Lucelli motioned to the pad. Silver picked up the pen and wrote: *Anything I find out in discovery they could trace back to me.*

Lucelli shrugged. "I've got faith in you, Richie. You'll figure it out."

Richie Silver began to panic. He understood this request for what it was. He tried to determine which he feared most—Tommy Lucelli or, at best, the bar association. No contest.

He took the pen and scribbled again: *If I find out, what then?*

Lucelli took the pad back. He wrote: *Then call 201-555-3498. Ask for Alex. Tell Alex who the witness is, where the witness can be found.*

Richie Silver studied the message. Alex? Who was Alex? He began to ask the question, then he thought better of it. There were things he'd rather not know. There were a great many things they had already told him that he would have preferred not to have known.

"I'll do what I can," Silver said grimly. "Meanwhile, I'm going to try to get you out of here, Tommy. But my suspicion is that there won't be any bail in this."

"No?" Lucelli said, a note of outrage in his voice. "Is this America or what, Richie?"

Silver shrugged. "The judge will know who you are. It's a murder charge, and there's some bad case law now on bail. It came out of those pizza connection trials up in New York. I'll yell and scream, but they didn't bring you in just to let you back out a couple of hours later—not if they didn't even try to question you. Bail doesn't look good."

Tommy Lucelli sat back in his chair. "Just do the other thing. Do that and we'll be all right."

Richie Silver nodded. "I'll try, Tommy. But I'll try on the bail thing, too."

Tommy Lucelli smiled. "Hey," he said, "don't get your balls in an uproar. If they let me out on bail, fine. If they don't? Hey, that's show biz. Just work on the other thing, Richie. I can count on you, Richie, can't I? I need to know I can count on you."

Richie Silver nodded his head grimly. "You can count on me, Tommy."

Tommy Lucelli smiled. "Good man," the mob boss told his lawyer.

CHAPTER 10

"You're really a shithead," Murphy said.

"I know," Webster told him. "I'm sorry."

"I don't want to hear sorry. Why the hell didn't you tell me?"

"I thought nobody would find out. It was years ago, for Christ's sake. It was in another life. I thought maybe nobody would have a record of it anymore. I'm using a different name now. How could they even connect me with something that happened in another state so long ago under a different name?"

Murphy shook his head wearily. Dumb, he thought—world-class dumb. He and Webster were separated by a wire-mesh screen in the visiting area of Holmesburg Prison, Philadelphia's city jail. Holmesburg was an incredibly threatening structure that rose up next to the Delaware Expressway in Northeast Philadelphia. The building had all the architectural charm of Castle Dracula, and inside it was worse—vastly worse. Webster was dressed in prison garb—a blue work shirt and jeans—and Murphy wore a gray suit that was so tight on him that his eyes were almost bulging out. And he'd missed breakfast that morning, too, which did nothing for his mood.

"Schmuck," Murphy said slowly, "they got you through your fingerprints. They took your fingerprints when they booked you, then they sent a computerized image of them to the FBI. The FBI has this big computer that's used for no other purpose except to store the fingerprints of everybody in this country who's ever been fingerprinted for any reason. The computer runs through its files and, poof, they've got your ass."

Webster was aghast. "But how the hell do they do that? How does a computer compare fingerprints?"

"Look," Murphy said patiently, "it's not all that tough. The computer here reduces your fingerprints to an array of numbers. The computer measures the whorls—the number of them, their distance from one another, their thickness, that kind of thing—and creates a numerical pattern. No two numerical patterns from any two sets of fingerprints will be the same. Then the FBI computer runs that numerical pattern through its memory banks until it comes up with the one in its files that fits. It works every time. If they've got you in the FBI computer, they can match it perfectly in somewhere between twenty seconds and—in a real tough case—maybe two minutes. Who do you think you're screwing around with here, for Christ's sake? You don't lie about something that can be checked against the FBI computer. And you don't ever lie to me, asshole. I'm your lawyer."

Webster's face was a study in utter misery. "I'm sorry," he said again. "Look, can you get me out of here? This is a horrible place. I can't stay here."

"You're staying," Murphy told him. "There's no bail for you after you pulled this kind of shit. You lie to a judge in open court and he tends to take it personally."

"Will I get the same judge at my trial?" Webster asked in alarm.

Murphy shook his head. "No. I'm checking the docket, waiting for a judge that I like to get free. I'll make it a point not to let the case be presided over by the guy you lied to. I'm in no hurry to find myself in his courtroom for a while. The guy I'm hoping to get is a good defendant's judge, and he's a straight guy, too. I'll tell you, though, you perjure yourself in his courtroom and you'll be a very old man with a long, gray beard when you get out of the can."

"I won't. I'll tell the truth. Can you get this guy you want?"

"He's got another murder trial going right now, but it should be winding down soon. There are problems with an early trial, but if you're willing to go for one, it's possible that I can get this case in front of him."

"Then let's do it," Webster said. "I can't stay long in this place. I thought that prison in California was rough. I've had to fight off three guys since I've been here."

Murphy smiled cruelly. "Eastern jails aren't like jails anywhere else," he said. "Most of the guys in here awaiting trial or serving a sentence for a misdemeanor would be lifers in any state west of Pittsburgh. They've got to be real badasses in this state by the time anybody decides to put them away for a little while."

"Tell me about it," Webster said. "I'll take an early trial. Just get me the hell out of here."

"You realize that an early trial means I'll have less time to prepare."

"So will the DA."

"That's true. On the other hand, he's got some nice

stuff already. You've got no alibi for the day of the killing."

"I went to the movies."

"Prove it," Murphy said.

"Well, maybe the girl at the ticket window will recognize me."

"Don't count on it. Unless there was something special about you, Mike, she's not even going to look at your face. I'll try it, but don't get your hopes up on that one. Two, they've got your record—"

"Can they even mention that in court?"

"Technically, no. But they'll try to slip it in. The judge will tell the jury to disregard it, and the jury will, of course, make it a point to remember every word. That's the way you play that game."

"Shit," Webster said.

"Well, if you get convicted, that sort of thing would give me grounds to move for a mistrial."

"And I'd still be sitting here."

"Right," Murphy told him. "They've also got your prints on that kitchen knife that was sticking out of Lynn's chest. I'm sort of curious about that one myself. How did that happen?"

Webster held out his hands in helplessness. "I don't know. When I opened the trunk and saw her there, I must have tried to pull the knife out of her. I . . . I was all rattled. I couldn't believe what I was seeing."

"Yeah," Murphy said, "well, the only problem is that the only prints on it were yours. Whoever stuck it in her must have wiped it clean. That's going to be my pitch, anyway."

Webster said, "It doesn't look good, does it?"

"It could be worse. I've got some leg work to do, but I can probably establish that you were at least near the movie theater that day. That'll lend some credibility to your story. Two, the bad back helps. If I can establish by medical testimony that you couldn't have lifted Lynn's body into the trunk, then that'll count for something. I'll have to send a doctor out here to examine you."

"I'll be here," Webster said. "I don't plan on going anywhere for a while."

"The whole thrust of our defense," Murphy told him, "will be reasonable doubt. It's the only thing we've got right now. I'm going to try to find some other angle before we actually get into court, but for now reasonable doubt is it."

Webster said nothing. Murphy could tell that his client wasn't hopeful. Neither, frankly, was Murphy. Which brought him to his next point.

"I think it's time we talked about my fee," Murphy said.

"Sure," Webster told him. "Whatever you charge. I'm in no position to bargain."

Murphy said, "Well—separate and distinct from what you owe me for arranging bail—my fee for murder is usually eight grand. That's up front, Mike."

Webster paled. "I don't have it."

"You told me you've got about four."

"Yeah, I've got four. That's all I've got."

"All right," Murphy said. "You go to the jail administration. They'll give you a form to fill out that'll give me permission to take the four grand out of your account. You can give me the rest of it according to a fee schedule we'll set up after I get you off."

Webster smiled slightly. "And what if I get convicted?"

Murphy shrugged. "Then you'll still be legally

obligated to pay me the balance of the fee, but you won't bother, will you? What am I going to do, sue you? Am I going to have you put in jail? You'll already be in jail."

"That's a cheery thought," Webster said.

"That's just one of the joys of criminal work," Murphy told him. "If the client loses, so does the attorney. That's why most lawyers insist on their fees in full, up front, before the case goes to trial. Half the guys in this jail, they're awaiting trial while their mothers and fathers and brothers and sisters and wives and girlfriends are out committing crimes to get up the cash to pay the legal fee up front. If I were like most lawyers in this town, you'd sit right here in this hellhole until you found some way to get me the full eight grand. I wouldn't do a thing for you before you got me the cash up front—and in full."

"Couldn't I get a public defender or something?"

"You could do that," Murphy conceded. "And the public defender would plead you guilty because he's got too many other cases to give you any kind of a defense."

"All right," Webster said. "What you're saying is that you're cutting me a break."

"Only because I'm a prince," Murphy told him. "Now, tell me about this manslaughter beef out in California."

Webster wiped his face with his hands. Then he leaned back in his chair.

"I was working on this place near Fresno," he said. "We grew grapes for Gallo—you know, the stuff they put in their jug wines. I liked the work, and I liked the product, too, if you know what I mean."

"You had a drinking problem?" Murphy said.

Webster smiled ruefully. "Yeah, well . . . you know how some guys use alcohol as a crutch? I used it more like a wheelchair. So did my old man—before it killed him. I guess you inherit a taste for it. I don't touch the stuff anymore, not even a beer. I haven't had a drop since that trouble out there. Shit, I was just a kid then. I didn't have any brains at all."

"The trouble . . ." Murphy prodded.

"Yeah, right. I had this wife then. She was bad news right from the start. She was pretty, and she was smart, but she decided early on after she married me that she wanted more out of life than being married to a farm worker who was boozed up four nights a week. She started playing around. I came home one night—drunk, I guess—and caught her in the sack with another guy. There was a fight, and the other guy fell down a flight of stairs. He broke his neck."

"That's it?"

Webster nodded. "That's it. I'd never been in trouble before, not for nothing. But here was this guy dead with his pants down around his ankles, and I got manslaughter second degree. I did my time at Vacaville. That's where I had my back operation, in fact. When I got out on parole, I went back home and found my wife shacked up with another guy. It was either fight him or split. I just decided to take off."

"Jump parole, you mean?"

"Yeah. I never figured on going back there. I figured what the hell. I just wanted to get a new life going. So I came to Philadelphia."

"Why Philadelphia?"

"The cheapest air fare from Fresno to the East Coast."

"How'd you end up with the job at Brian's farm?"

Murphy asked.

"When I first got here, I got a job as a janitor at one of the big office buildings in Center City. There was this older guy who ran a big insurance agency, and I cleaned his office. He was a decent guy. We got to talking one night when he was working late and it turned out he had this gentleman's farm out on in Phoenixville. I told him I used to do farm work. He offered me a job working there, and I jumped at it. I hated living and working in the city. I'd always worked outdoors before. So, I worked there for a few years, and when the guy retired to Florida and sold the farm to Brian I got kept on. I'm good on a farm. I know planting and stuff, and I'm good with livestock. I work my ass off, Frank. I've always been a good worker. Nobody could say I wasn't that."

"You said that Mike Webster isn't your real name," Murphy said. "What is it?"

"Mike Caldwell. Webster was my mother's maiden name."

"I need your full name."

"Michael Edward Caldwell. But I don't use that name anymore. I'm Mike Webster now."

Murphy scribbled in his notebook. Webster fell silent. His gaze fell to the floor. After a moment, he said, "Everything was fine until Lynn showed up. I was doing okay until that happened. All that stuff was behind me for keeps."

"Not anymore," Murphy told him.

Webster looked up. "No, I guess not. I didn't kill her. Somebody's got to believe that. Do you believe me, Frank?"

Murphy ran his hand through his thick gray hair. "Well, Mike," he said, "I'm trying real hard."

121

CHAPTER 11

The day had been bad enough already—no breakfast, the jailhouse meeting with Webster. Then, to get things really rolling, the Toronado ran out of gas on the way back to the office. Murphy had to walk eight long blocks on a disturbingly warm spring day and give the doped-out freak at the gas station a twenty-dollar deposit before he'd part with a five-gallon can of gas. Then he had to hike back to the car to put enough fuel in it to get it back to the station and recover his twenty bucks from the space cadet.

He'd already known that the speedometer on the Toronado was screwed up. He'd learned that a month earlier when he'd gotten nailed for speeding even though the speedometer said he was well within the limit. Now the gas gauge was clearly reading incorrectly. Murphy began thinking about a new car. All the way back to his office he thought about it. Then he thought about what they were charging for new cars, and he thought about Patricia's tuition and he muttered a number of words to himself that would have gotten his knuckles rapped if he'd still been in parochial school.

He arrived at his office just before noon with his stomach growling and a deep scowl on his face.

"Good morning," Esmeralda said brightly. "And don't we look cheery today?"

Murphy grunted.

Esmeralda followed him into his private office and rattled off his messages while he turned on the Mister Coffee and thought about the bottle of bourbon behind the real estate law book.

"You had a call from your daughter," Esmeralda said. "She wants you to get back to her. You had a call from Lieutenant Wilder, who said you should get back to him right away."

"All right," Murphy said. "Do two things for me. First, get me a copy of the paper."

"You've got bets down already?" Esmeralda asked him. "Baseball season just started."

"Please," Murphy said. "I just want to keep up on the fluctuations in the international monetary supply."

"Right," Esmeralda said.

"Besides," Murphy told her, "there's no point spread on baseball. I want you to call the California State Department of Corrections in Sacramento and find out how we'd go about getting the prison records—especially the medical records—of a Michael Edward Caldwell, who did some time in Vacaville State Penitentiary on a manslaughter charge."

Esmeralda took notes. "Got it."

"And get Wilder for me, too."

"I've got things you just gave me to do," she protested. "Did you break your fingers this morning?"

"You know," Murphy told her, lighting a cigarette, "if I was looking for abuse I could move back in with my wife."

Esmeralda moved back outside to her desk as Murphy prepared a cup of coffee. He was punching it up with a dose of bourbon when she rang him.

"Lieutenant's Wilder's on the line."

Murphy hit the button. "Hi, Jim. What's up?"

"I just got orders that I'm reporting to you on special assignment. How did you actually manage to swing that?"

"It's a long story. I'll give you the details later, but the deal is that we've got to put this guy Berger into protective custody."

"Did you know that Lucelli got picked up yesterday?"

"I heard it was going to happen."

"It happened," Wilder said. "It's in this morning's paper, too."

Murphy's lips pursed beneath his moustache. "All right, then we've got to get Berger on ice quick. I also have to get a deposition from him for Fletcher. I'll call Berger and tell him to get down to my office right away. Can you think of where we might put him for a few weeks or even a month or so?"

Wilder said, "I've got a thought. Remember Joe Otis?"

"Uniformed lieutenant in West Philly?"

"That's him. He took his retirement back around the first of the year, and now he's police chief in some little burg up near Scranton. It's only a couple of hours away, but he might have a spot where we can hide Berger. I can call him, tell him we need a spot, and he won't ask a lot of questions."

"Sounds good. Suppose you make your arrangements and figure on meeting me and Berger here at my office around four. I'll have him ready to go, and you can take him up there. You know you've got to stay

124

with him."

"I know," Wilder said. "This isn't going to make a big hit at home. Annabelle had plans for me this weekend."

"I can take over on weekends for a while. You just got to stay with him during the week. I can't stay up there Monday through Friday because I've got cases to handle in court."

"Yeah," Wilder said. "You can't let all them scumbags down, can you?"

"Hey," Murphy said, "they're my scumbags. They pay the rent. You got that nice city check rolling in every week."

"Okay. I'll call Joe and then I'll go home and get some stuff, then I'll meet you at your office at four."

"Catch you later," Murphy said, hitting the button and then dialing the number Berger had left him. The phone rang only once.

"Caravelle," a woman's voice said. Murphy could hear the sound of tinkling glassware and the hum of voices in the background.

"Mr. Berger, please."

"Who's calling?"

"You can tell him it's Frank Murphy."

"One moment please."

Murphy waited, drumming his fingers on the desktop. Then Berger came on. "Hello."

"Frank Murphy, Mr. Berger. Things are moving."

"Moving? I read the newspapers. The *momzer* has been arrested. Good."

"Yes," Murphy said, "it's good. But that means it's time for us to put you somewhere where his friends can't get at you. Remember I told you we'd have to do that."

125

"I remember. My bag is packed."

"Come to my office this afternoon about two-thirty. I have to take a preliminary statement from you. Then a friend of mine, a Lieutenant Wilder, is going to take you somewhere where you'll be safe. It's going to be a couple of weeks at least, Mr. Berger."

"Weeks, months. Who cares? It's been years I've waited for this."

"I'll see you here at two-thirty."

"With bells on," Irving Berger said.

Murphy hung up and dialed the number of his former home in Mount Airy. Mary Ellen answered.

"I was going to call you," she said. "Patricia said you drove her home the other night with a murderer in the car. Is that true, Frank?"

"He's an accused murderer. There's a difference."

"Not much difference to me," she said.

In this case, maybe none at all, Murphy thought. But he didn't say it. He did say, "She was perfectly safe, Mary Ellen."

"Frank," she told him, "if you want to drive around on dark nights with killers in your car, that's your business. When you bring our daughter along with you, then it's mine. Please be kind enough to keep your lovely collection of law clients away from Patricia from now on. If she has to meet any rapists, I'd rather she arranged her own introductions, if you don't mind."

"Is she there?" Murphy asked weakly.

"What for? Do you have an armed robber you'd like to fix her up with?"

Murphy gritted his teeth. Mary Ellen had a tongue she could use to trim a hedge.

"I'm returning her call," he said finally.

"I'll get her," Mary Ellen said. "I mean it, Frank.

Keep those creeps of yours away from her."

"Yes, dear," Murphy said.

Patricia came on the phone a moment later. "Hi. Want to buy me lunch tomorrow?"

"I'd love to," Murphy told her, "but I've got a full schedule."

"Daddy, I'm going back to school in a few days."

Murphy thought about the next day's workload. "Look, I've got to go back out to that farm and do a few things. Then I've got to go interview Judy Kavanaugh at that school she goes to. If you don't mind watching me work all morning and afternoon then I'll pick you up around ten."

"Will you take me someplace nice?"

"Isn't it enough that I send you someplace nice for an education? I was more or less thinking about McDonald's."

"You've got to be kidding," Patricia said. "Barf, barf."

Murphy chuckled. "All right. Someplace decent."

"You're a nice daddy," she told him.

"When you tell your mother be sure to point out to her that it'll just be you and me and that there are no plans to include anybody with a prison record. She's getting touchy about things like that."

"I'll tell her. See you at ten tomorrow. Bring Winston, okay?"

"Yeah, why not? He'd like the ride."

"Bye, bye," Patricia said.

Murphy hung up the phone and rubbed his ear. He was spending so much time on the phone lately he was developing ears like Esmeralda's husband, the boxer. While he'd been on the phone with his daughter, Esmeralda had dropped a copy of the *Inquirer* on his

127

desk. Murphy scanned the front page. It contained a sketchy story on Lucelli's arrest. Neither the police nor the DA were giving out details, which was fine with Murphy. Aside from that, the *Inquirer*'s front page was full of crap out of Central America and shenanigans in Harrisburg. Murphy scanned that and then went directly to Clark DeLeon's column in the B-section. DeLeon's specialty was infuriating cat owners. Today he was writing about how the catapult had gotten its name. According to DeLeon, the device had been invented for the sole purpose of propelling cats over high walls.

"Tomorrow," his last line read, "we'll talk about the catheter."

Murphy moved back to Sports. He was into a story of monumental importance—a piece on Mike Schmidt's performance early in the season—when Esmeralda buzzed him again.

"Yes," Murphy said.

"Mr. Toddman on line one."

Murphy hit the button. "Hi, Paul."

"I just got a call from Quick Silver. He's representing Lucelli."

"There's a marriage made in heaven. What's he want?"

"He wants a meeting with me. He wants to talk about a plea bargain."

"No shit," Murphy said.

"I think he's just out to find out what he can find out."

"No question about it."

Toddman said, "I thought that since you're now on the payroll for six grand a week you might like to sit in."

Murphy pondered the proposition. "I wonder if it's

128

such a good idea to let him know I'm involved with this."

"He'll find out anyway," Toddman pointed out. "If we're going to pay you, then your name is going to show up on the voucher sheets in connection with the case. They're public information. And at six grand a week, it won't take long for the word to get around, believe me. So come on in here and earn some of the money, Frank. Why should I have to put up with all this shit by myself?"

"Can we make it late? I'm taking depositions from our witness this afternoon. I'll have Esmeralda type them up overnight and drop them on your desk first thing in the morning."

"How long are you going to refer to the witness as the witness? Just when do you plan on letting me know who the fucking witness is?"

"I'll tell you when we get together this afternoon if you like."

"Well, that's real big of you, Frank—especially considering that I'm going to find out tomorrow morning anyway, when I get the depositions. I guess it doesn't make much difference now. I've already risked a false arrest suit on this witness, whoever he is."

"Or she," Murphy said.

"Is it a she?"

"Since you've talked to me in such a disrespectful tone, you can wait until you see the depositions to find out."

"Up yours," Toddman said. "Is four-thirty okay for you?"

"Fine."

"You're really a *putz*, Frank," Toddman said.

"It's all part of my charm," Murphy told him.

CHAPTER 12

"Where is this place you're taking me?" Irving Berger asked.

Jim Wilder, in the driver's seat of his unmarked, city-owned Dodge, said, "It's up in the country, a couple of hours away. Just sit back and relax, Mr. Berger. Everything is under control."

Berger sat back in his seat and looked at the city streets as Wilder artfully negotiated the raceway around City Hall. It was the confluence of the city's two busiest streets—Broad and Market—and it had taken a sadistic genius to build City Hall squarely in the middle of them, creating a traffic nightmare unparalleled in North America. To top it all off, there was always heavy construction underway somewhere in the loop around the baroque building. At times like this—it was the beginning of the evening rush hour—the roadway around City Hall was filled with slow-moving cars, trucks, and buses which were, in turn, filled with drivers who shook fists or made other angry, even more inelegant gestures or, on occasion, got out of their cars and beat the hell out of one another.

Irving Berger never drove his car in Center City. These days, even getting behind the wheel brought forth heartbreaking memories. Periodically, when driving from his home in Elkins Park to his restaurant in Northeast Philadelphia, he sometimes thought about what would happen if he simply floored the gas pedal in his Buick Park Avenue, aimed the car at a tree and closed his eyes. It was a terrible temptation. In a sense, he supposed—thinking about the two hours of questioning to which Murphy had just subjected him in his office before sending him away with Wilder—that's what Berger was doing now. This well-dressed black man in the unmarked police car next to him was protecting him and, at the same time, abetting him in his suicidal tendencies.

"Strange," Irving Berger muttered to himself.

"What?" Wilder said.

"Nothing. I said nothing, I was only thinking."

"What were you thinking about, Mr. Berger?" Wilder asked him.

"Call me Irving. Everybody calls me Irving—even the dishwashers at the restaurant call me that. Mr. Berger was my father, he should rest in peace. A good man, my father."

"Call me Jim, then," Wilder said, maneuvering the Dodge up North Broad on his way to Vine Street and then out to the Delaware Expressway. "I never knew mine."

"Never knew your what?"

"My father. He got killed in a robbery when I was a kid. It was in a grocery store in North Philadelphia, and there was some shooting."

131

"And that's why you're a policeman?" Berger asked. "Because a robber killed your father?"

Wilder smiled slightly. "Not quite. My old man was the robber. He was a junkie. The grocer had a thirty-eight under the counter, and that's all she wrote. My mother was never right after that. My grandmother ended up raising me. She just died a couple of years back. Some lady, she was."

"Nu," Berger said.

Wilder looked at him. "What's that mean?"

Now it was Berger's turn to smile. "What does *nu* mean? Good question. There's no word in English."

"What language is it?"

"Yiddish. Forgive me, I still think in Yiddish after all these years. *Nu* means whatever you want it to mean in Yiddish. Somebody says, 'Did you hear that Goldfarb ran away with Steinberg's wife?' And you say, *'Nu!'* Somebody says, 'Kessel has a son who's a *schmendrick.'* And you say, *'Nu.'* You understand?"

"Nu," Wilder said.

"Does that mean yes or no?"

"You tell me," Wilder said.

Berger chuckled. "So, you're a policeman because your father was a robber? Is that it?"

Wilder shrugged. "Might be, deep down inside. Mostly I think I'm a cop because I like things neat. I like them orderly. Cops keep life orderly for people. We try to, anyway. The odds are stacked against us. I saw this article in a magazine the other day. The attorney general's office in California decided to track about a quarter million guys who turned eighteen in 1974 and follow them until they turned twenty-nine. Those are the prime years for criminals. They just picked these guys at random. You know what they

132

found out?"

"What?" Irving Berger said.

"They found out that one in three of the guys ended up arrested. One in three! Can you imagine that? One in six of them were arrested for something serious—like rape or murder or robbery. And half the guys who got arrested got arrested more than once."

Irving Berger grunted and shook his head.

"And those are only the guys who got caught," Wilder pointed out. "In most crimes—I mean, like nine out of ten—you don't bust anybody. Did I say I like order? I'm in the wrong line of work."

Irving Berger said, "Some things are more important than order."

"Like what?"

Berger produced an Anthony and Cleopatra panatella. "Do you mind if I smoke?"

"Be my guest."

"Would you like one?" Berger said, lighting up.

"Nope. I quit a year ago."

"Too late for me," Berger said, cracking the window.

They drove in silence for a while. Wilder got to the Delaware Expressway and gave the Dodge the gas. Unmarked or not, the uniformed guys would spot the Dodge for what it was and let it go. Wilder cranked it up to seventy in the left-hand lane, driving with an effortless skill born of years behind the wheel of a prowl car, trying to break out of the city before rush hour began in earnest. After a few miles, Wilder noticed the old man gazing out the window, lost in thought. It didn't do to let witnesses in protective custody think too much. Sometimes a detailed examination of their predicament tended to weaken their testimony.

"So," Wilder said, "what's more important than order?"

Berger was stirred from his reflection. "Hmm? Oh. Well, many things. Order isn't everything. I learned that in Cologne—before you were born, probably."

"I was born just as the war was ending."

"I wish I had been," Irving Berger said quietly.

"You were a Jew in Germany before the war, right? My old man was a black in Georgia before civil rights. The Klan hung my uncle—strung him right up. My old man, he never got over that. He was pissed off at white people till the day he got killed. A white guy shot him, too."

"How do you feel about white people, then?" Berger asked.

Wilder laughed. "Don't worry. I'm harmless."

"You didn't answer my question."

Wilder cast a glance in Berger's direction. "I got nothing against white people unless they got something against me. Then we got a problem."

"Does that happen much? Do you come across white people who seem to have something against you?"

"In my line of work? No, not more than five or six times a day. It comes with the territory."

"The man who shot your father," Berger asked, "was he a Jew, like me?"

"He was a Jew, yeah. My part of North Philly was Jewish until black folks started to move in. The Jews took one look at us and moved out to the suburbs in a big hurry. But this guy, he still had his grocery store in the neighborhood. He came in every morning and opened up and did business and then he went home at night. Before the neighborhood went black, he'd lived in an apartment over the store. I don't know where he lived after he moved. Was he like you? No. He was a frightened man. That's why he had the gun under the counter. You don't seem to be scared much of anything, Irving. Why not, I wonder—considering what you're into?"

"I've been into worse," Irving Berger said. "Before the war, they came and took us away. They sent us to a camp. You understand what I mean, a camp?"

"I understand."

Berger sat back against the vinyl seat, pulling on his cigar, remembering. He seldom recalled such matters —at least, not willingly. "I was a boy in my teens. My father was a merchant in Cologne. We had a little store. We sold giftware. Like your grocer, we lived in an apartment over the store. First they made us wear the yellow stars on our coats. They were big, yellow, Jewish stars. Then one day they came and took us away. Just like that. They knocked on the door and told us to pack and we went—my mother, my father, and my little sisters. They put us on a train, in a boxcar, and we rode the train for a long time. It was fall, and the weather was getting cold. We froze in that car. And then we got to the camp."

The old man was silent for a moment as he called forth the images. Wilder said, "Then what?"

Berger answered in a low, raspy voice. "Then we stayed. Five years I was in that camp. They shaved our heads every month or so. Lice. There was not much food. We slept in a barracks. We wore uniforms with stripes on them. After a while, they took me away to work because I was the strongest. I was the only one who survived. Why me? I ask that all the time. God knows. One of these days I'm going to get to ask Him. Why me, I'm going to say? What was on your mind with all that? I can hardly wait to hear what He says."

"You asked me if I have problems with white people," Wilder said. "Do you have problems with Germans?"

Berger nodded. "I won't buy German goods. I won't do business with them."

"It's a whole new generation over there now," Wilder pointed out.

"I'm not a new generation."

"Does it make you feel good to feel that way?" Wilder asked him.

"It makes me feel better than I would if I didn't feel this way. I know it makes no sense. A lot of things people think and feel make no sense. Why should I apologize for this one? You don't understand."

"Oh, I understand. I just don't see the point in it."

"There's no point in a lot of things. Why—"

"Why should you apologize for the way you feel having no point? Right?"

"Right," Berger said. "You know, you're a smart man. Did you go to school?"

"College, you mean? I went nights. I've got a degree in English."

"Good, good. My Ellen, she was never very good in English. But the sciences? A whiz, she was. Very smart."

"Ellen was your daughter?"

Berger nodded. "She was my daughter, yes."

Wilder found the Pennsylvania Turnpike, got on the Northeast extension and hit the gas hard. It was mostly uphill from there on in, but he had the Dodge cruising at close to eighty. This was a police car, with a special engine and handling package. Wilder's personal car was a Ford Tempo with a tiny, four-cylinder engine.

His wife used that one. He used the city Dodge, night and day. It was a perk they'd given him when he'd made detective lieutenant—a perk he liked, too.

After a while, as the sky over the mountains north of the city darkened, Berger said, "How much farther?"

"A couple of hours yet. Maybe less if I stomp it a bit."

"Will you tell me where I'm going now?"

Wilder said, "You're going to a little town called Sparta, about forty minutes outside Scranton. It's an old mining town built on the side of a mountain. I was there once, a few years back, to pick up a prisoner. You and I are going to be living in a small summer camp for kids. The place won't open up for another couple of months. We'll have all the privacy we need, and we'll be out of the way. That's what we're after—someplace out of the way."

"Is there TV?"

"I checked. There's TV. We'll be staying in the camp director's cabin. It has electric heat. It won't be plush, but it's better than putting you in some crummy apartment in Philadelphia somewhere and having cops all around. If we did that they might hear about it. Here, only two people know where you'll be—Frank and me. Not even the DA knows."

Wilder paused for a moment. "Well, actually three people. The police chief in Sparta used to be a Philly cop. He set this up for us, but he doesn't know who we're going to be keeping there."

"Can this man be trusted?" Irving Berger asked.

Wilder nodded. "He's a straight shooter."

"You know this man well, do you?"

Wilder caught more than a note of suspicion in the old man's voice. "I've known him for ten or twelve years. He was my last desk sergeant when I was in uniform. There's no way to do something like this without either putting at least some trust in somebody you know or arousing a lot of suspicion in somebody you don't know. This'll be fine."

Berger said nothing. He finished his cigar while Wilder played with the Dodge's radio, trying to find a clear station. After a while, Berger said, "How much do you trust Mr. Murphy?"

Wilder glanced over at him in surprise. "You ask me that? You're the guy who went to him instead of to the DA. How much do you trust him?"

"I don't trust anybody," Berger said. "If you were me, who would you trust?"

"Nobody," Wilder admitted. "But you can trust me, and you can trust Murphy. We were patrol partners for six years. You get pretty close to a guy when you work together like that. Frank's a funny guy. He's bright as hell, and he's got a lot of energy. All the time I've known him he's been going to school every minute in his off hours—except lately, since he got his law degree. Now all he does is work and try to earn enough money to keep his daughter in college."

"He has a daughter?" Berger said with interest.

"Yep. Smart kid. He's crazy about her."

"Yes," Berger said. "I know what that's like. My daughter, my Ellen, she was everything to me. She came to me late in life, like a gift you don't expect. Then in a second she was gone, like her mother. Go figure. I can't."

Wilder felt a powerful urge to change the conversation. "How did you happen to come to America, Irving?"

138

Berger stroked his little moustache. "After the war, there was no Israel then, or I would have gone there. I thought about Palestine, but it was so hard to get in. This was easier, so I came here. It was a place to feel a little safe. I met Sophie on the boat. We came here from New York because she had cousins. Her cousin Nathan, he had a little diner. I went to work for him. When Nathan decided to retire, I bought the business from him and expanded it. It's a nice place now. You know the Caravelle?"

Wilder nodded. "I worked the Northeast for a year or so. We used to stop in there and get coffee and strawberry shortcake. Great strawberry shortcake."

Berger smiled. "That was Sophie. She was a marvelous baker. She was an artist. We did fine. We bought a nice house. Did you ever know Sophie when you stopped in my place?"

"I don't think so."

"A little woman," Berger insisted. "She looked like Gracie Allen, only with glasses sometimes."

"Maybe I remember her," Wilder said, not remembering at all.

"I thought so. You ever saw Sophie, you'd remember. Are you married?"

"Yeah. My wife is a social worker. We've been married sixteen years."

"Children?"

Wilder shook his head.

"That's either a blessing or a curse," Berger told him.

"Probably a blessing," said Wilder, not believing it. "I remember a line I learned in college. 'The first half of our lives are ruined by our parents and the second half by our children.'"

139

"It's not true."

"I know," Wilder said. "We can't have kids together. That's why I rationalize it, I suppose. What happened that night, Irving?"

"Which night?"

"The night your wife died."

Berger nibbled slightly on his lower lip. When he spoke, his voice was strained. "It was a Tuesday, very late. There was no business. We were all set to close up. All the help had gone home. I was in the back, paying bills. It was near the end of the month. Sophie was in front, ringing up the receipts and waiting for the last two customers to leave. They were two men, talking in a booth. I started to come out to ask her a question. There was a door between the dining room and the office in back. I put my hand on the door to push it and I heard a shot. Then, right away, I heard two more shots. I just froze. I couldn't move. I looked out the glass, and there was a man in a blue overcoat standing near the door. He had a shotgun. There was smoke in the air. I could smell it through the door. I know the smell of gunsmoke."

"Then what?"

"Then the man turned around and ran out. I saw his face. I saw his face very clear. He was only ten feet away. How could I not see his face?"

"And he didn't see you?"

"No. He never looked my way. He just looked in the booth. Then he was gone."

"So then what?" Wilder asked.

"So then I came out and looked in the booth and there were two dead men. They were covered with blood. This one man, he had a cigarette still in his

140

mouth. I thought my heart would burst, it beat so. Then I called for Sophie, but she didn't answer. Then I found her on the floor behind the register. She had no face. My Sophie had no face."

"And you saw the man? You're sure?"

"I see him in my dreams. All these years I've seen him in my dreams. He was the man I saw in the newspaper."

"You know," Wilder said, "if you say this in court you're going to put away the head mobster in this city. You know that."

"It doesn't matter to me," Irving Berger said. "It doesn't matter to me what else he's done. He killed Sophie. That's why I want him. I was always going to tell about him. I was going to wait until Ellen was grown up and had her education. Then I was going to tell her what I had to do and send her to Israel and then come and tell what I'd seen. I promised that to Sophie when I was sitting *shiva*. I swore to her I would do it. I had to keep silent all those years, for Ellen's sake. You understand?"

"I understand," Wilder said.

"Now I can speak. It's not the way I wanted. But now I can speak, and then I can die. I must not die, though, until I've spoken. I must not die until then. I'm in your hands."

"You're in good hands," Wilder said grimly.

The rest of the way into Sparta, the two men did not speak. Neither felt the need, and each was lost in his own thoughts. Irving Berger's were on his past. Jim Wilder's were on Irving Berger's future, on doing what he could to ensure that the old man would have one.

For a little while longer, at least.

141

CHAPTER 13

Richie Silver's face was grim when he entered Toddman's office on the third floor of City Hall. It was a smallish office, furnished with battered city issue, a startling contrast to Silver's own office three blocks away.

Richie Silver's lair was a vast sea of thick, rust-colored carpeting and chrome and glass furniture, accented with beige leather and hot and cold running secretaries in tight dresses. Richie was fussy about secretaries. They had to be young, pleasant and pretty, because it was good for business. It helped, too, if they had a high tolerance for Richie's advances. They didn't have to say yes—Richie wasn't a pig about it—but they had to say no with style, maybe with a small hint that if Richie weren't a married man they'd find him irresistible. The word had gone forth in Richie Silver's office that there was a right way and a wrong way to say no to the boss—that those who said yes would be favored with light work schedules and liberal vacations and those who couldn't bring themselves to say no in the proper fashion would soon be unemployed.

Here it was different. Toddman's secretary was a woman in her sixties with bodily dimensions roughly approximating those of an M-1 tank. She was smart, though, and she performed at a high level. Toddman sat in his shirtsleeves in an aged, high-backed leather chair and chewed on one of his huge cigars.

"You get lip cancer from those things, Paul," Silver said as he entered. "That's what killed Freud. It killed Ulysses S. Grant, too."

"Let me guess," Toddman said, extending his hand. "You were a history major as an undergraduate. Jesus, Richie, that's really impressive. Now tell me how General Custer got it, why don't you."

"Custer got it because he hung out with the wrong crowd," Murphy said from behind Silver.

Silver spun about.

"Hi, Richie," Murphy said. "Nice suit. Business must be good."

Silver turned back to Toddman. "What's he doing here?"

"He's under contract to the office," Toddman said.

"For what?"

Toddman turned to Murphy. "Tell him for what, Frank. I'd like to know myself."

"Moral support," Murphy said, sitting down in one of the chairs in front of Toddman's desk. "Fletcher decided that he couldn't make another move on this case without me. Ever since I left this office, you know, the whole place has turned to shit. Sit down, Richie. You're making me hurt my neck looking up at you."

Silver sat, surveying the situation. Toddman he knew, had dealt with often and respected. Murphy he knew less well, had dealt with not at all in such matters and didn't particularly care for. Silver tended to regard cops the way he regarded janitors—as necessary but essentially inferior beings. Murphy's recently acquired law degree and recent admission to the bar made him no less a cop. To Silver, such an accomplishment was roughly comparable to the auto mechanic obtaining a college degree by going to class nights. It was an admirable accomplishment, but it changed nothing. The auto mechanic would always be an auto mechanic, and the cop would always be a cop. Silver was who he was and had been for a long time. People like Murphy were who they were—no matter how hard they worked to change it.

"Who am I dealing with here?" he asked Toddman finally.

"The DA's office."

"And he's the DA's office?"

"On this case," Toddman said. "He's involved, anyway. So, spill it. What's on your mind, Richie?"

Silver shrugged in what was designed to be a disarming manner. "The usual. You've got a client of mine in custody, and I'm curious about what you've got on him."

Toddman sat back in his worn chair. He lit his dead cigar and blew out a puff of blue-black smoke. "Normally," the first assistant district attorney said, "I'm always more than happy to tell the defendant's attorney just what we have. Usually, when they find out the people have a bulletproof case, the defendant is willing to plead. Is your guy ready to plead, Richie? Is the boy godfather of South Philly looking for a deal?"

"It's possible," Quick Silver said. "Tommy's a

144

reasonable man. But he won't make a decision until he knows what he's up against."

Murphy looked at Toddman. Toddman shrugged. "Sound reasonable to you?" he asked Murphy.

Murphy lit a cigarette. The more tobacco smoke the better, he figured. That would drive Silver out of here sooner. "Well," he said, "I'm not the guy to ask. I've never had much of a reputation for being reasonable. If it was up to me, I'd tell Richie here to go fuck himself. Of course, that's just a personal opinion."

Silver frowned deeply and turned toward Toddman. "Is that what I'm supposed to tell my client?"

Murphy leaned forward and said, "You can tell Tommy that we've got him absolutely stone cold. He couldn't get out of this one with a can opener."

"Stone cold with what?" Silver insisted, his annoyance showing through at last.

"An eyewitness. It's a positive ID. It's ironclad. Tell your guy to get his toothbrush packed."

"What positive ID?" Silver countered. "You haven't even had Tommy in for a lineup."

"We don't need one," Murphy told him. "The witness is certain and positively unshakable."

"Do you have a deposition?" Silver demanded.

"Does a bull have balls?"

"Can I see the deposition?"

"When the trial begins," Murphy said. "Discovery isn't mandatory in criminal cases, Richie—as we all know."

"Who's the witness?"

"That waits, too."

"So we're supposed to go for a plea on nothing more than your word?" Silver said incredulously.

145

Toddman shrugged. "I don't much care what you do. For one thing, I'm not inclined to take a plea in this case to begin with. Your client isn't your garden-variety scumbag. He's a big-time, first-class scumbag, and you and I both know that this murder represents only the tiniest portion of the bullshit he's been responsible for over the years—him or his merry band of sociopaths. All a plea will buy you, Richie, is twenty years instead of the twenty-five-to-life we're talking about if we go all the way. If Tommy is willing to take a flat twenty, then I'll go to the DA with it. But he has to do it blind—on our say-so about that we've got is solid enough to ice it for us in a trial. That's the only deal I'd consider, and I can't promise that Fletcher would go along with that. These mainline guys, they've got a different view of the world, you know what I mean?"

Silver folded his hands in his lap and studied them for a long moment. Then he looked up. "He might go for the twenty, Paul. He really might. But he won't do it blind. He's got to know who the witness is and what the witness saw."

"What he's got to know," Murphy said quietly, "is who the witness is and where the witness might be found by some of Tommy's close personal friends. And that he's not going to find out. Not until the day we put the witness on the stand in front of a jury and the witness says what the witness has to say."

Toddman bit into his cigar and leaned over his desk. "I'd sure be upset if anything happened to this witness, Richie. I can't think of anything that would upset me more. Now, I realize that you might be nervous about how your client would react if he should happen to get convicted on this, but you should be at least as upset about what would happen to you if something were to happen to our witness. You might just get your ticket lifted, Richie, and you'd end up selling insurance nights. And that's for starters. The cops? It's hard to say what they might do. And they can play the same way Tommy's boys play. Or so I'm told. I wouldn't know about any of that stuff, myself."

"I would," Murphy volunteered.

Silver's face flushed visibly. "What's your connection, Frank?" he demanded. "Why am I talking to you?"

"Because I'm civic-minded."

Silver turned to Toddman. "A trial like this is going to cost this city a mint."

"Then we'll raise taxes," Toddman told him.

Silver knew when he was wasting his time. He stood up, his face the color of a watered zinfandel. "Well, it's clear that you guys don't want to negotiate. What you want to do is jerk me off and that's it."

Murphy suddenly grinned. He looked over at Toddman. "That must be why they call him Quick Silver," Murphy said.

"I didn't invite you, Richie," Toddman said in a low voice. "You called me, remember? That's the deal, and it won't get any better. Actually, I'm kind of hoping your client won't take it. I'm kind of hoping, in fact, that he gets the full load after a trial, goes to Graterford and stays there until he gets Alzheimer's."

"He won't take it blind," Silver said. "Give me what you've got and I'll take it to him. If it's good, I think I can talk him into going for it."

Toddman blew forth another plume of smoke. "See you in court, Richie."

147

"You want publicity on this," Silver accused. "Fletcher wants the publicity. Isn't that it?"

"Our Fletcher?" Murphy asked in feigned shock.

Silver turned and left without a word. Murphy stood up and scratched his head. He stretched. It had been a long day.

"A fishing trip," Murphy said.

"And a crude one at that," Toddman told him. "He won't be back."

"Well, they know that we think what we've got is pretty good. They know that much."

Toddman stood up and began to pace his office, hands in his pockets. He was a short, rumpled man with close-cropped black hair flecked with gray. "They'll go balls out to find the witness. That's their only hope now. How did the depositions go?"

"If he testifies in court the way he deposed, it's open and shut."

"I'll have to talk to him before the trial. You know I've got to do that."

"I know. When the time comes I'll tell you where he is. Shit, I'll take you there."

"You know, Frank," Toddman said, "it wouldn't be bad having you back in the office. You might find life different as an assistant DA than it was when you were chief investigator."

"As long as Fletcher is in office, no way."

"Well," Toddman said, "if we handle this right we might just get him out of here and into Harrisburg."

"What if Quick Silver comes back and says Tommy will plead anyway?"

Toddman laughed. "Then I'll tell him to stuff it. I want Fletcher on page one and the six o'clock news

148

every day while this trial is going on. I want him to come off like Tom Dewey. If we handle this right, the least that'll happen to him is that he'll get a judgeship. Either way, he's out of here."

"And you're in?" Murphy asked.

"What is it you Micks say? If there's a God in heaven."

"There's considerable debate over that," Murphy pointed out as he left.

The district attorney's suite of offices occupied the southwest corner of City Hall. Murphy's old office, now occupied by another detective lieutenant delighted to be here working nine to five, was just down the hall. Murphy followed the path to his old quarters and found Beverly Kavanaugh at her desk, just putting the cover over her typewriter and slipping her coffee cup into a desk drawer.

"My tax dollars at work," Murphy said.

"Hello, Frank," Beverly said. "What are you doing here? Looking for your old job back?"

"What?" Murphy said, pulling out his lighter and tossing it from hand to hand. "And give up show business?"

Beverly cocked her head at him quizzically. "I don't get it."

"Forget it," Murphy said. "It's an old joke, and it's not terribly tasteful."

"So let's hear it."

"You don't want to hear it."

"Yes, I do."

She did, too, Murphy knew. Beverly had a passion for tasteless humor. It was one of the personality traits that Murphy liked best about her. Murphy put down

149

the lighter and began to tell the story with both his voice and his hands.

"All right," Murphy said, standing back to give the story the proper body movement. When Murphy told a joke, he always made it a point to put on a show.

He said, "This guy is walking down the street and he sees this guy he knows. He says, 'Sam! Long time, no see. What are you doing with yourself?' and Sam says, 'I'm with the circus.' So the guy says, 'Yeah? What do you do with the circus?' and Sam says, 'I work with the elephants. Whenever an elephant has a bowel disorder, I have to put on this long rubber glove that stretches up to my shoulder. I stick my arm up the elephant's behind and pull out all the blocked-up crap, then I reach up in there with a garden hose and hose everything out and the elephant is fine.' And the guy says, 'Jesus! That's a horrible job. Why don't you get into another line of work?' And Sam gets this horrified expression on his face and says, 'What? And leave show business?'"

Beverly Kavanaugh rolled her eyes.

"I told you you wouldn't like it," Murphy said.

"Who says I didn't like it?" Beverly Kavanaugh told her old boss.

"I'll walk you out. I want to talk to you about something."

They started down the hall. Murphy said, "You remember Barry Weiner?"

"Your psychiatrist friend?"

"That's him. How would you like it if Barry talked to Judy?"

"What for?"

Murphy shrugged. "Second opinion. Barry's pretty

150

good. And he wouldn't charge you a nickel. It couldn't hurt."

They had reached the elevator. Beverly said, "I guess not. Do you want me to call him?"

"No," Murphy said, reaching for his cigarettes. "I'll take care of it. Shit, I left my lighter on your desk."

"I'll hold the elevator."

"Don't sweat it," Murphy told her. "I'll catch the next one."

"Call me on Barry Weiner," Beverly said, getting into the elevator. "Any Saturday would be fine."

"I'll get back to you," Murphy said as the door closed.

Then he walked back down the hall to the DA's suite of offices and went inside. He went to Beverly Kavanaugh's desk and found the lighter he had left atop her calendar. He slipped it into his pocket and then looked around carefully through the corners of his eyes. It was well after five. Nobody was in sight. Murphy walked around behind Beverly's desk, opened the top drawer and spied the coffee cup. He took out his handkerchief, reached into the drawer and folded it carefully around the cup. Then he pulled the cup out of the drawer, closed it carefully and slipped the meticulously wrapped coffee cup into his suitcoat pocket.

Then Frank Murphy went home to have dinner and watch the Phillies on TV.

CHAPTER 14

Alex bowed. Not a gesture of subservience, just a concession to civility.

"Good evening, Mr. Morgan. Missus Morgan. And how are you this evening?"

Morgan was a red-faced man of fifty in a Bill Blass blazer. His wife wore diamonds. "Just fine, Alex. We're hungry, though."

"Your table is ready. Just follow me, please."

Alex turned and walked with the muscular grace of a dancer across the elegant dining room. Alex had been a dancer—long ago, in another life. That was before other, more lucrative business arrangements had provided enough capital to open this restaurant. A gourmet restaurant on Route 22 in Summit. It was a sumptuous setting designed for sumptuous food, and the combination had made the reputation of L'Americain. Already it was considered by the knowledgeable to be a world-class restaurant, and it was all the more remarkable for being in New Jersey, not Manhattan. A world-class restaurant for suburbanites. A world-class restaurant with prices that weren't inflated by Manhattan rents. A novel concept.

Not bad, Alex was aware, though Alex had worked hard for it. He still worked hard for it, doing what was necessary. Nothing was free. Alex had figured that out a long time ago.

"Here we are. Your waiter will be Adolfo. I'll send the sommelier by shortly."

"Thank you," Morgan said. "No bread, please. I'm trying to take off a few pounds—although this is hardly the place to do that. Alex, I don't know how you stay so trim with a place like this."

Alex smiled, white teeth flashing against pale skin. "It's amazing what two hours a day in the gym does for you."

"I wish I had the time."

"You just have to make the time. Here's Adolfo. Enjoy your meal."

Alex walked back to the reservations desk. It was a week night, which meant that L'Americain would be busy but not swamped. This, in turn, meant that the quality of the food and service would be better than it was on Friday and Saturday nights when the staff was overworked. Alex liked week nights. This place existed for quality, after all. It had no other reason for existing at all, since it had barely broken even the previous two years.

Alex knew good food and wine. But business? That was another matter. Besides, even in the best places the bartenders stole. They pocketed money spent at the bar. They brought in their own bottles when they thought no one was looking. Under the best of circumstances, the restaurant business was a tough business—even the best of restaurants. It was a business of nickels and dimes, of buying and manufacturing and selling and—if you cared about it—some small artistic satisfaction. Alex loved it, even if the money wasn't spectacular. Besides, there were always other sources of income for someone with Alex's particular talents.

The phone calls came regularly. Alex was a student of fine dining, but if worse came to worse, there were other ways to make ends meet. When you had achieved a certain reputation in a particular field—when you offered a special service unmatched in your area—you were always in demand. Two, maybe three jobs a year were all that was required to keep L'Americain afloat. And that was all that interested Alex—keeping the restaurant afloat.

Even as the thoughts materialized, the phone rang at the desk. Alex studied it before answering. A call for a reservation or a call pertaining to the sideline. Alex always wondered when the phone rang.

"L'Americain," Alex said.

"I'd like to speak to Alex."

"This is Alex."

There was a momentary silence from the other end of the line. "This is Alex?"

"Yes, this is Alex."

"My name is Richard Silver, from Philadelphia."

"I was expecting to hear from you," Alex said. "I had word to expect it. Do you have the information I need?"

"Yes," Silver said. Then: "Well . . . no."

"Which is it?" Alex asked quietly.

"It's yes and no. I don't have the name I wanted. But

154

I have another name."

"And what name is that?"

"Frank Murphy."

"Who is?" Alex asked softly.

"A lawyer. He has some connection to the case. I'm not sure just what. I think maybe he's tied in with the witness. He could be, anyway."

Alex said nothing for a moment. Then: "And that's all you have?"

"That's what I've got," Richie Silver said with irritation. "I'm not used to this kind of work, you know. I'm a lawyer. I don't want anything to do with this sort of thing."

Alex ignored Silver's harsh tone of voice. "Tell me about Murphy."

"He's an ex-cop, new in practice. He used to work in the DA's office."

"Where does he live?"

"I don't know."

"Where's his office?"

"The Fidelity Building in Center City, Philadelphia."

"What does he look like?"

"I don't know," Richie Silver said, his voice a study in nervousness. "He's maybe forty-five, forty-six. He's six feet tall or so, going to fat, a big shock of gray hair, moustache, wears glasses once in a while. He chain smokes Camels. He looks like a cop."

"Thank you, Mr. Silver," Alex said.

"That's it?"

"That's it. I'll take it from here. Tell that to our friends, please."

"Are you sure you can handle it by yourself?" Richie Silver asked.

"I'm sure," Alex said, hanging up the phone. Then: "Adolfo."

The waiter came over. "I'm going upstairs now. You take over, please."

"I'll handle it."

"Adolfo, I'm going away for a while. I'll be leaving tonight or tomorrow morning."

"Oh? When'll you be back?"

"I'm not sure. I just feel the urge to get away for a while."

Adolfo was used to this routine. Still, he always asked. "Can I reach you anywhere?"

"I'll be traveling. I'll call you. I'll keep in touch."

Adolfo shrugged. His real name was Angelo, and he'd been a waiter a long time—in this place and places a lot worse. He knew the drill—had been through this before—and Alex paid him rather nicely to serve as backup.

"I'll keep an eye on things," Adolfo said. "You just have a nice vacation."

"You're so nice," Alex said, taking his hand and stroking it gently.

Adolfo carefully drew his hand away. "You better get that taken care of while you're on vacation."

Alex laughed. "You're so straight, Adolfo."

He shrugged and smiled sheepishly. It worked well. He was a handsome man, and the sheepish smile was part of his repertoire. "I got a wife and three kids, Alex. I live clean."

"Yes," Alex said. "And what a shame."

Alex climbed up the stairs to the apartment on the second floor. L'Americain was located in a 1910 farmhouse that had once, years before, been a private home. The traffic on Route 22 had made the place a commercial site since the Depression. Alex had once occupied a comfortable four-bedroom home in a posh nearby town—had inherited it, in fact—but now preferred to live over the store, just like the president. The house had been too large and too full of memories for only one person.

Over the store in this case consisted of a two-bedroom apartment with a large living room and a small kitchen, all furnished in Danish modern with small pieces Alex had ferreted out of antique shops in Greenwich Village. The apartment was quietly middle class with stray touches of real class. Alex didn't need more than that. This was a place to sleep, mostly. Life was lived downstairs or elsewhere. There was hardly a place on earth Alex hadn't visited in the past five years. Every year there were two trips abroad. It was all deductible. Searching for recipes, you know. The IRS winced, but it always passed as a legitimate expense. That was one of the reasons Alex had chosen the restaurant business as an outlet for the cash earned in other endeavors; the government subsidized your travel.

Alex went into the bedroom and produced a pale-green leather suitcase from beneath the bed. Into the suitcase went cosmetics, clothing, an alarm clock, a robe, some towels, and a sheaf of trade journals—some reading on which Alex had meant to keep up. In the back of the closet, Alex brought out another bag. This one was of cloth. Alex put it on the bed and opened it. Inside were a Remington .16-gauge pump-action shotgun with a sawed-off barrel, a Smith & Wesson .38-cal. snub-nosed police revolver, an aging but still

157

efficient Beretta .32 automatic, a small crossbow with a supply of needle-pointed bolts, a wire garrote, several knives of varying description, and an umbrella. Alex studied the inventory, then selected the shotgun, the umbrella, the Beretta, a small packet of .32-cal. shells, and a small, hard-covered case about the size of a paperback book. These were placed in the leather bag, along with the various personal items. All in all, the packing took less than ten minutes.

When the bag was packed—Alex seldom traveled with more than one bag—one of the ghosts came in. Alex was taken somewhat by surprise, because tonight there had been none of the nervousness that tended to precede the ghosts, none of the jumpiness that indicated that ghosts were around and looking for company.

The ghost just walked through the door of the bedroom and sat down in one of the two Queen Anne chairs near the window. The ghost was naked, except for a pair of dark dress socks. It was a chubby, balding man in its late forties with a small, blood-encrusted hole between its eyes. Alex studied it. Who was this one, now? The name escaped memory. It had been more than a decade ago, one of the first ones. A bisexual auto dealer from Detroit, Alex finally recalled. He'd been terribly surprised, which meant the job had been handled professionally. He'd never had a clue until Alex had suddenly leaned over him in bed, watched him smile in the wake of his orgasm and put the bullet squarely between the eyes that were staring now with such accusation.

"Aren't you cold?" Alex said softly to the ghost.

The ghost didn't respond. They never responded,

none of them. He just stared at Alex, accusing with his eyes, the way all of them did. None of them ever spoke, they just stared. At first, when they had begun appearing a few years before, they had frightened Alex. At first it had been utterly terrifying. Now it was just an annoyance, nothing to be scared of. The ghost watched as Alex changed into jeans, a sweater, and sneakers. The ghost never said a word. As Alex snapped the leather suitcase shut, another ghost came in from the bathroom. This one was a tall, lean black man of not quite thirty, a pimp from Paterson, New Jersey, in a pale blue leisure suit. He was recent, not more than a year or two ago. This ghost was somewhat more unsightly, having been the victim of the Remington shotgun at close range. He sat down in the other Queen Anne chair, trying to look accusing with what was left of his face. He was a regular, and he didn't bother Alex at all anymore. He showed up all the time. The fat, naked guy, he hadn't been around in months.

Alex pulled the bag off the bed and hefted it. Not too heavy. Easy enough to carry downstairs to the Volvo. A flick of the hand killed the lights. In the doorway, Alex looked back at the ghosts. The two of them were sitting there in the dark. The pimp had lit one of those little cigars he'd liked to smoke.

"That's bad for your health," Alex said.

The ghosts remained silent. They just stared.

"Hey," Alex called softly, and with a smile, "fuck you guys if you can't take a joke."

CHAPTER 15

Murphy dreamed again.

This time he dreamed of being back in the navy—specifically at the Great Lakes Naval Training Center, where he had undergone basic training and developed such an intense hatred of all things and individuals military. He dreamed of his last day there, waiting in the icy pre-dawn for the bus that would take him away from the scene of his torment.

"That guy in there," one of his companions told him, jerking a thumb toward the day room, "he's from Philly, like you."

"No shit?" Murphy said.

Murphy went inside and asked the guy if it was true that he was from Philly. The guy was one of the training petty officers, a smallish man not much older than Murphy himself. Murphy had seen the guy around and not been aware that he was a fellow Philadelphian. As far as Murphy had been concerned, he'd simply been one of "them"—one of the assholes Uncle Sam had seen fit to inflict on Murphy during his initiation into military life. Now, as he was leaving for sea duty, Murphy felt a sudden kinship for this man with whom he shared some common experience—a kinship he hadn't felt for any other human being with whom he'd had the slightest contact at Great Lakes.

"Yeah," the petty officer said, eying Murphy with training supervisor eyes. "I'm from Philly. You know, you look pretty sloppy going out of here, sailor. Square up that hat."

When this had actually happened, Murphy had looked at the petty officer for a moment in pure shock, stunned that his gesture of friendship had been so rudely rejected. That was the military—more assholes per square foot than any other collection of humanity on earth. Murphy had straightened up his hat and gone back outside to wait for his bus.

In his dream, though, Murphy dropped his seabag, leaped over the desk and beat the petty officer senseless. He did it lavishly, battering the man until his face was no more than a bloody jelly. When Murphy awakened from dreaming about a scene from his life that had taken place twenty-eight years earlier—one that would now be forever revised in his favor in his subconscious memory—he felt strangely refreshed. He loved dreams like that, dreams about what he should have done. He would have a dream like that maybe twice a year, and they always tended to perk him up. He came out of bed whistling. Winston, on the floor beside the bed, eyed him with suspicion. Murphy bent down and scratched the bulldog's ears.

"Hello there, baby bow-wow," Murphy said cheerily.

Winston snorted in distrust. Dogs and young children are creatures of routine. In the ten months or so that he had shared quarters with Murphy, Winston had become accustomed to Murphy awaking grudgingly and communicating for the first fifteen minutes with unintelligible grunts and muttered monosyllabic curses as he lurched about the littered apartment in his underwear, lighting cigarettes and trying to make coffee.

Today, however, Murphy went first to the bathroom. Winston heard him flip on the shower and then heard him sing a hopeless version of "Wings of Love" while he washed and shaved. Then Murphy came out of the bathroom, naked and hair neatly combed. To dress, he had to dig through the pile of clean underwear and socks he kept in one corner of the bedroom, then find a dress shirt in a clear plastic bag from the Chinese laundry over on Spruce Street. Murphy put on the underwear, the socks and the crisp dress shirt. From his closet he selected a gray, pinstriped suit—Murphy always hung up suits; getting them pressed after leaving them on the floor ran into too much money—and put that on. Then he found a tie he liked hanging from a half-open dresser drawer, managed to get it tied and found a pair of matching shoes from the dozen pairs that lay under the bed or scattered about in heaps of dirty underwear and discarded clothing.

At the end of the process, he looked fairly respectable, although the room was still a disaster area, which was how he liked it. As a kid at home, Murphy had always been required to keep his room neat and clean. His mother had been a stickler for that, and so had the navy. Since going out on his own, he had evolved proudly into the consummate slob. Barry Weiner, his psychiatrist friend, had once told him that his slovenliness was a gesture of revolt against parental authority and that it was unseemly in a man nearly forty-six years old. The fact that Barry was also a slob—that his office at the University of Pennsylvania Hospital looked vaguely like it had been struck by a shell from the *U.S.S. New Jersey*—had not gone unmentioned in this conversation, but Murphy supposed that Weiner was probably correct. He'd realized long ago that adults tend to spend their lives either in constant imitation of their parents or in more or less direct revolt against their values. Murphy's life was a combination of the two. He figured that made him well adjusted.

He walked the dog and got a cup of coffee and some cheese danish at the corner deli in the process. Then he found the Toronado with its rust-freckled fenders where he had left it the night before fairly well blocked in between a Mercedes 450 SEL in front and a new Chevy Corsica in the rear. He unlocked the door, put the dog in the rear seat and spent the next ten minutes freeing the vehicle—rocking it back and forth between its captors, banging its big bumpers into their small ones, until he could get out. A tugboat would have helped, he reflected, as he started out toward Mount Airy to pick up Patricia.

It was a glorious morning in late April, Murphy's favorite time of year. Winter in Philadelphia was a gray affair, with chilling moisture in the air. Summer was blazingly hot. The only times the city was really bearable were in the spring or fall, and the dying leaves of autumn tended to depress Murphy, for all their beauty.

It took him not quite forty minutes to reach the

house in Mount Airy. It was a brick house with a small front porch and a bay window protruding from the living room. The entire block was composed of nearly identical houses built just after World War II. Murphy's house—and that's how he still thought of it, even though he no longer lived there—was nicely landscaped with mature shrubs he had mostly planted himself and then nourished over the years with healthy doses of peat moss, plant food, and dried cow shit. Mary Ellen's wagon was in the driveway. Murphy pulled in behind it, got out and rang the bell. Mary Ellen answered, as lovely as any woman past forty could be.

"Patricia's almost ready," she said. "Want some coffee?"

"Sure," Murphy said, coming in.

"Where's the dog?"

"Asleep in the car."

"Well, bring him in, too. I've got some leftovers I saved for him."

Murphy went back out to the Toronado and roused the sleeping bulldog. Winston came into the house with his stubby tail whirling like a helicopter rotor and his blunt claws clicking across the slate-covered foyer.

Mary Ellen bent down. "Hi, sweetie," she said brightly.

Winston just shook all over in greeting. Mary Ellen hugged him while he snorted and sprayed dog spit in all directions. Murphy noted silently that his own greeting from his estranged wife had been far less affectionate. What really annoyed him was that Mary Ellen had detested the first bulldog he'd owned, the first Winston Churchill, but she seemed to be in love with this one. Of course, the fact that this young dog had been a gift from both Mary Ellen and Patricia last fall clearly played a role in her change of heart—that and the fact that Mary Ellen didn't live with this dog the way she'd lived with the first one. Come to think of it, Murphy reflected, Mary Ellen had been somewhat nicer to him since she'd thrown him out, too.

"Forget him and get me some coffee," Murphy groused.

"Oh, screw you," Mary Ellen said, kissing the bulldog on his wrinkled brow.

"Well, if you're willing to do that," Murphy said, "you can give him the coffee."

His wife frowned—same old delightful sense of humor, Murphy thought—and went into the kitchen with the bulldog in tow. She opened the refrigerator and pulled out a plate of beef scraps. Winston caught the scent and barked anxiously. Mary Ellen put the plate on the floor in front of him, and Winston Churchill proceeded to give an exhibition in canine gustatorial bliss, slobbering shamelessly while he sucked in snakelike rolls of waxy beef fat through his immense jaws.

"Coffee?" Murphy asked politely. "Where's Patricia?"

"Drying her hair. She knows you're here."

Patricia's voice came from upstairs: "I can hear you talking about me. You said 'she.' I'll be right down."

Murphy sat at the kitchen table while Mary Ellen served him a cup of coffee.

"Where are you taking her today?" Mary Ellen asked. "Got a dope pusher or two you'd like her to meet?"

"I'm just going out to do some digging 'round. We

shouldn't bump into a soul you wouldn't be proud to have her associate with."

"No armed robbers?" Mary Ellen persisted. "No hookers?"

"Give it a rest, Mary Ellen. Please?"

She sat back in her kitchen chair. "As long as the point has been made."

"Making points with inadequate emphasis has never been among your failings," Murphy told her.

"Does today's adventure involve your Mr. Webster?"

"Yeah. I'm going out to his place to see if I can't find some evidence to place him somewhere else at the time of the Rice woman's murder. He says he went shopping and bought some clothes. The receipt might have the date and time on it, depending on the type of cash register it came from."

"Do you have a time of death on her yet?"

It was a good question. Murphy wasn't surprised. When they had lived together, Murphy had often discussed his cases with his wife. Mary Ellen had a sharp mind, and—after all their years together—possessed more than a passing knowledge of police work and related investigative procedures. For an eighth-grade English teacher, she wasn't a bad detective. She had good instincts.

"Not yet," Murphy told her. "I've got to go see Weinberg and see what he can tell me. I'm going to do that tomorrow if I can."

"Do you still think your client is innocent?"

"He says he is."

"Do you think he is?"

Murphy lit a Camel, and Mary Ellen—a reformed smoker for more than a decade now—reflexively got up and found an ashtray for him.

"I don't know," Murphy said. "What I do know is that at least two other people who might have done it don't seem to be able to establish witnesses for where they were the night of the murder."

"Who are they?"

"Brian and Beverly Kavanaugh."

Mary Ellen was aghast. "Don't tell me that you suspect Beverly."

Murphy shrugged. "I suspect everybody. Where were you last Saturday night, by the way?"

"Very funny. I'm serious."

"Well, Beverly had good reason to hate Lynn Rice. Beverly is a big, strong girl. She could certainly lift the body into the trunk of a car. Lynn Rice was tiny, you know. And Beverly claims she was home alone all night, even though I tried to call her and didn't get an answer. She says she heard the phone, but she was in the tub."

"But you don't think it could really be her?"

"It could be, yes. Whether it really was is another matter. And Brian claims he spent the night in his office, doing paperwork. Again, no witnesses. Maybe he did, and maybe he didn't. Maybe he went back out to the farm later."

"How about your client?" Mary Ellen asked.

"He says he went shopping and then went to the movies."

"Any witnesses for his alibi?"

"Not so far. I'm working on it."

"Of the three of them," Mary Ellen said, "it sounds to me like your client would be the likeliest candidate."

"Then give me a motive."

Mary Ellen sat back in her chair. "Oh, let's say a man and a woman alone, the man makes an advance. The woman rejects it, threatens to tell the man's boss. The man gets scared or mad or both, does something dumb."

"It's possible," Murphy admitted, sipping his coffee. "They're all possible."

"What would be Brian's motive?"

"Maybe Brian has second thoughts about the marriage. Maybe he starts to worry on the effect the remarriage will have on the kid. Maybe he comes back that night to talk it over, and he and Lynn have a vicious fight about it. This one has a lot of maybes in it, Mary Ellen. I have a lot of digging around to do."

Patricia came bounding into the kitchen. She greeted her father with a kiss on top of his head, then she fell to her knees in front of Winston and threw her arms wide.

"Baby, baby, baby," she said to the bulldog.

Winston snorted in glee and came grunting into her arms.

"The two of you are spoiling that goddamned dog," Murphy complained, to no avail. Patricia was rolling on the floor with Winston, pulling on his ears while he snarled in mock combat.

"He's such a dollface," Patricia said.

"It's time to get rolling," Murphy told her. "Grab something to eat."

Patricia took a doughnut, and the three of them— Murphy, his daughter and his dog—were on the road in less than two minutes. On the way, Murphy took a pass by Temple Stadium, where he had taken Patricia for years on Saturday afternoon to watch Temple football. He steered the Toronado onto Route 73 and headed toward the turnpike and Phoenixville while Patricia played with the radio, coming up with music Murphy had trouble facing anytime, much less early in the day. The music was the price for her company. He paid it gladly. At the end of the week, she'd be back at college, and his only contact with her would be limited to letters and an occasional phone call—and not many of those. His daughter had her own very full life now, and Murphy knew he'd never get used to the idea.

You raise kids so they can be admirable adults, but when they almost get there you start to wish that somehow you'd managed to stunt their growth just before puberty—that you could have them always as they had been a few years after they had been reliably toilet trained. That's when you had been all-knowing, all-powerful and generally perfect, and they had loved you without question or reservation.

Murphy looked over at his daughter as they drove, casting glances at her out of the corner of his eye. He had missed her terribly when he'd first moved out. Now, with her gone most of the year, he missed her even more. What strange sequence of events, he wondered, had led to the reality of the three of them—him, Patricia, and Mary Ellen—living in three different places? It was amazing how people could screw up their lives to such a degree. He wondered what it might take to get Mary Ellen to take him back in the house. A miracle, he concluded as he thought about it.

He and Patricia talked about nothing in particular as they drove to Brian Kavanaugh's farm. They arrived just after ten, and Murphy was surprised to see Brian's Austin Healey parked outside the big house. Brian came out the door as Murphy pulled in. Brian was dressed in jeans, and he was unshaven. The man didn't look good.

"I would have thought you'd be in Center City skinning the suckers," Murphy told him as he got out of the car.

"I didn't feel much like going in this week," Brian said. "I'd already made arrangements to take some time off, so I'm taking it. What are you doing here?"

"I'm here to get some stuff for Webster. I've got the key to his place. Mind if I go inside?"

"Be my guest," Brian Kavanaugh said.

Webster's cottage was a two-room affair with what turned out to be a startlingly pretty view of the farm's rolling fields from the bedroom window. Patricia stayed outside, throwing a stick for Winston to retrieve on his stubby legs. Brian Kavanaugh followed Murphy inside, a development that left Murphy somewhat displeased. He would have preferred to go through the cottage by himself, slowly digging through every drawer, analyzing every scrap of paper—just nosing around, which was both his personal and professional inclination. As it was, he looked around only until he found a department store bag on the dresser in the bedroom. Inside it were a pair of Wrangler jeans and a set of three Jockey brand briefs housed in a plastic package. Murphy studied the receipt. It bore a store's name, a date, and a number Murphy couldn't figure out, but no time was stamped on it. He frowned and placed it carefully atop the dresser. Then, despite Brian Kavanaugh surveying him from the doorway, he looked around the place. He checked out the closets and drawers and found only clothing—most of it designed for working outdoors. In the bedroom closet he found a blue blazer and a pair of gray dress slacks hanging on a wooden hanger along with a light-blue knit tie folded over the shoulders. In the closet near the front door, he found a trenchcoat that clearly had been worn but little.

"Is the furniture yours or his?" Murphy asked Kavanaugh.

"Mine. It came with the place, just like most of the stuff in the big house."

The living room was furnished in Sears best, with a plaid Early American sofa and matching chairs and a coffee table of dark, heavy pine. Murphy bent over the coffee table and picked up an ashtray by the edges. It was from Caesar's Palace in Atlantic City.

"How about this?" Murphy asked, tossing the ashtray casually to Brian Kavanaugh.

Kavanaugh, taken by surprise, deftly caught the ashtray. He studied it carefully. "I don't know where this came from. It might have been here when Mike moved in. It might have been something he picked up on a trip to Atlantic City."

Kavanaugh put the ashtray back on the table. Murphy gazed around the place.

"You know," he said, "it's strange. There's not a personal item in this cottage—no pictures, no photographs. It's like a hotel room. Funny that a guy would live this way."

Kavanaugh shrugged. "He was a guy living under a false identity."

"Even so . . ." Murphy said.

"Did you find what you're looking for?"

"I guess," Murphy said. "I didn't find much, that's

for sure."

The two men went outside. Kavanaugh began to lock the door behind him. As he did, Murphy snapped his fingers.

"Shit, Brian. I've got to go back inside. I forgot something."

Frowning, Kavanaugh opened the door again, and Murphy went back inside. He emerged a moment later brandishing the cash register receipt.

"I'm losing it," Murphy said with an embarrassed smile. "I left it on the dresser. This is what I came all the way out here for."

"That's it?" Brian Kavanaugh said. "You've got everything now?"

"Everything I need," Murphy told him.

Before all this

"So what do you do, Phil?" she said, stretching against the pillow in the dim light from the bathroom.

Phil Bonsignore—that was his real name, Ellie had assured her—merely smiled at her. "I'm a member of the College of Cardinals. Right after this, I've got to call Pope Paul. He told me to see if I could get him tickets to the Yankees game tomorrow."

Alma smiled and shook her head. "Seriously, what do you do?"

Phil Bonsignore gazed at her for a moment and said nothing. Then he got out of bed stark naked, turned on the lamp on the night table and went to the telephone.

"I'll show you," he told her. "Yes. This is Mr. Bonsignore in fourteen-eighty-seven. I'd like you to send up two six ounce filets of Pacific salmon, lightly broiled. Not too much, please. Send up a side of hollandaise, too, and don't load it up with flour. If it needs some bulk, use some arrowroot instead. Tell the kitchen I'll know the difference. I'd also like some steamed green beans almondine and some *pommes dauphinoise* . . . What? I don't care if it's not on the menu. Just charge me what you like, but give me what I'm ordering. You take it up with the chef. I don't think he'll mind . . . What? . . . All right, you slice up a bunch of potatoes, very thin. You sprinkle them with garlic, salt, and pepper. Then you add enough heavy cream to cover the potatoes. You bake them for a while and then add maybe a half cup of shredded Gruyere. If you don't have that, then use Swiss—imported Swiss— but it's better with Gruyere. Then top it with seasoned bread crumbs and broil the top until it's crispy. That's *pommes dauphinoise* . . . Fine, if it takes a while then it takes a while. And when you bring it up, also bring a bottle of Heron Hill Otter Springs chardonnay, any year. If you don't have that, then make it a Sutter Mill white zinfandel. Bring some coffee, too. Decaffeinated, please. Yes, fine. Thank you."

He hung up and walked back to the bed. Alma watched him as he walked. He was worth watching. Phil Bonsignore had to be in his mid-forties, anyway. But he was trim and well set up, his stomach as flat as a board. He was pleasant and confident, and he had a surprising touch. Usually, nothing much happened to Alma when she was working, even when she was with one of her regulars. Oh, every once in a while, maybe, when she was in the mood. But it was the rarest of occurrences. Tonight she had come five times—a record with a client, especially a new one. Pretty close to a record with anybody for Alma, if the truth be told. Usually she just tended to business.

"So," Alma said. "That's supposed to tell me what you do? You order from room service for a living? Is that it?"

He smiled. "No. I own a restaurant."

"No kidding," Alma said. "Where?"

"Jersey. You ought to drop over sometime. I'd love to have you."

Alma chuckled. "You've already had me. Twice."

"That's true," Phil said, lighting a cigarette. "And it was about the most pleasurable experience I've had in a long time. You're not from New York, are you?"

"No. How can you tell?"

"Accent. I'd say somewhere in the Midwest."

"Minnesota."

"What brought you to New York?"

"Show business," Alma said. "I'm an actress when I'm not doing this." Then she giggled. "Of course, I do this a lot."

He gazed at her through the swirl of cigarette smoke. "How'd you end up doing this?"

Alma laughed. It was a joke. You thought a question like this was a hopeless cliché until you actually became a hooker. Then you found out that every other guy you did it with would ask you.

"What's a nice girl like me doing in a job like this?" Alma said. "Is that the question?"

"No," Phil said. "You're not a nice girl or you wouldn't be here. And I'm not a nice guy, or I wouldn't, either."

"What are you doing here?" Alma asked him, motioning toward the wedding ring he wore. "The old lady shut you off for a while?"

He shook his head and stubbed out the Marlboro. "No. She died a few years back. You wouldn't think women could die in childbirth anymore, but they do. The baby died, too, which they told me is kind of rare

175

these days."

Alma looked down at the sheets. Then, without a word, she got out of bed. She went into the bathroom, looked into the mirror and swore silently to herself. Then she came out and said, "I'm sorry, Phil. I've got this big mouth that's always getting me in trouble."

"Don't worry about it, Al," Phil Bonsignore said. "I've gotten used to the idea by now."

"Do me a favor?" Alma asked. "Don't call me Al. I don't like that name. I've got my reasons."

He looked at her quizzically. "You like Alma better? Jesus, nobody's named Alma. No offense, babe."

"I don't like Alma much," she admitted. "I thought about changing it when I came to New York—you know, for professional reasons. But then I thought, if they can't take me for what I am, the hell with them. And, sure enough, they didn't take me. You can call me anything you want to call me, but don't call me Al. Okay?"

Phil took her hand and patted it. "Fine. I'll think of something to call you. Meanwhile, how would you like to turn on that TV set? The news ought to be on right about now."

Alma turned on the set and climbed back into bed, snuggling against him. He had her for the night. There was much more to go. As the hotel air conditioner whirred, keeping out the August heat, Alma watched Richard Nixon on television being hugged by Sammy Davis, Jr., during some function at the Republican National Convention in Miami. Politics bored her. Alma yawned.

"Don't go to sleep," Phil told her. "Food's coming."

"Wake me when it comes," she said. "I'm out of it.

You rang my bell once too often, Phil."

He gathered her in his arms. To her surprise, Alma liked it. She liked him, too, which was not common. Alma rarely had any use for her clients.

"You're nice," she told him.

"We'll have to do this again," he said.

"Anytime," Alma Pale told him.

CHAPTER 16

Lunch was at the Berwyn Inn, a few miles from Judy Kavanaugh's posh private school in Devon and worlds away from the neighborhood in which Murphy had grown up. He had sprung from Fishtown, a rowhouse Philadelphia neighborhood populated mainly by working-class ethnics who believed in two guiding principles: one, that hard work would bring you all that your heart desires and, two, that the Phillies would take the World Series next year.

As far as the second principle was concerned, Murphy had long ago written off a world championship for the Phillies as an impossible dream. He was a fan, but he wasn't deranged. The first? Hard work helped, but Murphy had even greater faith in dumb luck. Luck was a virtue Murphy admired, and he was deeply aware that he'd never had any—no good luck and, thank God—no outstandingly bad luck. Nobody had ever given him a thing. He'd fought and clawed for whatever he possessed in the way of worldly goods or stature in society. But then he'd never had anything important taken away from him, either. He'd been born able-bodied, and he'd never sustained a crippling injury or suffered a serious illness. He'd been born with a quick mind, and he knew its worth. On the other hand, he'd been granted no particular talent—he'd been only a fair schoolboy athlete, for instance, and he couldn't sing or dance.

The modest circumstances of his upbringing had effectively prevented him from dreaming big enough dreams at an early enough age to do anything with them. But he'd come from solid people who'd instilled in him a sense of industry and drive for some measure of respectability. He'd been fortunate enough, too, to have been born the right color. Jim Wilder was Murphy's best friend, and Murphy thought he had some idea of how lucky he'd been that he hadn't found himself with the social handicap with which Wilder had to wrestle every day.

Murphy wasn't rich, and he wasn't poor. He still had all his hair, but it was gray. He had a bright and pretty wife, but she'd thrown him out. He had a marvelous and beguiling daughter, but she was close to being a grownup and gone from him forever. He'd never had a son, and that disappointed him deeply. On the other hand, the son might have turned out to be a creep, and then what would he have done?

As far as Murphy was concerned, luck was a wash in his case—one side balanced the other. Besides, he was pushing forty-six. What was, was. In addition, there would come a point when it would be all downhill. His body would eventually betray him. He had seen it happen to his father. He'd seen the old man begin to suffer from diabetes, to lose the vision in one eye, and the powerful body that had enabled him to earn a living. Murphy had seen the old man slowly begin to lose out on life's pleasures—no more booze or tobacco. No more big nights out with his friends. After his first heart attack, the old man had even lost bowling, which he'd loved.

"This is how God prepares you for death, Frank," the old man had said during his last months. "He takes away the things you enjoy, one by one. He takes away your friends and turns the world into something strange where you don't much enjoy things anymore or understand what the hell is going on. That way, when he decides to take you, you don't really mind. God's pretty smart, if you think about it."

Murphy didn't know about that. However approving his old man had been, Murphy had noted a few compelling flaws in the vast, eternal plan. Be that as it may, however, he had to admit that God had worked genuine magic in creating the young woman who sat across the table from him in the Berwyn Inn. Patricia was, in Murphy's eyes, close to being the ideal human being—except for the smart mouth she'd inherited from her mother.

"What'll you have?" he asked her.

"The duck in cherry sauce."

Murphy made a face. "You can have it."

"How about you?"

Murphy gazed at the menu, struggling to decipher the French. "I think I'll have the luncheon steak."

Patricia shook her head. "That's all you eat—red meat and eggs and shellfish in cream sauces. I shudder to think what your blood vessels look like."

"At least they're not clogged up with cherry sauce."

"I wish you'd watch what you eat," she told him.

"It's bad enough having to watch the crap you eat."

Patricia sipped from her water glass. Murphy knew her moods—he'd certainly had them inflicted on him enough during the early years of her puberty.

"What's bugging you?" he demanded.

"Nothing."

"Something," he insisted.

She looked up at him. "When are you and Mom going to stop screwing around and get back together?"

Murphy looked heavenward, as if for assistance. "Now there's a question," he said.

"How about an answer?"

Murphy lit a Camel. "I should think that at this point you'd forget it. I moved out more than two years ago. Have you detected a groundswell of support for me moving back in? Is there something I've missed?"

"You were getting along pretty well last summer."

"Yeah, as long as we weren't trying to share the same roof. Look, we lived together more than twenty years. I got on her nerves for most of that time, and I guarantee you that she got on mine. She's not willing to try it again. And, frankly, I don't think I could go through moving out again. It was tough enough the first time."

"Then why don't you just get divorced and go your separate ways?"

Murphy shrugged. "Maybe we will when you're gone for keeps. We've talked about it."

Patricia looked at her father squarely. "Do you still love her?"

Murphy frowned. "I'd just as soon get off this line of conversation. Can't we talk about your love life? On second thought, don't tell me about it. I'd rather

182

not know."

"I'm serious."

"So am I," he told her. "What you do is your own affair."

Patricia looked at her nails. An inspection of the fingernails indicated a serious statement of policy coming up. Murphy dreaded it.

"The problem with both of you," Patricia said finally, "is that you both think you have forever to work everything out. You both think that one of these days you'll sit down to talk and you'll finally work everything out. And if you keep on like this, you'll run out of time. One of you will die, and the other one will be left with all sorts of things you meant to say but just couldn't find the opportunity to get out. You'll keep this shit up until it's too late."

"Don't say shit in a classy restaurant," her father said. "It's not ladylike."

"What is it you really want, Daddy?"

Murphy pondered the question. "A thirty-year-old, deaf-mute nymphomaniac with a million bucks and a liquor store. But they're hard to come by."

Patricia shook her head wearily.

"Here comes the waiter," Murphy said. "Order your cherry duck and stop giving me such a bad time."

The rest of the meal was pleasant for both of them. Patricia gave up on trying to get her father to discuss the subject seriously, and Murphy got her talking about living away from home for the first time. It was the first extended conversation he'd had the opportunity to have with her since driving her all the way to Skidmore College in upstate New York the previous fall. On that occasion, they had talked the full five hours in the car. On this one, they ended up spending two and a half hours at the table, chatting long after the remains of the meal had been cleared away and the check arrived. Finally Murphy excused himself and made a phone call to Beverly Kavanaugh.

"I'm close to Judy's school," he told her, "and I thought I'd drop by to see how she's doing. Do I have to make a reservation or anything? Will they call you, or what?"

"I think I'd have to call them," Beverly said. "She's just about through with classes this time of day anyway. What do you want to see her about, Frank?"

"I want to find out what she can tell me about Mike Webster's relationship with Lynn Rice. The prosecution will question her anyway, Beverly. If anybody knows that, you do. I'd like the first shot at her if I can get it. You know I'll treat her just fine."

"All right," she said. "I'll call the school and tell them you're not just some pervert."

"Thanks for the endorsement," he said.

Murphy hung up and immediately dialed another number he'd scribbled in his address book the day before. The operator came on, and he gave her his credit card number.

Then: "Hello."

"Jim? Frank. How is it up there?"

"Pretty fucking bleak, if you want the truth. We got a black and white TV set, and no cable. All I can get are the Scranton stations. Plus, we're living on canned goods and frozen dinners. For a guy who runs a restaurant, Berger turns out to be a fairly shitty chef. He always hired people to do the cooking, he tells me. Say, when are you planning to come on up here and do your share of the guarding? I wouldn't mind getting home next weekend."

"I might make it this weekend. I'll have to let you know."

Wilder said, "How long have I been working with you? Coming up on seventeen or eighteen years now?"

"Closer to twenty," Murphy said.

"Well," Wilder told him, "I don't know how you manage it, Frank, but every time we get into a deal like this I end up picking the cotton and you end up rocking on the veranda sipping mint juleps."

"The important thing is that you derive satisfaction from your work," Murphy told him. "How's Berger doing?"

"Him? He's loving it. He watches TV all day. When he's not doing that he wanders around the woods all day listening to the fucking robins chirp and then sits on the dock watching the water birds. This joint is on a little lake, you know. It's probably full of 'gators."

"What's the layout like?"

It was a serious question, Wilder knew, and he answered it seriously. "The camp's way up on this hillside overlooking the lake—lots of trees and stuff. The road up from the lake is pretty tricky, but the place is hard to see from down below. I took the liberty of taking down the sign for the place about fifteen seconds after we got here. It's got a big mess hall building, which is shut up, a year-round cabin—which we're in— and maybe fifteen or twenty summer cabins for kids. They're all boarded up. I've got a barricade on the road up from the lake. You can move the barricade out of the way, but it makes noise. We keep the lights down low at night. We're talking desolate, man."

"Sounds like Otis set us up just right. What do you have for hardware?"

"I got my service revolver, and I took a twelve-gauge pump and an M-sixteen from the arsenal. I got enough shells to stand off an army, too. What I didn't bring was enough to read, and I don't want to go into town to get anything. Brothers tend to stand out a bit in this neighborhood, if you get my meaning."

"You getting along okay with Berger?" Murphy asked.

"Just fine. He's seen a lot, Frank. He's an interesting guy, too. Turns out he knows more about boxing than any guy I've ever met. I never would have figured that. I sure don't want anything to happen to that old man."

"How often does Otis check in?"

"He calls every day about this time. I thought you were him. He comes by in a prowl car every third day or so. The first time, I forgot to tell him about the barricade. He started to move it, and when I heard the noise I almost blasted him with the M-sixteen. Scared the shit out of him. So now we got us a password."

"What is it?"

"It's Sugar Ray. He was Berger's favorite fighter."

"Which one?"

"Both of them."

"I've got to go now," Murphy said. "I'll be back in touch. And when I come up I'll bring you some books."

"Bring me *Mila 18*, if you can find it. I read *Exodus*, but I never got to read that one. Talking to Irving got my interest up."

"You got it. Keep cool now."

"I'm always cool," Wilder informed him.

Murphy went back to the table. The waiter had

186

taken Murphy's credit card and returned it with the receipt. Murphy folded up his copy—he would lie about lunch on his income tax return—and then carefully ripped up the carbons.

"Why do you do that?" Patricia asked him.

"Somebody could get my credit card number off the carbons. Then they could use it to order stuff by phone. I had a client who specialized in that. He had all the stuff shipped to a post office box and switched boxes every month."

"Where's your client now?"

"Paying his debt to society. He never paid me, though. Come on. We've got to go see Judy Kavanaugh."

CHAPTER 17

As a young man, an impoverished Limerick day laborer named Brendan Mulcahy had robbed a churchbox to buy bread for his widowed mother and younger sister. As an old man, rich beyond his wildest dreams after a career as a politically connected building contractor in Philadelphia, he found himself the employer of some shrewd tax lawyers. After earnest conversation with these tax lawyers, Brendan Mulcahy found it in his heart to donate his drafty and horribly expensive thirty-eight-room mansion in Devon to the church as compensation for his youthful indiscretion.

The building had been used for some years as a convent, but in the late 1950s the same group of Irish lawyers who had represented the now late and only mildly lamented Mr. Mulcahy pointed out that, to the archdiocese, the mansion could be put to better and more profitable use. Their idea: a boarding school for young ladies from prosperous families who wanted their troublesome daughters exposed to the terrors of a Catholic education. Thus was Our Lady of Light school born.

The school was housed in a two-and-a-half-story Georgian-style structure of reddish-brown brick. Murphy got chills just driving up to the place. It had been a long time since he'd been inside a Catholic school. He remembered his own parochial school education well, and he had insisted that Patricia attend public schools, where the teachers would be less likely to slap her hands with a ruler for wearing patent leather shoes. He piloted the Toronado up the circular driveway in front of the imposing building, parked and got out. Patricia opened her door and let Winston loose in the front yard. The dog had slept in the car during lunch, and he was brimming over with energy.

"I'd better stay out here and watch him," Patricia said as Winston bounced around in front of her playfully.

"I'll bring Judy outside here, then," Murphy said.

He went through the huge double doors and found himself in a towering vestibule beneath a ceiling two stories high. Murphy walked down a long hall before finding a door marked Principal. Inside he found a severely dressed but rather pretty woman of about forty behind a desk on the telephone. The woman put her hand over the phone.

"I'll be right with you," she said. "Please sit down."

Murphy sat. On the wall behind the woman was a painting of *Veronica's Veil*. On another wall was a color photograph of Pope John Paul II and on the third wall, between two windows, was a color photo of John Cardinal Krol, the recently retired archbishop of Philadelphia. Murphy had met Krol once, at a PBA dinner. The cardinal had been drinking bourbon, and Murphy had decided that he probably wasn't such a

189

bad guy.

"Thank you, officer," the woman was saying. "Yes, if you could bring it out I'd be very grateful. Yes. Thank you." She hung up the phone and looked at Murphy. Murphy looked back and noticed the crucifix attached to the collar of the woman's dark suit.

"How do you do," she said. "I'm Sister Joan. How may I help you?"

Murphy stood up. He wasn't accustomed to sitting in the presence of nuns. On the other hand, he'd never gotten used to the idea that nuns had hair. Sister Joan's hair was a rich chestnut attractively frosted with gray, he noted. Murphy had liked nuns better in their penguin uniforms and rimless glasses. They hadn't looked like women then, and that had seemed only right.

"I'm Frank Murphy, sister. I'm here to see Judy Kavanaugh. Her mother should have called you by now."

"Yes, she did, Mr. Murphy. Judy is in her room. I'll have her sent down. I'm just going to run an errand. You can talk to her here."

"I thought I'd take her out front and talk to her there, if you don't mind."

The nun smiled. It was one of those indulgent, sickly sweet smiles they issued nuns along with their crosses. Murphy remembered the smile well. He also remembered nuns' skill with thimbles that made your brains scramble when they were bounced off your forehead. Looking back on it, Murphy was sure that he had had a grid mark on his forehead until he had been fifteen or so. He remembered one aged nun in particular, Sister Mary Joseph, who had delivered such lightning-fast, lethal blows with her thimble that she had been nicknamed the Green Hornet. So far Sister Joan had only smiled at him, but Murphy knew she might just bat him one in the very next instant. Nuns were like that.

"I'm sorry," Sister Joan said, "but Judy isn't permitted out of the building for two weeks. She's on restriction."

"Oh," Murphy said in surprise. "What for, if I might ask?"

"She was out of her room after bed check last weekend. She was caught out on the grounds. That's against the rules, I'm afraid."

"Only two weeks?" Murphy said. "I remember a time when that would have meant at least a broken arm."

Murphy chuckled at his own joke. The nun did not.

"Things have changed a bit since our day, Mr. Murphy. The Church has even called a halt to the Inquisition, you know."

"I heard," Murphy said. "The pope's going soft, if you ask me."

Sister Joan frowned, calling forth a wealth of memories Murphy thought he'd successfully sublimated. "I'll have Judy sent down to see you."

"Thank you, sister," Murphy said, smiling awkwardly. "I was just making a little joke."

"Were you now?" Sister Joan said, leaving the office. Murphy had visions of her coming back with a priest, and then he'd really be in trouble, but he decided he was being paranoid. She'd probably just leave him to God. Murphy could crack his jokes in purgatory for a few hundred years. Then we'd see how funny he thought he was.

Murphy glanced over the books in Sister Joan's bookcase. There was a Latin text, one on social studies, several English books, a paperback copy of *The Shoes of the Fisherman;* another, somewhat smaller novel entitled *The Bulletin,* which looked interesting; a Duoay version of the Bible, and the inevitable Baltimore Catechism. Just like old times, Murphy thought.

"Hello, Mr. Murphy."

He turned at the sound of Judy's voice and saw her standing in the doorway. Murphy smiled as winningly as possible.

"Hi," he said. "I hear you've been a bad girl."

"Don't tell my mother," Judy pleaded. "Please?"

"Hey," Murphy told her. "I'm a lawyer. I make a living not telling on people—especially to their mothers. How have you been, Judy?"

"Fine," the girl said.

Murphy motioned to a chair. "Sit down, honey. I have things I have to talk to you about."

Judy sat. She was dressed in her school uniform: a white blouse with rolled-up sleeves and a dark-green pleated skirt. Murphy remembered the uniform well. Catholicism produced regimented memories.

"Did anybody tell you why I'm here?" he asked.

"No."

"I'm representing Mike Webster. You know that he's been charged with Lynn's murder, don't you?"

Judy nodded. The girl seemed tense to Murphy. On the other hand, she had always seemed tense, every time he'd ever met her. Beverly and Brian had raised a profoundly twitchy kid.

"Judy," he said slowly, "I think Mike is innocent. I

don't think he could ever do what they charged him with. What do you think?"

She thought for a moment before answering. "I don't think Mike could hurt anybody," she said finally.

"No, I'm sure he couldn't," Murphy responded, purposely neglecting to mention a guy with his pants around his ankles who had been knocked down a stairwell in Fresno, California, with troublesome results. "How did you like Lynn, Judy?"

The girl looked at the floor. "I didn't like her much."

"Did Mike like her?"

"I don't know."

"Well, did he ever indicate to you that he didn't like her?"

"No."

"Did you ever see them talk together?"

"Yes."

"And how were they when you saw them? Were they friendly?"

"I don't know."

"Well, were they unfriendly? Did they ever argue in front of you?"

"No."

"Did you ever hear Mike say anything to Lynn that would indicate to you that he was mad at her?"

"No."

"Did Lynn ever say anything to Mike that indicated that she was mad at him?"

Judy nodded. "Once. A couple of times, actually."

"What did she say?"

"She said that Mike was nothing. I heard her say that once."

"When?"

"I don't know."

"Recently?"

"A few weeks ago, maybe."

"Do you remember the circumstances?"

"No."

"Did anybody else hear it? Did your father hear it?"

"No. They were different when Daddy was around."

"How do you mean, different? Different in what way?"

Judy shrugged. "They didn't talk as much when he was there."

"Did they talk much when he wasn't there?"

"No," she said, "not all that much."

Murphy ground his teeth together. "Did you ever see Mike and Lynn having a long conversation?"

"Once or twice."

"What was it about?"

"I don't know. I was standing a ways away."

"What did Lynn call Mike?"

Judy looked at him in mystification. "Huh?"

"How did she address him? What name did she use?"

"Mike. She called him Mike."

"And what did he call her?"

"He called her Lynn. Except when my dad was around. Then he called her Miss Rice."

"He called her Miss Rice when your father was around, and he called her Lynn when they were alone? Is that right?"

"Yes."

Murphy frowned beneath his moustache. "And you never saw them argue? You never heard them exchange a harsh word?"

"I heard Mike tell her once that she couldn't marry Daddy."

"He told her what?" Murphy said.

"Mike told her one time that she shouldn't marry Daddy."

"You said 'couldn't.'"

Judy shook her head. "Maybe he said 'couldn't.' I don't remember."

"When was that?"

"I don't know."

Murphy took a deep breath. "Judy, is there anything you want to tell me? Anything at all?"

"No."

"How did you feel about your father and Lynn getting married?"

The girl's lower lip trembled. "I didn't want Daddy to marry her."

"Why not?"

"I wanted Daddy to marry my mother again."

"Did a man talk to you recently? A doctor?"

"Yes."

"What did you talk about?"

"Nothing. We talked about . . . things."

"What kind of things?"

"Nothing important."

"Did he talk to you about your father marrying Lynn?"

"Yes."

"And what did you tell him?"

The girl said nothing.

"Did you tell him you might hurt yourself if your father married Lynn?"

"Yes!"

"Just relax, Judy. Don't get excited. I'm your friend. I'm your mother's friend, and I'm your friend, too. You can trust me."

The girl began to weep.

"Stop crying, Judy," Murphy said quietly.

"You got me upset," Judy accused.

"I'm sorry. I didn't mean to. I apologize."

"Okay."

Murphy walked around the little office for a moment while the girl collected herself. A fun way to make a living, he thought to himself. Then he turned back to her. "Are you okay now?"

"Yes."

"Judy, I have a friend I'd like to have talk to you."

"I don't want to talk to anybody else."

"This is okay," Murphy assured her. "My friend is a doctor, only he's probably nicer than the doctor you talked to before. His name is Barry Weiner. I want to take you to see him Saturday morning."

"I don't want to go."

"Your mother said it's okay, Judy. You can ask her."

The girl stared at the floor for a moment. "If my mother said it's okay, then I'll go."

"I'll pick you up at your mother's place Saturday morning about nine, okay?"

"Okay."

"What did you do to get in trouble with Sister Joan?"

"Nothing."

"You must have done something. She said you were out on the grounds the other night when you were supposed to be in your room. Is that true?"

"I took a walk."

196

"Where did you walk to?"

"Nowhere."

"Who did you go with?"

"Nobody. I just wanted to walk by myself."

"You're sure?"

Judy nodded.

"What night was this?"

"Are you going to tell my mother?"

"I said I wouldn't," Murphy told her. "You can trust me."

"Saturday."

"Why were you out on the grounds Saturday?"

"I felt like it."

"Do you leave your room a lot when you're supposed to stay in it?"

"Sometimes."

"Did they ever catch you before?"

"No. I don't want to talk anymore."

"What did you do when you left your room?"

"I don't want to talk anymore. I want to go back upstairs."

"All right, Judy. I'll pick you up at your house Saturday morning. Okay?"

"Okay."

"And I won't tell your mother about your trouble with Sister Joan. Promise."

"Thank you," Judy said, and left.

Murphy sat alone in the nun's office for a moment, thinking. He stared at the wall—stared through it, really. His mind hummed and whirred inside his head. Sometimes Murphy thought he could actually hear its gears turning. Then he got up, lit a cigarette in the principal's office just to see what it would feel like and went outside to his car, his daughter, and his dog. The car was precisely where he had left it. Patricia and Winston were off a distance, playing in an open courtyard. Murphy watched them, the awkward bulldog and the graceful young woman who had—only a moment or two before, he was sure—been a little girl. Murphy just couldn't get used to seeing her look like that. She had been his for such a short time.

Now there was this boy at Skidmore, somebody named Teddy. Murphy had never met anybody named Teddy that he'd liked, and he was sure that this Teddy would be no exception. On the other hand, he'd never liked any of the boys who had dated Patricia. He remembered the first one who had shown up—a pimply-faced kid who'd come to the house when Patricia was fourteen to take her to a freshman mixer. Murphy had opened the front door and glared at the kid.

"Hello, rapist," he'd muttered.

The kid had paled visibly, and from upstairs he had heard Patricia's anguished wail of horror. Murphy had never quite lived that one down. He supposed he never would.

As he stood on the steps of the school, smoking his Camel and watching his daughter romp with the dog some forty yards away, a dark blue Plymouth Voyager van pulled into the long driveway, followed closely by a Devon police cruiser. He watched the cars carefully as they traveled down the tree-lined driveway and pulled in front of the steps directly behind the Toronado. A uniformed police officer stepped out of the van and a dark-complected man in a knit sport jacket got out of the cruiser. A plainclothes cop, Murphy knew. In the city, the plainclothes cops looked and dressed like the scum they chased. Here in the suburbs, the plainclothes cops looked like plainclothes cops. It was television, he supposed. All these guys really did was break up domestic squabbles and bust suburban punk kids for vandalism. Once in a while they'd roust some hookers who'd set up shop in a motel or nail a college kid with a lid of grass. Tough duty, Murphy thought.

The uniform went back to the prowl car and got behind the wheel while the plainclothes officer headed toward the steps and Murphy. He was a chubby guy around forty with dark hair and a gold chain around his neck.

"Excuse me," the plainclothes officer said. "Can you tell me where I can find Sister Joan?"

"You're the police?" Murphy asked.

"I'm Sergeant Garfalo."

Murphy stuck out his hand. "Frank Murphy. I'm the lawyer. I just talked to Sister Joan inside."

Garfalo took the hand. Murphy had carefully phrased his introduction. He was, indeed, Frank Murphy. He was a lawyer. And he had just talked to Sister Joan. But he was not the school's lawyer, which was the impression he hoped he'd conveyed.

"You'll have to sign this, Mr. Murphy," Garfalo said, producing a folded piece of legal-sized paper from an inside pocket and handing it to him.

Murphy studied the document. It was a standard property release form. It acknowledged that the school's van had been reported stolen and had been found that morning parked about a mile from the site of the alleged theft, which was the school.

"Is the vehicle damaged?" Murphy asked.

Garfalo shook his head. "Not a scratch on it. The

keys are in the ignition."

Murphy nodded. Then he handed the form back to the plainclothes officer. "I think Sister Joan ought to sign the release, since she's readily available. Her office is inside and to the left. It all looks like it's in order to me."

Garfalo frowned and took back the form. "It's in order. What's not to be in order?"

"Any idea who took it?" Murphy asked.

"Some fucking kids, I'm sure," Garfalo said. "The kids in this neighborhood, if it ain't nailed down, they'll fucking take it."

"Rich little bastards," Murphy said.

"You fucking said it," Garfalo said, going up the stairs and inside the school.

Murphy, his cigarette protruding jauntily from his mouth, went to the car and honked the horn. Patricia sprinted to him. The dog followed, his short, bowed legs pumping.

"Time to go," Murphy said.

"Will you put out that cigarette?" Patricia asked him. "How are you supposed to be a positive male role model when you're doing that to your lungs right in front of me?"

Reluctantly, Murphy stubbed out the cigarette.

"Every day you remind me more of your mother," he said, climbing into the car.

Murphy dropped Patricia off at the house in Mount Airy and made his way through traffic back to Center City. He was forced to park in a garage for six bucks, and when he got into his office Esmeralda was on the phone with her husband, the boxer.

"Any calls?" he asked her.

Esmeralda looked up from the phone. "Mr. Toddman."

"Get him for me. On second thought, I'll dial myself. You might break a nail or something."

Esmeralda put her thumb to her nose and flopped her fingers in Murphy's direction.

Murphy went into his office, hung up his coat, loosened his tie and dialed Toddman's number. Toddman came on the line quickly.

"We're getting around to setting a trial date on your guy Webster," Toddman said. "What do you want—sooner or later?"

"I don't want a trial at all," Murphy told him. "And I don't think you do, either. Look, I've been nosing around on this. You guys don't have all that much."

Toddman laughed. "We've got everything except a video tape of him stabbing her. Who are you kidding?"

"Paul, at least two other people had motive and opportunity."

"Like who?"

"Like Brian Kavanaugh. He says he spent the night of the murder at his office in Center City. Witnesses? Zip."

"Motive?"

"Lovers quarrel."

"Bullshit, Frank. Who's the other one?"

"Beverly."

"You've got to be kidding."

"She has no alibi for that night. And if anybody had motive it was her. Aside from which, my guy has a bad back. I don't think he could have lifted the Rice woman into the truck."

Toddman said, "Lynn Rice weighed one hundred and two pounds, according to the autopsy report. Any able-bodied man could lift her, and Webster looks able-bodied to me."

"When did you see him?"

"I didn't," Toddman said. "It's a figure of speech."

"Well, he's not," Murphy told him. "But Brian is. And Beverly is a bear. She must come in at close to one-forty, and she's all muscle. She could probably kick the shit out of both of us."

"Forget it," Toddman said simply.

Murphy sighed into the phone. "So you've stopped looking, then."

"We stopped looking the minute we found your guy with the body in his trunk and his fingerprints on the knife. Beverly? Get serious, Frank."

"Then I'll go late on the trial," Murphy said. "I'd hoped to go early, but now I'll need to do some more work on it, and I've got this Lucelli stuff to think about."

"I'll pencil you in for late. You'll get notice. Take it easy, Frank."

Murphy hung up and poured himself a small but welcome shot of bourbon. He spent the next hour doing paperwork and thinking about the Lucelli case. He'd have to go up there this weekend and relieve Wilder. It was not a prospect that appealed to him. Murphy hated the country in general and especially the woods. Animals lived there, and you couldn't go into a bar without sticking out like Richard Pryor at a KKK rally unless you happened to be wearing a John Deere hat and a flannel shirt.

He went over papers Esmeralda had prepared for a divorce case Murphy was handling for a lady cop he knew named Zsa Zsa. She kept changing her mind about going through with it. Murphy had been screwing around with this case for nearly a year, watching Zsa Zsa change her mind time and again. The worst part was that she was slow pay and Murphy owed her a few favors so he didn't feel right about pushing her for the money. The world would be a much simpler place, he reflected, if Zsa Zsa had entered a convent right out of high school. Murphy's life would be vastly simpler, and so would the lives of her legions of ex-husbands. He tried to picture Zsa Zsa as Sister Joan, but he couldn't get the image into proper focus. The phone rang and he answered it himself on the fourth ring. He had no idea what Esmeralda might be doing.

"Frank Murphy," he said.

"It's Paul. Bad news."

"This is turning out to be a fairly shitty day," Murphy observed.

"Fletcher wants an early trial on Webster, and he's going to prosecute this one personally."

"What for?" Murphy demanded in outrage.

"He said to tell you it's because you piss him off," Toddman explained.

"Oh," Murphy said softly. "Well, I guess I do at that."

CHAPTER 18

Murphy was annoyed.

Annoyed not so much at the prospect of an early trial for Mike Webster—although that was reason enough, given all the new developments—but annoyed because the early trial was nothing more or less than Fletcher Lake's mechanism for striking out at him, a gesture of revenge prompted by Murphy's impudence over breakfast and on other occasions.

When Murphy had worked as Fletcher Lake's chief investigator, he had tried—honestly tried—to remain loyal to the man. Murphy had been around long enough to understand that loyalty was a valuable commodity, especially when you held down a job that was essentially political. Loyalty was the classic political litmus test—loyalty to party policy, to party officials, to party candidates. Murphy had even changed his registration to Republican to please his new boss—although he'd changed back to the party of his father and grandfather the minute he'd gone into private practice.

Murphy had understood that loyalty to the Republicans and to Lake had been part of the bargain Murphy had made when he'd moved from the Major Crimes Unit into the DA's office under Toddman's sponsorship. But working for Fletcher Lake had stretched Murphy's capacity for loyalty—political, personal, and institutional—beyond its breaking point. Lake had represented all that Murphy despised in politicians and much of what he despised in humanity. The man had turned out to be hopelessly vain and venal, fairly inept as a lawyer and talented primarily in fooling the great unwashed. He'd also been petty and vindictive to a fault and lecherous to a degree that offended Murphy's Irish Catholic soul.

Murphy was no feminist—he tended to see women more as the natural oppressors of men rather than the other way around—but Lake's unfaithfulness to his wife, his casual and callous dismissal of women who paid him the compliment of giving themselves to him, his seeming refusal to grant women anything that even resembled human status, had repelled Frank Murphy from the start. Murphy soon learned that Fletcher Lake's two nicknames—Lake the Snake and Fletcher the Lecher—had been well earned.

Added to that had been Lake's autocratic and overbearing manner with his staff. Lake had gone easy on Toddman, whom he knew he needed to actually run the office. He'd even kept on Toddman as first assistant district attorney even though Toddman was a Democrat, which was the clearest possible indication of how much Lake valued the man. But his treatment of others—Murphy included—bordered on sheer viciousness.

Some aides and staffers tolerated it. Some even seemed to relish it, under the assumption that if they could put up with Lake's abuse long enough they might somehow manage to get slated for elective office and end up with their own staffs of hard-working bureaucrats to pick on. But it had been more than Murphy could bear.

The police department had not been free of assholes, to be sure. But those assholes had been forced to bow to competence. A good detective—a detective who produced results without resorting too blatantly to the tactics of the people he chased—had generally been left alone to pursue his craft. A truly good detective was given freedom unknown in any other line of work Murphy could imagine. In the DA's office, however, Murphy had found himself increasingly performing tasks that were designed primarily to further Fletcher Lake's political ambitions. The crusher had come a few years before when Lake had promised a room full of reporters that a particularly vicious random killer would be captured within a week and—in private, later—threatened to fire Murphy unless he managed to pull off that particular miracle, which hadn't even been in his line of work at the time.

As chief investigator for the DA, Murphy had to supervise arresting officers, to see that the evidence they gathered was solid enough to sustain a conviction, and to see that they didn't beat up a suspect to such a conspicuous degree that his confession would be ruled inadmissible. Murphy had gone into the DA's office under Toddman's sponsorship so he could finally work regular hours and get out of the business of chasing around creeps in the middle of the night.

In the end, Murphy had managed to catch the killer, but he and Wilder both had ended up in the hospital as a result. During his weeks of recuperation, Murphy had decided that enough was enough and made arrangements to rent office space from another lawyer. Then, from his apartment, where he collected disability checks, Murphy had quietly spread the word around the department that he would do cheap criminal work and handle cops' personal legal work—that meant a disproportionately high number of divorces and wife-beating beefs—at a reduced rate. Then Murphy had gone into Fletcher Lake's elegantly furnished office and suggested to the city's most popular public official that he perform an anatomically impossible sex act, a gesture that had not been appreciated at the time and was clearly still an issue of some contention between the two men.

And Mike Webster would suffer for that. Mike Webster would go on trial for murder before Murphy was ready to defend him because Frank Murphy had told Fletcher Lake to go fuck himself. That struck Murphy as essentially unfair. It strengthened his resolve to someday get Fletcher Lake, and it strengthened his resolve to get Mike Webster off. An acquittal for Mike Webster would please Murphy no end, even if he didn't get paid for it. Defeating Fletcher Lake in open court would be payment enough. Not that Murphy had any intention of telling that to Webster. Satisfaction—no matter how gratifying—wouldn't pay Patricia's tuition.

These were the thoughts that passed through Frank Murphy's mind after he ended his telephone conversation with Toddman. He sat in his high-backed judge's chair, his mind working, dissecting his hatred of Fletcher Lake and congratulating himself on his good taste in enemies. When he was finished with that exercise, he began to focus on the business at hand. That meant a phone call. He knew better than to ask Esmeralda to dial. She was, he was sure, too busy with the poor man's Mike Tyson. Murphy looked up the number himself. Then he called Brian Kavanaugh.

"What's on your mind, Frank?" Kavanaugh asked.

"I thought you'd like to know. Mike Webster will be going to trial in a few weeks."

"Whew! That's pretty fast. I thought there was a backlog in the courts in this city."

"There is," Murphy said, "unless the DA really wants to get his ass moving on a particular case. Fletcher Lake wants Webster badly, due mostly to the nature of our personal relationship, which, in a word, sucks."

"How will I know when the case comes to trial?"

"You'll get word. You're going to be a witness. Among other things, I'm going to want to call you as a character witness for Mike."

There was a moment's silence on Kavanaugh's end of the line. "I'm not sure I'd like that. You may be convinced of his innocence. You get paid to be convinced. But I don't, and I'm not."

Murphy said, "I'm not going to ask you about your opinion of his guilt or innocence. I'm going to ask you what you know about the guy. And you've already told me that's all good. Your personal contact with him is what I'll want you to testify to."

"I don't think I want to testify for Mike," Kavanaugh said.

"You don't get the picture," Murphy told him, an edge creeping into his voice. "It won't be your choice. I can call you whether you like it or not. And I will."

Murphy could hear Brian Kavanaugh bristle over the phone. "Is that why you called me, Frank? To push me around?"

"No," Murphy said quietly. "I called you so you could make whatever modifications in your schedule might be called for. I called you because I'm a nice guy. I was hoping you might be, too. I just left your daughter a few hours ago. She thinks you're a decent guy, Brian. That was good enough for me."

"What were you doing with Judy?"

"Just talking," Murphy said. "Judy's in a bit of trouble with the school, you know. It seems she took the school's mini-van out for a joy ride."

"No reason for them to worry about that," Kavanaugh said. "The kid drives better than you do, probably. I taught her myself—out on the farm. She's been driving my Austin Healey for better than a year."

"She's pretty young for driving, isn't she?" Murphy asked.

"She can handle a car," Kavanaugh said, "or a van, if it comes to that. If she can drive my Healey, she can drive anything. That thing doesn't even have synchromesh in first. You have to double-clutch the damn thing just to get it going. Listen, I don't want her involved in this, Frank. I don't want her involved at all. If you want the truth, I'd just as soon you stayed the hell away from her while all this is going on. No offense, but that's how I feel about it."

"When did you teach her to drive?" Murphy asked. "Patricia has her license, but I wouldn't ride with her unless I made a Novena first."

He was greeted by a stony silence from Kavanaugh's end of the line. Then: "What are you trying to do, Frank?"

"You're a suspicious sort, aren't you?" Murphy said.

"Don't give me that shit. You're trying to implicate Judy, aren't you? Come on, Frank. Level with me."

Murphy said, "Do you really think Judy could hurt anybody? You're her father, for Christ's sake."

Kavanaugh was silent for a long time. Then, voice quivering, he said, "What a schmuck you are. You are a total asshole, Frank. You're trying to tie my daughter to this just to get your client off?"

"Brian . . ." Murphy began.

"Fuck you!" Brian Kavanaugh said, his voice rising to a bellow.

Quietly, Murphy said, "A man with a less forgiving nature might take offense at that."

"You stay away from my daughter. Do you hear me? You stay the hell away from her. You're trying to make Judy out to be a murderer, you son of a bitch!"

"Settle down," Murphy said sharply. "You're making a fool of yourself, Brian. I didn't say anything like that."

Kavanaugh said, "You stay away from my daughter. I'm warning you, Murphy. I thought you were a friend of the family. You're only a friend to whoever is paying your fee, you rotten shit."

Murphy began to respond, but Kavanaugh slammed down the phone before he could get out a word. Murphy looked at the dead phone for a moment. Then, slowly, he hung it up.

So, Murphy thought, he had taught her how to drive. Wasn't that intriguing?

CHAPTER 19

"He's not available right now," said Angie, the receptionist. "He's busy in room two."

Murphy nodded. Room two was one of the autopsy rooms on the lower floor of the city medical examiner's two-floor complex in Philadelphia General Hospital. Murphy knew it well. He'd been in all three autopsy rooms over the years. None of them was terribly pleasant, but each was memorable in its own way.

Room one was the main autopsy room, equipped with four stainless-steel tables, each with its own electrical outlets, its own sink and scale and other equipment. Often, all four tables were in use at the same time. On such occasions the place reminded Murphy of a large butcher shop, just as a pathologist performing an autopsy reminded him of a butcher boning a chicken. Room three was specially designed for performing autopsies on people who had died of infectious diseases or for bodies in advanced stages of decomposition. The room was like a cave, with no windows and completely airtight. It was also equipped with special fans and air-conditioning equipment, which sucked out foul air or infected gases and drew them to an incinerator in the basement, where they were burned.

Room two contained a single table, and it was the chief medical examiner's private preserve. The room was never used by any of the staff pathologists, only by Marvin Weinberg himself, the ill-tempered old man who had run the medical examiner's office since the days when Murphy's voice cracked as he made indecent propositions to high school cheerleaders.

"He's cutting today?" Murphy asked the receptionist. "What's the occasion, Angie?"

Angie popped her gum, a habit Murphy had never found particularly attractive in a woman and one which especially did little to add to the allure of Angie, who bore a startling resemblance to Peter Falk in a beehive hairdo. "This detective has a stabbing, and he wants us to tell him if the knife he found is the murder weapon. The Doc took this one himself because he wanted to try something new."

"Hmmm," Murphy said. "What do you think he'd say if I just walked in and watched?"

Angie shrugged. "I don't know, Frank. You know what an old crank he is. He might come out and chew on my fanny good for letting you in there."

"Don't sweat it, Angie," Murphy told her. "I'll keep him off your back."

Murphy started down the hall toward the elevator that would take him to room two. Angie called after him, "Don't tell him I said you could go in. Tell him I was in the ladies' room or something and you just went in on your own."

213

Murphy turned and winked. "I can handle that surly old fart."

Weinberg was a positive terror. He'd been born nasty, and his mood had steadily deteriorated for the past seventy years or so. For more than twenty years, he had been widely acknowledged as the finest forensic pathologist on earth, which had done little for either his humor or his humility. Weinberg was assured of his genius and equally assured that virtually all the rest of humanity was beneath contempt. Slicing up corpses had probably done it to him, Murphy supposed—studying in minute detail year after year the horrors people inflict on themselves or on one another.

But for reasons Murphy had never been able to fathom, the old man had always seemed to like Murphy—had liked him from the day nearly fifteen years before when Murphy had watched Weinberg perform an autopsy and humiliate an unpleasant detective lieutenant named Herb Braun who had been under the mistaken impression that he'd been dealing with a shooting case. The lieutenant had based this conclusion on the presence of a bullet hole in the victim's forehead, but Weinberg had deftly opened the skull, removed the brain and announced that the victim definitely had not died of a bullet wound.

"What?" the lieutenant had said. "That's a fucking bullet hole, Doc, I've seen five hundred of them."

Weinberg's eyes had narrowed. His white brows had flown together like a thunderclap. Then he had leaned over the corpse and said, "There's no exit wound, Herbie. There's no bullet in the cranial cavity or in the brain tissue. The wound is only eleven centimeters deep. There's no trace of powder burns. There's no trace of lead particles visible to the naked eye. If this guy was shot, where did the bullet go, Herbie? Did it melt, for Christ's sake?"

The lieutenant had shrugged. "You tell me. If a bullet didn't make that hole, what did?"

"A shoe, Herbie," Weinberg had said quietly.

The lieutenant had cocked his head. "What?"

"My guess is that a spike heel made this wound," Weinberg had said, pointing at it. "This guy said something his wife or girlfriend didn't like, and she hit him in the forehead with her spike heel. It punctured the skull and went into the right frontal lobe of the cerebrum. Of course, a wound like that wouldn't bother you, Herbie. You've got no upper brain to begin with."

The lieutenant had stormed out of the autopsy room. Murphy, a new detective just out of a West Philly prowl car, immediately had gone back to the victim's home, taken every one of the widow's high-heeled shoes he could find and turned them over to the police lab. A lab technician had found blood and brain tissue on the heel of one of them, and the DA had cleared the case with a plea to manslaughter second that same afternoon. Murphy had returned to Weinberg's office with a bottle of bourbon, and the two of them had killed it in the old man's office, chortling gleefully over what a dumb shit Herbie Braun was. They had been fast friends ever since, a relationship maintained by their free and open exchange of insults. Murphy walked into room two with one handy.

"Hey," he said as he entered, "I thought the stiff was supposed to be lying down. Oh, sorry, Doc. I didn't recognize you at first."

215

Weinberg looked up from his lab table. The old man was dressed in surgical greens, and his Florida tan almost managed to cover the large liver spots on each of his naked arms. He glared at Murphy and said, "My tax dollars at work. Oh, that's right, isn't it, Murphy? You're not suckling on the municipal tit anymore. You're on your own now, chasing meat wagons and tampering with juries. How could I have forgotten?"

Standing next to Weinberg was Mario Fortunato, a new detective Murphy knew slightly. Fortunato, then in uniform, had been involved in the capture of the Center City stomper two Christmases ago, the case that had driven Murphy out of the DA's office and into private practice. A third person also occupied the room: a black youth of perhaps fifteen. He was on the table, dead, his flesh a dark grayish-brown color, the hue of death.

"What have we got here?" Murphy asked.

"Stabbing victim," Fortunato said. "This kid got it this morning in some kind of gang clash at Germantown High. We've got two suspects in custody. Only they each have knives, and whichever one did it must have wiped his clean before we got there. He must have washed the goddamn thing clean in a water fountain, because the lab can't find a trace of blood on either of them. We're trying to figure out which knife did the job so we know who to charge with murder two and who to charge with felony murder."

Murphy nodded. Murder two was the bigger charge. Felony murder was reserved for accomplices, people who had participated in a crime that had led to the murder but who had not been directly responsible for the death of the victim. The charm of the felony murder

216

charge was that it usually induced the perpetrator to plead guilty to a lesser charge in exchange for spilling his guts on his partner. The charge, relatively new under Pennsylvania law, was a prosecutor's dream come true.

"Barium sulfate?" Murphy asked Weinberg.

The old man shook his head. "I've got a better idea," he sa'' and went back to work at his lab table.

Fortunato watched in curiosity. "What's barium sulfate?" Fortunato asked Murphy. "He won't tell me diddley."

"Quiet," Weinberg snarled over his shoulder. "I'm an old man, and my hands shake. You want me to hurt myself with this Bunsen burner?"

Murphy took Fortunato around the autopsy table to the other side of the disinterested corpse.

"The usual drill," Murphy said quietly, "is to pour barium sulfate into the wound. That's the stuff you drink when they give you an upper GI series—you know, those X-rays of your stomach when they're looking for an ulcer? What he usually does is pour that stuff into a stab wound and then X-ray it from a few different angles. That'll give you a perfect view of the knife blade that did the damage, and you can get a precise measurement of the wound at the same time. I don't know what he's doing instead of that. He's always screwing around with these things. You ought to see him with poisonings. He really goes whacko over those. How do you like plainclothes work, Mario?"

"Well, it's different. I'm learning lots of stuff. This medical stuff is weird."

"The miracles of modern science," Murphy said. "The scumbags don't have a chance. Funny we can't catch more of them, isn't it?"

"There!" Weinberg announced triumphantly from his lab bench.

The two men—the new detective and the former one—turned as the old man stood up, turned and approached the corpse, carrying a steaming test tube in a pair of stainless steel tongs. He poured the test tube's contents into the wound. Smoke rose from the teenager's naked chest, and Murphy's nose was assailed by the stench of cooking human flesh. It made his stomach churn. Fortunato paled visibly. Weinberg grinned.

"That'll do it," he said.

"What the hell are you doing?" Murphy demanded, waving away the wisps of smoke rising from the corpse's chest. "What is that crap?"

"You'll see," Weinberg said, studying the wound.

They waited several minutes, no one speaking. Then Weinberg turned to his lab table and produced a set of forceps. He leaned over the corpse, dug at the wound for a moment and pulled what appeared to be a knife blade out of the boy's chest. He held it up and studied it in the light.

"What's that?" Fortunato said. "Where'd it come from?"

"I made it out of Wood's metal," Weinberg said, eying the blade critically. "I just melted a test tube full of the stuff and poured it directly into the wound. If I'm right—and don't have any doubt about that, gentlemen—this metal that hardened in the wound will conform precisely to the shape of the murder weapon."

Weinberg handed the sliver of metal to Fortunato. "Now, detective, you take this piece of metal back to headquarters and compare it to the blades of the two knives in question. It'll be a precise match with one of them, and then you'll know who did what—who actually did the stabbing and with which weapon. Jesus, I'm smart. I truly am. I amaze even myself sometimes."

Fortunato grasped the sliver of metal with his fingertips. He wrapped it carefully in his handkerchief and put it in an inside jacket pocket.

"Thanks, Doc," he said, and left hurriedly.

Weinberg watched him go and then turned to his sink and washed his hands. "Eager, that one," Weinberg said over his shoulder. "Remember when we were eager, Murphy? How long ago was that?"

"In your case," Murphy said, "it must have been sometime during the Reformation."

"Hah!" Weinberg laughed. It was his standard laugh—one short snort that managed to convey derision and amusement simultaneously, and in more or less equal amounts. He dried his hands on a city issue towel and turned around. He produced one of the curved pipes he favored and lit it with a wooden match he struck on the sole of his shoe.

"So," Weinberg said, puffing to get his pipe going. "What are you doing here, anyway? Hiding from the bar association? Some outraged client you fleeced want his money back?"

"Not quite," Murphy said. "If you're finished here, let's go up to your office and talk for a few minutes."

Weinberg led the way. They left room two and its disinterested occupant and took the elevator to the next upper floor. The medical examiner's complex took in thousands of square feet in the city-owned hospital. Murphy followed as Weinberg stalked through it to his office—past the photo lab and X-ray rooms, past the neuropathology and toxicology labs, past the huge refrigerated room that contained corpse chambers, past the staging area where bodies were brought in to be sliced into tiny pieces, which were weighed, analyzed, subjected to a whole spectrum of chemical analysis and—eventually—provided the evidence of cause of death. The whole complex was a monument to mortality, to the fleeting character of human life. Murphy had spent countless hours here, and he knew the value of the work done within these walls. The place gave him the creeps anyway. It was only human nature that it should. On the way, they passed Angie, and the old man snarled an order to her to have the corpse in room two returned to refrigeration.

Weinberg's office was largely unchanged from the second Eisenhower administration. The floor was covered with a Persian rug that bore the marks of thirty years of heavy traffic. The walls were darkly paneled, and the desk—roughly the size of the U.S.S. *Nimitz*—was battered and covered with papers Weinberg rarely looked at. He was notoriously contemptuous of the most routine paperwork. The office was, in fact, littered with paper of all description: professional journals, autopsy reports, piles of letters from lawyers from around the world offering the old man stunning sums for his work as an expert witness, copies of *Golf Digest* that reflected Weinberg's one nonprofessional passion, newspapers, *Time* magazines dating back to the Vietnam era. Murphy, a slob of legendary proportions, admired the mess. Even the bookcases were sloppy. Weinberg's leather-bound copies of the

220

complete works of Sherlock Holmes were stacked haphazardly, evidence of the old man's regular study of them. Dust had gathered in thick layers on the large jars filled with floating bits of humanity preserved in chemicals. Weinberg even had the fetus of a two-headed calf in one of them. He had shown it to Murphy once, and Murphy had almost lost his expensive Le Bec Fin lunch as a result.

The old man settled behind his desk, nearly hidden behind the mountain of paper. He gestured to Murphy to sit down in one of the two ancient Queen Anne chairs reserved for the rare guest.

"What's on your mind, Francis?" the medical examiner asked. "Aside from which horse at Liberty Bell has been dosed with the most potent dope?"

Murphy leaned back in the chair and lit a Camel. "I might need some help in a case I'm handling."

Weinberg laughed, flashing his tobacco-stained teeth. "Murphy, I have more court work than I know what to do with. Do you know where I have to be on Friday? Las Vegas. There's some sort of malpractice case out there that demands my incomparable attention. And there's a good fight card at the Sands Friday night. I can catch a late flight back and be on the first tee at nine in the morning Saturday."

Murphy said, "Actually, I wasn't figuring on just having you testify. I was figuring on having you do a little lab work first—to see if I even want you to testify."

"You definitely (puff) can't afford me (puff)," Weinberg said.

Murphy looked at the old man and said, "I could really use some expert help on this one."

Weinberg's face was expressionless. Murphy had never before asked him for a favor that required more than a few minutes of the medical examiner's time. Weinberg was not renowned for his generosity.

"Why don't you tell me what you want?" the old man said finally.

Murphy got up and began pacing. He tended to do that when he was agitated. "I've got a case where a guy is charged with a stabbing. They found the body in the trunk of his car with the knife still in place, and they found his fingerprints on the murder weapon."

"Evidence like that, and you're not going to plead this case?"

"No, not if I can help it. I'm starting to get a pretty solid idea that he didn't do it. I just can't prove it, is all."

"I'd say you have a major problem, Francis. You don't need me. You need Merlin."

Murphy smiled. "He's not available. You're next on the list."

"What do you need?"

"First," Murphy said, "do you still have custody of the body of a Lynn Rice."

"I don't know. I'll check." Weinberg got on the phone. "Angie, check for me on whether we have a stabbing victim named Lynn Rice. Get back to me right away." He hung up. "So, if we still have her, so what?"

"I'll get back to the body," Murphy said. "First, there's the murder weapon. That's in police custody. I can't get it for a lab study without a court order. But you can. You might even still have it, if you have the body."

"We might," Weinberg admitted. "We probably dusted the thing for prints here with the detectives

222

present. What's wrong with a court order so you can have a private lab give it a going-over?"

"Nothing. I could get one easily enough. But if I did, it would alert the DA to the fact that I'd been nosing around the weapon. And I'd prefer not to alert the DA, since I'm going up in court on this one with Lake the Snake himself. I'd just as soon Lake's people didn't know I'd ever had anything done with the weapon. Let them think that I've accepted that my client's prints were the only ones on it. You, on the other hand, you could say you need it to check how it matches with the wound. Shit, you could say anything. They'd give it to you if you just asked for it. Aside from which, you really wouldn't be doing anything for me. You'd just be doing your job diligently."

"One catch to that," Weinberg said. "I'm supposed to be on their side, remember?"

"Says who?" Murphy demanded. "You're supposed to be on the side of the truth. All I want is the truth. And the police lab won't do any more than they have to to make their case. They never do. That's the way it works in every aspect of a police investigation. Once the cops get something that points them in a specific direction, they don't bust their humps to disprove their own case. It's human nature. I know that because I was like that, too. You aren't even aware of it at the time. I never realized it until I was on the outside."

Weinberg nodded. He knew Murphy spoke the truth. "And what am I supposed to do with the knife once I get it into my lab. Just dust for prints again? That's already been done."

Murphy drew on his cigarette. "Do you have a fancy microscope you could use to scan the knife handle for prints that the police lab might not have noticed? I'm talking about fragmentary prints."

"I have a TEM," Weinberg said.

"What the hell is that?"

"It's an electronic microscope—a transmission electron microscope, to be precise."

"That's better than a regular microscope?"

Weinberg looked at Murphy with barely disguised pity for his inadequate intellect. "It'll magnify up to twenty-five hundred times," he said patiently.

"So you could see even the barest detail of a latent print?"

"In theory. We use it here to do tissue studies. But I suppose we could use it to study a knife hilt. Either the TEM or the SEM. That's a scanning electron microscope. We have one of those, too. If there's a decent latent print fragment, we should probably be able to find it."

"Good," Murphy said. "Look, here's the problem: The weapon is a kitchen knife. The only prints on it—I mean, the only ones—belong to my client, who would never have occasion to use that knife. He doesn't live in the house it came from. Now, does it make sense to you that there would be no prints on the hilt of a kitchen knife? Even if the thing had just been taken out of the dishwasher, there would still be traces of a print on it from somebody who used it to slice up a tomato or something. With no prints, that tells me that somebody wiped it down before my guy touched it. If somebody wiped it down, somebody else with a fancy microscope might be able to find some kind of fragment—some faded impression—something."

"It's possible," Weinberg conceded.

The phone rang and Weinberg picked it up. "Yes? Fine. Good." He hung up. "We still have the body. It's scheduled to go out of here later this afternoon to the funeral home."

"Good," Murphy said. "How would you like to try something fancy?"

"Like?" Weinberg inquired.

"The last time we all played poker—you and me and Wilder and Toddman—you mentioned something you'd read about that they're doing in England to take prints off flesh."

"Yes, I remember that."

"Have you ever tried it?"

"No, but the technique isn't all that complicated. What they're doing over there is dusting corpses with a fine lead powder and then subjecting them to X-ray. They've managed in a few cases to take fingerprints from flesh, which everybody used to think was impossible."

"Could you do that with Lynn Rice's corpse? You see, here's the deal: Whoever killed her did it in the kitchen of her house. Then he—or she—dragged the body outside and dumped it into the trunk of a car. That was the car my client was caught driving the next day. Whoever dragged the body out might have touched her someplace where it would show up. Maybe she was dragged by the wrists, for example. Also, if you still have her clothes, you might give them the same sort of treatment."

Weinberg chewed thoughtfully on his pipe stem. "Prints on cloth are tough, Francis—very tough."

"I know."

"And what if I don't find any prints at all, either on

225

the body or on the knife?"

"If you don't find any other prints on the knife," Murphy said, "then that indicates the weapon was wiped down carefully before my client touched it. That counts in his favor. If you don't find any on the body, then I just won't ask about that in court."

Weinberg pondered the proposition. Then he said, "All right, on one condition."

Murphy knew what was coming and what it meant. "You want me to question you on direct and not on cross."

"That's right. Under city regulations, I'm not eligible for an expert witness fee if you elicit the information from me as the state's witness."

"How much do you want?" Murphy asked.

"My usual fee is five thousand a day, plus expenses."

"I'm only getting eight myself," Murphy pleaded, "and I'll have to wait a long time for that even if I get this guy off. If I don't get him off, I'll have to pay you out of my own pocket."

Weinberg merely smiled at him. Murphy sighed. He should have known better than to have expected mercy at the hands of Marvin Weinberg. Making a living in this business was no picnic.

"All right, Doc," he said. "Feel free to bankrupt me. It's a deal."

"Look at the bright side, Francis. You can win it all back from me at poker."

Murphy shook his head wearily. Of the four of them who gathered once a month for poker, Weinberg was far and away the best player. The old man was a positive shark with cards.

"One more thing," Murphy said. "I'll be sending over

226

a coffee mug and an ashtray, all wrapped up. I'd like you to dust them for prints. Then, if you find prints on either the knife or the corpse, I'd like you to compare them with the prints you find on those two items."

Weinberg's eyebrows rose. "You have other suspects, then?"

"Three others. But I only have print samples from two of them right now. I'll get you the third print sample on Monday morning."

Weinberg stood up. It was a dismissal.

"Well, I have stiffs to cut up, Francis. I'll see what I can do for you, though. And to show you what a kind-hearted soul I am, I won't even bill you for this consultation."

"Gee, thanks, Doc," Murphy said. "You're a prince."

CHAPTER 20

The cat was going to be a problem, Alex knew.

It was a big Siamese—an enormous Siamese, actually, about the size of a cocker spaniel on steroids—and it put out dander the way an atomic reactor put out radiation.

"Aaaaa-chooo!" Alex said. "Excuse me, please."

"You must be catching a cold," Emma Fronczek said.

"Could be," Alex said, eying the big cat as it sprawled on the windowsill and well aware of what had kicked off the sneezing fit. "My eyes have been watering a bit all morning."

"Well," Emma Fronczek said, "you ought to go home and go to bed. It's all this rain we're having today. You make sure you keep your umbrella up when you go out."

"I will," Alex said, sniffling and patting the umbrella. "But first I have to tell you about your prize."

Emma Fronczek sat forward eagerly. "I was so

pleased when I got the letter. I just couldn't believe it. I've only been to Europe once, you know, years ago. That was when George was alive. We went for our fifteenth wedding anniversary. We took a bus tour of France and Germany and the low countries. We always meant to go back, but we never did. And I always wanted to go to Italy. We never got there."

"Well," Alex said. "Here's your chance."

"Tell me again how my name was selected," Emma said. "I still don't understand that."

"Nothing more complicated than random chance," Alex explained. "The computer picked you from hundreds of thousands of other names on the Social Security lists. You were just one of the lucky ones."

Emma clasped her fat hands together in glee. "I can't believe it. I just can't believe it."

Alex said, "Oh, you can believe it. Now let me explain how this works . . ."

Alex went on for perhaps five minutes, describing the hotel accommodations in Rome and Milan, explaining that the travel firm that Alex represented awarded only a dozen such trips nationwide every year, for promotional purposes. Would Emma mind terribly if her name and face appeared prominently in several national magazine advertisements? No? Very good. Emma Fronczek nodded constantly, bobbing her head like one of those dog decorations you sometimes see in the rear windows of cars.

"And," Alex added, "it's a trip for two. You can take along anybody else you want to accompany you."

For the first time, Emma looked perturbed. "Well," she said slowly, "I don't have anybody to take."

"You don't?" Alex said. "Not even to Italy?"

Emma shrugged. "I don't have any family left. Just Snookie."

"Snookie?"

Emma gestured toward the enormous cat.

"Oh," Alex said softly, sneezing again. "Well, I'll tell you what you can do. You can take the cash for the second trip. Would that be all right?"

"Oh, that would be wonderful. That would be just wonderful."

"I wonder," Alex said, "if I could use your bathroom for just a moment. Would you mind? You just look through this brochure here, and I'll be right back."

"Go ahead," said the deliriously happy Emma Fronczek. "It's right around the corner there."

Alex found the bathroom and closed the door. This would just take a moment. The real work had been getting in here in the first place.

Alex had studied the occupants of this building for several days, watching who came in and who went out. Of the six apartments in the brownstone building on Schuylkill Avenue, only one tenant seemed to have no visitors and to leave only for quick trips to the corner grocery store. That had been Emma Fronczek. A letter generated by a word processor Alex had bought at a Center City computer store had followed—a letter informing Emma Fronczek she had won a trip to Europe. It had informed her that Alex would be calling at a precise time and day. The ploy had worked perfectly. It had gotten Alex into the apartment, and once in the apartment the next step was to get into the bathroom. Thank God for the rain. It had made the umbrella a plausible piece of equipment.

Alex unscrewed the tip of the umbrella with delicate fingers. It was careful work. Alex tried not to sneeze, no mean feat with cat dander everywhere. A sneeze here, a jab of the needle imbedded in the umbrella's point into Alex's finger, and that would be the end of this job. It would be the end of Alex, too, which was not on the agenda.

The umbrella had cost several thousand dollars in Brussels three years before, during a restaurant tour of the continent, but it had been worth every penny. Alex had used it twice now. The first time the target had been a federal prosecutor in Brooklyn. The poison injected by the tiny spring-operated device in the umbrella's tip in that instance had been ricin, a substance chemically extracted from castor beans and fatal in a dose even as small as one hundred millionths of a gram. Alex had simply bumped into the prosecutor in a crowd in the federal courthouse in Brooklyn and stuck him with the tip of the umbrella. A tiny hollow metal ball, no larger than a pinhead and with minute holes on four sides, had been injected into the target's flesh, in an upper leg muscle.

Over the course of a few hours, the ricin had seeped out of the tiny pellet into the target's circulatory system. Over the course of the next twenty-four hours, the prosecutor had grown progressively sicker until he finally passed out at his desk in the U.S. courthouse. He had been taken by ambulance to the hospital, where he had hung on for another twenty-four hours before expiring. The effects of ricin mimicked cardio-vascular collapse, although the victim had been left with a suspiciously high white blood cell count. Nobody had ever proved anything, however, which had been the point. It had been important for that death to be attributed to natural causes, and it had been.

Today's task called for something faster acting. Alex had selected hydrocyanic acid—cyanide. Its drawback was that it was easily detectable, but it had the virtue of instantaneous results. Alex positioned the tiny metal pellet with great care. There were certain mistakes it didn't do to make.

"How about restaurants?" Emma Fronczek said as Alex emerged from the bathroom. "Does the trip cover my meals?"

"Oh, yes," Alex said, standing behind Emma and jabbing her lightly between the shoulder blades with the tip of the umbrella.

Emma said nothing. She merely snapped upward as though she'd been struck by lightning. Every muscle in her body flexed and tensed for a long moment. The sudden contraction bent her nearly backward in her chair. Then something in her brain gave way—some pathway for electrical current through her brain cells. The rictus evaporated, and she fell forward, hard, on the coffee table, making a bit more noise than Alex cared for. The old woman slid off the table to the floor, scattering magazines about the worn carpeting and rolling over on her back as she hit. Her eyes bulged slightly, and her mouth worked for a few seconds as her face turned a vivid pink. That was one of the effects of cyanide as well. The skin turned pink—a result of cyanhemoglobin in the blood—and the corpse was left with the smell of bitter almonds.

Alex stood over Emma Fronczek, watching her

closely. The old woman was dead in less than ten seconds, staring sightlessly at Alex, her mouth torn open in a silent scream of horror. Over on the windowsill, Snookie watched all this with no comprehension and monumental disinterest. The cat yawned, displaying needly teeth.

Alex went to the phone and dialed.

"Yeah."

"Vito, please."

"Who's callin'?"

"Tell him it's Alex."

"Wait a minute."

In a moment, the familiar voice came on. "What have you got?"

"Some cleanup for you. Have somebody buy a big steamer trunk and then rent a big truck. Have them come to this address"—Alex provided it—"and bring the trunk up to the front apartment on the second floor. I'll be here. This has to be done today. And have the men dressed in work clothes, please. Coveralls would be nice."

There was silence for a moment at the other end. Then: "Is this it already?"

"No. This was part of getting set up."

"It'll take a couple of hours," Vito said.

"Just as long as it's today."

Alex hung up and studied the apartment. The furniture was old, and the place could hardly be characterized as elegant. Alex went into the kitchen and opened the cabinets. All pre-prepared food, mostly cans of Campbell's chunky soup. Alex would have to do some shopping later today, after the trunk was taken out. It would be either shop or starve. And the windows would have to be opened to release the cat dander. Alex's lungs were filling up rapidly.

The cat came into the kitchen and made its way leisurely to a litter box in one corner. It squatted in the sand, its tail twitching, and glared at the intruder. Alex toyed for a moment with the umbrella tip, adjusting it for more use and stifling a sneeze as the work was performed.

Then: "Nice kitty. Here kitty, kitty."

Before all this

Alma's decision to quit the escort service and move in with Phil Bonsignore came as no surprise to Ellie, who had been through such hardships before. Ellie accepted such developments as a professional hazard. You sent a woman out to sleep with a man for money, and every once in a while it turned out that she liked the man more than she liked the money. It was less common that the man developed a genuine interest in the woman, but it had been known to happen. And when it happened, the woman usually moved on to other endeavors.

Unless she was totally crazy, that is, which a good many hookers were.

But Alma wasn't crazy. Not that Ellie had noticed, anyway. And in Alma's case, movement out of the profession had been overdue. Twice in the previous year she had been busted, nailed by undercover cops who had first sampled the wares and then confiscated the merchandise. Ellie, who had been in this line of work since the beginning of the Kennedy presidency, could tell when the girls were getting itchy. Being busted twice in less than a year tended to make them itchy even if they hadn't been itchy to begin with, which a lot of them were. The streetwalkers on Eighth Avenue, they didn't mind getting busted. They didn't mind much of anything, since most of them were junkies and completely out to lunch. They were the ones with the clap and the crud and God alone knew what else. High-priced call girls like Alma were a different matter altogether. After a while, when they got a few miles on them, they started to look for a man to settle down with.

But Phil Bonsignore? Ellie had her doubts about the wisdom of that move.

"Do you know about him?" she asked Alma. "Do you know what kind of guy he really is?"

"He's a decent guy with a dead wife who runs a restaurant," Alma said. "He's lonely. So am I. So what's the big deal, Ellie?"

Ellie, forty-seven and wise beyond her years, said, "Phil's connected, Alma. Do you know what that means, when I say he's connected?"

"So, he's connected. So what? A lot of people are connected."

Ellie shook her head. "You don't know what I mean, do you?"

"I know," Alma said. "He knows some people. You know some people, too, right? That's how you stay in business and that's how you know about Phil's connections. What's your point, Ellie?"

Ellie held up her hands to show that she meant no offense. "Hey," she said, "no point. No point at all."

Alma was sitting on the sofa in Ellie's office. The

236

escort service operated out of a SoHo loft you could park a bus in. Ellie lived in the place and worked out of it, too. She was past the age when she went on calls herself, but she made a decent living out of the service, and she ran a good business. She took care of her girls. She paid them well, provided them with health care and motherly advice and was acutely aware that if she didn't run this business somebody else would—somebody who would probably treat these girls the way Ellie herself had been treated when she had been young, which hadn't been very well. Every once in a while she came across a girl who reminded her of herself when she'd been younger—a girl just a bit too sharp and with too much drive and independence to really be in this line of work. A girl like Alma, for example.

Ellie had come to New York in the late fifties from Upstate New York, looking for a career in modeling. Her problem was that, as a kid, she'd gotten into the habit of eating at least once a day, hardly a sure thing as a struggling model, so she'd ended up a whore and never made any apologies for it. Her parents had never known. For years they had thought that Ellie was a successful advertising executive, and the money she had sent them every month had contributed to that myth. Now they were dead anyway. Ellie had a younger sister who was married to a Methodist minister in Ohio, and Ellie sometimes suspected that her sister had figured out the truth, since she avoided all contact with her, except for the ritual exchange of Christmas cards. Those were the breaks, Ellie supposed. Meanwhile, she was running a business and trying to be the best human being she knew how to be under the circumstances. To

Ellie, that meant offering advice when advice seemed called for.

"You've got your mind set on this," Ellie said.

Alma nodded. "I've had it, Ellie. What the hell am I going to do with myself? Am I going to go into business like you? Am I going to go back to Minnesota? I've got to do something."

"No more acting, then?"

Alma laughed. "What acting? I could never even get a walk-on. That was my big dream. I was going to be the next Julie Andrews. What a joke."

"Yeah," Ellie said, "well, I was going to be Susie Parker, remember her? She was the fifties version of Christie Brinkley. That was a joke, too. I should never have left Horseheads."

"Horseheads?"

"That's the town I grew up in."

"Funny name," Alma said.

"The name came from an Indian village that was there before they built the town. The soldiers were coming in to kill the Indians, only winter came first. The Indians sat there all winter with nothing to eat except their horses. When spring came, they stuck all the horses' heads on poles around the village and got the hell out of there. The place got to be known as Horseheads. I should have stayed there. You should have stayed in wherever you came from, too."

"St. Cloud," Alma said. "Only I couldn't stay. I shot my stepfather."

"Oh?" Ellie said. "Did you kill him?"

"No. I only shot him in the leg. He'd been all over me since I was a kid. When I was fourteen, he got me pregnant, only I miscarried in the bathroom. But I said then that if he came at me again I'd get him. He did, and I did. So I had to leave. I was going to leave anyway. I took his money and his gun and caught a bus for Chicago. Then I took another bus to New York. The money went fast enough, but I've still got the pistol. If I ever see him again, I'll use it on him."

Ellie said nothing for a moment. Then she said, "You've got your mind made up?"

"Oh, yeah," Alma said. "I'll be all right with Phil. Don't worry about me."

"I won't then," Ellie said.

But she would. Ellie worried about all of them. They were her girls, after all.

Phil lived in Jersey. He lived in a four-bedroom house in Short Hills with a pool in the backyard and a Buick Riviera in the driveway. There was room for all his stuff and all the stuff Alma had amassed in her apartment on the Upper West Side, where the rent was going out of sight to begin with. She packed herself up, rented a van and moved in on a Monday, when Phil's restaurant was closed. He was waiting for her when she got there.

"I'll want to get some kind of job," she told him that night, as they sat in front of the fire drinking wine.

"Work in my place," Phil told her. "I'll teach you how to run a decent restaurant."

"I hate restaurants," Alma said. "My stepfather ran a hot dog stand back in Minnesota. He used to make me work there on weekends."

"This is different," he assured her. "I run a class joint."

"I just can't figure out how a guy like you got into the restaurant business," Alma said. "You don't strike me as the type."

"No?" he said. "What's the type?"

"I don't know. Somebody different from you."

He leaned back. "Well," he told her, "I wanted my own business. I wanted the sort of business where I could come and go as I pleased. I wanted a business where you had cash coming in. Also, I like good food. Don't you like good food, Al?"

"Stop with the Al," she said. "No, I never cared much about food. Working in my stepfather's hot dog stand cured me of that."

"This is a different type of joint. Come work with me. You'll see."

"No hot dogs?" Alma asked him. "No chopped onions? None of that?"

"Class," Phil told her as he pulled her close. "Strictly class."

CHAPTER 21

One of the staples of Murphy's childhood memories was the neighborhood grocery store he had frequented as a child in Fishtown. The owners had been Mr. and Mrs. Kasabian, a childless Armenian couple doing business in a largely Irish neighborhood. Looking back on it, Murphy realized that Mr. Kasabian was one of those rare men who had learned an important trick for maintaining a happy marriage. His trick was to do precisely what he was told. Mr. Kasabian's job had been to stock the shelves, make the deliveries, sweep up and keep his mouth shut—chores he performed dutifully, if unenthusiastically.

Mrs. Kasabian had run the place. She had dealt with the suppliers, charming them when it seemed appropriate, terrorizing them when she deemed it necessary. She had decided on how food would be displayed, and—most important—she handled all the money. She had been a big woman in a flowered-print dress, high-top black shoes and a shabby, grayish-green sweater. She had often worn a white apron over her usual outfit, and her hands had been rough and strong from wielding the heavy cleaver behind the meat counter.

Murphy had never seen anybody like Mrs. Kasabian in the televised family situation comedies of his childhood. There had been no one like Mrs. Kasabian on "Ozzie and Harriet" or "Father Knows Best." It only showed how flawed and unrealistic those programs had been. Murphy took a special delight in a T-shirt he had seen a few weeks ago hanging in the window of a trendy Center City boutique. It had shown Ward and June and Wally and the Beaver, all smiling their television smiles. Only the Beaver had been wearing a green Mohawk haircut, a safety pin in one ear, and displaying a face painted with red and yellow lightning bolts. The caption read, "Mom, Dad, I think there's something wrong with the Beave." Mrs. Kasabian, Murphy was sure, would get a big kick out of that image if she were still alive. And she might be, somewhere. She would be quite old, but she had always given Murphy the impression that when Death came bopping around one day to collect her he'd suddenly find himself with his hands full.

At the time, the woman had seemed to Murphy the very eyes of age, but in retrospect he realized she had probably been in her mid-forties—the same age he was now. Her store had been a neighborhood gathering place, and she had dispensed—along with the food and liberal credit—an abundance of warmth and old world philosophy. Murphy recalled his mother once complaining to her about all the dissension in the world after World War II, and Mrs. Kasabian had responded: "If everybody pulled in the same direction, the earth would tip over."

Her merchandise had been arranged in no apparent order, and it was profoundly appealing as a result. The smell of sharp cheese had mixed gloriously with the rich odors of garlic and freshly baked coffee cake. Adequate refrigeration in Mrs. Kasabian's store had been no more than a wish. Penny candy had rested in sticky disarray in rectangular glass jars. Newspapers had been piled in heaps next to the front counter. The uneven wooden floor had been worn and grime encrusted. The place had been poorly lit and warmly dark.

Mrs. Kasabian had been well aware that she served a clientele for whom missing even one weekly paycheck would have spelled utter financial disaster, so she had dispensed credit liberally just to keep the goods moving. Murphy remembered going into the store on more than one occasion for milk and bread and telling Mrs. Kasabian his mother would pay her the following week. He never knew if the money actually got paid, although he suspected it had. Murphy's mother would have sold her body on Market Street before she left a debt unpaid.

The market in which Murphy now shopped was a dramatic departure from the corner grocery store of his childhood. It was a sleek and shiny chain store where the odors of food were sealed in behind clear plastic, as if they might offend. The market was brightly illuminated with long fluorescent bulbs attached to the ceiling four miles above. Prepackaged meals came frozen, hard and stiff as marble in bright colored boxes. Packaged displays towered like skyscrapers at the end of each aisle. Only the open bins of produce seemed the same, and the produce department alone was several times the size of the Kasabians' entire store. Murphy wondered what Mrs. Kasabian would make of passion fruit and avocados and whole pineapples and coconuts. He wondered what she would think of yams and bean sprouts. As he grew older, Murphy realized, culture shock was battering him with increasingly unmerciful zeal. He didn't look forward to old age. Even if he quit smoking and took care of himself, all he could look forward to was getting sick and dying, and he would go through the entire process hopelessly confused by how the world around him had changed in every minute detail.

Murphy cruised the market behind his shopping cart with a Camel stuck in his mouth. He hadn't been home yet, and he was vaguely disturbed at himself for shopping for food when he hadn't eaten in five hours. His stomach gurgled and bubbled, and he was buying too much. He stocked up on Lean Cuisine, knowing even as he did so that it would take four or five of the damn things to make a decent meal. He laid in a good supply of frozen pizza, his primary staple in life. He bought some spinach tortellini and the necessary cheese and cream to make Alfredo sauce. He picked up some white seedless grapes from California and a huge bunch of asparagus. He got four pounds of potato salad from the deli and six large cans of white albacore tuna. He bought some frozen burritos and a quart of heavenly hash ice cream. Murphy picked up two dozen eggs and a plastic bottle full of liquid margarine.

He figured he had picked up enough food to last him for a few days and lighten his wallet by about a hundred bucks when he saw the woman. She took his breath away. It didn't happen to him often, but when it happened it was always a memorable experience. Murphy stopped his cart and just gaped at her. She was utterly stunning, and Murphy felt sixteen years old again.

The woman was tall, nearly as tall as he was. Her age was hard to place. She could be anywhere from her late twenties to thirty-five. She wore jeans and a sweatshirt, and her reddish hair hung loose down her back, the way Murphy liked it. Her skin was pale and smooth even without makeup. She was about to do something so stupid that Murphy could hardly believe it. As he watched, she reached down to a can of Wise potato sticks situated on one of the lower rungs of an enormous display, pulled it out, and the entire display came toppling down on her. Blue and white can after blue and white can came crashing down on the supermarket's beige-tiled floor. The woman staggered backward, stepped on one of the cans and fell hard. Murphy was at her side in the briefest fraction of a second. Helplessly, she waved her shapely arms and legs in the sea of potato sticks, and Murphy grabbed one of them.

"Let me help," he said, and did, pulling her to her feet as a supermarket clerk rushed to their side.

"Anybody hurt here?" the clerk demanded, as if daring the woman to have suffered injury.

"I . . . I'm all right, I think," the woman said shakily.

"If you're all right, ma'am," the clerk said quickly, "I have a form I'd like you to sign."

Murphy's eyes narrowed. "A release form?" he demanded.

"It's just a formality," the clerk said nervously. Then, to the woman: "You're sure you're all right, now?"

245

"I think s—"

"I'm this lady's lawyer," Murphy snapped. "She's not going to sign anything until she sees a physician. This display is clearly dangerous. What's going on in the heads of you people, piling something like this eight feet high?"

The clerk, who was barely more than a boy, paled visibly. "Let me get the store manager, sir. I'll be right back. Now, don't go anywhere, you two."

The clerk ran off. Murphy said, "Are you sure you're all right?"

She nodded and smiled weakly. "Aside from the fact that I feel like a complete asshole, yes. I'm fine."

Murphy laughed aloud. "Here," he said, bending down and picking up one of the cans, "take your potato sticks. You've earned them."

"Thank you. Are you really a lawyer?"

"Yes, and don't sign a thing these guys stick in your face. You really ought to see a doctor, you know. A fall like that can leave you with problems that don't show up until later. In fact, I can recommend a doctor, if you'd like."

"I'd like to think about it."

"I'm Frank Murphy."

She smiled. "Alexandra Fronczek. Alex, they call me."

"I have a neighbor named Fronczek. Emma Fronczek. She lives in the next apartment."

"That's my aunt."

"No kidding?" Murphy said. "I like your aunt. She's a marvelous lady."

This was a lie. Murphy regarded Mrs. Fronczek as an annoying busybody, and her cat tended to frighten

246

Winston, who was, despite his bloodlines, nobody's fighter.

Alex said, "Well, you won't have her to put up with for a month. She's left for Europe."

"Europe?"

"Yes, she won a trip in some contest she entered. I'm watching her apartment for her."

This is what I got because I went to mass, Murphy thought to himself. He made a mental note to go to confession.

"I have my car outside," Murphy said. "I'd be more than happy to give you and your groceries a lift home. I mean, we are living in the same building."

"That would be nice of you," Alex Fronczek said with a smile that made Murphy's knees buckle.

"Well," he said brightly, "let's get checked out, eh?"

Murphy couldn't resist showing off at the checkout counter. The clerk returned with the manager, a harried-looking man about Murphy's own age in a green blazer. The manager tried to placate Murphy while a checkout clerk rang through Murphy's order.

"The form is purely routine, sir," the manager said. "It's a standard accident form we file with our regional office."

"No dice," Murphy said. "My client signs nothing. You know, you've got cans all over the floor back there."

"It's being picked up right now," the manager assured him.

"You've only got one of these items," the checkout clerk told Murphy, holding up a can of corn. "They're two for ninety-nine."

"I just want one," Murphy said.

247

"Okay, that's fifty cents."

"That's not the one I want," Murphy said. "I want the one for forty-nine cents."

The checkout clerk, a teenager who looked to Murphy like a young Charles Manson, said, "One is fifty cents. You only get one for forty-nine cents if you buy two of them."

"That doesn't make sense," Murphy said. "If they're two for ninety-nine, then one of them has to be forty-nine cents. That's the one I want. Let somebody else buy the fifty-cent one."

The checkout clerk looked at the manager with panic in his eyes. "Mr. Rhodes . . ." he said.

Rhodes, the supermarket manager, glared at Murphy. "Give it to him for forty-nine. Now, you people are not going to sign the form, right?"

"Not until my client sees a doctor."

The manager turned on his heel and stomped off in a rage. Alex Fronczek, in the next line, smirked visibly. "Are you always like this?" she asked Murphy with obvious amusement.

"I'm not always this successful at it," he admitted. "Say, what are you doing for dinner, if you don't mind my asking? We can drop off the groceries and I'll take you out somewhere. How's that sound?"

"I don't know," Alex said. "I think I'm more in the mood to cook. Believe it or not, I'm a fairly adequate chef. I assume that your place has a kitchen?"

"Fully equipped," Murphy said, pondering a full return to the church.

CHAPTER 22

Wilder had thought about it, and he had decided that the television show he detested above all others—and this took in some real territory—was "Miami Vice." Normally, having developed a love for books at a relatively late age, Wilder didn't watch much television. When he relaxed at all, which wasn't often, he tended to read—unless there was a Seventy-Sixers game on, or a Phillies game.

The problem now, though, was that he had read everything he'd brought along with him, and it had turned out that Irving Berger was a television addict. He started out watching "Good Morning America" and then progressed to "Donahue" and "Sally Jessy Raphael" and then to reruns of "Mash." Berger would quit at noon, wander the woods or fish during the afternoon soaps and get back in front of the set in time for "Quincy" at four.

From there until bedtime, with a half hour out for whatever the two of them could manage to cook up from the mountain of canned goods and frozen food

Joe Otis had stocked the place with, Berger was glued to the TV set. Since Wilder didn't like to get too far away from him—or too far from the road in and the telephone—he was stuck watching, too. Sometimes Wilder could pry the old man away from the TV set long enough for a few quick games of pinochle or longer bouts at the chess board. But not on Friday night. Never on Friday.

Normally the old man watched "Dallas" at nine on Fridays, but reception at the camp was limited after the sun disappeared. The CBS station out of Scranton that carried "Dallas" came in with snow and an iffy sound. The ABC station couldn't be found at all. And the only program they could get on a rainy spring evening was "Miami Vice," which made Wilder ill just to think about. Two hippy-dippy detectives in designer clothes blasting around Miami in a Ferrari nailing a dozen drug dealers armed with Uzis every week. Just like real life.

"Watch this one," Berger said. "Watch how Tubbs handles this guy."

"You've seen this one before?" Wilder asked in surprise. "I thought you were a 'Dallas' man."

"I tape 'Miami Vice,'" Berger confided. "I watch it at ten instead of nine. So tonight, I watch 'Stingray' instead."

"Gee," Wilder said, frowning, "good thinking, Irving."

"You don't like cop shows?" Berger asked.

"One, I liked, a few years back. The 'Blue Knight,' I think it was. That one was okay."

"Not even 'Hill Street Blues' you didn't like when it was on?"

"It was better than this," Wilder conceded.

"Someday," Irving Berger said, "they're going to make a television show about a restaurant. I'll try to get a job as a consultant. I could show them how it really is."

"They don't care how it really is. Look at the suit on that dude."

"I wore a suit like that before the war," Berger said.

"That suit costs what a car cost before the war." Wilder watched Crockett and Tubbs. He tapped his fingers on the arm of his chair. He was twitchy. He needed to get home—to see Annabelle and sleep in his own bed. Wilder had never liked being away from home, even when he had been a marine. As he'd grown older, he liked it even less. Annabelle tried on every vacation to get him to travel when all he wanted to do was lie around the house, drink beer, and read. Once she had gotten him to go along with it. They had gone to Florida to tour the Epcot Center. Wilder had gone back to work chasing criminals, grateful for the opportunity to get some rest. Epcot, somebody in Florida told him, actually stood for Every Person Comes Out Tired. Aptly named, Wilder thought. He couldn't pass by a picture of Mickey Mouse now without spitting at it. Wilder liked it at home in Germantown, in the row house he had just about rebuilt over the past fifteen years. Well, Murphy would be there soon and Wilder would get the weekend off. It was more than two hours back to the city, but he would welcome the drive and the escape from Crockett and Tubbs.

The phone rang. Wilder grabbed it. He put it to his ear and said nothing. It was habit. At a crime scene, when a phone rang a cop would answer it and say nothing. You could find out the damndest things just holding a phone silently. Here—away from home and on the job—he instinctively did the same thing.

"Jim?" Murphy said.

"I'm here. Where're you?"

"That's why I'm calling."

"Oh, shit," Wilder said.

"I'll be up Sunday."

"Why not tonight, dammit? You said you'd relieve me this weekend. Sunday doesn't leave me enough time to get home."

"It's not my fault. Toddman wants to come up and take a statement from Berger. Aside from that, I've got a trial starting in another week, and I've got a witness I want to run past Barry Weiner. The only day I can do that is tomorrow."

"I don't care about the problems of your private practice, Frank. Hell, you're getting paid for this. I'm not."

"I'm doing the best I can, Jim."

"You bet," Wilder said, steaming. "Did I just hear something there?"

"Like what?"

"I did hear something," Wilder said. "You got a woman with you? I can hear her singing off in the background, for Christ's sake."

"That's the radio."

"Bullshit."

"Oh, you must mean Patricia. She's in the kitchen."

"That ain't Patricia," Wilder said with genuine menace. "For one thing, she'd be back at school by now."

"Well," Murphy said, "it's just a friend."

"A friend! I'm up here in the goddamn wilderness

252

with bears and wolves and shit all around outside and you got a friend with you in your nice, cozy city apartment? Man, you are too much. You are too fucking much. Now just when are you getting up here?"

"Sunday," Murphy said mildly. "I'll be there Sunday. I'll bring some good beer, too."

"You just be sure to bring your ass so I can kick it up around your shoulders," Wilder said.

"How did anybody with such a rotten disposition ever reach such a high rank?" Murphy asked into the phone.

Then he realized that Wilder had just slammed it down and probably missed the entire remark. Murphy looked for a moment at the dead phone and hung it up. He found his cigarettes in the darkness of his profoundly messy bedroom, lit one and stood up. Frank Murphy stretched. He was stiff and sore from unaccustomed exercise, but it was the kind of exercise he liked and had enjoyed too little of lately. Buck naked, he stepped carefully over piles of clothing and made his way into the hallway, through the living room and into the kitchen. Alex Fronczek, dressed similarly except for an apron that said Kissin' Don't Last; Cookin' Do—a gift to Murphy last Christmas from Patricia—was standing over a kitchen counter pounding veal with a wooden mallet. She looked up from her task and smiled at Murphy.

"Now I'll cook," she said with an evil grin.

Murphy gazed at her appreciatively. "I never had a nude woman cook me dinner before."

Alex Fronczek dragged the veal through egg batter. "There's a first time for everything," she said.

CHAPTER 23

When he'd met Alex Fronczek, Murphy hadn't been feeling particularly irresistible.

That's because he knew he wasn't. The last decade or so of his marriage had driven home to him with disturbing clarity the reality that he possessed any number of personality flaws that made him something of a long shot for the swordsman's hall of fame. Not to mention the fact that he had a beer gut that rivaled the one on that accountant on "Cheers." He also was pushing forty-six and sported a head of hair that looked like a dandelion gone to seed. Gray hair looked terrific on John Forsythe. On Murphy, it just looked old, which was how he'd been feeling lately.

His several months of living with a younger woman after leaving Mary Ellen hadn't particularly helped Murphy's self-esteem in the romance department either. That was because the woman he'd picked as a roommate, Nancy Elliott, had been so hopelessly desperate that her ready acceptance of Murphy had rendered her taste decidedly suspect. And she hadn't lasted all that long, anyway, before departing for the company of a younger man who was apparently less annoying. Since she'd cut out, Murphy hadn't noticed an overabundance of women throwing themselves at his feet as he walked by belching from too much food, tobacco, and booze. But every once in a while he would start to miss feminine companionship, both physical and emotional.

The truth was that Murphy liked women, even though they tended to piss him off. He knew they were all really the same. They had different faces only so you could tell them apart. But he liked them nonetheless. Women didn't think the way men did. They didn't react the same way. These traits, which made them maddening, also made them appealing. Murphy had friends who were women, and that was one thing. But platonic friendships with women were satisfying only to a certain degree. However gratifying they might be in and of themselves, such friendships lacked the intimacy Murphy was capable of developing only in the course of a romantic relationship.

He didn't intellectualize it, but he was aware that male and female friendships were dramatically different in character. Men, by nature, seldom confided in one another. No matter how close he might be to another man, Murphy was incapable of any willing display of weakness to anyone of the same gender. Women, on the other hand, accepted weakness in a friend, male or female. They seemed to demand it, in fact. Their friendships with one another seemed to be based largely on mutual displays of unhappiness, and they seemed to welcome similar displays from men anxious to exhibit their sensitivity. This was fine with

Murphy, because every once in a while he felt the vague urge to complain to somebody about how miserable he sometimes felt about himself and life in general. He could expose that part of himself only to a woman, and not to a woman he knew only in a platonic sense.

Only after some sort of romantic relationship had been established—he generally defined this as a sexual encounter—could Murphy manage to lower his guard and truly reveal his myriad weaknesses to a woman as he never would to another man. He supposed, when he thought about it, that the roots of the whole process were Darwinian. If Darwin had been right, that the strongest males tended to attract the greatest number of females, then it stood to reason that somewhere in the distant, prehistoric past the strongest men would have kept harems. That would have meant that women would have had to develop mechanisms for living with other women—confiding in one another for the sake of bonding and competing with one another nonviolently at the same time—and that a man would have developed a marked reluctance to display weakness of any kind to another male, who might then be prompted to try to take over his harem.

Whatever the reasons—biological or cultural or some combination of the two—Murphy found that he needed a woman to talk to on an intimate basis. And a precondition for that was sexual contact with her, which had its own virtues even if they never got around to talking. So it was that even in middle age, with his youthful Niagara of hormones slowed to a manageable trickle, Murphy still occasionally mustered the guts to give it a try, to make a pass—a task he knew he performed as ineptly now as he had when he'd been sixteen and wondering of creatures as marvelous as girls really possessed anything as base as sex organs.

Still, everything seemed to work beautifully with Alex Fronczek. She smiled appreciatively at his wisecracks, seemed warm and friendly and even complimented his car.

"You can't beat a big car like this for comfort," she said as they loaded the groceries in the Tornado's yawning trunk.

"Our military has invaded islands smaller than this car," he told her, "but I like it. It's about ready for Medicare now, and I'm going to have to replace it one of these days. It's going to break my heart, too."

They talked pleasantly during the drive back to their apartment house and while Murphy circled the block looking for a parking space. Alex said she was from New York. She described herself as an aging Broadway hoofer between shows.

"Not all that aging, certainly," Murphy said.

"Thirty-seven," she told him.

"You're kidding?" Murphy said in genuine shock.

She laughed. "Don't I wish."

"You look terrific."

"I work at it. It's my job. I just finished a show. I'll ache for a month."

"What show?"

"A musical version of the life of Wild Bill Hickok. It was called *Wild Bill*. It was way off-Broadway. We ran not quite five months."

"That's pretty good, is it?"

She nodded. "Five months of regular work? That's terrific. I was all set to starve for a while until Aunt

257

Emma called me up and said she'd won this crazy trip and asked me if I'd come down and watch her place for a month. I've been subletting in SoHo since last September, and the real tenant is coming back home the beginning of next month. This was like a godsend. I might even find some work here. Philadelphia has a few theater companies. And if I don't, I could use the rest. And the money. Aunt Emma is even paying me to watch the place."

"Have you ever been to Philly before?" Murphy asked her.

"Never. I'm from Minnesota. I've lived two places in my life: Minneapolis and Manhattan. I envy Aunt Emma. I've never been to Europe. I've never even been out of the country."

By this time, Murphy had miraculously found a spot not ten steps from the door of their building. They were unloading groceries.

"I've never been to Europe either," he said. "I spent some time in the Far East, courtesy of my Uncle Sam, but that's about it. And most of that time was spent aboard ship."

"What kind of ship?"

"Warship," Murphy told her. "I was on the U.S.S. *Elmira*."

"I was on a big ship once. I worked for a few months on one of those passenger ships out of New York that take people on cruises to nowhere. You just go out and cruise around for a few days. I was in a company that put on shows for the passengers every night."

They climbed the stairs to the second floor. Murphy opened the door to his apartment and went in first. The moment he flipped on the light he wished he'd cleaned up the place a bit. Alex came in behind him, and he could hear her intake of breath when she saw the incredible devastation of Murphy's living quarters. He looked at her sheepishly.

"The maid didn't make it today," he said, smiling weakly.

Whatever shock Alex Fronczek might have felt, she shook it off quickly. "Looks like my place in New York," she said, smiling, "only neater."

Murphy kicked his way through the piles of clothing and newspapers to the kitchen table, swept it clear of empty Chinese food containers and deposited the groceries.

"I'll run around and straighten up," he said. "Can I get you a drink or something?"

"Sure," she said. "What have you got?"

"Heineken's and bourbon."

"What kind of bourbon?"

"Jim Beam."

"That'll do. Straight, please, with one ice cube. Do you mind if I smoke?"

I've found her, Murphy thought. The perfect woman—if she liked boxing, that was.

Murphy put on some music—an easy-listening FM station—while she sat on the sofa, smoking and sipping Jim Beam.

"You know," she said, "there's some stuff on the market that tastes pretty much like this but is a hell of a lot cheaper."

"What's that?"

"A bourbon called Charter Oak."

Murphy filed that information away. "You never hear the consumer reporters on TV giving out with

259

useful information like that," he said.

Then, inexplicably, he suddenly ran out of things to say. This had happened to him several times before in life, usually at moments like this when he had hoped to be at his wittiest. Confused, and his face beginning to flush, he ran around the apartment picking up piles of crap and stuffing it into the overloaded trash can he kept under the sink.

"I'll be with you in a second," he said.

"Don't rush. I'm enjoying the violins."

Murphy managed—out of nervous energy more than anything else—to make the living room and kitchen relatively presentable in just a few minutes. Then he poured himself a stiff drink, feeling sillier and more nervous by the moment, and sat down in the chair facing Alex Fronczek, who seemed as relaxed and confident as Murphy felt jumpy and jerky.

"Well," he said finally, "so you like Philly so far?"

"Just fine," she said, leaning back on the sofa in an almost sleepy manner.

"Good town," Murphy said. "I'll have to show you some of it."

She nodded lazily. "Fine."

"You like sports?" he asked, desperate.

"Sure."

"What do you think of the Phillies' chances this year?"

"No pennant."

"No, I guess not. No pitching. That's the problem."

She nodded.

Murphy sat in the chair. He lit a cigarette. The silence hung between them like a thunderhead. Murphy drummed his fingers on the arm of the chair.

260

He tried, but he couldn't think of a thing to say. Why did these things happen to him? With a man, he could have talked all night. In a courtroom in front of a jury, nobody could have shut him up. Here, with this pretty woman four feet away, his mind was an utter blank. He wasn't cut out for this stuff, Murphy knew. He'd never had a problem talking to Mary Ellen, which was probably why he'd married her. On the other hand, Mary Ellen had howled at birth and never shut up since, so he wasn't sure how much that experience counted for.

The two of them sat there listening to the FM violins and drinking bourbon for what seemed like hours before a Johnny Mathis song came on.

"Chances are," Mathis sang, "that I wear a silly grin the moment you come into view . . ."

"I like this song," Alex said, stretching languidly on the sofa.

"Me, too," Murphy said. "This guy has always been good."

". . . Chances are you think that I'm in love with you . . ."

Alex stood up suddenly. She smiled down at Murphy. "This is silly," she said, putting down her drink. "Would you like to dance with me? I think it might help break the ice."

Murphy, surprised and delighted, stubbed out his Camel. He stood up.

"Hey, listen," he said, "whatever works for you."

He put out his arms for her.

And that, thank God, pretty much got things going.

CHAPTER 24

"Well, hello," the blond woman said as she opened the door. "How are you?"

"I'm fine, Ella," Murphy said.

"I'm not talking to you," Ella told him. "I know you're okay. I'm talking to you."

"I'm fine," Judy Kavanaugh said.

Ella smiled benignly. It was her usual expression. "I'm Ella."

"I'm Judy."

"Come on in," Ella said, holding the door wide.

The apartment Ella shared with Barry Weiner occupied a corner of Society Hill Towers that gave them a stunning view of the city, which was gleaming beneath them in the spring morning sunlight. Murphy gently nudged Judy Kavanaugh, and they walked inside to the beige-tiled entranceway and then onto the thick carpeting of the living room.

"I assume he's here," Murphy said.

"I'll go get him," Ella said. "You two just go in and sit down."

Murphy and Judy moved into the living room and

onto the facing love seats next to the balcony. Judy stared at the top of the table and said nothing. Murphy frowned. The kid hadn't said six words since he'd picked her up at her mother's place a half hour before. It was early on a Saturday morning, and he was tempted to write it off to that. Patricia at the same age, he recalled, had slept like the dead and awakened badly in the morning. Sometimes Murphy had pondered the purchase of a pulmotor to rouse her.

"You're going to like Barry," Murphy told her.

Judy merely nodded.

Barry Weiner came in a few moments later, looking—as he always did—as though he'd just spent the previous half hour in a rotary clothes dryer. Weiner was a skinny, hunch-backed man in his mid-fifties who bore a startling resemblance to Woody Allen masquerading as a homeless bum. Weiner had the same thick glasses, the same weak chin, the same receding hairline. Only in Weiner's case, what hair was left was streaked with gray and tended to stick out in various directions. Murphy looked sloppy enough in baggy chinos, scuffed Docksiders, and an old blue oxford-cloth button-down with frayed collar and cuffs, but he always managed to look neater than Weiner even when the psychiatrist was dressed to kill. In this case, at his home on a Saturday morning, Weiner hadn't even made the effort. He wore corduroy jeans, a University of Pennsylvania T-shirt, and a cardiac pacemaker device on his belt, a souvenir of one mild and one truly vicious heart attack, the last and more serious only five months before.

"Hello, Frank," Weiner said. "This is your friend, Judy?"

"This is her. Judy, this is Dr. Weiner."

"Forget that doctor stuff," Weiner said. "Just call me Barry. Is that okay?"

"Okay," Judy said.

Weiner turned to Murphy. "You can get lost now, Frank, if you would. Ella's in the kitchen if you'd like some coffee."

"Fine," Murphy said.

He found Ella cutting up a honeydew melon. She was roughly twenty-five years younger than Weiner, and she looked like a young Mary Travers with some beef on her. Ella was ostensibly a graduate student in psychology at Penn, where Weiner taught when he wasn't testifying as an expert witness either for the defense or the prosecution. That was how Murphy had met him some years earlier. At the time, Weiner had been drinking heavily—it had been his hobby—and Ella had just moved in with him in a last-gasp effort to save his life. So far, she had accomplished that task by studiously struggling to manage his diet, forcing him to get enough rest, engaging in a never-ending campaign to curtail his boozing and smoking, and loving him with such devotion and self-sacrifice that Murphy had been forced to classify her as a cultural freak.

She was a pretty and placid young woman caring daily for a failing grandfather with two ex-wives and a heart condition instead of living her own life, bearing her own children, pursuing her own needs and desires. Murphy often wondered if she had a sister. This was the kind of companionship he wanted when his body finally betrayed him—a woman whose interest in him extended no further than utter and total devotion.

"Is that for me?" he asked.

"Since when do you eat melon?" Ella asked him.

"When I'm hungry, I'll eat anything that won't break my teeth."

"I have some whole-grain cereal, if that interests you," Ella said.

Murphy made a face. "I need something heavy in blood fats. You want to get out of here for a while? He'd just as soon talk to her alone, and you've made me enough meals when I've dropped by. I'll buy you breakfast."

Ella beamed. "That's a deal," she said, flipping off the coffeepot.

Murphy took Ella to the Harvey House, which was open twenty-four hours a day and served pancakes you could use in discus competition. They ate and talked and after a while Murphy asked Ella how Weiner was doing. Her ever-present smile faded slightly.

"He's taking it easier since the last attack," she said. "I have to ride his ass all the time, and it drives him crazy, but he's taking somewhat care of himself now. He keeps telling me it's all a waste of time. He says that neither his father or grandfather made it to sixty, and he's reconciled to the fact that he won't either. But he likes all the fussing over him. Barry's really just a big baby."

Murphy nodded. "I worry about him. He's my best friend. One of them, anyway. When you think about the way he's abused himself all these years—all the boozing and smoking and carousing—it's a wonder he's still around."

Ella laughed aloud. "Look who's talking."

"Yeah," Murphy said, "but I'm tough. He's just a little-shit shrink. And he should never drink, anyway.

Everybody knows that Jews can't drink. It's genetic. With me, it's different. I'm Irish. I was born with liquor on my breath."

Ella chuckled. She chuckled better than anybody else he'd ever met, Murphy supposed. Ella found life endlessly amusing, and he'd never seen her in a bad mood. He'd seen her angry—especially when she caught Weiner smoking—but never depressed, never feeling sorry for herself, never surly. Murphy knew there was something seriously wrong with her, but he didn't care. Weiner, in a private conversation, had once described Ella to Murphy as a "caretaker personality" with a compulsive need to be needed.

In the same conversation, Weiner had also described himself as a *putz,* which certainly appeared to be the case sometimes. Weiner's redeeming characteristics were his needle-sharp wit and immense intellect, which combined to make him terrific company. Murphy could forgive a good many sins if the sinner was companionable. When all was said and done, what you did in life was spend time with people. Murphy enjoyed spending time with Weiner, even if he did resent the older man's undeserved good fortune. Weiner enjoyed an inherited fortune, and while Murphy envied him for it, he sometimes thought he envied him more for Ella. Murphy would tolerate a heart condition if he could have an angel like Ella around to make him take his medicine, keep him relaxed and do all the work in bed.

It was several hours before they got back to the apartment in Society Hill. Weiner and Judy were still in the living room talking, but the conversation broke up as the door opened.

"Ate like pigs, right?" Weiner said. "Some fried eggs

with bacon? Some toast with real butter? Go ahead, 'fess up."

Murphy belched, purposely and loudly. It was a trick he'd learned as a kid, burping on purpose. He could also make himself fart at will, but he figured this wasn't the proper occasion.

"Ella, honey," Weiner said, "how would you like to take Judy downstairs and let her look at the riverfront? And keep her company, too, will you?"

The apartment house was located a block away from the Delaware River, a vast channel that was only about forty percent water this far downstream, and Murphy couldn't imagine why anybody would want to be close enough to it to suffer the stench of rotting garbage, raw sewage, discharged chemicals, and various levels of petroleum-product waste. Not to mention the wheezing of fish gasping for oxygen. But he knew—as did Ella—that Weiner wanted a little privacy with Murphy. Ella smiled again, this time at Judy.

"Want to watch the freighters come in?" she asked.

Judy Kavanaugh shrugged. "Sure."

"Half an hour ought to do it," Weiner told Ella.

"Got it. Come on, Judy."

After the girl and the woman had left, Weiner turned to Murphy and said, "Well, are you carrying?"

Murphy shook his head wearily and reached for his Camels. "I think two heart attacks would do it for me, Barry," he said, handing over a new pack he'd bought at the restaurant. "You really ought to give up these things."

"So should you," Weiner said, ripping the pack open greedily.

"Yeah, but you should quit more than I should quit."

267

Weiner lit the Camel and drew the smoke into his lungs gratefully. "Tell you what: When you have your heart attack, then we'll see how easily you quit. The problem with life, Frank, is that you've got to go on living while you're doing it. You quit doing everything you enjoy doing, and you're dead already."

"Rationalization," Murphy charged.

Weiner shrugged. "Well, it's probably true that I'm also a hopeless nicotine addict. But I prefer not to use that argument because it lacks a certain dignity. Let's go out on the balcony. If Ella smells smoke it'll be my ass. I could tell her that you did the smoking, but she'd never go for it. What time is it, anyway?"

Murphy glanced at his watch. "Not quite noon."

"Late enough for a drink," Weiner said. "You go on out. I'll bring the glasses and the bottle. Bourbon for you?"

"Fine. And some ice."

"Ice," Weiner sneered. "Candy-ass."

Murphy opened the sliding glass door and took a seat at the outdoor table Weiner kept on his balcony. Fourteen floors below him, the city lived its raucous life, cars crawling along, exhaust fumes rising. But up here the air was relatively clear. A pigeon flew by the balcony, barely five feet above Murphy's head, as graceful and lovely in the air as it was awkward and repulsive on pavement. Weiner came out with two glasses and a bottle of Wild Turkey, the cigarette stuck out of one corner of his mouth.

"Let's see how drunk we can get before Ella gets back," he said. "She gets worked up when I drink. Triglycerides, or some such crap. *L'chayim,* Frank."

"Skol," Murphy said.

"Do you know where that came from?"

"What? *L'chayim?* It means 'to life,' doesn't it?"

"More or less. I was talking about *Skol.* Of all people, you ought to know that one."

"Why's that?"

Weiner leaned back in his chair and drank and smoked. Murphy had always liked him best on such occasions. Weiner, sober, was only moderately entertaining and sometimes annoyingly imperious. Weiner with a drink or two in him was warmer, more vulnerable and a fountain of incidental knowledge that Murphy always found fascinating.

"It came from the Norsemen who conquered Ireland a thousand or so years ago. After a battle, the Vikings would cut off the top of an enemy's skull—sometimes he was dead at the time, but not always—and fill it with ale. Then they'd drink a toast to how much fun the battle had been. Their toast was 'Skull.' That's Skol."

"Fun guys, those Vikings," Murphy said.

"They brought civilization to your ancestors, Frank. Ireland had no central government then. There was a petty king on every block. When the Norse came in, they went around the country conquering first this region then that one. And when they'd finished, they realized that they'd have to go back and conquer the first guys again and repeat the process endlessly. So they built cities with walls around them to keep out the Irish rebels. It didn't work, but that's how Ireland ended up with lovely cities like Limerick and Cork."

"My grandfather came from Cork, and he apparently got the hell out with a fair measure of enthusiasm. Something tells me that whatever the Vikings did over there it probably left a bit to be desired.

"You've never been to Ireland?" Weiner asked in surprise. Weiner always seemed surprised at the narrowness of experience of just about everybody else.

"No," Murphy said, "and I'm in no hurry to go, either. Not until you can get a decent pepperoni pizza there, and I hear that small symbol of civilization is still missing from the scene."

Weiner nodded thoughtfully. "You get a lot of potatoes and mutton."

Murphy said, "All this is just captivating, Barry. Now why don't you tell me about that kid I brought to see you?"

"What do you want to know?"

"Is she disturbed?"

"Aren't we all, to one degree or another?" Weiner responded.

"Everybody but me," Murphy told him. "I'm a model of admirable adjustment. Somebody ought to put me in a textbook, now that I think about it. In her case, it's the degree that interests me."

Weiner's brow knit. "Bear in mind, I've had only one session with her, and she wasn't as responsive as she might have been. I conducted no tests, did no hard diagnostic work. Moreover, psychiatry is an art, not a hard science, and much of psychiatric diagnosis is highly subjective under the best of circumstances. Anything I might say, Frank, would be largely hypothesis."

Murphy had heard all this before. Weiner seldom rendered an opinion without qualifying it seven different ways—unless he was talking politics. Then he issued simple declarative sentences resplendent with

270

utter certainty about all sorts of matters on which he was only moderately informed. Plus, Weiner was a liberal, while Murphy instinctively adopted political positions somewhere between those of John Wayne and Genghis Khan.

"Okay," Murphy said, "anything you have to say will be regarded as baseless bullshit. Now say it."

"Well, the girl is having emotional difficulties. She'd probably meet all the tests for clinical depression."

"Is it because of her parents?"

Weiner nodded and lit another of Murphy's Camels. "Ostensibly. Clearly, that plays a part in it. But I have another theory about mood disorders."

"Which is?"

Weiner leaned forward over the table. "Well," he said, "the evidence has been building for some years now that all of us are virtual slaves to our genes to one degree or other. A good many of us, unfortunately, to a substantial degree. Whether you tend to put on weight easily, whether you tend toward addictive behavior—"

"Like you?"

"Like me. You, too. That's part of your charm. The point is that whether you go bald or gray early—it all seems to be largely a matter of having chosen the right or wrong parents. There's no real dispute over any of that. But in the past few years, as we've done more research on brain chemistry, there's developed a growing body of evidence that a good many emotional disorders are biologically based."

Murphy chuckled. "Biology is destiny, Barry? Have you mentioned this theory of yours to Ella? I'm sure she'd get a real charge out of it."

271

Weiner smiled ruefully. "I haven't put it in precisely those terms, no. But Ella's an honest person. She would understand, I have no doubt, that genetic tendency doesn't necessarily mean genetic inferiority. Humankind is indisputably prone to certain sorts of behavior, but that doesn't mean that we have to behave that way. Not unless we're in a vulnerable state, with our hormones running wild. That's why teenagers are so crazy, Frank. They have limited experience and strong urges to behave in primitive fashion. If we're lucky, they make it to adulthood without embarrassing themselves or their parents too badly. And most rebellious teenagers become rational adults. It's just a question of waiting them out."

Murphy chewed on his moustache. "Barry, what exactly are you saying?"

Weiner smiled condescendingly. "I keep forgetting, Frank, that you have difficulty with ethereal concepts. Like the Star Wars program, for example."

"Don't start that shit," Murphy warned. "It seems to scare the hell out of the Russians, and that's good enough for me. I say build two or three of the goddamn things, just to play it safe."

"Yes," Weiner said with great skepticism. "In any event, back to what I was saying: In most cases, we humans have the intellect to provide us with free will, once we understand why we want to behave in certain ways. That's one of the key factors that separates us from the lower orders. Not the only one, to be sure. We also have the capacity for imagination, which animals don't have. We can imagine the alteration of our environments. We have the capacity for abstract thought. Did I tell you about the paper I read

272

comparing the difference between human and animal intelligence? These people out at Stanford—"

"Barry . . ." Murphy began.

"Come off it, Frank," Weiner said disapprovingly. "This is interesting. You might just learn something. Now, these people at Stanford conducted some tests using adult chimps and human children. They discovered that chimps and human beings up to about the age of five have about the same problem-solving capacity. You know, square pegs in square holes, round pegs in round holes. I'm talking about left-brain cognitive skills here."

"I don't know what the fuck you're talking about," Murphy volunteered in surly fashion.

Weiner ignored the dig, plowing forward, "What was interesting was what they did to test right-brain skills. At one point, they gave the children crayons and paper and the kids drew pictures. They created concrete representations of what they imagined. The chimps just ripped up the paper and ate the crayons. Do you get the significance of that?"

"The chimps were hungry? They thought they could get high from the crayons? They get off on colored wax? What?"

Weiner shook his head wearily. "No. The chimps were unable to imagine anything that wasn't actually there. To them, something either was or it wasn't. They couldn't grasp the abstract. The human children, on the other hand, could conceive of the hypothetical and try to create it. That's what makes us different. We instinctively struggle to improve our environments— build cities, harness electricity. As a species, we can't seem to be able psychologically to accept the given, the

273

available world. We can't live with imperfection. That capacity makes us strivers, as other life forms on this planet are not. But it also indicates a Darwinian predisposition for dissatisfaction. We seem to be biologically programmed for it. And some of us have more pronounced biological programming than others."

"That sounds like a lot of crap to me," Murphy said.

"Most of it probably is," Weiner admitted. "But not entirely. Did you know that originally Freud thought that mental disorder was largely biological, that modes of behavior like anxiety and paranoia had been inherited from our Ice Age ancestors? In those days, Freud reasoned, it was a species-desirable trait to spend all your time fretting about having enemies like sabre-toothed tigers. Cave people with the proper levels of anxiety and paranoia were less likely to end up as hot lunches. Instead, they survived, and they passed along a tendency toward emotional disorder to their young. The early Freud was essentially a Darwinist, Frank. That's why we're all so crazy now, when there's no need for it. Freud changed his mind later, of course. He decided that if you were deranged it had to do with how you got along with your parents—especially your mother—in the early stages of life. Now the new evidence about brain chemistry is beginning to make it look like he was right the first time out. Fascinating, isn't it?"

Murphy drummed his fingers on the table and sighed deeply. "So Judy Kavanaugh has emotional problems, right? Is that what I should get from all this?"

"Right," Weiner said, pouring more bourbon and grabbing another Camel.

274

"Do you think she's capable of taking her own life?"

Weiner lit and puffed. "Didn't I say that?"

"If you did, I missed it. On the other hand, I got lost somewhere back around the Ice Age, Barry."

"Well," Weiner said, "the answer is yes. She's filled with anger that her parents have split up. She's unhappy with the world as she finds it. And I tried to explain to you that it's a uniquely human trait to take direct action to alter an unacceptable environment. I think she's depressed enough to take her life if she felt it would sufficiently wound the people who hurt her. That's usually one of the prime motivations when a teenager commits suicide—to inflict pain on those who inflicted pain on the teenager. But given her state of mind—her clear and vivid rage at whoever she thinks is responsible for disturbing her environment—my own suspicion is that suicide would be her less preferred course of action."

"What would be her most preferred?"

Weiner looked at Murphy with open surprise. "I thought I'd made that clear," he said in a tone of mild disapproval. "Murder, Frank. I'm talking about murder."

CHAPTER 25

She was waiting when Murphy got back. Alex, in parachute pants and a designer sweatshirt, was sitting on the sofa in a pile of newspapers reading a year-old copy of *Newsweek* she'd found amid the litter. He was somewhat surprised—and perversely pleased—that she had made no effort whatever to clean up the apartment. Nancy had been a compulsive cleaner. She'd picked things up as soon as Murphy had thrown them down. It had driven Murphy crazy. He'd felt as though he was living in a surgical ward. He was unable to relax unless his surroundings were in total disarray. As far as Murphy was concerned, San Francisco would never have become as screwed-up a city as he perceived it to be if they hadn't been so fanatical about straightening up after the earthquake.

"You had a call," Alex told him. "Somebody named Doc. He said you could reach him at the meat cooler, whatever that means."

"I've got to get back to him right away," Murphy said. "Give me a minute."

Murphy went directly to the rolltop desk along one wall of the living room. He lifted the top, and to her astonishment Alex noted that the desktop was a model of order: papers neatly piled, pencils protruding neatly from the top of a plastic cup, paperclips lying in a desk tray in almost military formation. She had just witnessed one of the stunning contradictions that were so much a part of Frank Murphy. His habits in life were sloppy; his habits in work were compulsively neat. He sat down at the desk, picked up the phone extension he kept in it and dialed a number.

"Give me the Doc, please," he said. "Tell him it's Frank Murphy."

"Who is this guy?" Alex asked him.

"He's a doctor," Murphy explained.

"Hello."

"Hi, Doc. Frank. What are you doing in on a Saturday? I thought you were going to Vegas."

"That was yesterday," Weinberg growled. "I got back late last night and came in here this morning. I do all my outside work on my own time. They're not going to get me for theft of city services. I know they'd like to, but they won't. Goddamn politicians. I missed a good fight out there to come back here and help you out, you ought to know—not that you're likely to appreciate it."

"I appreciate it," Murphy said, truly surprised by the old man's gesture of generosity. "What have you got?"

"I did that lab work we talked about. Your guess was right. There were prints on Lynn Rice's wrists. They showed up quite clearly on the X-rays after I dusted the flesh with lead powder. That's a good technique. I'm going to use it again."

"Do they match the prints on either of the two

277

objects I sent your way—the ashtray or the coffee mug?"

"I haven't dusted those items yet. Once I do, I'll give you my opinion, but I'm not the expert witness you want on that score. You can count on me to testify about how I obtained the prints off the Rice woman's body, but I'm not as respected as a fingerprint expert as I am in pathology, you know. I'll offer my opinion on the stand, but you'd be wise to get somebody else to back up any comparison I make. Also, aren't you supposed to get me a third item to dust for prints as well?"

"Yes," Murphy said, thinking about the glass Weiner had given Judy Kavanaugh that morning from which she had drunk some fruit juice during the interview. Murphy had clipped it on the way out of Weiner's place. "I can drop it by today, if you like."

"Why don't you? I'll dust everything up and provide you with full sets of what I found on the Rice woman's wrists and the items you supplied me. I'll give you full blowups of the prints from all the sources. I'll give you my judgment, but you really should have a second witness with special training in fingerprints. That might be a problem, too."

"No sweat," Murphy said, realizing that the old man was giving him good advice and giving it to him twice to make sure that Murphy didn't screw this up.

"Oh?" Weinberg said. "Do you really figure you can get somebody from the police lab? Have you forgotten whose side they're on? Not yours, Frank, believe me."

"I know, Doc. But I think I can get backup from a guy I know who's with the Jersey State Police lab in Trenton. Just give me everything you come up with on the prints, and I'll work on the backup opinion. I think I can even get my guy in Jersey to use the computer in Trenton to back up his judgment. What about the knife?"

"That's tougher," Weinberg said. "It was probably wiped before Webster touched it. I can see what could be traces of latent fingerprint smears under the transmission electron microscope, but I don't have enough yet to provide a comparison with the stuff from the cup and the ashtray. Don't forget, this thing only shows a millionth of an inch in area on full power. It's not designed for this sort of use. I'll have to play with it for a while, and even then I can't guarantee anything on the knife hilt using equipment designed for tissue studies."

Murphy frowned. "Well, do what you can. If you can give me comparison prints off the corpse's wrist, that might be enough. I would like the insurance of the knife hilt, though."

"I can testify with probable certainty that it's been wiped, at the very least. Of course, the prosecution could always speculate that Webster stabbed her, wiped the prints off the knife immediately afterward and then—when he opened the trunk—touched the hilt again by mistake."

"Would you swallow that if you were a juror?" Murphy asked.

"I might. People do stupid things when they're upset. If anybody has seen proof of that, it's me."

"Well," Murphy said, "let's hope Lake isn't bright enough to think of anything like that. I'll drop off this last item right now. It's a glass."

"Leave it with the security officer in the lobby,"

Weinberg told him. "Make sure the stupid bastard doesn't handle it, though."

"Right," Murphy said, and hung up. He turned to Alex. "Want to take a little ride?"

"To where?"

"I've got to drop something off. Then I thought maybe you'd like to see some of the city's classier sights."

She shrugged and tossed the magazine aside. "Should I dress up?"

"I'm just thinking of the art museum. And maybe the Rodin Museum on the parkway. I'm going like this."

Alex eyed Murphy's baggy pants and worn shirt. She stood up. "I'm ready, then. Next to you, I'm dressed like Princess Di."

Murphy dropped off Weiner's glass to the security guard in the lobby of Philadelphia General Hospital. Then he took Alex on a tour of the art museum. Murphy didn't understand much of what was inside the place, but he hoped that the very idea of the tour would leave her with the impression that he was a man of some culture, which he knew he was not. He did like the Rodin Museum a short distance away, however. The sculpture there—art in tangible, three-dimensional form—always moved him when he saw it.

Alex stared a long time at the copy of *The Thinker* on display there.

"What TV show does that make me think of?" she asked Murphy.

"'Dobie Gillis.'"

"That's right. He always sat in front of this statue when he talked to the audience. It was a dopey show."

Murphy nodded. "The show was dopey, but the

statue—the original, that is—must be really something. Just imagine what's involved in creating something like that."

"How tough can it be?" Alex asked. "You just take a hammer and chisel, and then you chip away everything that doesn't look like *The Thinker.*"

He smiled. "Something tells me there's probably more to it than that. Just look at that thing. Jesus."

She looked at him strangely. "I wouldn't have taken you for the kind of man who liked art."

"I don't know much about it," he admitted. "But I got turned on to sculpture in 1964, when I saw *The Pieta* at the World's Fair in New York. I think it was in the Italian pavilion. The Vatican had sent it over with serious reluctance. They had it behind a wall of bulletproof glass, and you went by it on a moving belt. You only got maybe thirty seconds to see the thing, but I never forgot it. It was incredible."

"Didn't somebody wreck *The Pieta* later on?" Alex asked. "Didn't somebody hit it with a hammer?"

Murphy sighed. "A crazy Hungarian named Lazlo Papp. The statue makes it over here all the way from Rome. They put it out in front of the nuttiest people in America, and nothing. They send it back to Rome and this psycho caves in Mary's face. They supposedly fixed it, but I'm sure it's not the same."

"That's a shame," Alex said.

"It's worse than a shame," Murphy said. "It's a crime. They should have executed the crazy bastard. Us and the Europeans, we don't know how to treat criminals anymore. The Russian have the right idea. Do you think they get recividists in the Gulag? The crazy Arabs, they know how to handle it. It's real tough

281

to go back to picking pockets if they've cut your hands off for doing it the first time. And rapists? I won't even tell you what they cut off those guys, but if any of them are able to pull that again they belong in Ripley's Believe It Or Not."

Alex laughed, a bubbling sound. "And you defend criminals? What's the prosecutor like? Torquemada?"

Murphy grinned sheepishly. "Just some old instincts coming out. That happens once in a while. I was a cop for a lot longer than I've been a lawyer."

"Really?" Alex said.

"Yeah. I've only been in practice for about eighteen months, since I passed the bar exam."

Alex sat down on a bench. She motioned for Murphy to sit beside her.

"Tell me all about it," she said. "What kind of cases do you handle?"

"Oh, you don't want to hear about all that crap."

"Yes, I do," Alex said. "You switched careers like that? I never knew anybody else who did anything like that. I'm fascinated. Tell me."

She was fascinated? That was good enough for Murphy. He talked. He sat on a bench in the Rodin Museum with a lovely woman and told her all about himself. He told her about his life as a police officer. He told her about his failed marriage, about his daughter away at college, about his tenure in the DA's office, about his struggles to get his practice going. He talked freely and with some gusto. Murphy liked talking about himself to pretty women who seemed interested. He made it a point to mention only the good parts.

"What kind of cases do you handle?" Alex asked.

Murphy shrugged. "What I can get. A lot of civil

work for cops. Cops get divorced a lot, and we don't seem to pay our bills all that well. Some criminal work from guys I used to bust every chance I got."

"I should think you'd be more comfortable as a prosecutor," Alex said.

Murphy shook his head. "Let me tell you about the DA we've got in this town," he said, and proceeded to do so.

"Sounds like a terrific guy," Alex said when he had finished.

"A prince. Maybe when he gets out of the DA's office I'll consider going back. Actually, I'm back now, in a way. I'm handling a case on a contract basis."

"No kidding."

"Yeah. Feels good, too. You know, working as defense counsel has fairly few real satisfactions. You get some guy, he should be sent away for twenty years, and you've had a good day if you get him off with three. That's what passes for personal satisfaction most days as criminal defense counsel. The fact is that most of the people who get arrested did it. Or they did something else worse at some point that they didn't get caught for. I understand better than most people the routine that everybody is entitled to his day in court and all that, and I know that the prosecution makes mistakes every once in a while. Not usually, but it happens. I've got one of them now, I think. But cases like that are relatively few and far between, and I generally feel more comfortable on the other side."

Alex took his hand. Murphy squeezed back.

"What sort of case are you working on for the DA now?" she asked.

Murphy went to light a Camel inside the museum,

but he caught the disapproving glare of a security guard. "Let's go somewhere where I can smoke this. Say, do you want to go someplace nice for dinner tonight? Or would you like to do Chinatown?"

"Chinatown would be fine," Alex said as they went outside. "Go on, tell me. What's this case you're doing for the prosecution?"

Murphy looked at her quizzically. "You really get off on this stuff, don't you?"

She squeezed his arm and pressed close to him as they walked. "It's just like on TV."

"Mob murder," Murphy said simply. "In fact, I have to attend to some business on it tomorrow. I'll be leaving early, back late."

"Where are you going?"

"A ways."

"Can I come?"

Murphy laughed. "You're a city girl, remember? Where I'm going you won't like it."

Alex filed that away.

CHAPTER 26

Alex stirred. Her awakenings were always quiet, almost stealthy. It was as though she sneaked out of sleep. Her eyes opened slowly, blinked twice and she was back in the real world.

Or was it the real world?

Another ghost was standing at the foot of the bed in which she lay with the snoring bulk of Frank Murphy. This ghost was a balding accountant who had lived in a fine house in Lake Forest, Illinois—a house in which Alex had killed him with his own revolver, a .38-cal. Colt snubnose he had kept in a dresser drawer in his bedroom. Since he had died naked, with a startled expression on his face, that was how he appeared now, eyes bulging in shock. If he was cold he didn't show it. Then again, Alex supposed, the accountant was beyond cold, beyond pain, beyond any sort of discomfort.

That still didn't make him pretty to look at, though. Alex had jammed the barrel of the the pistol into his open mouth and pulled the trigger. The angle had been a little off, unfortunately. As a result, where the accountant had sported a gleaming dome of skin in life, in death the top of his head was missing entirely. He stood before her with neither a top to his head nor pants. Alex did not find the combination inviting.

A goodly number of Alex's victims had left the world dressed as they had been when they had entered it. She had determined early on that men tended to be least on their guard during and immediately after sex. It had always struck her as best to conduct her real business under such circumstances. The technique had been undeniably effective, but it did make for disturbing visitations. Alex had never found anything particularly attractive about the male body. They had too much hair all over the place. Some men even had sprawling mats of thin hair on their backs. Men had—things— hanging off them that were interesting enough when they were impassioned but positively repelling in their flaccid states.

Repelling on a ghost, at least. Alex knew this one would soon leave, however. She glanced at the alarm clock and saw it was set to go off in just a minute. That would awaken Murphy, and the ghost would disappear. The ghosts never showed up when anybody else was around. She knew why. They knew that only Alex would understand why they were around. She sometimes wondered if they visited, too, the people who had retained her to take their lives. If so, none of her employers had ever mentioned it to her. And she, in turn, had never mentioned the ghosts to anybody either. To talk of them, to even acknowledge their existence to a living being, would be sure to give them some sort of satisfaction. They wanted recognition of some sort, she suspected, and if that was it they could go fuck themselves. They couldn't hurt her, so she wouldn't give them a thing. Why should she?

Alex wondered if the bulldog, who was sleeping on the sofa in the living room, had sensed the presence of the ghost. Clearly, she decided, the dog had not. The dog had made no sound, and she imagined that the realization that something as strange as the accountant was lurking around would have given the bulldog something of a start. Then again, it was possible that the gho—

Buzzzzzzzzzzz!

Murphy awakened with his usual aplomb. *"Arrgghhh,"* he said, groping toward the clock.

Alex reached over and stilled the buzzer. Then she snuggled close to the semi-comatose Murphy, who drew her to him.

"Wake up time," she said softly.

"Oh, shit," Murphy muttered resentfully.

"Come on, Frank," Alex said, sitting up. "You said you had to be somewhere today. You've got to get moving."

Murphy sat up, rubbing his eyes and grunting like a bear coming out of hibernation. He looked up through bleary eyes. "Okay," he grunted weakly.

Alex got out of bed, glorious in her nakedness. She glanced toward the door. No ghost. "I'll make some coffee."

Murphy looked up, taking in the sight. He smiled broadly, something he seldom did immediately after awakening, even weakly. "Stay like that," he told her.

She shook her head in good-natured disdain and picked up his blue oxford-cloth button-down shirt from where it lay on the floor next to the bed. "I'll freeze to death," she said, slipping it on. "Go ahead, get into the shower. I'll have coffee and an English muffin when you come out."

By the time Murphy had showered, shaved and dressed in jeans and another old blue oxford-cloth shirt, the apartment was redolent with the smell of fresh coffee and toasted muffins. He entered the kitchen with his first Camel of the day—always the very best one—hanging out from beneath his moustache. He saw Alex at the counter wearing his shirt. She was a tall woman, and the tail of the old shirt didn't quite cover the cheeks of her behind. Murphy came up behind her and cupped them gently with his hands. Alex, bearing a mug of coffee and a plate with the muffin, moved deftly away.

"Eat," she said, depositing the food on the kitchen table.

Murphy gave her an evil leer.

"That," she told him, pointing at the food.

Murphy frowned. "You're a lot more fun at night," he grumbled, taking his seat.

The coffee was marvelous, much better than the instant Murphy made for himself in his microwave. He soaked the muffin in liquid margarine, added some grape jelly for color and devoured it in two bites. Then he glanced at his watch and stood up.

"Time to go," he said. "How would you like to do me a favor and walk Winston?"

"Fine," Alex said. "When do you expect to be back?"

"Probably not until very late. Maybe after midnight."

"In that case," she said, "I'm going to get out of here

and spend some time at Aunt Emma's place."

"What the hell for?"

"That's the apartment I'm supposed to be watching, remember? I don't think I've been in there more than an hour since I met you that night at the market."

"So you won't be here when I get back tonight? Are you going to be awake?"

"Frank, where are you going, anyway? It's Sunday, for God's sake."

Murphy took her chin in his hand, kissed her gently on the lips. "Man's work, little lady," he said in his best Gary Cooper voice.

"Up yours," Alex said, kicking his leg with her naked foot. "I'm serious. Where are you going, anyway? Who's more important to you than I am?"

"Remember the mob murder I mentioned?"

"Yeah?" Alex said.

"It has to do with that," Murphy told her, kissing her forehead and heading for the door. "I'm off to serve the public."

"Take me with you."

"Not a chance."

"Then I'll be asleep," she called after him as he left.

The door closed. The accountant's ghost immediately came out of the bathroom and sat on the sofa. Alex glared angrily at the ghost.

"You guys are really beginning to annoy me," she said aloud.

Before all this

Because Alma was no dope, it didn't take her long to realize that Phil didn't support the Riviera, the big house in Short Hills, and his penchant for first-class travel out of the proceeds of the restaurant.

The restaurant, which Phil had named L'Americain, was located on a major highway less than a half hour from the house in which they lived. The place was not terribly large, and while it was reasonable by Manhattan standards—especially in comparison to the top of the line places with which it would have competed there—the market for such a restaurant in New Jersey was severely limited. In Manhattan there were people who dined nightly in fine restaurants. But in Jersey a place like L'Americain tended to attract a clientele consisting largely of middle-aged couples out to splurge on their anniversaries or spoiled rich college kids anxious to impress a special date. The service, atmosphere, and the food—especially the food—all were terrific. Phil did some business, but he paid only passing attention to the books, and it wasn't long before Alma realized that the lifestyle Phil lived—the trips the two of them took to Europe every summer, the islands in the winter—had very little to do with the restaurant.

"How do you do it?" she asked finally. "Where does the money come from?"

"Don't worry about it," Phil told her.

But she did worry about it. She had no income of her own, and she would have been crazy not to worry about Phil's, since it supported both of them in a style Alma had come to enjoy. She pressed him. It wasn't nagging exactly, but it was persuasive. And, since he truly loved her and had come to trust her as well, Phil eventually told her what he did for a living.

"I perform a business service," he said one night after some heavy pressure from Alma. "Somebody has a problem with somebody else, I take care of the problem."

Alma didn't get it at first. "What do you mean you take care of the problem?"

"What do you think I mean?"

"Tell me, Phil," she insisted.

He frowned. "All right. I was a soldier in Korea. I killed guys for my country. I got a silver star for it. So now I'm still a soldier. But I work in private industry."

"What do you mean? You kill people?"

"Yeah."

Alma didn't believe it. "How often?"

He shrugged. "Two, maybe three times a year. It depends."

"Who do you kill people for?"

"You guess," Phil said to her.

They were in bed in Short Hills, and it was late. Alma

studied him, not sure yet if this was for real or some kind of joke. If it was, he was doing a good job at it. "How did you get into this line of work?" she asked finally.

He shrugged. "A guy I knew in Korea. He looked me up after the war. He asked me if I was looking for something to do, which I was. I had a wife and no job. This guy, he loaned money, and sometimes people didn't pay what they owed. I helped him collect some of it. Then there was this one guy; he didn't have the money. The idea was that he was supposed to be a lesson for some other people. So I took care of him."

"You took care of him?" Alma said, in shock.

"Yeah," Phil said with irritation. "Do I have to draw you a picture, or what, Al? I took care of him."

"Don't get worked up," Alma said, and now she was starting to believe it. "I don't know what to think of all this."

He lay back in the bed. "So what's to think of it? You kill people for the army, they give you a medal. You kill guys in business, they send you to jail if you get caught. It's all the same thing, though. The guys I do, they know the score. They know what's going on. I don't go out on the fucking street and mug people, for Christ's sake. I'm like a soldier, only I work in private business. I'm a mercenary, is all."

Alma pondered it. "When was the last one?"

"The last one what?"

"The last one you . . . you did."

"March," Phil told her. "You remember when we were in Vegas? The night I went out for a while?"

Alma was stunned. "You killed a guy when we were in Vegas? While I was playing roulette?"

293

"Yeah. Why the hell do you think we went to Vegas in the first place? You know I don't like to gamble."

"I thought you wanted a little vacation. That's what you said."

"What am I going to tell you?" Phil demanded. "I've got to go to Vegas to kill a guy? Want to come along? Stop bugging me about this, Al."

"Don't call me Al," Alma said. "You know I don't like that, and I told you why. My stepfather was named Al."

"Well, I don't like Alma," Phil told her, and he was growing angry as he said it. "I've told you that. I'm nuts about everything about you except your name."

"What am I supposed to do?" Alma demanded, her own voice with an edge to it. She didn't know if it was prompted by his tone of voice or what he had just told her. "You want me to change my name?"

"Yeah," Phil said. "As long as we're playing true confessions—as long as I'm telling you stuff I shouldn't be telling you in the first place—yeah, I wouldn't mind it if you changed your name. Alma sucks, if you want the truth. It's an old lady's name, for Christ's sake."

She was silent for a moment. Then she said, "So what do you want me to be named?"

"Anything," Phil said. "Anything but Alma."

She snuggled close to him, nibbling on his ear. "You want to give me a new name?" she purred. "Is that what you want?"

Phil turned to her, touching her. "I don't care."

She touched him back, felt him quiver. "You name me. Go ahead."

He thought about it. "How about Alexandra. That's sort of like your real name, only it sounds better."

"Fine," she said, fondling him, stroking him, making him groan in a low voice. "You can call me Alexandra if you want to. But you have to do something for me."

"What?" he said, as she moved on top of him.

"Promise?"

"Ahhhh," Phil gasped. "What?"

"Next time you do somebody," Alexandra said, taking him inside her, "take me with you."

"Forget that doctor stuff," Weiner said. "Just call me

CHAPTER 27

Murphy pulled the Toronado in front of Paul Toddman's large stone house in East Oak Lane and considered, just for a moment, shutting off the engine and going up to the door to knock like a civilized human being. It was a moment of weakness, and he dismissed it. He leaned on the horn, a short, loud burst. In less than ten seconds, Toddman's door opened and the first assistant district attorney of the city and county of Philadelphia leaned out to give Frank Murphy the finger.

"I'll be out in a minute," Toddman called out, slamming the door as he withdrew.

Murphy lit a Camel and listened to an oldies tape Patricia had given him for Christmas. Aretha Franklin was proclaiming herself to be a "natch-yoo-ral wo-mun" when Toddman emerged from his door dressed in a suit and tie and carrying a briefcase. As Toddman got into the Toronado, Murphy turned off the tape deck and said, "I didn't know this was formal."

Toddman took in Murphy's casual attire. "Clearly,"

he said sourly. "Come on, let's go."

If there was one person for whom morning was an endless hardship, it was Paul Toddman. He always gave the impression that undergoing unnecessary surgery on his private parts would annoy him less than being forced by the necessities of making a living to leave his bed before the crack of noon. This was especially true on the rare occasions he was forced to work Sunday mornings, and today he resisted all Murphy's attempts at pleasant conversation, such as they were. Toddman merely sat in the passenger's seat, staring out the window and grunting occasionally, while Murphy made his way to the turnpike.

Finally, Murphy gave up and put the oldies tape back on. Aretha assured him that "What you want, Baby I got . . ." After that, somebody—Murphy couldn't remember who—came on and announced that he was a soul man, an admission that seemed to rouse considerable excitement from his backup group. Murphy was tapping the wheel in time with the music when Toddman said, "You can tell me who the witness is any time now, Frank."

"I'd rather talk about Webster."

"Forget Webster. One case at a time."

"If I give you enough proof to cast genuine doubt on Webster, what are the chances that you guys will come to your senses and drop the charges?"

Toddman shrugged. "I might. Fletcher won't, though. You can count on that."

"Will you at least push back the trial for a few months? I can't do a decent job for my guy with all this Lucelli crap on my mind."

"Like I said, it's up to Fletcher. Why don't you call

him up and reason with him, Frank? You know how highly Fletcher thinks of you."

Murphy shook his head. "You know," he said, "I think it's fairly shitty of him to take out his problems with me on my client."

"Yeah," Toddman said, "well, I think I might be more concerned about all that if I didn't think your client did it. Which he did, by the way."

"Three other people had motive, and two of them had opportunity. The third one had opportunity, too, I think."

"Nobody had motive like your guy had motive," Toddman told him.

"What do you mean by that?"

"For Christ's sake, Frank," Toddman said with irritation, "who's the witness against Lucelli? Who the hell is it?"

"The guy who owned the diner where the murders took place. His name's Berger. He saw the shootings."

For the first time all morning, Toddman perked up. "He saw the killings? With his own eyes he saw them?"

Murphy nodded. "Yep."

"Why didn't he tell the cops at the time?"

"He had his reasons."

"Good witness?" Toddman asked suspiciously. "No shit?"

"Self-made man. Lucid, rational. Holocaust survivor. I asked Wilder to run a make on him, just to play it safe. Nothing. This guy's like a gift from heaven."

"Why's he doing this now, after all these years?" Toddman demanded.

"His wife got caught in the crossfire and ended up dead. It's been eating away at him for a long time.

When his only child—a college kid, a daughter—got killed in a car crash a few months back, he figured he had nothing left to lose. He was in dead man's shoes."

"Dead man's shoes?" Toddman said. "What the hell is that?"

Murphy chuckled. "I keep forgetting. You were never on the street, were you? Penn undergraduate, Yale law. But you never were really out there where it all goes down."

"You're right," Toddman said, mildly annoyed. "I suffer under the handicap of a middle-class upbringing and a decent education. It's a wonder I ever got this far, isn't it? So what does that mean, dead man's shoes?"

"It's a street expression," Murphy told him. "It means you're in a situation you'd rather not be in, but it's something you can't avoid. You've just got to do what you've got to do—like Gary Cooper in *High Noon*. After the daughter got killed, Berger figured he couldn't avoid this—not if he ever wanted to sleep again."

"Dead man's shoes," Toddman said, shaking his head. "I never heard that one."

"Well, look at it this way: You're weak in street talk, and I never got to join the Hasty Pudding Society, or whatever it is."

"Neither did I. That's Harvard, asshole, not Yale."

"Asshole," Murphy mused. "Learn that at Yale, did you?"

"No," Toddman said, "I learned it from assholes like you."

It was just about lunchtime when they pulled into downtown Sparta. Downtown consisted of a single intersection with corners occupied by a hardware store, a Gulf station, a pharmacy, and a three-story office building with a cafe on the bottom floor.

"I'm hungry," Murphy said. "From what Wilder tells me, there's not much to eat where they are. He's doing most of the cooking, for one thing."

"Then let's stop at this grease palace," Toddman suggested.

Murphy pulled in front of the cafe, which was named Peggy's, according to the chipped sign painted on the glass. He killed the Toronado's engine and they went inside. The cafe had been there a long time. There were booths along the glass windows in front, and the counter along the back wall clearly went back to the forties. There was a timeless quality about old urban neighborhoods and small-town business districts that Murphy always noted. The stools at the counter were made of stainless steel and covered with thick plastic. The damned things were sunk into the old linoleum floor with six-inch bolts. They'd be there for another forty years, he was sure, when every McDonald's in America was a shambles of orange plastic and smashed glass. Two men in work clothes sat at the counter, drinking coffee and studying newspapers from Scranton. A woman in a pale-green tricot uniform and a black apron was behind the counter, washing down the area near the meat slicer.

Murphy and Toddman settled into a booth. The woman came around from the counter with handwritten menus in clear plastic covers. She was a wiry woman of perhaps forty, her dirty blond hair up atop her head and her face pleasant enough, although care-lined. Looking at her, Murphy thought of the Toronado—showing wear, to be sure, but still basically solid, a lot of miles left if nothing unexpected went wrong. That's how he thought of himself, too, which was one of the reasons he liked the car so much.

"Check this out, fellas," she said, "and I'll get you some coffee while you're making up your minds."

"No coffee for me," Toddman said, opening the menu. "What do you recommend?"

"Nothing that's tough to cook," she said. "I had a rough night last night."

Murphy laughed and pulled out his cigarettes and his Bic lighter. "How are the burgers?"

"Mostly meat," she said. "We serve them on hard rolls, too."

Murphy flicked the Bic several times, to no avail. He rummaged through his pockets for matches. "Tell you what," he said. "Give me two, and a side of fries. I'd like fried onions and cheese on the burgers, and burn the meat pretty good, if you will."

"Give me one," Toddman said, "and no fries. Got any cole slaw? And a Coke."

"Me, too, on that Coke," Murphy said.

"You got it," she said, memorizing the order, which didn't strike Murphy as much of a chore.

"By the way," he asked her, "got any matches?"

She reached into her apron pocket and tossed four packs on the table. Each was a bright yellow with the name of the cafe and its address and phone number on the face of the pack. "On the house," she said, and headed back for the counter.

Murphy lit a Camel with one pack of matches and stuffed the rest of them into his shirt pocket. He leaned across the table toward Toddman. "You know, watching you sit in that office and wait for Fletcher

302

Lake to move on to another office is like watching somebody commit suicide with toenail clippers. It takes forever; it might never work out and it clearly hurts every second. Why don't you just run against him and get it done with? Every criminal lawyer in town would be on your side."

"Hah!" Toddman said. "Nobody would be on my side unless they thought I could beat him, and I wouldn't have a chance of getting the nomination unless I had everybody on my side from the start. Nobody with any brains who makes a living out of criminal law in Philadelphia wants to get on the wrong side of the DA."

"I'm on the wrong side of the DA."

"I'm talking about people with brains and people who are making a living. You don't meet either test, Frank."

"I'm clearing almost as much as I made as a police lieutenant. And I don't have to take any guff from anybody, either."

"Big fucking deal," Toddman said. "Do you know how much a guy like Richie Silver pulls down? Can you even imagine? If Richie cleared less than half a million a year he'd burst into tears. That's a living to a lot of those guys, Frank. What you and I make is nickels and dimes."

"Why do you do it, then?"

"Why do I do what?"

"Why do you stay a prosecutor? You're the best courtroom lawyer in the city. If you could pull down that kind of bread on the outside, why not go for it?"

Toddman looked at Murphy somewhat mystified. "You ask me that? You see the kind of scumbags Richie

303

Silver represents. You could look your kid in the face representing those guys?"

"It's the system," Murphy said. "I think Richie's a creep, but he's part of a system that's better than any other system."

Toddman picked up the matches Murphy had left on the table and lit one of his huge cigars. "Let me tell you about this system of which you've lately become so enamored," Toddman said. "I had this case a few years back. I handled it myself. This guy—this rich guy, the son of a big doctor down in Richmond, Virginia—he's in town to buy some coke and a suitcase full of pills. He's got this rented car, and he's coming back from his score. He picks up this runaway girl on the Schuylkill and takes her back to this place he's staying in out in Manyunk. The girl was maybe fifteen, and screwed up from the word go.

"So this guy takes the coke and God knows what else. Then he takes her and ties her to his bed and, over the course of a three-day period, he rapes her twenty-eight times. All the time, he's doing coke, pills, all kinds of weird shit. After a while, he starts to think . . . Christ, I don't know what he starts to think.

"What he's doing is he's grinding up the pills in a bowl and licking his fingers and sticking them into the bowl, you know? And, in between, he's doing coke. While he's at all this—while the runaway is tied to the bed—he knocks out all her teeth and breaks four or five of her ribs. Then, just for laughs, he gets out a butcher knife and takes off each of her little fingers, just to see how loud she'll scream.

"He gets busted because he then throws the girl out into the street just as a prowl car is coming around the corner on a quiet Sunday in spring, just like this one. At this point, the guy was so stoned he couldn't talk. He turned out to have had a record you could stack up and do high dives off of. He'd done something like this before, too, down in Virginia, back in the early seventies, but his old man got it pleaded down to squat.

"And you know what? He gets off on this. You know why he gets off? He gets off because the girl never shows up for trial. She was crazy enough to begin with, and after that she was really nuts. And, in addition, he gets off because Richie Silver proves that the guy was never given his constitutional warning before the cops beat the shit out of him with their night sticks and took him into custody."

Murphy sighed loudly. All this had a familiar ring to him.

"The best we could do was possession," Toddman went on, "for which he got less than a year in Holmesburg. And you talk to me about how Richie Silver is just part of the system? You want to talk to me about how Richie pulling in God alone knows how much from this creep's rich old man is just part of the American system of justice? Give me a break, Frank, please. If I've got to pick a side—and we all do—I'll pick this one. It doesn't pay all that well, but it pays enough that I don't have to engage in that kind of shit."

Murphy nodded. He had his share of horror stories, too. He tried to forget them, but conversations like this brought them back.

"Be that as it may," Murphy said finally, "you're not always on the right side in these things. Every once in a while, you go after somebody who's genuinely innocent."

"Like who?"

"Webster."

Toddman rolled his eyes. "Give it a rest, for Christ's sake. Webster is as guilty as sin. He took that kitchen knife and stabbed that woman with it. Don't have any doubt about it."

"How do you know that?" Murphy demanded.

Toddman drew on his cigar. "Because I do."

"Oh," Murphy said, "that clears it all up for me. You're a fucking clairvoyant. You just read it in your cigar ashes."

Toddman gazed at him impassively. "Frank, I like you. Don't ask me why, but I do. But you're like all the rest of them. The first chance you get, you sell your soul for the money and the independence—in your case, maybe just the independence—and you try to pretend that the scumbags you represent are just like the rest of us. They're not. They're still scumbags, even if they came to you for help. It's all a delusion."

"If I've sold my soul for the money, then I got royally screwed," Murphy pointed out.

Toddman put down his cigar as the woman in the pale-green uniform brought the food.

"You've lost your belief in principle," Toddman said simply.

Murphy responded: "Maybe. But I still believe in interest." Then he turned to the woman serving the meal. "Can you help me with something? I'm trying to get to Camp Wintu. Which way do I go at this intersection?"

"Go down that way," the woman said, pointing out the window. "You go about six miles, and the camp is on your right. The lake'll be on your left, and the camp is up a steep road on the right, got it? There's a sign."

Not anymore, Murphy thought. Then he ate his burger.

Wilder's barrier was crude but formidable. It was a quarter-inch steel cable stretched between two trees at a height of four feet and decorated by a haphazard collection of pots and pans and—oddly—a set of Christmas bells. It was hung directly across the steeply pitched little road Murphy had found with such difficulty. Murphy would have needed a set of wrenches to disconnect the cable from the two trees to which it was attached, one on either side of the road, and the action would have been difficult without some noise—probably a lot. He stopped his car and said to Toddman, "We have to get out here."

"What the hell is this?" Toddman said, climbing out of the car.

"Wilder put this up. Watch."

Murphy banged a pot with his fist. The pot banged into another pot, which shook the steel cable, which made the bells jingle. The noise was incongruous in the wooded setting.

"Sit tight," Murphy told Toddman.

Wilder appeared a moment later, an M-16 across his arm. "Nice to see you," he told Murphy, and looking none too pleasant as he said it.

"Lovely spot," Murphy said, looking around at the dense woods on either side of the dirt road. "Truly lovely. You're a lucky man, Jim. Fresh air, sunshine, nice trees, bir—"

"Stuff it," Wilder said, lowering the rifle. "Hi, Paul."

Toddman nodded. "How's my witness?"

"In one piece. No thanks to chubby, here."

Murphy looked wounded. "You're a harsh and cruel man, Sergeant Wilder," he said.

Toddman looked up the road eagerly and reached into the car for his briefcase. He turned to Wilder. "Let's go. I've waited a long time to meet the guy who's going to help me put Tommy Lucelli away."

Murphy got back late, past 11:00. He was dead tired. He entered his building wearily, climbed the stairs slowly and put his key into the lock—all chores performed with enormous effort. It had been a long day, and Murphy wasn't seventeen years old anymore. Inside, he found Alex on the sofa, dozing in front of the TV set. Murphy smiled, closed the door gently and went to her side. He knelt next to her and kissed her gently on the forehead. She stirred and wrapped her arms around his neck.

"Mmmmmmm," she said. "About time."

Murphy nuzzled her neck. "I thought you were going back to your own place."

"I was," she said, "but your goddamn dog started howling. I had to come back in here to keep him quiet."

Murphy kissed her cheek. "As long as you're here, want to go to bed?"

"Sure," she said.

They kicked the sleeping bulldog off the bed, and—after making a shameless fuss over Murphy for the monumental act of returning home—Winston went into the living room to sleep on the sofa. Murphy shed his clothes, dropping them where he stood, and slipped into bed in his shorts. Alex stripped to her panties and climbed in with him. They both drifted off in short order.

Alex tossed for some hours. She slept fitfully. Finally, she awakened some time around three. She had told herself before sleep came to her that she would awaken about that time. It was an old trick, one she had mastered long ago. She had known for some time that her body possessed some kind of inner clock, and she took advantage of it every time it seemed necessary.

She sat up in bed. Murphy slept the sleep of the dead. He didn't move—hardly breathed, in fact. Alex got out of bed and stood mostly naked in the dim light of the bedroom, which was illuminated by the streetlight in the alley behind the building. She bent down and systematically went through the clothes Murphy had dropped on the floor—a ritual she had performed faithfully every night she had spent in this room, while Murphy had snored loudly. On all other nights, the task had proven fruitless. Tonight was different. Alex's persistence finally paid off. In the pocket of his old blue oxford-cloth shirt, she found the matches from Peggy's Cafe at the corner of Main and Lake in Sparta, Pa., phone number 717-555-6092.

Alex memorized all that was printed on the packs of matches. Then, as insurance, she slipped one pack under the bed, to be retrieved the following morning. After that, she lay back down next to Frank Murphy and slept.

Peacefully.

CHAPTER 28

How many days would it be? Let's see, now . . . Two hundred and thirty days a year times twelve years and add in about four months . . . that would be pretty close to three thousand days. Yeah, just about three thousand.

Jesus Jumping Christ, Profumo thought as he finished up his computation. Three thousand days of getting into his car in the morning—it was a new Nova every four years—driving half an hour up the turnpike, parking in the same sprawling lot and going into the same building to work in the same laboratory.

Thrilling, Profumo thought. He'd heard of groundhogs who lived more exciting lives.

He needed a trip badly, really needed it, this time. And—thank God, all his angels and American Express—one was coming up, provided he could get through the next two weeks without flipping out. Three thousand days. That was three times longer than Kennedy had been president. Somehow, Profumo had the impression that his work had made something less

310

of a dent in the fortunes of humanity. On the other hand, he'd done his bit. He was still doing it. Profumo would rather be here doing something worthwhile than just working to make somebody else rich. He didn't get much money, and he knew he never would. On the other hand, he did important work. He put creeps behind bars. At least, he did in a way.

He parked the car in its customary spot, near the rear of the lot so nobody would be likely to park next to him and bang a door into it, and walked into the building. State police headquarters in Ewing Township, just outside what Profumo liked to refer to as the former city of Trenton, was a three-story brick structure that could have passed for a large public school except for the cop cars all over the place and the state and American flags flying from the poles out front. He went in through a back entrance and took an elevator to his work station on the second floor. He nodded to the receptionist on the way to the doorway that bore his name. Profumo entered, hung up his poplin jacket, put on his white lab coat and started up the coffeepot on a table near the door. Then he settled down at his lab table and dug into the pile of work orders the receptionist had placed there for him.

Profumo worked in a small, private room with a window overlooking the back lot and an aged photograph on the wall of a somber, bespectacled man in a frock coat.

"Morning, Sir Edward," Profumo said to the portrait of his personal god, even if the guy had been a Limey. Then Profumo flipped on his computer terminal and began going through his papers. In just a few moments, he was lost in them.

Angelo Profumo was thirty-four years old, the father of two and the unquestioned authority in his house despite his height—or, rather, his lack of it. He stood five-foot-two and bought his clothing in the boy's department. He ranged between a size eighteen and a size twenty, depending on the cut and the manufacturer. He had realized early on that he was never going to be big, and the realization had annoyed him. He had been annoyed ever since, although he managed to hide it most of the time. Except today, of course. Profumo was in a particularly foul mood.

It was, he knew, the fact that it was Monday that was doing it to him. That and the trip. Profumo lived for his one trip abroad a year. This year it would be to Acapulco. It was the beginning of the off-season. The hotel rates would be bearable, and it was still early for the summer hike in air fares. Burritos, piña coladas, liquor from bottles with dead worms in them, some deep sea fishing, watching jerks diving off cliffs into the sea. It sounded like heaven to Profumo. Next year he was planning a trip to Australia. That's how he did it. He planned at least a year in advance, sometimes two. It was indisputably cheaper that way, but that wasn't the real reason he did it. He spent much of his time thinking about trips because if he didn't he would be reminded that he lived in New Jersey. Not that New Jersey was all that bad, regardless of what people liked to think, but it wasn't overly exciting, even in its best moments. How exciting could a place be when it named its high point High Point?

Profumo had his magnifying glass out, peering into it at a set of classic central pocket loops when the buzzer on his intercom sounded. Irritated by the distraction, Angelo Profumo hit his intercom button and said, "What?"

"Somebody here to see you," the receptionist said.

"Who is it?"

"A Mr. Francis P. Murphy. He's an attorney from Philadelphia, according to his card. He says he has an appointment, but he's not in the book."

"Send him in," Profumo snapped, and killed the intercom.

Murphy entered a moment later, wearing a gray glen plaid suit that had once fit him. Now his gut strained against it. He carried a manila envelope under one arm.

"Dr. Frankenstein, I presume," Murphy said. "Nice coat, Angelo. It lends you a certain mad scientist air."

Profumo, peering into his magnifying glass, never looked up. "You got the stuff for me?"

"Right here."

Profumo put down the glass and spun about to face Murphy. "Let's see," he said.

Murphy opened the envelope and laid out its contents on the lab table.

"You've got these sets," the lawyer explained. "These came from the coffee mug. These came from the drinking glass. These came from the ashtray. This came from the corpse. They're all more or less complete."

"I can tell which set matches right now," Profumo said, glancing at them. "You can see it yourself. Look at this whorl pattern, and look at the double loops here. They're twins. See it?"

Murphy studied the prints Profumo indicated. "No," he said finally. "I can't read these things."

Profumo looked at Murphy with open disdain. "A blind man could see this. Here, watch."

313

Profumo took the two sets of prints and laid them side by side on what looked like the glass face of a photocopying machine attached to his computer terminal. He pressed a button on the side of the machine, and Murphy became aware of a hushed humming issuing from the contraption.

"This thing going to blow up, or what?" Murphy said.

"What the computer is doing," Profumo said, "is reading both sets of prints and reducing them to binary digits. There, see on the screen? A match. They're identical. No sweat, Frank."

Murphy stared at the computer screen. A message printed there read "Positive."

"Takes no more than five seconds," Profumo said. "Like magic, isn't it? Even Sir Edward wouldn't believe it."

Murphy looked up from the computer screen. "Who?"

Profumo gestured toward the portrait on the wall. "Sir Edward. You don't remember who he is?"

Murphy shrugged. "Ty Cobb's coke supplier?" he guessed.

"Watch what you say about Sir Edward," Profumo cautioned.

"I remember," Murphy said. "I'm just pulling your chain. Meanwhile, though, I'd sort of like to get this taken care of so I can get the hell out of New Jersey, you know?"

"Screw you," Profumo said. "I've lived my whole life in Jersey."

"It shows, too," Murphy told him. "You know what's wrong with New Jersey? I thought about it while

314

I was driving up here this morning. The problem is that New Jersey doesn't exist."

Profumo cocked his head. "Say what?" he said.

"It doesn't exist," Murphy said. "Oh, I know that when I came across the Ben Franklin Bridge this morning, I saw this sign that said New Jersey exists and that I was in it all of a sudden. And it also said that whichever sticky-fingered politician who hasn't been indicted recently is governor this month. I saw all that. But it occurred to me that it's all sort of a fiction, just some meaningless lines on a map. If you live in South Jersey, you actually live in Philly. You get the Philly papers. You watch the Philly TV stations. If you live in North Jersey, you live in New York. New York papers. New York TV. Christ, they've even got a town up in North Jersey there called West New York. What more proof do you need? Does New York have a place called East New Jersey? Come on, Angelo, face it: where you live doesn't exist."

"New Jersey has got the Giants and the Jets," Profumo said.

"You don't have the Eagles."

"And thank God for that. Listen, when do I have to testify in this case? I've got a trip coming up in two weeks."

"How long a trip?"

"Two weeks. My wife and me."

Murphy thought about it. "Jury selection ought to take about a week. Then we've got opening statements, and the prosecution will present its case. That ought to take a few days, maybe a week. You should be okay. Can you leave me a number where I can reach you in an emergency?"

315

"I'm going to be in Mexico."

"Well," Murphy said, "They've got phones down there. No indoor toilets, but they've got phones. We should be okay on the time, anyway. Call my secretary and give her the number just in case. And call my office the minute you're back in town. Don't drink any of the water down there, okay? I'd hate to get you on the stand and have you keep running out to the john. You taking the kids?"

"Is the Pope Italian?"

"No, but he wears a beanie."

"There's your answer. They're staying with my wife's mother. I figure a couple of weeks with them and she'll stay the hell away from my house for six months after we get back. I won't have to see her again until Thanksgiving."

"Good," Murphy said. "You'll write me up a report and turn it in before you go away? You know, in case the plane crashes or something, I wouldn't want it to be a total disaster."

"I'll send it in," Profumo said.

"One more thing, Angelo. If I send you an item, could you dust it and run a make for me on the prints?"

"Is it involved with this case?" Profumo asked.

Murphy shook his head. "Something else. I could have the Philly cops do it, but since you're going to be doing this much anyway . . ."

"Tell you what," Profumo said, "I'll do it if you pay me my expert witness fee up front. I could us the cash in Acapulco."

"Deal," Murphy said.

Profumo smiled. "Sir Edward and I extend our thanks."

CHAPTER 29

The minute he realized what judge they'd drawn in the Webster case, Murphy knew he'd lucked out.

Fletcher Lake had pushed so hard for an early date that he'd neglected to check which common pleas court judge would be in line for the case. It turned out to be Joseph R. Luce, a smallish, quiet man in his early fifties with twinkling eyes behind horn-rimmed glasses—the judge Murphy had wanted from the very beginning. He spoke softly and angered slowly. He happened, like Lake, to be a mainliner, but that was all they had in common.

Joe Luce had gone on the bench eight years before, after a successful career as a lawyer for one of the blue-chip firms on Chestnut Street. He'd proven to be fairly lenient with first offenders, and Lake had singled him out several years after his election when the district attorney had given one of his impassioned televised press conferences to attack soft judges. Lake had dubbed the judge "Let 'em Go Joe" and "Turn 'em Loose Luce." The names hadn't stuck, since Luce had also turned out to be a terror with repeat offenders. But Murphy suspected that the judge remembered the incident.

Moreover, Murphy had built a decent relationship with the judge over the years. As a detective, Murphy had taken to seeking out Luce when he needed a signature on a search warrant. The last thing he'd wanted in such cases was for the case to be thrown out because the judge who'd signed the warrant had done so on the basis of evidence too thin to sustain a challenge to it. Luce had habitually grilled Murphy unmercifully before signing search warrants, and it had been such sessions—encounters that had sharpened Murphy's mind and turned him on to the law's subtleties—that had in large measure prompted him to take the law boards and enter Temple Law School. Joe Luce, as it had turned out, had been on the faculty, teaching criminal procedure, and the two men had become friends of a sort.

Luce made it a point not to socialize with Murphy or members of his circle—men like Wilder and Weiner, Weinberg and Toddman—people the judge was likely to encounter as he performed his duties on the bench. Moreover, Luce tended to move in somewhat different social circles. But Joe Luce liked Frank Murphy, and Murphy knew it. Luce was also known as a defendant's judge in all matters except sentencing. In a pinch, he always gave the defendant the benefit of the doubt in the conduct of a trial. As a result, he was considered a villain by the police and a hero by the appellate courts, which seldom reversed him. When he saw who his judge would be, Murphy was delighted.

Murphy worked hard on the case. It would be his

318

first big trial since passing the bar. He'd had one other murder case, and he'd gotten that client off before the trial stage by helping Wilder figure out who the real killer had been. As he looked back on that case, Murphy realized he'd cheated. He'd felt more confident working as a detective than as a lawyer. This would be his first real test as a trial attorney, and even though he was going up against Fletcher Lake, who was a notoriously bad legal scholar, Murphy was nervous. However ignorant of the law Lake might be—largely because he was intellectually lazy and worked vastly harder at obtaining the next office than concentrating on the duties of the one he held—the district attorney was nonetheless a good talker and a consummate showman. Given the right set of circumstances—a contest against an inexperienced defense counsel, for example—he might just manage to dazzle a jury. It was something to worry about.

Murphy briefly considered calling in another, more experienced lawyer to split his fee and to guide him as the trial unfolded. It would have been the most prudent course of action. But his fee would be so small in this case—possibly even nonexistent, given Murphy's expenses and Webster's financial condition—that it wasn't practical. Moreover, in the end, he couldn't bring himself to back down from a face-to-face showdown with Lake. He knew it was childish, but he also knew that Lake could have simply used Toddman as the prosecutor, in which case Murphy would have been dead meat. Paul Toddman was a shark in the courtroom, and Murphy would never have stood a chance.

Instead, Lake had taken on the task of personally

prosecuting Mike Webster in court, either out of misdirected ego, personal animosity at Murphy, or a combination of the two. In any event, the district attorney had put his ass on the line in this one, and Murphy had felt a powerful obligation to do the same. It occurred to him that in so doing, he might not be operating in the best interests of his client. He dismissed the thought. His job was to do his best. He would.

But it wouldn't be easy.

For starters, he had other cases to worry about. Webster's four grand didn't go far toward paying the bills, and Murphy had already shelled out chunks of that for use of Manny Strobel's bail money and to retain Profumo and Weinberg as expert witnesses. Moreover, Murphy had to worry about Zsa Zsa's divorce, somebody else's house closing, somebody else's will, somebody else's personal damage suit, somebody else's drunk driving arrest. That's where the steady income was to be found. And on weekends, Murphy was at Camp Wintu relieving Wilder. Every Friday night Murphy drove up the turnpike's northeast extension to spend two days sitting around the counselor's cabin at Camp Wintu playing gin rummy with Irving Berger. And getting his ass kicked almost every game. Sometimes Murphy wondered if there was anybody on earth who couldn't beat him at cards when he had things on his mind.

On week nights, there was Alex Fronczek to worry about. Murphy wanted to keep her close to him, and she complained bitterly about his weekend departures.

"Aunt Emma is coming back soon," she whined, "and I've got to go back to New York. If you've got to

320

take off every weekend, at least take me with you, Frank."

"I will one of these times," Murphy promised her. "But not this time. In a couple of weeks or so, okay?"

And Alex would make a face at him. But she never got really angry, which Murphy found strangely appealing in a woman. He'd always assumed that women tended, as a breed, to treasure anger, to prize it and nurture it like a child. But if Alex carried anger around with her, she kept it in check with no apparent effort. She did that very nicely, indeed.

Murphy was positively entranced by her capacity to forgive him just about any of the transgressions that had so maddened his estranged wife. Alex seemed to find his self-indulgent personal habits strangely amusing, his apparent lack of attention toward her generally understandable, his preoccupation with his clients' welfare admirable. She also liked his bulldog, even if Winston did tend to slobber on her. Too good to be true, Murphy thought.

Alex had even sat in the courtroom while Murphy had battled it out with Fletcher Lake over jury selection, which each man knew to be the most important part of the trial. The voir dire, the preliminary examination of prospective jurors, was a crucial process for each side. The prosecution and the defense each had a specified number of challenges for cause—dismissal of a juror because of some sort of innate prejudice in the case that came out in questioning. Each side also had a specified number of preemptive challenges: the right to dismiss a prospective juror for no specific reason.

On one occasion, Murphy found himself with the

opportunity to shake up Fletcher Lake a bit, and he was delighted that Alex was in the courtroom to watch him do his stuff.

Lake had been examining a prospective juror, a black woman in her late fifties in a print dress. Lake had asked her all the usual questions:

Had the woman read about the case, Lake asked.

"No. I don't read newspapers. They just depress me."

"Have you seen anything about it on television?" Lake asked.

"No. TV's busted. Been busted a long time now."

"Have you heard about it on the radio?"

"Don't listen to the radio. Nothin' on there but a bunch of junk."

"Do you know the defendant or did you know the victim?"

"Nope. Don't know nobody."

"Have you ever been the victim of a crime?"

The woman shook her head. "Just been lucky, I guess."

"How do you feel about capital punishment?" Lake asked her.

The woman shrugged. "Don't have no objections to it. If somebody did somethin' real bad—like killed somebody in cold blood or somethin'—capital punishment seem like it's okay with me."

Lake turned to Joe Luce on the bench. "This witness is acceptable to the people, Your Honor."

Murphy stood and said, "Preemption, Your Honor," and sat back down.

Fletcher Lake's face had glowed bright red. He had turned to Joe Luce and said, "Your Honor, this selection process has been dragging out all week. Mr.

Murphy has dismissed several jurors who seemed to me to be perfectly acceptable. The only explanation I can think of is that he's trying to drag out these proceedings because he knows he has no case. I demand that he explain to this court why he finds this juror unacceptable. This woman had no preconceived notions about the case, no objections to legal penalties. I want to know why Mr. Murphy is being so obstructionist."

Luce turned to Murphy. "Well?"

Murphy stood up. "I'm perfectly willing to outline my objections to this juror, Your Honor, if the prosecution is willing to let me retain this preemption and accept my reasons as just cause for dismissal."

"Mr. Lake?" Joe Luce asked.

"Fine, fine," Lake snapped. "Let's hear it."

Murphy approached the prospective juror. "Hi," he said.

"Hi, yourself," the woman said to him suspiciously.

"Ma'am," Murphy asked. "Were you ever a juror before?"

"Yes."

"When was that?"

"Long time ago."

"About eight years ago, would you say?"

The woman thought for a moment and then nodded. "Yep. About that."

"Was it another murder case? Was it a case in which a man was accused of murdering his business partner?"

"That was it, yes."

Murphy turned to Joe Luce. "I was the detective charged with investigating that case, Your Honor. I thought the suspect was innocent, but the DA's office insisted on prosecuting. The defendant was convicted—unjustly, I thought at the time. I still do. I don't want this woman on my jury."

Fletcher Lake's jaw dropped. "You remember this woman after eight years?" he demanded. "You remember one face out of twelve in a jury box from a case eight years ago?"

Murphy smiled. "The last time I looked at the Gettysburg Address was when I was eleven years old. Want to hear it, Fletcher? 'Four-score and seven years ago, our forefathers brought forth on this continent a new nation, conceived in liberty and dedicated to the proposition that all men are created equal. Now, we are engaged in a great civil war, testing whether that nation—or any nation so conceived and dedicated—can long en—' "

"Let him have his challenge for cause, Your Honor," Fletcher Lake said sourly.

Murphy said, "Want to hear the words to 'Sugarfoot'? Remember that show, Fletcher? 'Sugarfoot, Sugarfoot . . . Easy-lopin', cattle-ropin' Sugarfoot. Carefree as a-uh summer breeze, just ridin' along with a heart full of song and a rifle and a volume of the law . . .' "

"Your Honor," Lake protested, "make him cut this out, please."

"'You'll find him, on the side of law and order, from the Mexicali border, to the rolling hills of Ar-kan-saw-aw-aw . . .' "

"That'll do, Mr. Murphy," Joe Luce said.

"I can do 'Cheyenne,' too, Your Honor," Murphy volunteered.

"The court will take counsel's word for it," the judge said.

CHAPTER 30

Spring in Philadelphia tends to be an iffy commodity.

The city sits at just above sea level. Even though the ocean is some distance away, Philadelphia's weather is largely a captive of sea conditions. Truly bitter cold is rare even in the dead of winter. But in May, heat usually associated with August can come rolling across the vast flood plain of South Jersey and settle over Center City like the wet breath of a tropical depression—heat that routinely turns urban pavement into a griddle you can feel through heavy shoes, heat that stifles the breath and surrounds you like the swirling vapor of a steam room.

The May morning Mike Webster's trial began was unseasonably warm. Thick clouds formed—clouds fatter and more pregnant with moisture than the thin, grayish lace curtain clouds of winter. When the sopping May clouds hid the sun, the dripping heat was merely unpleasant. When they moved aside, the heat became nearly unbearable. The sun blared down and bit into the concrete as though it had teeth—an angry, yellowish-white fireball driving through the great, rolling rafts of clouds on which it rode.

Mike Webster's face showed the heat as he entered the courtroom with a sheriff's deputy on his arm. Murphy thought it might be the heat, at least. There was always the possibility that the dark circles under Webster's eyes that contrasted so vividly with his unflavored-yogurt complexion were the product of guilty sleeplessness. Murphy hoped not. He really needed that extra four grand Webster would owe him if Murphy got him off.

Fletcher Lake and Toddman had taken their places at the prosecution's table to Murphy's right. Lake wore a crisp gray suit, and every hair on his head was in place. He looked very smooth, very sharp. Murphy figured that was a mistake on the district attorney's part.

The jury was a typical Philadelphia jury: largely older, blue collar and not terribly prosperous. Prosperous people generally managed to get excused from jury duty, and the fate of the accused often rested on the whims, prejudices, and misunderstandings of the retired, the unemployed, and the hopelessly confused. Both Murphy and Lake had used the bulk of their preemptions on the better-educated and more charismatic of the jury pool. Neither prosecutor nor defense attorney wanted a jury that contained a prospective leadership figure. The lawyers wanted to do the leading, and they knew their chances were better if they selected a jury of born followers.

Murphy figured he could never match Fletcher Lake when it came to style and smoothness. His plan was to appeal to the jury as one of them, albeit as subtlely as possible. He wore a shapeless blue blazer and baggy gray trousers. His tie was, by design, slightly askew. His shoes were dull and unshined. There would come a time to dress up, to look sharp, like the DA. But that would come at the end of the trial, when he made his summation. Murphy first wanted to make friends with the jury, and it was his guess that Fletcher Lake's eight-hundred-dollar suit would make him few friends with this crowd.

"How are you doing?" Murphy asked Webster as the defendant sat down at the defense table.

"Nervous," Webster said.

"Try not to show it," Murphy said to him, smiling. "You look too nervous, and the jury will figure you've got something to be nervous about. Try to look calm and innocent."

"How do you look innocent?"

"By not looking guilty."

Webster turned and looked around the courtroom behind him. The place was filled with the type of crowd attracted by a murder trial: elderly people with nothing better to do, housewives who found a live courtroom vastly more entertaining than the soaps on television, and persons with a direct interest in the proceedings. In this case, that meant key witnesses and friends and family members of the deceased and/or the accused. Webster spotted Brian and Beverly Kavanaugh sitting on opposite sides of the courtroom. He saw Judy sitting next to her mother and next to Patricia. Seated next to Patricia was a pretty woman who was clearly a companion but whom Webster didn't recognize.

"You bring your fan club?" he asked Murphy.

327

"Who? Patricia? She said she wanted to see opening statements."

"Who's the fox next to her? She looks too young to be her mother."

"Oh, that's my mother," Murphy told him.

The bailiff came out of Joe Luce's chambers and said, "All rise. Common Pleas Court of the Commonwealth of Pennsylvania, city and county of Philadelphia, is now in session. The honorable Joseph R. Luce presiding."

Joe Luce came through the open door, looking somewhat self-conscious at the announcement and looking lost in his flowing black robe. He was not a large man, and Murphy always had the impression when watching Luce in full robes that he looked like a kid playing in one of his old man's overcoats. Luce took his seat and gaveled the court into order. The assemblage sat back down.

"Is the prosecution ready to proceed?" he asked.

"Yes, Your Honor," Lake said, just a touch louder than necessary. It was, Murphy recognized, the DA's press conference voice, the one he used for the TV cameras. Murphy hoped the jury noticed and it pissed them off. It pissed Murphy off, certainly.

Joe Luce sat back in his chair until just his head showed above the bench. "Then go ahead with your opening statement, Mr. Lake," he said.

Fletcher Lake stood up, buttoned his jacket and approached the jury, which watched him with wide and attentive eyes. This was the man they were so used to seeing on television, and now they were seeing him in person. His every gesture and voice inflection would strike a familiar chord with them. He knew they knew him, and he smiled warmly at them, as if greeting old friends.

"Ladies and gentlemen," Lake said, "I won't take up any more of your time here than is absolutely necessary. The evidence in this trial will make the people's case far more eloquently than I could, and I know that you're interested in actually hearing and seeing the evidence, not in hearing some lawyer tell you what he thinks about it."

Murphy almost smiled at the statement because he knew that Lake would now proceed to do precisely that. He would tell the jury what he thought—or, rather, what he wanted them to think—and he would try to do it in a fashion designed to make them think it, too, even before they heard the evidence.

Lake said, "You'll hear testimony from skilled professionals in law enforcement—from the best people in their fields on earth—testimony that will prove to you conclusively that this man . . ." Lake pointed accusingly at Webster. "Took the life of a young woman. He murdered her purposefully and brutally, by driving a kitchen knife into her heart. You'll hear evidence that will convince you, as it has convinced me, that only one person had the opportunity to commit this crime, that only one person had the motive to commit this crime, that only one person did, in fact, commit this crime. And he sits before you at this moment."

Murphy never took his eyes from Lake, but he felt Webster shift nervously in the next chair. Lake paused for just a moment, just long enough for the jury's eyes to move to Webster's pallid face, back to the district attorney's tanned one. Then he went on.

"Now, will the people produce an eyewitness who saw Mike Webster snuff out the life of Lynn Rice? I'm afraid not. Murder seldom takes place at high noon in City Hall courtyard before a lunchtime crowd. This particular murder took place in the kitchen of a house in a remote location—the house of Mike Webster's employer and Lynn Rice's fiancé. Only one eyewitness was available at the time. That was Lynn Rice, and the people's role in this trial is to speak for her, to speak for the victim who's unable to make the accusation against her murderer in person.

"Will the people produce a confession from Mike Webster? No. Mr. Webster has steadfastly maintained his innocence. He's done this in the face of over-whelming evidence to the contrary. He's done so throughout his weeks of incarceration in Holmesburg Prison, surrounded by other criminals who proclaim their innocence at every opportunity. And why, you might ask, was he remanded to Holmesburg Prison in the first place?"

Murphy was on his feet in a heartbeat. "Objection, Your Honor."

Fletcher Lake smiled knowingly to the jury. Murphy knew what he was trying to do. The district attorney was trying, in his very first time at bat, to slide into the record evidence of Webster's criminal record. It was prejudicial information, and Murphy knew that Luce would immediately tell the jury to disregard it. He also knew that the jury would do no such thing, regardless of the judge's instructions.

"Sustained," Joe Luce said. "You understand the objection, I think, Mr. Lake. The jury will disregard."

Lake smiled at the jury and nodded absently toward

the judge. He placed his well-manicured hands on the rail of the jury box.

"The evidence in this case," he went on, "will not be absolute. Absent an eyewitness of unimpeachable credibility, the people's evidence will, of necessity, be circumstantial. You'll hear a great deal about that from defense counsel. That doesn't mean, however, that it isn't evidence enough. The learned judge will instruct you in some detail before you begin your deliberations that the people are not obligated to make their case beyond all shadow of doubt. The people are obligated to make their case only beyond a reasonable doubt. And that we will do. We will do it because the evidence is there and because its total weight is nothing less than damning." Lake paused for effect. Then he said, "We will prove this case beyond a reasonable doubt—and you good people will return a verdict of guilty as charged—because the evidence requires it and the ghost of Lynn Rice demands that the people do justice in her memory. Thank you."

Fletcher Lake strode across the faded wooden floor of the courtroom and took his seat, fighting back a smug smile. Joe Luce nodded to Murphy, who stood up and walked leisurely over to the jury box, his hands in his back pockets and his eyes on the floor, as if he were pondering some great thought. When he reached the box, Murphy looked up at the jury and nodded in greeting.

"Hi," he said. He jerked a thumb in Lake's direction. "Pretty good, isn't he? Better than on TV."

Murphy turned and walked away from the jury box, wondering what the jury's reaction to that opening might be and feeling somewhat relieved when he heard a slight chuckle from the far end of the jury box. At the sound, Murphy turned and walked back. He was beginning to pace. He did that out of habit and natural inclination and because he knew it would keep the jury's eyes riveted on him—unless he went on too long. He didn't plan to. Lake had wisely been brief, and Murphy planned to be even briefer. Juries, he knew from long experience on the other side, had notoriously short attention spans.

"You know, I'm sure, who Mr. Lake is," Murphy said. "That is, unless you watch 'Wheel of Fortune' instead of the news every night. But let me tell you who I am. I'm Frank Murphy, and I've been practicing law only a little while now. In fact, this is the first time I've ever been in court to defend in a murder case. Now, you must be looking at this gray hair and this middle-aged belly and you must be thinking, This guy must have flunked every course in law school at least twelve times if this is his first murder case at his age. Well, to tell you the truth, I did something else before I became a lawyer. I was a cop for nearly twenty-five years. I went out on the street and caught crooks. The courtroom is new to me, but murder isn't. I've seen more murder victims and more murderers than anybody else in this room. I know that murderers come in all shapes and sizes. They're all ages and colors and sexes. They commit murder for any number of reasons. Some of them feel sorry about it afterward; some of them don't. Believe me, I know murderers."

Murphy walked over and stood next to Webster. He looked at the jury. "I know, too, that this man isn't a murderer. I know it because I've spent time with him. I've talked to him. I've gotten some insight into his soul. I hope you'll have that opportunity, too, as this trial goes on. Yes, somebody murdered Lynn Rice. Somebody stabbed her to death with a kitchen knife. But it wasn't this man—regardless of what Mr. Lake would have you believe."

Murphy stepped away from the defense table and walked back to the jury box. He paced in front of it, along the length of it and back to the other end.

"You've heard Mr. Lake over there talk about 'the people.' The 'people' this, and the 'people' that. That's what he said. What he meant to say, though, is 'the state.' You know the difference between the state and the people, don't you? The state is where you go to get your license plates renewed. The state is where you go to try to get your income tax refund on time. The state is the outfit that's supposed to fill the potholes in the Delaware Expressway—you know, the ones that break the axles on your cars when you come off the Spring Garden off-ramp. The state is the agency responsible for seeing to it that the subway cars are clean and that the bus seats don't have springs sticking out of them. The state is who sees to it that your children and grandchildren can't get a decent education in this city. That's who Mr. Lake represents—the state.

"Now, let me let you in on a little secret. You probably know it already, but let me tell you anyway. The state tends to screw up a lot. The state is huge and unfeeling, and most of the time if it has the slightest bit of sense it manages to hide it wonderfully.

"It's the state that Mr. Lake represents, not the people. That's you, and you know the difference. It's the state that's wrongfully accused Mike Webster in this case. It's the state who can't find the real killer and

333

wants to hang it on this poor guy rather than admit it's made a mistake. All the enormous power of the state has been thrown into action in this instance for one purpose: to prove beyond a reasonable doubt that Mike Webster is the guy who murdered Lynn Rice. And the state can't do that because it simply isn't true. Mike Webster is innocent of this crime. The evidence you'll see and hear presented here will prove that to you."

Murphy rubbed his moustache, looking into the jury's faces. They were watching him with rapt attention. He leaned on the jury box rail.

"In the end, I have no doubt, it won't be the state that sets Mike Webster free. It'll be you, the people. That's what this court system is all about—the common sense and good judgment of ordinary people like you and me against the awesome power of the state. I've had the opportunity, during jury selection, to speak to each and every one of you. You seem like good and sensible people, otherwise you wouldn't be on this jury. I have confidence that you'll weigh the evidence and do the right thing—you'll find Mike Webster not guilty of this crime that somebody else committed. Thank you."

Breathing deeply and chewing his lower lip, Murphy walked back to the defense table to find Webster staring at him, wide-eyed. Murphy sat down and leaned over to him.

"How do you think it went?" he asked.

"You didn't talk much about the evidence," Webster said uneasily.

"When the law and the evidence aren't on your side," Murphy whispered to his client, "it never hurts to preach a little anarchy."

334

Before all this

It would not have been an exaggeration to say that Yasenchak was panting.

Which had been the whole idea.

"I'm not sure I want to," Alexandra lied.

Yasenchak took her delicate hand in his, which bore more than a passing resemblance to a Hormel ham. "Sure you do," he told her. "Come on."

"I don't know," Alexandra said.

"Ah, come on," Yasenchak said.

He was not unattractive—in an anthropoid sort of way. He was probably not yet thirty, even though he looked older. That was because of his neck, which had to be nineteen inches around. It made his head look like an afterthought—an option added to his immense body to give him a human appearance. His head was nice. His face was nice. It was smooth and pleasant to look at. It almost made you forget the body, which was not unlike a beer keg with legs.

"Look, honey," Yasenchak said, "I like you. I wouldn't have expected to find somebody like you in a joint like this. Who would have guessed, right? Of all the gin joints in all the—"

"I know that one," Alexandra said. "That's from *Casablanca*. That's what Bogart said to Lauren Bacall, right?"

"To Ingrid Bergman," Yasenchak said.

"Same difference."

"Do you want to go up to my room or not?" he said, cupping her hand and stroking it with what must have passed for gentleness with him. To Alex, it felt like sandpaper. She didn't let it show.

"I don't think so," she said, coyly.

"Come on."

"I don't know you," she said. "I don't like going to guys' rooms when I don't know them."

"You know me well enough," he said, "and I want to get to know you better. Lots better. I got some good grass upstairs."

"Tell you what," she said. "We can go to my place instead. How's that sound?"

He shook his head. "My place is just upstairs. What's the big deal?"

"My place," she insisted. "You can drive. We can come back and get my car in the morning."

Yasenchak pondered it. "I don't know."

"One more thing," Alex said. "I'm . . . well, I'm a little short. You know what I mean?"

Yasenchak sat back in his chair. In the background, a band was playing, and the singer who thought she was Carly Simon clearly wasn't. He drummed his thick fingers on the table and studied her for a moment with a long, appraising glance. Then he said, "Atlantic City. You got to love Atlantic City."

Alex shrugged. "Everybody's got to make a living."

He reached behind him and produced a wallet. He opened it for her. In the dim light, Alex caught a glimpse of big bills. He closed it and put it away.

"Well?" he said.

"Only at my place, though," she said. "They don't like us to go up to the rooms here, you know?"

"Okay," he said.

Alex smiled at him. "Whenever you're ready."

In the parking lot, next to his Seville, he put his hands on her. Alex melted to him, astounded at the thickness of the man. He ran one huge hand up her skirt in the darkness. She clutched at the folds of his knit sport coat as his stubby fingers dug at her.

"Good," Yasenchak grunted as he found her, pressed her button.

"Yes," Alex said, the word coming in a gasp despite herself.

She almost closed her eyes as he went at her, almost sagged into him. She hadn't expected this reaction on her part. She saw the shadowy figure move silently around the front of the Seville. Alex ground her crotch into Yasenchak's hand, but pulled her upper body to one side as she did.

"Do it," she said.

"I am, baby," Yasenchak told her.

Phil's shot was muffled by the silencer. It came out as no more than a *phhhhtt* and a golfball-sized burst of orange-white flame in the darkness. Alex felt Yasenchak's head snap forward over her shoulder. At the same moment, she felt the huge body give and fall toward her. She pushed at it, and at the same time she stepped back, ripping his dead hand from beneath her skirt. He landed on the blacktop at her feet with a dull thud. Except for his head, which cracked loudly against the pavement, face first. Phil was at her side in a heartbeat.

"You okay?" he hissed.

Alex nodded, looking down at Yasenchak.

Phil knelt next to the bulk on the ground. Alex heard another *phhhhtt,* saw another burst of light. Then she felt Phil's hand hard on her wrist.

"Come on," he told her.

The car was rented. It was a Chevy. The radio was playing as soon as Phil turned the ignition key. They roared out of the parking lot, tires screeching onto Atlantic Avenue.

"Good," Phil said to her. "Very good. Very, very good."

They went several blocks, the radio playing Whitney Houston and Alex silent and quivering in the passenger seat. Then she said, "Pull over, Phil."

"What?"

"You have to pull over."

Phil glanced at her out of the corner of his eye. "Get serious, Alex."

"Please," she said to him, clutching at his arm.

Phil pulled the car into the parking lot of a closed convenience store a half block down. "What?" he said, turning to her. "Are you all right?"

Alex grabbed at the keys, killed the ignition. At the same moment, she rolled over the console of the rented Chevy into his arms. Her tongue entered his ear. Her hands were on his trousers.

"What the fu—" Phil began.

"I want it," she whispered to him, crawling on him,

338

pressing his hands on her body. "Now. Here."

"Crazy," Phil muttered.

She put her hands on his belt, bent her head down. Phil Bonsignore looked both ways out the car windows. Nothing. Atlantic Avenue was dead. Then he looked down at her, at what she was doing to him.

"Turned you on, did it?" he asked.

Alex replied wordlessly.

CHAPTER 31

Lake's first witness was the uniformed police officer who had arrested Webster at the Center City gas station. The officer was young, still in his twenties, and looked like a shorter version of Michael Jordan. His testimony was succinct and routine. Murphy declined to cross-examine. He did this for two reasons: One, with seven blacks on the jury he was going to make it a point not to browbeat any black witnesses unless he deemed it absolutely necessary; two, there was nothing in the cop's testimony to shake.

Lake's second witness, though, was another matter. After the cop finished up, Lake called a technician from the police lab to testify that the fingerprints found on the knife embedded in Lynn Rice's chest matched those of Mike Webster. The technician was an old hand named Tom Nelson, a burly man in a suit he wore only to weddings, funerals, and court appearances. Murphy had known him for twenty years. When Murphy got his shot at Nelson, he put on his most pleasant face as he approached the witness stand.

341

"Hi, Tom," Murphy said, reminding the jury once again that he wasn't just a mouthpiece for scum but for a former police officer who was on the side of the angels, just like the prosecution.

"Hi," Nelson said.

"I suppose I ought to call you Mr. Nelson, considering where we are. How are you today?"

"Fine."

"Now," Murphy said, "you testified that the prints you found on the hilt of the murder weapon—that's people's exhibit A, over there—matched the prints taken from Mike Webster at the time of his arrest. Is that right?"

Nelson nodded. "That's correct."

"Good," Murphy said. "Now, could you explain to the jury just how a fingerprint is made?"

"Yes," Nelson said. "Each fingerprint contains ridges and valleys that make up a pattern unique to that individual. Each ridge contains tiny pores, and the skin breathes through these pores and releases sweat and oil in the process. This layer of sweat and oil is left behind when a finger touches something."

"So you can take a fingerprint from any object somebody touches?"

"No," Nelson said. "We can't really take prints from human skin because the oil and sweat from the pores in the finger mixes with the oil and sweat on the skin it touches."

"I see. Are you aware of any technique that would permit the taking of fingerprints from human skin?"

"Yes. There's been some experimentation in Europe on it. They put some kind of powder on the skin and they X-ray it, I think."

"You're not too familiar with that technique, I take it."

"No."

"So you didn't use that technique on the body of Lynn Rice, right?"

"No."

"You made no attempt to take fingerprints from the corpse?"

"No."

"Did you make any attempt to take fingerprints from the victim's clothing?"

"No. Prints from fabric is very difficult."

"But you've done it before?" Murphy asked.

"Yes. We've tried it, anyway. We've had mixed results."

"Why didn't you try it in this case?"

"Because we got clear prints from the hilt of the knife."

"So you didn't go any further? You got what you figured you needed and that was it?"

Nelson began to look slightly uncomfortable. "Well, like I said, we got the print from the hilt—"

"And you stopped looking, right?" Murphy asked. "You didn't go the extra step to see if there might be other prints on the victim's skin, on the victim's clothing or anywhere else. Isn't that right?"

"I object, Your Honor," Fletcher Lake called out. "The witness has already answered that question."

"Sustained," Joe Luce said. "Move along, counselor."

"Sorry, Your Honor," Murphy said. "Now, Mr. Nelson, will you explain to the jury the process involved in taking a fingerprint?"

343

"Sure," Nelson said. "There are several ways, actually, but the most common is for the fingerprint technician to dust the area suspected of containing a print with a powder. If it's a dark surface, he uses talcum powder. If it's a light surface, he uses black graphite."

"What did you use on the knife hilt?"

"It was a black plastic, so I used a talcum."

"All right. Go ahead."

"Well, then you brush the powder over the print and you can see it. So then you take a grease pencil and you draw a circle around the print, and you make a note of the date and any classification marks. Then you put your initials next to it."

"Then what?" Murphy asked.

"Then you photograph the print."

"And then?"

"After that, you put a piece of transparent tape over the print and you flatten it out. After that, you peel off the tape and transfer the print to a fingerprint card."

"And the print you transfer to the card is what you use to compare to the prints taken from the suspect at the time of arrest, right?"

"Right. That's the most common method. Sometimes you use other techniques. For example, if you've got a print on a piece of absorbent material—paper, for example—you can use this chemical—"

"But you didn't do that in this case?"

"No, I just dusted."

"Let me ask you this," Murphy said. "If you'd used the chemical technique, is it possible that you might have picked up other prints on the knife hilt?"

"I don't know. Probably not."

"On what do you base that 'probably not'?"

"On twenty-two years of experience."

"So," Murphy said, "basically, that's a guess, right?"

"Objection," Lake called out.

"What is your objection, Mr. Lake?" Joe Luce asked.

"Mr. Murphy's characterization of Mr. Nelson's professional opinion as nothing more than a guess, Your Honor. Those are his words, not the witness's."

"It is a guess," Murphy responded.

"An educated one," Nelson interjected, like a fool.

"So it is a guess?" Murphy asked, pouncing like a cat after a mouse.

"Objection!" Lake called out.

"Sustained. Just answer the questions, Mr. Nelson," Joe Luce instructed. "Try to refrain from volunteering any side comments during debate by counsel."

"Yes, sir."

"Did you pick up any other marks on the knife hilt?" Murphy asked.

"No."

"None? No smudges or smears? Everything else was clean?"

"Well," Nelson said, "you always get smudges or smears as background to the print."

"Always?"

"Well, sometimes. Not always."

"But in this case you did?"

"Yeah. I got some background smears."

"And what did that signify to you, Mr. Nelson?"

Nelson shrugged. "Not a thing."

Murphy turned his back on the witness and faced the jury. "So those smears didn't indicate to you in any way, for example, that the knife hilt could have been wielded by another person and then wiped clean before my client touched it? Is that right?"

"Objection!"

"Overruled," Joe Luce said. "Go ahead, Mr. Murphy."

"Well?" Murphy said.

"Not necessarily," Nelson said.

"Ah," Murphy exclaimed, as if discovering some long-lost truth, "so it is possible that a person wiping prints off a knife hilt such as the one you examined—a person wiping off the oil and sweat you described—could leave smears such as those you picked up in dusting for Mike Webster's prints."

"Unlikely," Nelson said.

"Unlikely or impossible?" Murphy demanded.

Nelson paused. "Well, no. Not impossible. But goddamn unlikely."

"But not impossible?"

"Objection!" Lake said. "The witness has already answered the question."

"Sustained," Joe Luce said.

"Sorry, Your Honor," Murphy said. "Now, Mr. Nelson, did you subject the hilt of the knife in question to any other tests? Did you go over it with a scanning electron microscope, for example?"

"No."

"No? So, let me make sure I've got this straight. You dusted the hilt for prints, but you made no effort to obtain prints from the victim's body or clothing?"

"Right."

"And you didn't use chemical reagents like ninhydrin to test for latent prints on the knife hilt?"

"No."

"And you didn't associate the smears on the knife hilt with an attempt on anybody's part to wipe prints off the weapon before my client touched it?"

"No."

"And you didn't subject the hilt to microscopic examination?"

"None of that was called for," Nelson said with irritation. "The prints we got were—"

"Do you know who Sir Edward Henry was?" Murphy demanded.

Nelson looked at him in puzzlement. "Who?"

"Sir Edward Henry."

"Sorry. Never heard of him."

Murphy looked at Nelson in visible reproof. "Well, you certainly should have, I think. One more thing: Didn't it strike you strange that a kitchen knife—a knife presumably used every day by Lynn Rice and others—should contain only smudges beneath a clear set of my client's prints? Especially when you consider that my client would never touch that knife under normal circumstances while the victim and other people presumably would handle it daily? Didn't that strike you as even a little strange?"

"Objection!" Lake called out. "Calls for a conclusion on the part of the witness."

"Sustained."

Murphy felt warm and giddy inside. He'd done what he'd wanted to do.

"No further questions, Your Honor," he said, stifling a chuckle at Fletcher Lake's knitted brow.

* * *

347

Mike Webster ate lunch alone and scared in a holding cell just off the courtroom. Murphy ate in the cafeteria at Wanamaker's Department Store, across the street from City Hall, with Patricia and Alex. Patricia, back home for the summer after finishing her freshman final exams, had met Alex that morning before court and sat with her throughout the proceedings. Alex had been pleasant but reserved, a manner that had carried over to lunch. Murphy was pleased to note, however, that his daughter seemed flushed with excitement at seeing him perform in the courtroom.

"You were good," Patricia told him. "It came as a shock to me, if you want the truth, but you were really good."

Murphy tried to look bashful over his coffee and failed miserably. "I was, wasn't I? Did you understand any of that, by the way?"

"No," Patricia admitted. "I didn't get much of that stuff with the fingerprints, but you had that guy all confused."

"How about you?" Murphy asked Alex.

"I understood most of it, I think."

"Well," he said, "I don't think the jury did. But all I was trying to do was to set up testimony from witnesses to come and to leave in the jury's mind the possibility that the police lab could have done more than it did."

"Could they?" Alex asked.

Murphy nodded. "They could have. But there was no reason they should have. They got prints in their first crack at the murder weapon, and there's no reason to go further once you've done that. Bear in mind, too, that their job is to obtain evidence for the prosecution, not the defense. Once they get something the prosecution can use, why should they go further?"

"To find the truth?" Patricia suggested.

Murphy laughed. "There is no truth in a police investigation, sweetheart. There are only facts. It's up to the jury to fashion its own version of truth from the facts each side presents and the opinions expressed by the lawyers on each side."

Alex smiled slightly over her chicken salad plate. "You seem to have a fairly cynical view of the process, Frank."

"No," Murphy told her. "It's not a bad process. It's a lot better than determining guilt or innocence by having each side hire a knight to battle it out in a trial by arms. It's better than tying the defendant to a chair and submerging him in water to see if his version is correct."

"Who did that?" Patricia asked.

"The Puritans. They'd take a defendant and hold him under water for a few minutes. If he survived, it meant that Satan was protecting him. So they'd very quickly find him guilty of whatever he was charged with and burn him at the stake. If he drowned, it meant that he'd had no supernatural protection, so he was found innocent—although, unfortunately, dead. An interesting criminal justice system. I'm sure all the defense lawyers back then tried like hell to get their fees up front."

Alex smiled. "I have a question, Frank. It hasn't come up in the trial, but I'm curious. Does your client have any kind of alibi for the night of the murder?"

Murphy frowned. "Nothing that's much good. He went to a movie, but nobody who works at the theater remembers him from his photograph. He also bought some clothing at a store a long way away from the farm. I've got a register receipt with a date on it, but the date is all I have. The people at the store have no way to determine what time he made the purchase. The register isn't set for that. And none of the four clerks who manned the register that day could remember him from his picture, either. In theory, he could have bought the stuff at the store and headed right back to the farm and killed Lynn. I don't plan to get into any of that if I can avoid it."

Alex nodded. "Doesn't sound good. I hope you can avoid it."

"Me, too," Murphy said.

After lunch, Lake called Weinberg as a prosecution witness. The DA asked the old man to recite his credentials, which took about five minutes. Weinberg went through his education—Penn undergraduate followed by Penn Medical School—and listed all the special training he'd received in forensic pathology. He mentioned his board certification; the fact that he'd held down his current post for more than thirty years; the fact that he'd performed roughly ten thousand autopsies during that period. Under questioning, Lake managed to bring out Weinberg's reputation as one of—if not the—finest forensic pathologists in the world. Murphy sat back quietly during this procedure. Lake was doing his work for him. When Murphy called Weinberg for the defense later in the trial, the old man's reputation and credibility would already have been established by the prosecution.

Under Lake's questioning, Weinberg gave his testimony concerning time of death and detailed how Lynn

Rice had died.

"The murder weapon entered her chest just below the sternum," he said, "and punctured the thoracic portion of the great aorta with a wound roughly fourteen centimeters in length."

"Did she die immediately?" Lake asked.

"For all practical purposes, yes," Weinberg said. "A wound that size would have resulted in an immediate hemorrhage into the thoracic cavity. It would also have resulted in an immediate and sudden drop in blood pressure. She would have lost consciousness the moment the blood escaped the aorta, and then her heart—in all likelihood—would have gone into ventricular fibrillation from the sudden reduction in blood pressure."

"Would you explain to the jury what ventricular fibrillation is, doctor?"

"It's an erratic and wild beating of the heart. It's a disruption of the heart's electrical patterns. The heart loses its rhythm and pumps in an undisciplined fashion. It moves little or no blood during this process. That means that the victim died of a cutoff of blood to the brain. That process technically takes up to ten minutes, depending on the patient, although irreparable brain damage sets in within just a few minutes in most patients. This woman lost consciousness within seconds of the sudden drop in blood pressure brought on by the puncture of the aorta. Her heart may have gone on pumping erratically for several minutes, but in practical terms she was dead the moment the knife blade entered her body."

"Thank you, doctor," Lake said, and sat down.

Murphy got up to cross-examine. He did not approach Weinberg. Instead, Murphy decided to pace back and forth in front of the jury box as he asked his questions.

"Dr. Weinberg," he said, "would it have required a great deal of strength on the part of an attacker to inflict the sort of wound you observed during your examination of Lynn Rice's corpse?"

"No," Weinberg said. "The weapon was sharp, and it would have had no difficulty in penetrating the thoracic muscle sheath. After that, it would have gone through the peritoneum unimpeded and met its greatest resistance in the aorta itself. It only penetrated the aorta by a depth of nine centimeters or so, so there's no indication that it was wielded with any particular force."

"I see," Murphy said. "Tell me, could you determine from your examination if the weapon had been wielded by someone tall or short?"

"No. Sometimes you can make such determinations, but it's impossible to determine the angle at which Miss Rice was standing when she received the fatal blow. She could have been bent over slightly in a forward direction. She could have been leaning backward. That's the problem when a body is moved, as it was in this case. Absent other evidence, you can only speculate as to the position of the victim at the time of death."

"I see. No further questions, Your Honor, but I would like to retain the right to call this witness at a later time in this proceeding."

"Very well," Joe Luce said.

Lake's next witness was Brian Kavanaugh. Kavanaugh looked drawn and weary, and Murphy thought the man seemed a little nervous, which was hardly surprising. Lake handled him carefully. The

DA's goal here, Murphy knew, was to make Kavanaugh seem the desolate lover of the dead woman and, at the same time, elicit testimony from him that would inflict damage on Mike Webster. For his part, Webster had seemed to pay little attention to the expert testimony of the fingerprint technician and the pathologist—Murphy suspected that Webster lacked the smarts to follow much of it—but he was held in rapt attention by what his former boss had to say.

Kavanaugh detailed the history of his association with Webster. It was reasonably tame stuff after Weinberg's grimly clinical description of Lynn Rice's death, and Murphy noted that neither the judge nor the jury seemed terribly alert through it. That was fine with Murphy. He would just as soon have seen the judge and jury doze off completely during the testimony of all the prosecution witnesses. Kavanaugh's version of how Webster came to work on his farm coincided perfectly with what Webster had told Murphy. He also talked about how he had come to be engaged to Lynn Rice.

"I met her through the real estate firm I bought the farm through," he said. "I was separated, and she was new in town and very attractive, so I asked her out. We just had a terrific time from the start. It got serious fairly fast. We . . . we just clicked, right from the start."

"What was your impression of how she got along with Mike Webster?" Lake asked.

"Objection," Murphy said. "Form."

"Sustained," Joe Luce said. "Please rephrase, Mr. Lake."

Lake nodded, understanding the objection. As asked, the question had called for a conclusion—an impression—on Brian Kavanaugh's part. It wasn't a big point, but to Murphy it showed how sloppy the DA was as an attorney. Lake was a whiz in speeches—in opening and closing statements—but he was a schlep when it came to examining witnesses.

"Did Miss Rice ever indicate to you in any way that she was afraid of Mike Webster?"

"Well, not afraid," Kavanaugh said. "I know she didn't like him much. She suggested to me on several occasions that I ought to let Mike go and get somebody else to handle the farm."

"On what ground did she make this suggestion?"

"She said he seemed hostile."

"Hostile?" Lake asked.

Kavanaugh nodded. "She wasn't all that clear about it. She just didn't like him. It seemed to me to just be personal chemistry."

When Murphy's turn came, he asked, "Did you ever see any overt signs of hostility on the part of Mike Webster toward Lynn Rice?"

"Well, no."

"So that's why you didn't let him go when your fiancée suggested that you do so?"

"No," Kavanaugh said, "not completely. My daughter, Judy, was very fond of Mike. And Mike seemed to me to be a solid guy. On balance, I wasn't prepared to let him go at that point."

"How did Lynn—Miss Rice—respond to that?"

"She wasn't pleased."

"How did she express that?"

"She got quite angry."

"Is that how she tended to respond when she didn't get what she wanted?"

"I don't think that would be fair to say," Kavanaugh said. "Sometimes she could get a little testy. Nothing out of the ordinary, I wouldn't say."

"Thank you," Murphy said.

Joe Luce looked over at Fletcher Lake. "Any redirect?" he asked.

Lake came out of his chair as though propelled by a spring, saying, "Mr. Kavanaugh, you say that Mike Webster always struck you as a solid guy, isn't that right?"

"More or less, yes."

"When you hired him, when you decided to keep him on after taking possession of the farm, did you make any check of Mike Webster's background?"

Murphy felt the hair on the back of his neck start to tingle. He looked up at Joe Luce, who seemed distracted. It was after lunch, and the courtroom was warm.

"No," Kavanaugh said. "The previous owner had seemed well satisfied with him."

Fletcher Lake stalked toward the jury box and fixed the jurors with a steely gaze as he asked his next question. The question came out in strong tones, as though Lake were at a political rally addressing a large crowd.

"So you weren't aware, then," he said, "that Mike Webster wasn't Mike Webster at all—"

"Objection!" Murphy called out.

Lake never faltered. "That his real name was Michael Caldwell—"

"Objection, Your Honor!" Murphy shouted heatedly.

"Mr. Lake . . ." Joe Luce began, coming awake now up on the bench.

"And that he had served a prison term in Califo—"

"Objection, for Christ's sake!" Murphy bellowed.

"Sustained!" Joe Luce shouted, his face red. He

355

glared at Fletcher Lake, who was just turning around from facing a startled jury. "Mr. Lake, I'm calling a recess in this proceeding. I want to see both the prosecution and the defense in my chambers immediately."

Joe Luce slammed his gavel and stormed off the bench.

"What the hell is going on?" Webster asked.

Murphy, still fuming, said, "You just sit here and try to look like a choirboy."

He followed Lake and Toddman through the door beside the bench into Joe Luce's spacious chambers, lined with legal volumes and furnished in deep, dark leather. The judge was behind his desk, pulling off his robes to reveal the small man beneath them. Murphy thought he'd never seen mild-mannered Joe Luce so livid.

"Just what the hell are you doing out there, Fletcher?" he demanded. "You know that stuff is prejudicial."

"I'm sorry, Your Honor," Lake said, clearly not sorry at all. "But I'm going to introduce testimony later that has bearing—"

"Nobody gives a shit what you're going to introduce later," Murphy snarled. "You can't bring up his record unless I do."

"But you won't, will you?" Lake said.

"Fucking-A right I won't," Murphy shot back. "You might be the fastest zipper in City Hall, Fletcher, but if you think you—"

"Cut it out," Joe Luce snapped. Murphy shut up instantly. Luce glared at both lawyers.

"Now," he said, "here's what we're going to do: Fletcher, I'm going to go back into that courtroom and instruct the jury to disregard anything they heard concerning the defendant's old name and, especially, his prior record. They won't do that, of course, and we all know that, so the damage is done. What you've managed to accomplish here is to give Frank possible grounds for a mistrial. Now, if you pull anything like that again, I promise you two things. One, I'll declare a mistrial on the spot. Two, I'll slap you with a contempt of court citation so fast you won't have time to blink. Do you understand?"

"Yes, Your Honor," Lake said. "I apologize."

Luce glared at the district attorney for a moment and then turned to Toddman. "You keep this guy in line, Paul. If he wants to try the case himself, fine. But I won't tolerate that kind of thing in my courtroom. I just won't have it."

"I understand, Your Honor," Toddman said. His face was an even grimmer mass of deep, frowning, fleshy folds than usual. These were not Toddman's tactics. He'd never needed them.

Luce turned to Murphy. "Frank, you had ample reason to be upset. But don't scream 'for Christ's sake' at me again in my own courtroom."

Murphy nodded and smiled sheepishly. "Sorry, Joe."

Luce shook his head wearily. "And call me 'Your Honor,' please? I kissed a lot of ass to get this job."

"Sorry, Your Honor."

Joe Luce leaned back in his high-backed leather chair, took off his horn-rimmed glasses and rubbed his eyes with his fists.

"Fucking amateur night," the judge grumbled in a low voice.

CHAPTER 32

When Murphy returned to the courtroom, he found Mike Webster tapping his foot nervously, a worried expression settled deep on his face.

"You look like your dog died," Murphy told him, settling into his chair.

"What was that all about?"

"Just the DA playing games and the judge taking a nap. Unfortunately, they both happened at the same time. You just keep cool. They don't have much more left, and once they're finished I've got some expert witnesses lined up who ought to pretty much ice this thing. Actually, it's not going all that badly."

Webster seemed unconvinced. "Will they call me to testify?"

Murphy shook his head. "No. You can't be compelled to testify against yourself. They can't get a crack at you unless I put you on the stand first, and I don't think I'm going to have to—not the way things are going. Their whole case seems to revolve around the fact that they found Lynn in the trunk of the car you were driving and your fingerprints on the knife hilt. We can explain the first one—all I have to do is call Brian to explain the circumstances that put you behind the wheel of that car at that particular moment. As for the prints, we've already raised doubts about whether the knife hilt was wiped off by somebody else before you touched it when you found Lynn's corpse in the trunk, and my expert witnesses will strengthen that doubt. I think we'll be fine. Just remember, when this is over you still owe me four grand."

Despite his predicament, Webster smiled at the remark. "You never forget the bucks, do you?"

"Hey," Murphy said to his client, "is this America or what?"

Joe Luce emerged from his chambers a few moments later and called the court to order. He gave a three-minute lecture to the jury about their obligation to ignore anything they had heard after Murphy had voiced his first objection. The jury listened carefully to the instruction and, Murphy knew, paid no attention whatever to it.

"Any other witnesses, Mr. Lake?" Joe Luce said finally.

Lake rose. "The people call Bonnie McEwen."

Murphy turned and looked over his shoulder. Who the hell was this? Bonnie McEwen stood up from a spectators' bench about halfway back to the door and moved to the witness stand. She was a tiny woman in her mid-thirties with sun-bleached hair and a deep tan. Murphy had no idea what her connection with the case might be, and his eyes narrowed as he watched her sworn in. He hated this. He hated not knowing all the answers to all the questions in any courtroom situation. He focused all his attention on Bonnie McEwen as Lake began his examination.

"Where do you live, Mrs. McEwen?" Lake asked.

"Fresno, California."

"How long have you lived there?"

"All my life."

"Which is how long?" Lake asked, smiling slightly. "Forgive me, please."

Bonnie McEwen clearly was not pleased with having to answer that one. "Thirty-six years," she said stiffly.

"McEwen is your married name, is that right?"

"Yes."

"And what was your maiden name?"

"Rice," the woman said. "I was Bonnie Rice."

"And were you related to the victim in this case?"

"Yes. Lynn was my sister."

"I see," Fletcher Lake said. "Were you close with your sister?"

Bonnie Rice shook her head. "No, not in recent years. Lynn and I drifted apart after we each were married. She wasn't too fond of my husband, and I was not happy at all with hers. I hadn't seen her for several years until I got word of her death. That came from your office, Mr. Lake."

Lake coughed slightly. "Yes. So your sister was married, then?"

"Yes."

"And you didn't like her husband?"

"No."

"Why not, Mrs. McEwen?"

"Her husband was pretty much worthless, in my view. I had no use for him at all, not from the start. But Lynn was crazy about him—in the beginning, anyway.

360

We just didn't see eye-to-eye on that topic."

"I see," Lake said. "How long had your sister been divorced at the time of her death?"

"She never did get divorced."

"She was still married at the time of her murder?" Lake asked in mock surprise. Murphy didn't like the phony surprise, and he didn't like not knowing about this witness. How the hell had Lake run this woman down? Murphy wondered. And what did she have to do with anything. He chewed on his moustache.

"As far as I know she was," Bonnie Rice said. "If she ever got divorced, she didn't tell me about it."

"I see," Lake said, uttering the phrase again and really getting on Murphy's nerves with it. Murphy didn't care what Fletcher Lake saw. He didn't give a shit about it. Murphy was sweating. He cast a glance at Webster and felt his stomach drop down somewhere around his knees as he studied his client. Webster had looked bad before. Now he looked like his dog had died and taken along Webster's cat in a suicide pact. His face was drained of color, and Murphy thought for a moment that Webster was seriously ill.

"You all right?" he asked in alarm.

Webster merely nodded, his eyes fixed on Lynn Rice's sister.

"Tell me, Mrs. McEwen," Fletcher Lake said, "what kind of man—in your view—was your sister's husband?"

"He was a loser," Bonnie McEwen said. "He had no education. He worked with his hands, and what he did was unskilled labor. He boozed a lot. The guy had nothing going for him—not a thing. Lynn could have done better. She could have done a lot better. I told her

361

that, and she got mad as hell at me, but it was true. Plus, he was a drunk. She'd sold herself cheap, was the way I saw it. She did, too—after a while, that is."

"I see," Lake said, prompting Murphy's blood pressure to soar. "What happened to this husband of your sister's?"

Bonnie McEwen seemed almost triumphant as she said it. "He went to prison. He got drunk and killed a guy he caught with Lynn and they slapped him into Vacaville on manslaughter charges."

Oh, Jesus H. Christ on roller skates, Murphy thought. He turned back to Webster, who was near tears next to him. He thought about objecting, but then dismissed the idea. There was no way to get out of this. It was set in stone already. The jurors were on the edge of their chairs.

"And," Fletcher Lake boomed, "is that man—the man who married your sister and who later went to prison for killing another man he caught with her—in this courtroom?"

Bonnie McEwen said, "Yes."

"Would you be kind enough to point him out to the jury?" Fletcher Lake virtually shouted.

Bonnie Rice's finger rose and pointed directly at Mike Webster. "That man there," she said.

Whatever color Webster had left vanished abruptly. His face turned the color of soured buttermilk. He barely looked alive. Wearily, and with great effort, Murphy stood up at the defense table.

"Your Honor," he said weakly, "the defense requests a brief recess."

*　　　*　　　*

"You shithead!" Murphy raged. "You incredible asshole! What in Christ's name was going through your tiny mind?"

Webster, seated in a small chair at a small table in a small room off the courtroom, looked up helplessly. The man was near tears.

"I'm sorry," he said earnestly. "I'm sorry, Frank."

Murphy, his blood pressure somewhere up in the stratosphere, leaned over him, his big hands flat on the table in front of Webster. "Sorry? You're fucking sorry? I'm the one who's sorry. I'm sorry I ever took this goddamn case. I'm sorry I ever laid eyes on you. I'm sorry that when they first busted you they didn't let you escape and shoot you right between the shoulder blades, like we used to do in the old days. You're sorry? Jesus H. Christ!"

Murphy turned away, shaking his head and struggling mightily to calm down.

Webster said, "I didn't think anybody would find out. I thought it would be okay."

Murphy whirled on him. "Nobody would find out? You know what? Your intellect could find shelter in the shade of a fucking snow pea. They have homes for people like you, Mike. All the walls have big rubber pads, and they show 'Mr. Rogers' on TV all the time. How can a brain so small generate enough power to move those lips? That's what I want to know. Nobody would find out?" Murphy looked heavenward. "Give me a break," he pleaded. "What did I do to deserve this?" Then he turned back to Webster. "Shithead," he muttered.

Webster buried his face in his hands. In the grim silence that followed, Murphy paced the room furiously, struggling to calm down. This happened to him once in a while. It happened less often as he grew older, but it happened nonetheless. Murphy's rages were slow in coming, but they were ferocious when they arrived, and they were even slower to depart. He knew he'd be hours—days, maybe—before he got over this one. This one was truly a hummer. Murphy breathed deeply. He lit a Camel and sucked in the smoke. As the nicotine blasted into his circulatory system, Murphy silently dared his heart to attack him. He'd rip it out of his chest and stomp on it. They'd both go together. After a few moments of sucking on the cigarette, he had contained himself to the point where he decided to try conversation again. He sat down across the table from Webster and glared at him.

"Now, look," Murphy said, "let's get this straight once and for all. You lie to me just one more time—you forget to tell me just one more thing—and I quit this case. I'm out of it; you get it? I can put up with a lot. I can put up with a client who's guilty—"

"I'm not!" Webster said in sudden panic.

"Shut the fuck up," Murphy told him coldly. "I can put up with a guy who's guilty. I can put up with a guy who's probably going to be guilty at some point in the future if I manage to get him off this time. I can put up with dumb clients. I can put up with clients who are slow pay. But I can't put up with a guy who lies to me. I can't defend a guy who sends me out there to look like a total jerk. Now you tell me the story—the real story. And you'd better make it good. I still might take a hike. I haven't made up my mind yet."

Webster nodded, his head bobbing up and down repeatedly. "All right. I'm sorry. I was dumb—a shithead, just like you said. Just don't walk out on me now, Frank, please. If you ditch me, I've got—"

"Let's hear it," Murphy snapped.

"Okay, okay. Lynn was my wife. At first, it was okay. But then she started screwing around, and I started hitting the sauce. Or maybe it was the other way around. Maybe I started drinking too much first. I don't know. Anyway, it was like I told you. I caught her with this guy, and that thing happened, and after I got out I just split, came back East here. It was all like I told you—except for Lynn."

"How'd she find you?"

"I wrote her once for some money. I didn't figure I'd get it, but I needed it bad, and it was worth a shot. I didn't think she'd tell anybody about me jumping parole. She wasn't the kind to go running to the cops. The next thing I knew, she was at the farm. I almost fell over. I asked her what she wanted."

"And?"

"She didn't know what she wanted. She just decided to find me."

"That doesn't make any sense," Murphy told him.

"I know. But that's the way she was. She'd always done crazy things for no reason. You want the truth, I think she liked me better after I did time. I think it turned her on. I'm telling you, she was nuts in a lot of ways. So's Bonnie, by the way, but that's another story."

"How's Bonnie nuts?"

"Oh," Webster said, "she was into that EST crap back in the seventies. She was into Jesus for a while. Bonnie had always been a little wacky. So was Lynn, but it was different. It's hard to explain. Lynn . . . she was wild. She liked to take chances all the time. Anyway, I think the thing that made her come cross-country to be with me even though I didn't want her anymore was that I was a fugitive. Does that make any sense to you?"

Murphy shrugged. "I don't pretend to understand why women do a lot of things. Go ahead."

Webster said, "So I told her I wanted her to get lost, but she wouldn't do it. She got this apartment in Phoenixville. Then she bought that fancy car—"

"Where'd she get the money for all that?"

"She sold our house in Fresno. She got enough out of that to set herself up pretty nice. She finally ended up getting a job in that real estate office. Then one day Brian came in and ended up buying the farm and he hit on Lynn and Lynn hit back. I think she did it at first just to get at me. You know, coming out to the farm and hanging all over Brian with me watching, treating me like hired help in front of him and Judy, and knowing I couldn't do or say anything about it."

"How'd you feel about that?" Murphy asked him.

"It pissed me off. How would you feel about it? But that wasn't the worst part. The worst part was when she decided to get Brian to marry her. I told her that she was nuts, that she couldn't marry the guy. She already had a husband, for Christ's sake—me. But she liked the idea of all those bucks Brian has. There was nothing I could do about it. But then when Judy got so worked up about Brian getting married, I tried to get her to give it up. The whole thing was crazy. But Lynn was crazy. You get what I mean? She'd do anything if she decided she wanted to do it, and she didn't give a shit about anybody else. It was just what she wanted, and nothing else counted."

"So you killed her," Murphy said.

"No," Webster shouted, breaking into genuine tears this time. "I didn't do it, Frank. It happened just like I told you."

"Why didn't you tell me about Lynn to begin with?"

"I was afraid to, for one thing. I figured that if I told you or the cops then you'd know who I was and the best that would happen was that I'd get shipped back to California to go back to Vacaville. Besides, if I told this story in the beginning everybody would have figured I'd really killed her."

"What do you think that jury believes right now, Mike? The fact that they found out that she was married to you through testimony like that is going to be just about impossible to overcome. What Lake did was provide support for what had been the weakest part of his case—motive. Before Bonnie testified, Lake didn't have any motive. Now he has a zinger. He even managed to get in your previous conviction."

"Can't you cross-examine her and show the jury what a jerk she is?" Webster asked.

"It doesn't matter if she's a jerk. What she testified to was the truth. I can shake the testimony of an expert witness who hasn't done his homework. I can get the full truth out of a witness when the DA has him testify to only part of it. I can show the jury that a liar is a liar. But what am I going to do with a witness who plunks her ass in the chair and kills my whole case with the truth? I'm not even going to cross-examine her. God alone knows what other damage she might do if she gets the chance. No, I'm just going to have to go with what I've got coming up later and hope it's enough.

And it might not be, Mike. We might just lose this one. It's time you faced up to that."

Webster's lower lip trembled. Murphy could actually see the thrill of terror shoot through the man. He saw the big blood vessel on the side of Webster's neck begin to twitch. "I didn't do it," he whispered hoarsely.

Murphy stood up. "No, I don't think you did. If you go to the slammer for this, it won't be because you're guilty. It'll just be because you're stupid. And you know what? That's how a lot of guys get there."

Before all this

The first sign of Phil's problem was a weakness in the right hand.

"What the hell is this?" Phil said at breakfast one morning.

Alex, making a western omelet as he had taught her to make one—expertly—looked over her shoulder casually and said, "What?"

"I can't get a decent grip on this glass of orange juice. I can't hold it. I'm trying, but I can't pick it up."

"What do you mean you can't pick it up?"

He didn't answer. He just stared at his hand, which was wrapped around the five-ounce glass of orange juice like a wilted leaf of iceberg lettuce. He tried again to lift the glass, but his fingers slid up and over the brim. Phil's expression was one of mixed curiosity and panic.

"I just can't pick it up," he told her. "I can't get my hand to close on it tight enough."

Alex turned down the heat and went over to the kitchen table. Phil's hand was like a dead fish, limp and lifeless. She held it in her own hands and inspected it.

"Make a fist," she told him.

He did—weakly. His fingertips barely touched his palm.

"This is weird shit," Phil Bonsignore said quietly.

"How long has this been going on?" Alex asked him.

"Just happened."

"Does it hurt?"

He shook his head. "No. Everything feels fine. But I can't squeeze my hand shut. I must have pinched a nerve or something in my sleep."

"Then it should hurt."

"Well, it doesn't," Phil said quietly. "It just won't work, is all."

"Want to see a doctor?" Alex asked him.

"If it doesn't get better pretty soon," he said.

It didn't.

CHAPTER 33

The rest of the afternoon passed in predictable fashion.

Fletcher Lake spent more than an hour examining Bonnie Rice McEwen. Some of his questions were leading and downright amateurish, but Murphy deemed it the wiser course of action to let Lake finish with this witness without interruption and get her the hell off the stand. When the time came for him to cross-examine, he declined in a quiet voice, and Joe Luce decided to call it a day. The sheriff's deputies took Webster away for another night of city hospitality in Holmesburg Prison as Murphy stuffed his papers into his briefcase under the smirking gaze of Fletcher Lake. Before he left the courtroom, the DA stopped by the defense table.

"Not much like law school, is it, Frank?" he asked.

"Not all that different," Murphy told him. "We had assholes in law school, too, Fletcher. They all seemed to have their cheeks polished and their teeth simonized, just like you."

Lake's smirk faltered for just a moment. Then he laughed, a sign that Murphy's insults weren't worthy of his annoyance. Murphy knew this was a facade. Murphy had been born with a talent—a sometimes troublesome talent—for irritating other people, even when he didn't mean to. But he irritated no other person on earth the way he irritated Fletcher Lake. Except Mary Ellen, he supposed. But the district attorney came in a close second behind Murphy's estranged wife, and with Lake Murphy was really trying. The district attorney left without another word. Toddman nodded in Murphy's direction and followed his boss.

Had the day gone well—as Murphy had expected it to go when he'd entered court after lunch—he'd have taken Alex and Patricia out to dinner. Murphy had seen too little of Patricia the past few years. First she'd hit puberty and discovered a disturbingly full life of her own outside the family circle. From the time she'd turned fourteen she'd been little more in Murphy's life than a blur of fancy sportswear, a peck on the cheek and a cloud of perfume. Then he'd moved out on Mary Ellen—been thrown out, actually—and then Patricia had gone off to Skidmore, five hours away by car. Ordinarily, he'd have been delighted at the opportunity to take out his daughter and this pretty woman who had entered his life so recently, but not tonight. Murphy's mood was vile, and Patricia sensed it. She took the bus home, and Murphy moped, brooded and drank bourbon in sullen silence while Alex prepared a feast of tortellini alfredo, one of Murphy's favorites, in his sloppy apartment.

"Frank," Alex asked from the kitchen, "do you have any wine in this place? There's nothing in the refrigerator."

"Faggot drink," Murphy grumbled.

Alex came around the corner into the living room. She was wearing cutoffs and one of Murphy's Temple T-shirts. She put her hands on her hips. "Aren't you a mean old fart, though?" she said. "I've got some in my place. I'll be right back. You'll like it, I promise."

Murphy grunted noncommittally.

Alex went out the door, leaving it slightly ajar, and walked the few steps down the hall to Emma Fronczek's place. She opened the door with Emma's key and was only mildly surprised when she found Emma inside, sitting on the sofa stroking Snookie. This was Emma's first appearance since her death, but Alex had been expecting her. However unprepossessing Emma might be, at least she was less repelling than the pimp with the ruined face and the naked accountant with the hole in the top of his head.

"Hello, Mrs. Fronczek," Alex said casually, going for the refrigerator.

Inside she found a bottle of New York State wine she particularly liked—Heron Hill Otter Spring chardonnay, one of Phil's favorites. She tucked it under her arm and passed by Emma and the cat as they sat silently on the sofa, staring at her with two sets of dead eyes.

"See you later, Mrs. Fronczek," Alex said, slipping out the door and locking it behind her.

Alex strode barefoot down the darkened hall to

Murphy's open door. She was halfway in before she realized that Murphy was at his desk, his back to her, on the phone.

"How's he holding up?" Murphy was asking.

Alex stepped back outside the door and flattened herself against the wall, clutching the wine bottle between her breasts.

"Good," Murphy said. "What? (Pause) Yeah, probably. The way things are going, I should be finished up by this weekend. Unless I get a break here, the jury is going to take a fast twenty minutes to convict my guy. (Pause) No, he isn't. (Pause) Because I know he isn't, Jim, that's how. (Pause) Just fine. (Pause) I will. What do you think, I was born yesterday? You worry about what you've got to worry about. I'll handle my part. Listen, by the way, have you got anything left to drink at that goddamn camp? You want me to bring anything when I come up? (Pause) Fine. I'll do that. You're sure he's okay, now? He's been up there a while now. He's got to be thinking about what he's gotten himself into. (Pause) All right, good. (Pause) I'll be up Friday night, then. Try not to let him fall into the lake and drown between now and then, okay? (Pause) Yeah, right. Be cool, my man."

Murphy hung up the phone as Alex entered with the wine. He turned in his chair and frowned. She came over and flopped into his lap.

"What can I do to cheer you up?" she asked.

Murphy's frown never wavered. "Nothing much with your clothes on."

"You're a pig, Frank," Alex told him in serious tones.

"Yeah, I know," he said. "Forgive me and feed me, okay?"

Alex snuggled against him. "Not necessarily in that order. You eat my dinner, and then maybe I'll forgive you."

"And then you'll take your clothes off?" Murphy asked hopefully.

CHAPTER 34

"I'm not going to make it today, Daddy," Patricia said over the phone. "I must have eaten something bad last night."

Murphy, shaving with the portable razor as he spoke, said, "How serious is it, do you think? Do you think you ought to see a doctor?"

"I'll be all right, but I don't think it would be a good idea to get too far from the bathroom, if you know what I mean. Mom is here. Do you want to talk to her?"

"Yeah, put her on."

There was a moment's pause. Then: "Hello, Frank."

"Is the kid all right?" Murphy asked anxiously.

"She'll be fine. I'm going to be here all day with her. If it looks like more than it looks like now I'll take her to a doctor. I don't think it will, though."

"All right. Keep an eye on her."

Mary Ellen was silent for a moment. Then she said, "Patricia tells me you've got a new girlfriend."

Thanks, Patricia, Murphy thought. He said, "Sort of."

"Would I like her?"

"I doubt it," Murphy said.

"Then you must be getting along just fine with her, Frank," Mary Ellen said. Then she hung up.

Murphy held the phone away from his face and stared at it for a moment. Not an auspicious beginning to the day. He went back into the bathroom, brushed his teeth and tied his tie. With an unlit cigarette in his mouth, he was gathering up his briefcase when Alex came through the door. She wore one of those flowery summer dresses in shades of blue and yellow that made her pale skin gleam. When she'd left his apartment to go back to Emma Fronczek's to change, she'd been in the same worn cutoffs and shabby Temple T-shirt she'd worn at dinner the night before. The transformation was nothing less than startling. Murphy caught his breath when he saw her. This was a truly stunning woman, he realized again.

"Ready to do battle?" Alex asked.

Murphy lit his Camel with his free hand. "One quick call," he said.

Murphy dialed his office and got Esmeralda. His secretary might not do much at work, but she always got there early so she could not do much on time, and for that he was grateful.

"Did you reach Profumo?" he asked.

"Got him last night," Esmeralda said. "He'd just gotten in. He'll be there this morning."

"Good. I'll need him."

"I guess you will. Have you seen the *Inquirer* yet this morning?"

"No. They got a story on the trial?"

"Yes, back inside the metropolitan section. From the

way it reads, you must have gotten beaten up pretty badly in round one."

"Today is round two," Murphy told her with noticeable irritation. "Is that the way you talk to your pug husband?"

Esmeralda laughed. "He's never made it to round two."

"I'll tell him you said that," Murphy said, and hung up. He turned to Alex. "Let's go."

They were fortunate enough to find a Yellow cab cruising down the street just outside the door to the apartment building, which gave Murphy an excuse not to walk to City Hall in what was already an unpleasantly hot day. When Murphy arrived in the courtroom, he got Alex a seat in the front and found Webster already waiting for him at the defense table. From his appearance, Webster hadn't slept all night.

"Lighten up," Murphy instructed him. "You keep on looking so glum and the jury's got no choice but to think you're guilty."

"They already think that," Webster said in a flat, emotionless tone.

"Well, I'm going to change their minds today. You do your part, and I'll do mine."

Fletcher Lake and Paul Toddman entered not more than thirty seconds later. This time Lake was attired in a sleek, double-breasted suit that contrasted dramatically with Murphy's too-tight gray sharkskin. Toddman, as always, looked as though he'd bought his suit from Goodwill Industries a decade or two before. He approached Murphy at the defense table as Lake took his place at the prosecution's headquarters across the aisle.

"We've got a date on Lucelli," Toddman said. "It starts next Monday, if we can finish this up this week."

"We ought to be able to do that," Murphy said.

"How's Berger? Have you heard?"

"I talked to Wilder last night. Everything is cool."

"Everything?" Toddman asked.

Murphy's eyes met those of the first assistant district attorney. "It's all cool," he said quietly.

Toddman nodded. "Good. I'm counting on you, Frank."

The jury began filing in, and Toddman moved back to his seat next to Fletcher Lake. In a moment, the bailiff entered and announced Joe Luce. The judge came out of his chambers, took the bench and gaveled the trial into order.

"Your next witness, Mr. Lake?" he said.

Lake rose. In a voice louder than necessary, he said, "The people feels it's proved its case beyond a reasonable doubt, Your Honor."

"Does that mean you rest?" Luce said with just the slightest trace of annoyance in his voice. There was a right way and a wrong way to do these things, the judge knew, and when you rested, you rested. You didn't make a speech.

"Yes," Fletcher Lake said. "The people rests, Your Honor."

Joe Luce frowned deeply. Then he turned to the defense table. "Mr. Murphy," he said.

Murphy stood up. "Your Honor, the defense calls Dr. Marvin Weinberg back to the stand."

"Dr. Marvin Weinberg," the bailiff intoned.

The old man slowly got up from his aisle seat and made his way to the witness stand.

"Raise your right hand, please," the bailiff instructed as Weinberg settled into his chair.

"I've already been sworn in, you idiot," Weinberg growled.

The bailiff looked helplessly toward Luce, who sighed and nodded. "The court stipulates that the witness has already been sworn," the judge said. "It's a courtesy, doctor, as I'm sure you're aware. Proceed."

Weinberg merely glowered. Murphy walked over to him.

"Morning, doc," he said.

Weinberg was never at his best in the morning, Murphy knew. In fact, Murphy was hard-pressed to imagine when Weinberg might be at his best. The pathologist merely grunted. So much for the amenities. Murphy said, "Doctor, in the course of your examination of Lynn Rice's body, did you have occasion to test the corpse for fingerprints?"

"I did."

"Under what circumstances?"

"At the request of defense counsel."

"So," Murphy said, "the prosecution never made a specific request for fingerprint analysis of the victim's corpse?"

"Not that I'm aware of, no."

"Isn't it fairly difficult to obtain fingerprints from flesh?"

"Yes," Weinberg said. "Fingerprints are the product of grease and sweat left on a surface by a human hand. They don't show up using normal fingerprint methods, since the surface on which they're located has its own surface of sweat and grease. But there's a fairly new technique I'd heard about, and I tried it in this case."

"Would you explain that technique to the jury?" Murphy asked.

"Yes. I covered areas of the corpse with a fine lead powder and X-rayed them. The X-rays gave me a fingerprint image on the skin of the victim."

"Where on the corpse did you locate these latent fingerprints?" Murphy asked.

"On the victim's wrists."

"On her wrists?"

"That's correct."

"And what did the discovery of the fingerprints on the wrists indicate to you?"

"Objection!" Fletcher Lake called out. "The question calls for a conclusion on the part of the witness."

Murphy shook his head in despair at Fletcher Lake's stupidity. "Your Honor, the prosecution has already established through testimony it elicited itself that the witness is probably the foremost expert on forensic pathology alive today. The prosecution called him for the explicit purpose of giving testimony that represented the conclusions he drew from examining the body of the victim. That's all I'm asking him to do. He testifies as to his conclusions for a living. That's what the city pays him for."

Despite himself, Luce could barely stifle a grin. The judge turned to the DA. "A response, Mr. Lake?"

Fletcher Lake looked perplexed. "Well," he said lamely, "I still object."

"Overruled. Proceed, Mr. Murphy."

Shaking his head for the benefit of the jury at Fletcher Lake's ineptitude, Murphy said, "Thank you, Your Honor. Doctor, please answer the question."

Weinberg leaned back in the witness's chair. "Based

on my professional training and my many decades of investigating such violent deaths, it's my considered opinion that the fingerprints indicate that someone had grasped the victim by her wrists."

Not precisely the answer Murphy had been seeking. He tried again. "Before or after death?"

"I can't say."

"Well, could it have been after death?"

"Certainly."

"Could it have happened after the person who grasped her wrists first drove a kitchen knife into her chest? Could it have happened when he or she then dragged the body outside the scene of the murder and to the trunk of a waiting car?"

"It's entirely possible," Weinberg said.

"Could those fingerprints have belonged to the murderer?"

"They most assuredly could have."

"In your professional judgment—based on your experience, your knowledge of the case, and your examination of the victim's corpse—is it likely that the person who dragged the corpse outside and the person who wielded the weapon could have been—"

"Objection!" Lake called out. "This goes beyond the witness's expert conclusions."

"I agree," Joe Luce said. "Sustained."

"Doctor," Murphy then asked, "in the course of your examination, did you locate any other fingerprints that might have bearing on this case?"

"I did."

"And where were those fingerprints?"

"I found fingerprints on the cuffs of the blouse the victim was wearing at the time of her death."

382

"How did those fingerprints compare with those you discovered on the flesh of her wrists?"

"Well, prints obtained from fabric will differ in clarity and character from those obtained through the X-ray method from flesh, but they seemed to me to be a fair match."

"Objection," Lake said. "The witness is not an expert in fingerprint classification."

"Sustained," Luce said. "The jury will disregard."

Like hell, Murphy thought. He said, "In the course of your work on this case, did you have occasion to examine the murder weapon, doctor?"

"I did. I subjected the weapon to analysis on a sophisticated electronic microscope that scans areas as small as a millionth of an inch."

"And what did this show you?"

"It showed me what appeared to be latent fingerprint fragments beneath those that have been identified as those of the defendant."

"Objection!" Lake called out, this time with discernible irritation. "Same grounds."

"Sustained," Joe Luce repeated. "The jury will disregard."

Bullshit, Murphy thought. He said, "Did it appear to you that those fragments had been left behind when the hilt of the knife had been wiped off in an effort to obscure them?"

"Objection!"

"Sustained."

"Could that have been the case?"

"Objection!"

"Sustained. Cut it out, please, Mr. Murphy."

"I'm sorry, Your Honor. I'll get away from that,

then." Murphy walked back to the defense table, pulled a manila envelope from his briefcase and walked back to the witness stand. "Doctor, would you open the envelope, please?" Weiner opened it and examined its contents. Murphy said, "Do you recognize what's inside?"

"I do."

"And what might that be?"

"These are X-rays from several angles of the lumbar region of a human spine, along with copies of medical records. They're the same ones you asked me to examine in the course of preparing for my testimony today."

Murphy turned and faced the jury. He said, "Doctor, in your professional opinion, what would be likely to happen to the owner of this spine if he were to bend in any significant manner and lift a dead weight of more than one hundred pounds to shoulder height?"

"The spine displays evidence of severe disk disease that would create pain in the form of pressure on the S-One nerve, the largest nerve leading from the spinal column down the left leg. Pressure on the nerve would cause it to swell, which would create muscle spasms in its vicinity. The likelihood would be that the patient would probably be in severe pain within several hours—possibly as long as twelve hours—after attempting a lift like the one you described. It's not possible to say that this would absolutely be the case. Nerves sometimes produce pain for no apparent reason, and other times they fail to produce pain when X-rays say they should. But the likelihood is that the patient with that spine who attempted a lift such as you describe would end up in almost crippling pain."

Murphy took back the X-rays. He turned to Joe Luce. "Your Honor, these X-rays will be defense Exhibit A. Let the record show, please, that these X-rays are of the spine of my client, taken while he was a patient in a California corrections medical facility. Accompanying them is his medical history as it pertains to his back—a history that makes clear that the likelihood of Mike Webster having dragged Lynn Rice's body from the house to the car, then lifting it and dropping it in the trunk without putting himself in traction is highly remote."

"Objection!" Lake called out. "Is that Mr. Murphy's considered medical opinion?"

"Sustained. Let your expert witnesses draw the conclusions, please. Don't do it for them."

"Very well, Your Honor. Now, doctor, in the course of this investigation, did you have the occasion to examine any other objects related to this case and to obtain fingerprint impressions from them?"

"I did."

"And what were those objects?"

"They were a coffee mug, an ashtray, and a drinking glass."

"And," Murphy asked, "in your judgment, did any of the fingerprints you obtained from those objects match the prints you found on the victim's wr—"

"Objection!" Lake virtually bellowed. "Mr. Murphy is continuing to ask the witness to make judgments on fingerprint classifications that the witness is not equipped to make even though you've sustained my objections on those grounds."

Murphy thought he detected a note of panic in the DA's voice, and a glance in Lake's direction confirmed that suspicion. Murphy almost squirmed in delight. He wished Patricia were on hand to see this.

"Sustained," Joe Luce said, but Murphy knew it didn't make any difference. The jury had gotten the point, unless they were so hopelessly dumb that nothing anybody said or did made any difference. It was possible. Juries were like that, sometimes.

"No further questions," Murphy said, and sat down.

Fletcher Lake got up slowly in his elegant suit, consulting his notes and his brow furrowed. Finally, he said, "Doctor, this technique with the lead—have you ever used it before?"

"No," Weinberg told him. "First time."

"Ah," Lake said. "So you based your conclusions on a technique with which you weren't intimately familiar?"

"I didn't say that. I said I'd never used it before. That doesn't mean I'm not familiar with it. I've never died before, either, but I'm certainly familiar with death."

Murphy watched Lake's brow break out in a patina of sweat. For the next ten minutes, the DA tried valiantly. He tried to establish that the prints on Lynn Rice's wrists could have been Webster's, which was what Murphy had hoped he would do. He also tried to undermine the professional credibility of the man whose professional virtues he had touted to the jury just the day before. But Marvin Weinberg had been testifying as an expert witness when Fletcher Lake was stuffing the ballot box for student council. It was no contest from the beginning—especially on testimony of a scientific nature. Lake scored no points. In fact, Weinberg was beating him up rather badly when Lake caught Toddman's quasi-frantic signal to let it all go.

All Lake was doing was digging himself a deeper hole into which to fall. Finally the DA said, "No further questions," and sat down. Murphy could tell that the DA was steaming.

"Nothing on redirect, Your Honor," Murphy said.

"You may step down, then, doctor," Joe Luce told Weinberg.

The old man was out of the chair before the judge began the sentence. "I already knew that," he grunted to Joe Luce as he left the witness stand.

Weinberg passed by Murphy without a word as the defense lawyer called Profumo as his next witness. Profumo was resplendent in his Acapulco tan and a bright red sport jacket. Murphy thought he looked like a midget fox hunter. He spent a few moments asking the little man about his credentials, establishing him as a legitimate expert, before getting down to his testimony.

"Did you have occasion to compare the fingerprints Dr. Weinberg obtained from the corpse of Lynn Rice—from her wrists and from the cuffs of her blouse—with those of the defendant, Michael Webster?"

"I did," Profumo said.

"Did they match?"

"They did not."

"And how did they differ?" Murphy asked.

"They differed substantially," Profumo said. "There are one thousand twenty-four primary fingerprint classifications. The print can be further classified by the various pattern types of each finger until the number of possible variations runs into the thousands and thousands. In addition to that, fine details of the fingerprint pattern—I'm talking about the number of ridges in a loop or a whorl—can form sub-secondary classifications. There's just no way I could even begin to tell you in how many ways the prints differed, but they did. There were hundreds of differences."

"Well," Murphy said, "did the prints Dr. Weinberg obtained from the corpse match any of these you obtained from the three objects I asked you to check— the coffee mug, the ashtray, and the drinking glass?"

"Yes," Profumo said. "One set I obtained from those objects was a perfect match."

"So," Murphy said, "the prints Dr. Weinberg obtained from Miss Rice's body matched perfectly with the prints you obtained from either the coffee mug, the ashtray, or the drinking glass. Is that correct?"

"It is," Profumo said.

"And how did you ascertain that the prints matched?" Murphy said.

"I compared the fingerprint impressions using the computer in my laboratory at New Jersey State Police headquarters in Trenton."

"Would you explain—briefly, please—how that computer works?"

"Yes," Profumo said. "The computer scans each print through a viewing screen. It then reduces the various characteristics of each print to a mathematical code and compares the numbers."

"Would you—as an expert witness in fingerprint identification—classify this method as foolproof?"

"I would."

"Thank you, Mr. Profumo," Murphy said. "Your Honor, I'd like to enter into evidence the three objects in question—the coffee mug, the ashtray, and the drinking glass. I'd like to offer into evidence, too, the report prepared by Mr. Profumo comparing the various fingerprints obtained by Dr. Weinberg from the corpse of the victim, her clothing, and the objects I've just mentioned."

"Very well," Joe Luce said, motioning to the court attendant. "The exhibits will be appropriately marked."

"Also," Murphy said, "I'd like to reserve the right to call this witness again for further testimony."

"You may do that," Joe Luce said. "Would the prosecution like to cross-examine?"

Fletcher Lake, perspiration soaked through his custom-made shirt and the armpits of his double-breasted suit, said, "Not at this time, Your Honor."

"One more thing, Your Honor," Murphy said hurriedly, angry at himself for almost forgetting. "Mr. Profumo, can you tell the jury who Sir Edward Henry was? The prosecution's expert didn't seem to know."

"Yes," Profumo said. "The first man to use thumbprints as a means of identification in criminal cases was Sir William Herschel, who worked for the British government in Bengal. That was back in 1858. His work was expanded on by Sir Francis Galton back in England. He was the founder of the science of eugenics. That's the science of selective breeding. They were the people who realized that fingerprints were unique to every person."

"And Sir Edward?" Murphy prodded.

"Sir Edward R. Henry was inspector general of the Bengal police about forty years after Sir Francis did his work. Sir Edward built on the work of those earlier men. By 1901, he'd developed a classification system

389

for fingerprints for use by Scotland Yard and other police agencies. It's the same classification system we use today, with minor variations. Sir Edward was the father of our modern science of fingerprint identification. The man was a genius, and he's my personal hero."

"Does it surprise you that any genuine fingerprint expert would not know who Sir Edward Henry was?" Murphy asked.

"Well," Profumo responded, "some guys function more as technicians than scientists, if you know what I mean."

Murphy smiled broadly at Profumo. If there hadn't been so many people watching, he would have kissed the little man.

"That's all, Your Honor," Murphy said.

Joe Luce slammed down his gavel. "Court adjourned until two this afternoon," he announced.

CHAPTER 35

Immediately after Joe Luce gaveled court into recess—as the bailiff took a more confident and relaxed Mike Webster back to his holding cell for lunch—Paul Toddman was at Murphy's side.

"Whose prints are they?" he demanded.

"I should tell you?" Murphy said. "I shouldn't just bring it out in testimony?"

"Whose?" Toddman asked again.

Murphy shook his head as he stuffed papers into his briefcase. "No dice, Paul. You guys wanted a trial, you got a trial. I told you from the beginning that you had the wrong guy, but nobody would listen."

"Don't be a jerk. You're in no position to be so cocky, Frank. We've still got your guy's fingerprints on the murder weapon, the body in the car he was driving, and the sister's testimony."

"If you're on such solid ground," Murphy asked, "then why are you over here bugging me? You want me to tell you? Reasonable doubt, that's why."

Toddman frowned. "What might seem like reasonable doubt to you and what might seem like reasonable doubt to the jury could be two different things. I'm trying to help you out here, in case you don't realize it."

"No, you're not. You're trying to help Fletcher out. What you see here is Fletcher losing a case and maybe looking bad on page one of the *Inquirer*. You're over here figuring that maybe I'll take a plea. Isn't that right?"

Toddman shrugged. "I can get you manslaughter three. If he behaves himself, it's less than four years."

Murphy gazed at the first assistant district attorney in disgust. "No way."

"Have it your way. Just remember this. I've been around juries all my adult life. You never know what they're going to do. These people sit around here for two months at a stretch for twelve bucks a day plus two dollars for bus fare, and by the time they actually get on a case they're mad as hell at everybody. Sometimes they take that out on the defendants—especially in murder cases. Juries are like everybody else, Frank. They figure that if somebody got arrested, he probably did it. That presumption of innocence crap is pure bullshit. The reality is that we don't have to prove our case beyond a reasonable doubt. You've got to prove your client's innocence beyond a reasonable doubt. That's the way the system really works. Maybe you've already managed to do that. But unless you've got something else pretty big up your sleeve, I wouldn't count on it. If you're smart, you'll take what you can get. This is a sure thing, and there aren't many of those you come across in life."

Murphy snapped his briefcase shut. "I'm hungry," he told Toddman. "See you back in court this afternoon,

Mr. Prosecutor."

Toddman turned wordlessly and went back to his boss to report Murphy's response to the offer. Murphy, less euphoric than he had been only a moment before, found Alex waiting for him at the door of the courtroom. She took his arm as they started down the hall.

"That seemed to go pretty well for you," she told him.

"Maybe," Murphy said in a low voice. "We're only in the backstretch, though. It's too early to tell. Where do you want to eat?"

"How about that Italian place down on Walnut Street you took me to the other night?"

"Fine," Murphy said.

He was comparatively silent and brooding through the six-block walk and lunch in Freddie's, a basement restaurant decorated with Chianti bottles and prints of gondoliers in striped T-shirts. Alex tried to cheer him with small talk. When that failed, she turned to conversation about the case.

"How much longer do you think the trial will go?" she asked him.

"That depends on how long Fletcher goes at Profumo. He could drag that cross-examination out all afternoon. Then I'd call my last witness tomorrow morning, and he'd cross, then summations. We should finish up no later than tomorrow afternoon, but we might even get it done today. That would mean that the jury would get the case late this afternoon."

"That quickly?"

"Could happen."

She leaned across the table. "You know, this has

been absolutely fascinating for me. I've never seen a trial up close like this before."

"Me, either," Murphy pointed out. "You know, I think maybe I've made a big mistake in this. I should have called in a more experienced guy to work with me. I'm doing okay in the courtroom, but as these things go on you come across decisions you haven't had the opportunity to make before, and it would have been nice to have had somebody to consult with."

Alex squeezed his hand. "You're doing fine on your own."

"I wonder."

"You're one of those people who seems to work better by himself. I know, because I'm like that, too." She sat up in her seat and put her napkin on the table. "Speaking of that, I've got to call my agent in New York. He said he might have something for me pretty soon. You sit tight. I'll be right back."

Murphy sat alone at the table over the remains of his veal parmigiana, smoking, nursing an old-fashioned and thinking. Toddman was right. Presumption of innocence was bullshit. It was something to worry about, and Murphy was worried about it. He was doing the very best he could do. That McEwen woman had been a tough blow, though. She'd done real damage. When he'd gone into this, Murphy had figured that his best strategy would be to hammer away at the fact that the prosecution's investigation had been less complete than it might have been and the fact that no clear motive had been established for Mike Webster to murder Lynn Rice. As it had turned out, he'd established the first point rather convincingly, but he'd lost the second. He could see where a jury might convict Webster even if they thought the authorities had done a shoddy job of investigating the case. Stranger things had happened. Murphy knew what he had left to do, and he knew, too, that the success of what he had left to do depended on the reactions not of the jury but of other people. The last thing he wanted to do was to count on a jury. Despite the platitudes of his opening statement, Murphy had no faith whatever in the primary principle on which the jury system was based: the good sense of average people. If average people were so smart, then why was a *putz* like Fletcher Lake sitting at the prosecution table?

Alex was back in a few minutes, and the expression on her face was not encouraging.

"What's the matter?" Murphy asked her as she sat back down.

"I've got to go back to New York."

"What?" he said. "When?"

She gazed at him, her lovely face filled with disappointment. "Today. I've got an audition for a new show first thing tomorrow morning, and my agent says there's a part that's just perfect for me. I know the director, and I've got a real chance at it."

"Oh, shit," Murphy said.

"I've got to work, Frank. This is what I do."

"I know, I know," Murphy said. "But the timing of this really sucks. When will I get to see you again?"

"Maybe this weekend. I'll try to get back down here."

"I'm out of town this weekend."

She looked at him and said, "If I get the part—and it looks like I will—I'll be starting rehearsals next Monday. Maybe you can come up to New York."

He shook his head. "Not next week. I've got a new

trial starting Monday."

Alex leaned back in her chair. "This doesn't look all that good, does it? It looks like it might be a while before we get together again."

"And you have to leave today?" Murphy asked.

She nodded. "I've got to get back, get unpacked into a friend's place and get myself ready for tomorrow morning. I need a lot of sleep the night before an audition, even if the fix is already in."

Murphy shook his head and looked down at his empty old-fashioned glass. "Well," he said, "I guess I'll just have another one of these."

Murphy didn't have time to walk Alex back to the apartment building. He kissed her good-bye, and rather passionately, on the street outside the restaurant, prompting no small amount of amusement from onlookers.

"Hey, pal," said one man in work clothes passing by with a group, "give her a little feel for me, okay?"

Murphy felt a little foolish at his age behaving like a moonstruck teenager on Walnut Street at lunch hour, but there was nothing to be done about it. Alex left him, and he watched her for a moment as she strode off down the street, graceful as a gazelle with her dancer's body. She waved back at him as she turned the corner to go down Seventeenth.

The moment she was out of sight, Murphy turned and virtually ran the six blocks back to City Hall. It was nearly ninety, and he was wearing the worsted wool glen plaid and slogging along his briefcase. On top of that, there was the forty pounds of lard he wore around his waist to worry about. By the time Murphy got to City Hall and into the elevator to the DA's office, he was soaked with sweat, the contents of an entire brewery pouring from his skin and through his clothes. He got out of the elevator and roared down the hall to Toddman's office.

"Where is he?" Murphy demanded of Toddman's hulking secretary.

"I don't know. He didn't come back after court this morning. He must have gone to lunch with Mr. Lake."

"Where?" Murphy gasped.

"I have no idea, Frank," the secretary said, "but he'll be back in court when the case opens again. Are you all right? You look all out of breath."

Murphy, chest heaving and heart pounding, collapsed into a chair. He glanced at his watch. There was still more than twenty minutes to go before court was to be resumed. Joe Luce liked to work out at midday at the YMCA, and consequently believed in long lunch hours. That was one of the advantages in being a judge. You made your own schedule and everybody else conformed to it.

Murphy sat in the chair and waited for his body to recover from the six-block run in the blazing heat. And all for nothing, too.

Toddman's secretary peered at him in genuine concern. "Do you want me to call a doctor, Frank?"

Murphy shook his head. "I'll be fine."

He was, too, although it took ten minutes before his breath came back and the air conditioner turned his wet clothes into an icy sheath. He got up and found his way up to the courtroom on the floor above. Murphy was waiting there when the spectators began to file back in. Lake and Toddman were at the rear of the line. As the bailiff brought Webster back to his position at the defense table, Murphy got up and moved to the prosecution's side.

"Paul," he said, ignoring Fletcher Lake.

Toddman turned toward him. "You want to try to work a little something out now?" he said.

Murphy shook his head. "No, no, that's not it. It's something else."

"What?"

"It's not cool anymore," Murphy told the first assistant district attorney.

"What?" Toddman said, puzzled. Then he realized what Murphy was telling him. "Oh, shit," he said. Without another word, Paul Toddman hurried from the courtroom.

Fletcher Lake, digging through his notes, looked up as Toddman disappeared out the door. A startled expression crossed his face. He turned to Murphy.

"Where'd Paul go?" the district attorney asked.

Murphy shrugged. "Beats me, Fletcher. Maybe he's got a tip on a horse. I guess you're on your own this afternoon."

Lake's startled expression changed instantly to one of genuine alarm. He stood up and made a move to start down the aisle to the door after Toddman.

At that moment, however, the bailiff intoned: "All rise."

Murphy and Lake took their positions in the courtroom.

Before all this

His whole life, whatever his other failings, Phil Bonsignore had been a man of action—a man who'd done things rather than talked about them.

He'd always kept his own counsel. He'd never pried. He'd never been much for small talk. In his half-century or so on this planet, he'd confided in precisely three human beings: his dead mother, his dead wife, and Alex—and in them only rarely. Now, in a hospital bed, the single activity left him was the one in which he'd always exhibited the least enthusiasm. He was left only with the power of speech. And he had nothing much to say, unless he wanted some small favor from a nurse or Alex. Facing death—and fairly soon, too—Phil still couldn't think of a great deal to talk about.

"I'd like some water," he said from his bed.

"Ice?" Alex asked him.

"No," he told her. "Just water. My throat's dry."

Alex went and got the water. It had been some time now—more than a year since he had been diagnosed—but she still hadn't gotten used to the idea that Phil had

ALS. That old politician—that Senator Javits—he had ALS. She'd heard that somewhere. But he was an old man, and it was expected that something would go wrong with him. Lew Gehrig, the ballplayer, he'd had ALS. That's what had killed him. But that had been before Alex had even been born. Both men were fictional characters as far as she was concerned. Who had ever heard of something like ameotropic lateral sclerosis?

Who'd ever heard of somebody with a disease that nobody understood, that nobody knew the cause of, a disease that simply took away the power of muscular movement until your lungs stopped working and you couldn't breathe anymore—until you just suffocated in a world full of air to breathe. Who'd ever heard of something like that?

Phil had never heard of it until they'd told him he had it. They'd told him with sad expressions on their faces. They'd been sad because they hadn't had the foggiest notion of what to do for him. There was nothing to do for him. There was nothing any of them could do to make it go away.

Alex came back from the bath attached to Phil's hospital room with a glass of water. She'd let the water run until it had gotten very cold. She sat on the bed next to Phil, held his head up and let the water trickle into his mouth and down his throat. He could no longer swallow. Any fluid he managed to take in he absorbed through the power of gravity or through the tubes they had sticking into him.

"Okay?" she said.

Phil tried to nod, failed. Alex put the glass on the hospital night table. Phil gasped for a moment, the water moving down his alimentary canal. His eyes bulged. His normal expression gradually returned. Alex held his hand. He'd been here for two weeks now. They had the oxygen mask on him periodically, but not all the time. They were hoping, she knew, that he'd die without it—die quickly and with a minimum of hassle for everybody. The doctor hadn't been in for two days. Alex knew it made no difference. So did Phil.

"How you doing?" Alex asked him.

Phil merely smiled, no more than a weak grimace. "Okay. I keep worrying about you."

"Don't worry about me," Alex said. "I'm the last person you have to worry about."

"I worry, anyhow. You know you're getting the house and the restaurant. I told you that, didn't I?"

"You told me."

"There's money, too," he said. "Not a lot of it, though. I always lived pretty good."

"Take it easy," she told him.

"Anybody call me lately?" he asked.

"Nobody important."

"Who called?" he asked, his mind instantly alert even though nothing else was working. That was the horror of ALS. Everything else failed. The mind kept humming along, like a curse.

"Who?" he demanded.

"Nobody."

"Come on, Alex," Phil said. "Don't bullshit me now."

She paused. Then she said, "A guy named Augie. I talked to him."

"And . . ."

She shrugged. "I can handle it."

"That's what you told him?" Phil asked.

"Yeah."

"What did he say?"

"He said okay. He seemed satisfied. You'll have to help me, though. You'll have to teach me."

"It'll be hard to teach you from here," he told her.

"Just tell me what you know," Alex said. "I've watched. I've helped. But I don't know what I don't know."

Phil said nothing for a little while. Then his mouth twitched. It might have been a smile. Alex couldn't be sure.

"There's not much to know," Phil said. "It ain't brain surgery. You just got to be careful, mostly. Especially a woman's got to be careful. It's no game. There's no rules."

"You've told me that before."

"Don't forget it," Phil said. "But you'll be all right. You'll do fine. You've got the most important thing."

"What's that?"

"You're willing," Phil said. "That's ninety percent of it, Alex. You got to be willing to do it. Not many women are. I don't know what made you that way, but you are."

Alex squeezed his limp hand, patted it, stroked it.

"I know," she said.

CHAPTER 36

When the bell over the cafe door sounded in late afternoon, Peggy Cooper was doing paperwork in the back. It was too late for lunch, too early for dinner and too nice a day for the pensioners who sometimes hung around the joint to sit anywhere but on benches over in the town square, near the band box. That's how Peggy Cooper knew that whoever had just come in the place was from out of town. Sparta was no bigger than the palm of your hand, and she knew the community's rhythms and routines fairly intimately. She ought to. She'd spent forty-one years learning them.

The customer turned out to be a tall, pretty woman wearing worn jeans and a T-shirt that said Just Visiting This Planet. A flashy new Volvo sedan was parked directly outside the cafe, and Peggy didn't know anybody who had a Volvo. This was pickup country—pickups and your occasional Lincoln town car, when somebody was doing extraordinarily well, which wasn't very often.

"Hi there," Peggy said pleasantly, passing the menu

403

across the counter. "I'll get you some coffee, if you like, while you check this out."

"Tea, please," the woman said. "With some lemon, if you have it."

"Sure thing," Peggy told her.

She tried not to show it, but Peggy Cooper was tired. She'd opened up at six, and she'd be here until eight before she shut down. Long days and not much money. On the other hand, things could be worse. Peggy knew that because she carried around with her vivid memories of when they had been worse. She poured tea into a thick porcelain mug with a maroon stripe around the rim. She put it on the counter in front of the customer.

"Make up your mind yet?" Peggy asked.

"Tuna salad on whole wheat."

"Chips and pickle?" Peggy asked.

"Pickle. No chips, please. Is this your place? Do you own it?"

Peggy turned to the sandwich board behind her and went to work on the tuna on whole wheat. "Yeah. It used to be my husband's. He was a fair bit older than me. He died and left it to me."

"I'm in the restaurant business," the customer said, sipping her tea. "I got my place the same way. It can be a tough haul sometimes, I know."

Peggy laughed. "You could say that. This sure isn't much of a business. After I pay my food suppliers and my utilities and my taxes it doesn't bring in much more than grocery money. But I own my house free and clear—Ken carried mortgage insurance—and I drive an old clunker, like most people around here. All I really need is pin money and a few bucks for groceries at home. I eat most of my meals here, at wholesale prices. You want mayo on this?"

"Just a touch, please."

"Your place like this?" Peggy asked.

"A little bigger. It's in Jersey, up near New York."

Peggy deftly sliced the pickle with her heavy knife. She slit it down the middle and arranged the halves on the plate, on either side of the sandwich.

"Bigger and fancier, I'll bet," Peggy said, delivering the sandwich. "You don't look much like the hash-slinging type to me."

Alex smiled over her mug of tea. "I've done my share. I've done my share of a lot of things, believe me. You do what you have to do to get by."

"Don't I know it," Peggy Cooper said. "At least if you own something you don't have to worry about somebody taking it away from you. I could probably make more money waiting tables out on the highway, but this is mine, for what it's worth. That's a good feeling."

"I know what you mean."

"You said you're from Jersey? What are you doing around here?"

"Looking for some property. I heard there's a camp around here that's for sale."

"A camp? You mean like a summer home?"

Alex shook her head. "No, I think it would be more like a summer camp of some kind. I just heard about it. Is there anything like that around here?"

Peggy shrugged. "There's Camp Wintu. That's out on the lake. That's the Kingston YMCA camp. I didn't know it was for sale, though."

Alex shrugged. "I was told it was—or that it might

405

be. I thought I'd take a look at it, anyway. How do I get there?"

"You go out that road in front—just the way your car is pointing—and follow it for five or six miles. The lake'll be on your left, and the camp'll be on your right. There's a sign on their road, if the snowplow didn't get it over the winter."

The woman ate and they talked.

"I grew up in a town sort of like this," the woman said. "It was a little bigger, but not much. That was out in Minnesota. We had a little cafe like this. The Iron Horse Cafe. They served great potato salad."

"I get mine in big plastic jars from the food supplier," Peggy admitted. "I used to make it myself, but they can make it cheaper and better. Macaroni salad, too. I just don't bother with it anymore."

"I buy some dishes pre-prepared and frozen," the woman said, "but not much. We try to do everything from scratch as much as possible."

"How much help have you got?"

"Eight waiters and a kitchen crew of four," the woman said.

"Big place," Peggy told her.

"Not too big. I don't want it to get very big. You get too big, and you've got quality problems."

"Hah!" Peggy said. "I'm small, and *I* got quality problems. I got all kinds of problems."

They talked about the frustrations and satisfactions of the restaurant business while the woman finished her sandwich. The customer listened, actually, and more than once in the conversation Peggy had the impression that she was thinking about something else. That was okay with Peggy. She just asked that every once in

406

a while somebody would listen to what she had to say. She didn't much care if they actually *heard* it. The woman ate up during the increasingly one-sided conversation. Then she said, "How do I get to this Camp Wintu again?"

Peggy turned over a place mat and drew a map with her ballpoint pen. The woman studied it for a moment, then folded it up and put it in her pocketbook. She left a five-dollar bill on the counter, which meant a tip for Peggy she could fold up and put in her wallet instead of dropping into her change purse.

"Nice talking to you," the woman said as she left. "Good luck with the business."

"Have a nice day," Peggy Cooper said.

She said that to everybody, of course. But this time Peggy Cooper meant it. Nice girl, she thought as she gathered up the customer's dishes.

CHAPTER 37

"Your Honor," Murphy said, "the defense calls Judy Kavanaugh to the stand."

"Judy Kavanaugh," the bailiff called out.

Judy, sitting next to Beverly, looked wide-eyed at her mother. Murphy saw Beverly's hand clutch at the sleeve of the girl's white blouse. Then the fingers relaxed, and Beverly nodded at her daughter. Tentatively, Judy got up and walked down the aisle, through the gate that separated the lawyers' arena from the spectators, and took her seat on the witness stand. Her "yes" was barely audible as she was sworn in. She looked to Murphy like a terrified doe, eyes large and the color drained from her face.

"Judy," he began, "do you like Mike Webster?"

"Yes," the girl whispered.

"Please speak up," Joe Luce said.

"Yes," Judy responded in a more forceful tone.

"How did you feel about Lynn Rice?"

"I didn't like her much."

"Were you upset at the prospect of your father

marrying her?"

"Yes."

"Did that prospect upset you badly?"

"Yes."

"Did you threaten to take your own life when you learned about your father's plans?"

Judy hesitated. "Well . . ."

"Judy," Murphy said, "did you tell a doctor at the school you attend that you'd kill yourself if your father married Lynn?"

"Yes."

"Speak up, please," Joe Luce repeated.

"Yes," Judy said in a loud voice.

"Good," Murphy said. "Now, let's just calm down a bit, Judy. Okay? Are you familiar with the van the school owns?"

"Yes."

"That van was stolen the night Lynn Rice was murdered. Are you aware of that?"

The girl looked down at her hands. "I heard about it."

"You heard about it?"

"Yes."

"You stole the van, didn't you, Judy?"

"No."

"You stole it, didn't you?"

"No!"

"You stole it, and you drove to the farm in it, didn't you? What would you say if I were to tell you that your fingerprints were found in the van, Judy—your fingerprints on the steering wheel? What would you say then?"

The girl's face reddened visibly. She said nothing.

"Tell the truth, Judy," Murphy said softly.

"Yes," she shouted angrily. "I took the van. I drove it around for a while, but I didn't go to the farm. I just took it for a joy ride. But the red light came on the dashboard, so I left it a few blocks from the school and walked back."

Murphy heard a gasp from behind him, and he recognized it as Beverly's. He never looked back.

"Why did you take the van?"

The girl shrugged. "A lot of us have taken the van at night. Sister always leaves the keys in it out front."

"So your story is that you just took it out for a joy ride, and it behaved badly and you ditched it, right?"

"Yes."

"And you didn't like Lynn, did you? You hated her. Isn't that right? Didn't you hate her?"

"Objection!" Fletcher Lake called out. "This child has answered the question already."

"Sustained," Joe Luce said.

Murphy turned and walked slowly away from the witness stand. He raised his eyes to the audience. Brian Kavanaugh's face was an angry red. Beverly's was drawn and tense. Mike Webster, at the defense table, was watching intently. Murphy turned back to the girl.

"Judy," he said, "do you remember Dr. Weiner?"

"No," the girl said with open hostility. Her eyes were narrowed with hatred for Murphy.

"Sure you do," he said casually. "He's the psychiatrist I took you to see. Do you remember him now that I've refreshed your memory? Or do you want me to call Dr. Weiner and have him testify?"

"I remember him," Judy Kavanaugh said sullenly.

"You talked to Dr. Weiner a long time, didn't you?"

"Yes."

"And what did you tell him?"

Judy was silent.

"What did you tell him?" Murphy demanded.

"Lots of things."

"Did you tell him about how you felt about Lynn?"

"Yes."

"Did you tell him that the prospect of your father marrying Lynn had you upset?"

"Yes."

"Did you tell him that there had been moments when you'd thought about killing Lynn to keep her from marrying your father?"

"Objection!" Fletcher Lake called out.

"On what grounds, Mr. Lake?" Joe Luce asked.

"Hearsay, Your Honor."

Murphy and the judge exchanged baffled glances.

"Hearsay?" Joe Luce asked. "I don't understand."

"Neither does he," Murphy offered.

"Well," the district attorney said, "Mr. Murphy is badgering the witness, then."

"Overruled," Joe said. "Proceed."

Murphy frowned. Lake's real objective in objecting had been to provide Judy Kavanaugh with a few moments to think, to break the rhythm of Murphy's examination. The ploy had succeeded well enough. Murphy decided to go at this from another angle and work his way back to this point again.

"Judy," he said, "how big are you?"

"What?"

"How tall are you?" How much do you weigh?"

"I'm five-five. I weigh one-eighteen."

"You're a big girl for your age. Are you strong?"

411

"I guess."

"You're a lot bigger than Lynn Rice was, aren't you?"

"Yes."

"If you'd wanted to, you could have done physical harm to Lynn, couldn't you?"

"Objection!"

"Oh, knock it off, Fletcher," Murphy snarled.

Luce banged his gavel. "Let's have a little order here, gentlemen. Mr. Lake, I do hope you have some grounds for this objection."

"He's badgering her," Lake complained.

"I asked her a question," Murphy said. "What with all this badgering crap?"

Luce frowned. "A little more propriety please, Mr. Murphy. Mr. Lake, I'm overruling this objection. Please refrain from interrupting these proceedings again unless you're objecting on a point of law. Do you understand?"

"Yes, Your Honor."

"Proceed," Joe Luce said.

"You could have done her harm, couldn't you, Judy?"

"No."

"You already admitted you stole the van that night. You could have driven to the farm, stabbed Lynn to death and put her body in the trunk of the BMW, couldn't you?"

"No!"

"Didn't you tell Dr. Weiner that you'd considered killing Lynn? Didn't you tell him that?"

"No!"

"I'll put him on the stand," Murphy threatened.

"You did tell him that, didn't you? Didn't you?"

Then Beverly Kavanaugh's voice shot through the courtroom. It was high and shrill. "Leave her alone, Frank! Stop it!"

Joe Luce's gavel slammed down. Over it, Murphy could hear Brian Kavanaugh shout out, "You son of a bitch, Murphy!"

Luce banged down the gavel five times, rapidly and one after the other.

"I want order in this courtroom," he bellowed.

"I want my daughter left alone," Beverly cried out, her voice a virtual wail.

"Your Honor," Murphy said. "I'd like to suggest a brief recess in your chambers with both sides as well as Mr. and Mrs. Kavanaugh." He cast a glance at Brian Kavanaugh's red face and enraged expression. He added, "It might be a good idea to have a couple of the bailiffs there, too."

Joe Luce surveyed the situation. "Very well," he said. "Recess for fifteen minutes."

The gavel sounded, and in a few moments the group had gathered in the judge's chambers. Beverly was in tears, and Brian Kavanaugh was so furious he couldn't sit still. He was up and pacing. Fletcher Lake, naked without Toddman at his side, had nothing to say.

"Well?" Joe Luce said, settling behind his desk.

"Frank," Beverly said, her voice shaky, "Judy couldn't have done this. You know she couldn't have done it."

"Do I?" Murphy said. "She did take the van. She admitted it. She had motive and opportunity. And the kid is as unstable as hell, Bev. You know it, and I know it. The whole courtroom could see it. And she did tell

Barry that she'd considered murder to keep Brian from marrying Lynn. She did say that."

"She also said she'd considered suicide," Brian Kavanaugh responded angrily. "She said a lot of things. She's a confused kid, for Christ's sake. You're just using her to get Webster off. You're going to try to hang it on a confused kid to free your client."

"My obligation is to my client, Brian," Murphy said quietly. "That's my only obligation. And I'll do whatever is necessary to carry out my obligation to him."

"Even if it means smearing Judy?" Kavanaugh demanded.

Murphy nodded. "Even that. And I have a good many more questions to ask her once we go back out there. I can keep this going for a while."

Beverly shook her head. "You're reprehensible, Frank."

"I'm doing my job," Murphy said grimly.

Beverly Kavanaugh looked at him, saw the resolve in his eyes and dropped her own. Then, very softly, she said, "Well, you can let it go now. I killed Lynn. I'm the one who did it."

For a moment there was silence in the book-lined room. Fletcher Lake's face had gone ashen. He looked as though he was about to throw up. Then, very quietly, Murphy said, "Tell us about it, Bev."

She looked up and away from all of them, tears streaming down her cheeks in a torrent. "I . . . I drove out there to talk to Lynn. We were in the kitchen. I tried to tell her that her marrying Brian could drive Judy off the deep end. She didn't believe it. She didn't believe it or didn't care. I don't know which. We got into an

414

argument, and she said some horrible things, awful things. I . . . I don't know what happened to me. The knife was there on the counter. I just picked it up and . . . That's what happened. Then I dragged her body out to the car and locked it in the trunk. That's all. That's what happened. I didn't mean to hurt her. I didn't mean to. It just happened . . ."

She put her hands to her face and began to weep loudly.

Joe Luce turned to Fletcher Lake. "Fletcher," he said, "under the circumstances, it appears as though your office should consid—"

"Not so fast," Murphy snapped. "The only problem with all this is that Beverly's fingerprints weren't the ones Doc Weinberg found on the victim's wrists. In court out there, I'd never identified the person who owned those prints, but they weren't yours, Beverly. You know that."

She looked over at Murphy, makeup hopelessly smeared. "They couldn't have been Judy's," she whispered. "They couldn't have been."

"No," Murphy said. "They weren't. And those dopey suburban cops never dusted that van for prints, either. I took a shot at that one—just like I took a shot at putting her on the stand to see what everybody's reaction would be."

"You told the girl on the stand that the police had taken her prints from the van," Lake accused heatedly.

"I did not," Murphy said. "I framed the question in the hypothetical. I never said they had her prints from the van. I asked her what she would say if I told her they had her prints. And I never identified the person who had grasped Lynn Rice's wrists."

"Well," Joe Luce said, "who was it?"

Murphy turned his gaze to Brian Kavanaugh. "The prints on Lynn Rice's wrists were yours, Brian. Of course, you already knew that. You knew that because you're the one who murdered Lynn, dragged her out to the car and stuffed her in the trunk for Mike to drive her corpse to the shore for you. Tell me, what were you going to do with it once it got there? Were you going to bury her out in the Pine Barrens somewhere? Were you going to weigh her down and dump her into the bay? What was the plan, Brian?"

All eyes in the room focused on Brian Kavanaugh. His lips were a thin line. His gaze shifted from one face to the other. He said nothing. His silence was answer enough.

"Brian . . ." Beverly began, her voice a hushed whisper.

"You don't have to say anything, Brian," Murphy told him. "If I were your lawyer, I'd advise you to do just what you're doing, which is to keep quiet. The fact is, there are good excuses for your fingerprints on Lynn's wrists. You were lovers. You could have simply held her lightly by the wrists while you kissed her good-bye that afternoon. The fingerprints don't prove a thing from a legal standpoint."

Kavanaugh said nothing.

"Good," Murphy said. "Good plan. You don't have to say a word, and you'd be a dope if you did. Now, let me tell you what I'm going to do. I'm going back into that courtroom, and I'm going to put your daughter back on the stand. And I'm going to do the very best I can to beat her bloody. She's not wrapped too tight, and she's just a kid for starters. I might even get her so confused that she'll confess to it right on the stand. Wouldn't that be a sight? If nothing else, it would make the papers. And it certainly would get Mike off. No jury is going to convict somebody when another person confesses to the murder on the witness stand during the trial. How does that sound, Brian? Want to see that happen? I can arrange it. You just watch me."

For a long moment, Brian Kavanaugh maintained his silence. His eyes scanned the faces of them all: the tear-stained face of his estranged wife, the expressionless face of Joe Luce, the ghastly pale face of Fletcher Lake, the grimly set face of Frank Murphy. Then Brian Kavanaugh's chest heaved an enormous sigh. The sound issued from him like wind from a bellows. As the air left him, he seemed to shrink in size. He moved, almost staggered, over to the window of Joe Luce's chambers and looked out over the city. Philadelphia was enshrouded in a cloud of early summer haze that diffused the sunlight and gave the skyline the air of a Monet painting. He never looked at any of them, merely peered out at the rising spire of Liberty Place on West Market Street. He spoke in a dull monotone as the pale sun illuminated his face.

"It was your fault, Frank," he said. "After you left, I started thinking about what you'd said about Judy and how upset she was at the prospect of me and Lynn getting married. What got me, I think, was the image you conjured up of Judy hanging from a shower head. I remembered seeing that in that movie, what was it, *An Officer and a Gentleman?* I remembered how they'd made up that guy who'd hung himself. He was all pasty and white, hanging there naked. An image of Judy like that kept bouncing into my head. It scared the hell out of me. I started to talk to Lynn about it, but the conversation wasn't going anywhere. So I told her we'd go down to the shore to talk about it—someplace where we could relax, a change of scene. Then I went into town to do some paperwork and to think about it for a while. The more I thought about it, the more I was convinced that we ought to hold off. After a decision like that, I couldn't wait for another day or two to resolve it with her. So I drove back out to the farm to talk it over with Lynn. We were in the kitchen. It got pretty nasty."

Brian Kavanaugh threw back his head and took a deep breath. He was braced against the window frame with both arms extended out in front of him. He never looked at them. He never looked at any of them.

"I don't remember exactly how it happened," he said. "Lynn had a nasty temper. I think she came at me with the knife first, if you want the truth. I remember grabbing her wrists and throwing her back against the counter and just pulling the knife out of her hand. She was like a maniac. It was like she'd lost her mind. I remember thinking at that moment that the whole episode was like a revelation. I realized that marrying her was a nutty idea, that I'd never seen her act like this, and thank God I was getting a chance to see it before I tied myself to her for life. Then she came at me again, and all of a sudden she was backing away, and the knife was in her chest. Her eyes were bulging out. Then they rolled back in her head and she just went down with a thump. I looked at her. Her eyes were wide open. She was stone dead. I knew that. I just couldn't believe it."

Beverly said, "Brian . . ."

He turned to her. He smiled a rueful smile. Murphy

418

suspected that the man was a little bit off his rocker at that moment.

"I'm sorry, Bev," Brian Kavanaugh said. "I never meant for anything like this to happen. When we got married, I never figured I'd do anything but spend my whole life with you. Look at me. I'm forty-four years old. My net worth exceeds a million and a half bucks. I've got thirty employees at the brokerage. My old man, if he could see me now, he'd just about fall over. He never made more than a hundred and sixty bucks a week in his life. How did I screw it all up so badly, I wonder? That's all I could think about when I saw Lynn lying there dead. How the hell did I manage to screw it all up so much? My daughter is half nuts. My wife hates me. And the woman I thought was going to help me put it all back together was a vicious psycho and dead to boot. I just couldn't believe it.

"All I could think about was getting it all cleaned up, somehow. I was going to get rid of Lynn's body and make some excuse for where she had gone. Then I was going to try to get back with you, and maybe the two of us, somehow, could find a way to help Judy. I never wished Mike any harm. But when he got caught with Lynn's body in the trunk of the car, what the hell was I supposed to do? All I wanted out of this when I saw how bad it had gotten was to protect you and Judy. That's all I wanted."

"Why did you wipe down the knife hilt?" Murphy asked him.

Brian Kavanaugh shrugged. "I don't know. I guess I wasn't even aware that I did it. So I guess I just wiped it off in case somebody found Lynn's body before I got to get rid of it. There wasn't very much blood. That surprised me. I guess it was mostly internal bleeding. You'd have thought there would have been more blood, wouldn't you?"

Brian Kavanaugh continued to stare out the window, saying nothing. Murphy could only imagine what was going on in his mind. Whatever it might be, it wasn't Murphy's business.

"Fletcher?" Murphy said finally.

Fletcher Lake emerged as if from a trance. He gazed blankly at Murphy for a moment, then to Joe Luce.

"Your Honor," he said weakly, "the people move to drop charges against Michael Webster."

"Very well," Joe Luce said. "There is, however, the matter of jumping parole in California. We'll have to conduct a bail hearing for him on that charge, and then see what California wants to do about extradition."

"I'll represent him on that," Murphy said, back to business now. "But right now I've got to get out of here. I have other business now that won't wait."

"All right, Frank," Joe Luce said. "We can handle that ourselves, I think."

Murphy stood up. He looked over at Beverly, his throat throbbing at her agony. "Bev . . ." he began.

She looked up, her face ruined by tears and her expression hopelessly forlorn.

"It's all right, Frank," she said.

"No, it's not," Murphy said, "but some day it will be again. You know I did what I had to do. I didn't have any choice. Excuse me, Your Honor, but I really do have to get the hell out of here."

"So, go," Joe Luce said.

CHAPTER 38

A barricade, she thought.

It hung at windshield level in the fading sunlight across the perilous dirt road that snaked up the hillside from the lake. She studied it. It was a ridiculous contraption of quarter-inch steel cable strung between two trees and festooned with pots and pans and old cowbells. A noise machine, she decided. An alarm system.

Alex, peering through the Volvo's bug-specked windshield, saw at once the folly of trying to dismantle the barricade in silence. She would need a set of tools to unfasten the cable, then bolt cutters to sever it. And none of that could be performed in silence—even if she had the tools, which she didn't. By now, Alex was startlingly efficient with the tools of her trade. With standard tools, though, she had no skill, and she didn't carry them in her car. She didn't even have a lug wrench for her tires.

Alex had no idea how much farther she would have to go on foot if she abandoned the car here, had no idea what she might encounter farther along. Perhaps there were more alarms, more traps. She knew this, though. She knew that if she was going to have to go in on foot, she would await the cover of night, which would be along fairly soon. Playing in the darkened woods was not her idea of recreation, but wherever they had the witness would be lit after sundown. From the darkness of the woods, she could see where they were while they would have no idea where she might be—if, in fact, they even suspected that she might be out there. Then she smiled at the thought.

No, they might suspect someone. Surely, they would suspect that someone might be coming, sometime. But they would never suspect her. She could walk up to the door and knock on it. They could look at her and still they wouldn't suspect her. No one had ever suspected her, not until it was too late, which had turned out to be her greatest strength—the one Phil had never anticipated. He had been a naturally suspicious man, so he had suspected everyone—regardless of age, gender, or physical equipment. But most other people never suspected that a woman could do what she could do— would be willing to do it.

There were men bigger, stronger and at least as clever. But, for the most part, they tended to be less willing. Most men who were willing tended to be too easy to spot—too careless, too crazy. Alex was the perfect blend. They never suspected her—never suspected her willingness—not until it was too late.

Perhaps that was why they kept coming back to haunt her. Perhaps it was because they felt foolish and betrayed. It might even be because they couldn't quite believe they were really dead, that they had been overcome by such as her, and they kept hanging around to make sure it was really she who had done it. But it had been she, undisputedly. Alex had never missed. And she had never kept count, either. That might be bad luck.

Thinking such thoughts, Alex backed the Volvo carefully down the steep dirt road to the paved two-lane thoroughfare that ran along the lake. Down the lake road she had spotted a summer home, not yet open for the season but with an inviting driveway. She would leave the Volvo there and walk back, carrying the tools of her trade. Not knowing what she might encounter, she planned to come well equipped.

Then she would climb up the hillside through the woods, slowly and carefully, making as little noise as possible. She would take as much care and as much time as necessary. There were, she was sure, not more than a few men guarding the witness, whoever he might be. If there were more guarding the witness, they would have kept him someplace closer to the courtrooms in City Hall, and Murphy would not have had to run back and forth to this place on weekends to relieve whoever had the job during the week. That indicated only a few, although Alex had no way of knowing for sure how many. Also, she was aware, she had no way of knowing which of them might be the guards and which might be the guarded. Moreover, she didn't expect to have time to inquire. There was only one solution to that problem. She would simply have to kill whoever she happened to encounter.

Alex was willing to do that.

CHAPTER 39

"You act so nervous," Irving Berger said over Dan Rather's voice on the TV set. "Why so nervous? Nervous is bad for your blood pressure."

Wilder said nothing. He merely peered out the front window, off into the darkening shadows of the forest. Visibility was diminishing. The M-16 was nearby. He didn't respond to Berger's question. Berger was used to that. When Wilder got nervous, he also got silent. And Wilder had been nervous much of the afternoon. Berger didn't know why, and Wilder made no effort to enlighten him. Actually, while nervousness was Wilder's natural state while on such assignments, he was now tuned to a fine fever pitch because of Toddman's call a few hours before.

"Listen," Toddman had told him, "something might be going down."

"Like what?" Wilder had demanded.

"I don't know what. Murphy's been hinting around for a couple of weeks now that there was some kind of problem brewing, but he wouldn't tell me what the hell it was. All he'd say was that it was all cool, that he had things under control. I've tried to press him on it, but he wouldn't tell me what it was all about. You know what he's like, Jim. On something like this, he doesn't trust anybody. He doesn't tell anybody anything. Then, just a few minutes ago, he told me it wasn't cool anymore. We were in court, and there was no time to go into details, but I thought I'd let you know right away. It might not mean a goddamn thing, but I've alerted the state police to stay on top of things. I didn't tell them why, but they're ready if you need them. You got the phone number there?"

"I got it," Wilder said. "That bastard. He never told me anything was going on. Not a word. Where the fuck is he now?"

"In court, last time I looked. We've got a murder case going upstairs. Look, it might be nothing, Jim. I haven't had a chance to talk to him yet, and I won't unless there's a recess. I just wanted to get to you first. I want Berger healthy and talkative."

"You're making me nervous," Wilder told him, "and I don't know what about. What am I supposed to make out of all this?"

"I don't know," Toddman admitted, "but I thought I'd let you know what I know. If it turns out to be a false alarm, I'll give you a ring."

So Wilder had gone and found Berger, who had been sitting under an oak tree up the mountainside reading *Time*. He had hustled the old man into the house and waited for Toddman's second call. It had come sometime later, as the shadows from the forest had deepened.

"I can't find Murphy," Toddman said. "He won his

425

case and disappeared. He's not at his office, and there's no answer at his apartment. He's probably out drunk somewhere. He left Fletcher for dead this afternoon. You can imagine how he would have reacted to that."

"Look," Wilder said, "have I got a problem here or what?"

"I don't know. Probably not."

"I'm not going to sleep tonight," Wilder said. "I hope everybody's happy."

Berger seemed remarkably unconcerned. The weeks of isolation on this mountainside had left the old man mellow and uncharacteristically laid back. This had been the longest period of inactivity in his life, and it had been the first in which he had enjoyed the opportunity to wander through wooded groves of oak and birch and poplar and elm. He had grown to love the smell of the woods, the sound of the waves slapping the shoreline down below the main road, the sunlight glinting off the waves and up through the trees. Berger had his books, his TV set, his memories, more peace and solitude than he had ever experienced, and he had Wilder for companionship to boot, even though Wilder was periodically given to these bouts of nervousness in which he would peer out the window with his weaponry close at hand. Berger was beyond nervousness. He was even beyond fatalism. He had, for some time now, viewed himself as a dead man. He was doing what he could do, and maybe that would be enough to get Sophie's killer and maybe it wouldn't. What would happen would happen. It was out of Berger's hands now. It was in God's. Not that Berger had all that much faith in God's ability to avoid screwing this up, but what could he do? Irving Berger had done what he could do. Now he would relax.

That's what he was doing, feet up in front of the television set watching the Bill Cosby Show, when the alarm sounded. Wilder's bizarre contraption down on the road went off with a horrible racket. It was loud enough to startle even Irving Berger. He sat upright in his recliner. Wilder simply went for the M-16 and snapped at Berger, "On the floor, Irving. Lie down on your belly and don't move a muscle."

The darkness outside was nearly complete now, and Wilder, hunched over, moved quickly around the little camp director's cottage, turning off lights. From down the road, he heard a second sound—a loud, crunching sound of heavy machinery crashing suddenly through underbrush. The noise was startling, and then it abruptly departed. Wilder strained his ears. Nothing. He could hear nothing.

"Kill that TV," he told Berger. "That gives off too much light."

With all the lights off inside, the woods outside seemed somewhat brighter, but not so much that it made any great difference. Wilder cradled the M-16 in his arms and knelt beside the front window, peering outside carefully. The window was open slightly, and he could hear the evening breezes rustle through leaves in the treetops above the cottage. Wilder strained his ears. He was a city dweller, not a woodsman, but he had been a marine, and he had been trained for combat outdoors. He listened hard. Then, in a moment or two, he heard it, coming from the direction of the road. Yes, he could hear it, quite definitely.

Footsteps. He could hear footsteps.

Wilder's glands kicked in. Adrenaline shot into his

circulatory system. His stomach fluttered. His heart rate increased. He checked the magazine in the M-16. He flicked the weapon from safety to semiautomatic. He was careful not to move it by accident to the next notch, to fully automatic. He remembered a guy, some redneck kid, on the firing range at Parris Island who'd done that. The redneck had been firing from the standing position, taken a break, and forgotten to move the switch back to safety. Then, when he'd moved forward a few moments later to fire from the sitting position, he'd inadvertently turned the rifle to full automatic. So, instead of squeezing off one shot at a time, the kid had instead let go with a burst of eight shots that had caught him by surprise and driven the muzzle of the weapon straight up in the air, where it drove a line of slugs through the corrugated steel roof over the firing line. Trainees and DIs alike had scrambled for safety. Afterward, the DIs had just about killed the poor son of a bitch. Wilder was very careful never to go to automat—

What the hell was wrong with him? What a time to let his mind wander. Wilder cursed himself silently and peered down the barrel of the M-16, using the circular military sight to scan the woods in the direction of the footsteps, which were growing ever louder. Then, coming along the road, he saw a shadow, a shape. He laid the sight over the shadow with great care. Wilder's finger lightly stroked the M-16's trigger.

Then: "Jim? You there? Sugar Ray, for Christ's sake."

Wilder knew that voice. He moved his finger off the trigger, although he kept the rifle pointing in Murphy's general direction.

"At least you remembered the password, Frank," he called out. "Just what the hell do you think you're doing?"

"Turn on a light or something," Murphy called out. "I can't see a goddamn thing. I just about killed myself a minute ago."

Wilder turned to Berger, who was stretched out on the floor. "Irving, get a light on, will you?"

The old man got up heavily. "So much excitement," he muttered. "Who needs excitement?"

Wilder didn't see the blood until Murphy got to the door. It ran down the side of Murphy's face and stained his white shirt and the jacket of his glen plaid suit. Murphy was covered with dirt.

"What the hell happened to you?" Wilder demanded, setting aside the rifle. "Irving, get a wet cloth for him, okay?"

Wilder took Murphy's arm and directed him to a chair. The big man seemed slightly dazed and extremely angry.

"I forgot about your goddamn Rube Goldberg alarm system down there hung between two trees," Murphy said. "I just came barreling up the road in the dark and ran smack into it with the Toronado. The cable broke the windshield and shot glass all over me. So then I tried to back up, and I ended up backing right off the goddamn road, down the hillside. The car rolled over. I was hanging there upside down in the seat belt. I finally undid the goddamn thing and fell on the headliner of the car. Then I crawled out. The whole top of my Toronado is caved in like a safe fell on it. Just what I needed."

"You got a nasty cut up here near the hairline,"

Wilder said, examining the injury. "Irving, there's a first aid kit in the trunk of my car out there. Could you go out and get it for me?"

"Keys?" Irving Berger asked.

"In my tan jacket in the other room," Wilder said.

"How are you doing, Mr. Berger?" Murphy asked him.

"Better than you," Berger observed.

"I really liked that fucking car, too," Murphy said. "The insurance company is going to total it on me. I know those bastards'll do it. The book value isn't enough to cover the repairs."

"Hold still," Wilder told him, holding a wet dish towel to the wound. "You're bleeding like a pig."

"You know," Murphy said, "I had a fairly good day going until just a couple of minutes ago."

Berger went by them, keys jangling in one hand. Wilder said, "Toddman called me this afternoon. What did you mean when you told him it's not cool anymore?"

"Long story," Murphy said. "Look, I think it's time we got him the hell out of here. The trial starts next week. I went out this afternoon and got us a safe house in West Philly. I stocked it with food. It's a good place—bars on the windows and stuff, big bolt on the back door. I came up to get you guys and lead you right to the place."

"Why? What's been going on?"

Murphy felt at his wound with his fingers. It hurt like hell.

"I got involved with this woman," he said. "She moved into the other apartment on my floor. A real show-stopper, Jim. Really gorgeous. She tells me she's an actress from New York, and she's in town to watch her aunt's apartment while her aunt is out of the country. And guess what? She finds me irresistible, likes everything about me. She thinks I'm the cleverest human being she ever came across."

"She's got to be either a psycho or a plant," Wilder said.

"Thanks, asshole," Murphy said, and his irritation was genuine. "But that's how I started to figure it, too—after a while, anyway. I mean, there just isn't a woman on earth as perfect as this one seemed to be. There isn't one for me, anyway. So first I checked her with Actor's Equity in New York. They'd never heard of her. After that, just to play it safe, I had Profumo run a check on her prints. You remember Profumo?"

"The globe-trotting Italian midget from Trenton? That the guy?"

"Yeah."

"And what did he come up with?" Wilder demanded, dabbing with a wet paper towel at Murphy's rather nasty cut.

"She's on file in Washington. Her real name turns out to be Alma Pale. She's from some little burg out in Minnesota. She had two convictions in Manhattan for prostitution a long time back. That's all that was on record, but the only thing she hadn't lied to me about was her age."

"Why didn't you tell me or Toddman?" Wilder demanded.

"Tell you what? Tell you I had a new girlfriend and I'd found out she had a background she lied to me about? Big deal. It made more sense just to keep an eye on her. Then, today—during that murder trial I had going—she just split. She said she had to go back to New York for an acting job. It might be something; it might be nothing. But I don't like it. I think we ought to move him right away."

Wilder frowned. "Is there any way she could know about this place?"

"I don't think so. On the other hand, I wasn't all that careful around her at first. There didn't seem to be any reason to figure her in any of this."

Wilder's expression was grim. "I hope you didn't screw this up, Frank."

Murphy's head was killing him. He said, "I hope not, too. I hope—"

And that's when Irving Berger cried out from the darkness outside the camp director's cottage.

CHAPTER 40

After he plunged out of the cottage—and after his
eyes adjusted to the inky night—the first thing Wilder
saw was Berger, stretched out on the ground next to the
unmarked prowl car.

Berger was dead, Wilder knew.

The detective let loose a low, snarling sound, barely
human. Of all the things he hadn't wanted to foul up.
He took a step forward from the doorway, sensing
Murphy's presence behind him.

"Is he . . ." Murphy began.

But before the question could be finished, the old
man was moving, hands crawling up the car door,
scrambling to his feet, his face a sallow beacon in the
darkness. Wilder held the M-16 in one hand and
clutched firmly with the other one at Berger's upper
arm. Wilder's fingers dug into the old man's flesh as the
detective dragged him roughly away from the car and
toward the cottage. Murphy was there with them,
bleeding again and not much help, more or less
staggering along beside them, now bending over

suddenly, now coming up erect. He said, "What was it, Irving?"

Berger's voice was shaky. "A lady. I was leaning into the trunk. This lady, she came around the car. She poked something at me. I thought she was a dream for a minute. What's a lady doing out here?"

"What did she do?" Murphy demanded as they got him inside. Wilder dropped the old man into the recliner and killed every light in the place once again, moving around the enclosed space in a frenzy, his mouth working as he swore silently to himself. Murphy had seen Wilder furious before. In situations like this, it was a sight that always reassured him.

"She poked something at me," Berger gasped. "I . . . I grabbed at it. I knocked it away. It was a spear, I think. She startled me, coming out of the dark that way."

Murphy held it up for them to see. "I found this on the ground. Was it this she tried to spear you with?"

Wilder eyed the object. "An umbrella?"

"I don't know," Irving Berger said. "Could be. I didn't see so clear. I just hit it away and tried to run, but I fell down. Where is she?"

"There was nobody there when I got to you," Wilder said.

"Turn on a light for me, Jim," Murphy instructed.

"No way. If somebody's out there, I don't want a light on. That's probably why I didn't see whoever it was when I went out, because I'd been in here with the light in my eyes."

Murphy sat down heavily on the floor. He moved on his behind, shifting sideways like a crab, to the wall a few feet away and beneath the window. Then he lit his

434

Bic lighter, which blazed like a blowtorch in the shadows. It gave Murphy's bloody face an eerie cast.

"Look at this thing," he said.

Wilder got down and slid like a black cloud across the floor. "You lie down, Irving," he said. "What, Frank?"

"Look at the end of this thing."

"What the hell is that?"

"It's some kind of needle," Murphy said. He slapped at Wilder's inquisitive hand. "Don't touch it, for Christ's sake. Look at this thing. It's spring mounted."

"She was trying to kill somebody with an umbrella?" Wilder demanded.

"I'll put money on it that there's a one real hummer of a poison in this," Murphy said. "Jesus Christ, think about it. If she'd stuck him with it and it's something fast-acting, we'd never even have known anybody was out there. Irving wouldn't have come back, and we'd have gone out to find him dead on the ground next to the car. There'd have been no marks on him, no blood. We'd probably have figured he'd had a heart attack or something. We wouldn't even have gone looking out there for anybody."

"Turn out the lighter," Wilder said. "Those thing'll blow up in your face. Haven't you read the papers about those plastic lighters?"

Murphy killed the flame and dropped the lighter into his shirt pocket, next to the Camels, one of which he wouldn't have minded having at that precise moment. "Oh?" he said. "Are we going to hold a little seminar on consumer affairs right now? How do you feel about those Audi Five Thousands always locking in drive? This is a terrific time to discuss that, isn't it, Jimmy?"

"Stuff it," Wilder spat out. "Look, she's out there, and she might not be out there by herself. We're like fish in a barrel in here. I'm going out after them."

"You can't see shit out there," Murphy pointed out.

"I can see what they can see, and I've got an automatic weapon. If I even hear a twig snap, I'm going to spray the woods with M-16 fire. You don't need spotlights to do that. Are you carrying?"

"No," Murphy said. "I didn't bring anything with me. Who knew?"

"From the look of things," Wilder said, "you should have. Irving, do me a favor. You go into the bedroom and come back with the shotgun and my service revolver. Stay low, okay?"

"Got it," Berger said, and crawled off in the darkness.

"Stay with him," Wilder told Murphy. "Before I come back in, you'll hear me say 'Sugar Ray.' If somebody comes in that door without saying that first, let go in their direction, you dig?"

"Fine," Murphy said as Berger returned with the weaponry. Murphy propped the shotgun up beside him against the wall and took the revolver in his right hand. The black plastic grip felt slippery in his palm.

"Jim," he said quietly. "I really did figure I had it under control. If she could put it together and end up here, she's got to be pretty good. That umbrella thing, she's a pro. You watch your buns out there."

Wilder's teeth flashed in the darkness. It might have been a smile. "I may not be the toughest dude in the world," he said, "but I never met even one woman whose ass I couldn't kick if it came to that."

"Then you and I've met some different women,"

Murphy told him. "I'm serious. Be cool, now."

Then Wilder was gone.

Murphy and Berger sat in the darkness, listening to one another breathe. Murphy clutched at the pistol grip. It was a perfect match to the one he had in the lower right-hand drawer of his rolltop desk at home, the service revolver he'd neglected to turn in when he'd retired from the force. He had always scored well with it on the pistol range, but on the only occasion he'd fired the gun at another human being he'd managed to miss by six feet and blow out the windshield of a Mercedes-Benz. That mistake had cost him a broken collarbone and assorted other injuries. The memory was a vivid one. He was bleeding even more tonight than he had on that night. He wondered idly if he'd managed to give himself a concussion when he'd rolled over the Toronado. He was going to miss that car, rusty fenders and all.

"You hear anything outside?" Irving Berger whispered.

Murphy listened. "No."

"Do you think Jim is all right?" the old man asked.

"He's the last guy you need to worry about," Murphy said in what he hoped was a reassuring tone. "Wilder's the toughest little son of a bitch you ever saw. And he's got a gun you could stop an elephant with. Did you ever see an M-16 in action, Irving?"

"No." The old man's voice sounded strained. Little wonder, Murphy thought.

"It fires a small slug," Murphy told him, keeping his voice low. "The slug isn't much bigger than a twenty-two. But it hits with serious velocity. You hit a guy in the foot and it's even money that the shock of the impact will kill him. That rifle's a pisser."

"A what?" Irving Berger said.

"A pisser," Murphy said. "That means something good, Irving. How are you doing, by the way?"

"All right," the old man said. "I was frightened ou there, you know. Who would have guessed that I coul be frightened after all this?"

"It's nothing to be ashamed of. She caught you when you weren't ready for it. That kind of fear is a reflex."

"Reflex?" Irving Berger said. "Yes, I suppose, if hadn't gotten scared I might not have run. So that' good."

"I'd say that's good," Murphy told him.

"Still, who would have guessed that I could be frightened. I felt no fear all through this. I keep thinking death holds no terror for me, and yet I felt fear when it came close. And I didn't even know it wa death. I didn't know what it was. Just a lady, I thought Why a lady, Mr. Murphy? Why would they send a lady after me? So strange."

"They sent a woman because they knew we'd b slower to suspect her. They were right, too. Men are foolish about women, Irving. They can be as warped a we are, and yet it always surprises us when they turn out that way."

"What will you do with this lady if you catch her?" Berger asked.

"Take her in—if she'll let us."

"Sssshh!" Irving Berger said. "I heard something."

Murphy strained his ears. He heard the wind in th trees. The wind was kicking up, and it made the leave sing. He listened hard. He heard nothing else. All hi senses were alert, though—even those he couldn'

438

describe. Those were the ones he'd always valued most.

"Is she still out there, do you think?" Berger asked.

"We're not going to take any chances on that," Murphy told him, "but my guess is no. She probably thinks she got you already and took off. If not, she's got to realize that she blew her chance. Jimmy'll be back in a few minutes, and we can make ourselves scarce when he gets here."

Murphy could sense Irving Berger's relief in the darkness. He couldn't see the old man, and nothing audible came from him to convey that message. Still, it came to Murphy in the air, as so many revelations had come to him over the years. It was nothing more than Murphy's instinct that told him that Irving Berger's tension was departing.

And it was nothing more than Murphy's instinct that prompted his own tension level to rise as he spoke. Had Berger been listening closely, he would have heard more than Murphy's reassuring words. He would have heard Murphy uttering them just a bit more loudly than necessary. Murphy had done that not because he had heard or sensed anything concrete but because his instinct had told him to. And, as the knob on the door leading outside began to turn with agonizing slowness, Murphy's instinct gave him other instructions. Those instructions were—

—to make a sudden grab at the shotgun propped up against the wall beside him, to pump a shell into the chamber, to roll to his knees into the darkened middle of the room and unleash a single, deafening blast through the thin, plywood door that led to the tiny covered porch outside.

The flash of the shotgun blast was a million dance

points of light burning into the back walls of Murphy's eyes, containing all the colors of the rainbow illuminating the small room for the briefest moment like the glare of a spotlight. The sound in that enclosed space was a thunderclap, a momentous assault on the eardrums that struck both men like a blow. Murphy could feel the heat, the wave of sheer force, of the twelve-gauge as it erupted in his hands. The surge of power it gave him was godlike in its dimension. The shot sprayed out, leaving countless little holes in the plywood summer door.

Then there was only silence—the hushed silence of the void. It lingered for what seemed like an eternity before Irving Berger could muster speech.

"My God!" he gasped from the floor.

Murphy knelt unmoving with the shotgun clutched in his hands, his senses awed by the force of its ejaculation. His arms quivered from it. And, from outside—in the all-consuming silence that followed— he discerned a faint sound.

It was a low, whining moan, delivered in a voice he had heard so recently cry out similarly in passion, a brief exhaust of air through vocal cords that would never leave his memory. The sounds of agony and pleasure mixed in his consciousness, and he felt rather than heard a similar cry issue from his own lips. He dropped the shotgun to the floor. It clattered hollowly on the dry boards. Then Murphy scrambled awkwardly, dizzily to his feet and threw open the ruined door. He plunged out blindly into the blackness.

"Alex!" he cried out.

She was at his feet, a crumpled shadow in the dirt just off the porch. His hands went to her face, came away

440

wet. He leaned over the form below him, a horror at what he had done crawling up within him, from his vitals to his brain. His hand touched hers. He felt the Beretta beneath her fingers, cold and insignificant. It counted for nothing.

"Alex," Murphy whispered.

Her voice was weak but clear. It came out as a gurgle, a liquid melody that hung in his ears. It was not at all accusing, which surprised him. It almost seemed to be tinged with . . . what could he call it? Gratitude?

"I promise, Frank," Alex got out. "I won't come back to haunt you."

Murphy wondered what she could possibly have meant by that.

CHAPTER 41

He dozed.

He never would have thought it possible, given the circumstances. But Irving Berger was an old man. He had slept badly the night before in the shabby house in West Philadelphia where Murphy and Wilder had guarded him. Besides, he had nodded off with disturbing ease in recent years. It was almost as though his consciousness was fading from him, along with his vitality, the fire that flickered ever lower in the furnace of his being. It was aging, he knew—part of slipping away as the world grew colder and more strange.

Murphy, sitting on the worn leather sofa in Toddman's City Hall office, saw the old man's head nod, heard the stifled snore. For a brief moment Murphy felt a thrill of fear shoot through him. Not now, he thought. Not after all this.

And then the fear passed. The old man had merely fallen asleep sitting upright in one of Toddman's profoundly uncomfortable office chairs. Murphy watched him. Berger's lined face was peaceful. After a while, Murphy stood up and went into the outer office. He lit a Camel just as Wilder—fresh from the Lucelli trial a floor below them—walked back in the door. The flesh around his right eye swelled out to the size of a tangerine.

"That hasn't gone down a bit," Murphy told him. "You really look like shit, Jim."

Wilder frowned. "You don't look so fucking terrific yourself, asshole—even without the head wound."

Murphy touched the Band-Aid over his left eye. He smiled ruefully. "I thought this gave me a kind of Gerry Cooney look," he said.

Wilder merely frowned. Murphy figured that—given what he'd done to himself—Wilder would probably be pissed off until sometime around the turn of the century.

"Irving still okay in there?" Wilder asked.

"Fine. He fell asleep. Can you believe that? He's going to testify in ten minutes, and he's nodded off. That old man is a fairly cool character."

Wilder's expression was grim. "Yeah, he's all right. What's Toddman got cooked up for him when he finishes? I mean, how's he going to keep Irving from getting iced?"

Murphy shook his head. "I don't know. And I don't want to. My guess is that they'll give him a new driver's license under a phony name and ship him out to California or down to Florida with the help of the feds. Arizona, maybe. Who knows? I do know that Toddman was making the financial arrangements to have his home and business sold, so I imagine he'll go wherever he's going to go with enough cash to live comfortably enough."

"He don't care about that, you know," Wilder said. "All he cares about is this thing today—getting his licks in at Lucelli."

Murphy glanced at his watch. "He ought to get his chance pretty soon. Toddman told me to have him here by eleven. It's after that now. How's it going downstairs?"

Wilder shrugged. "Okay. Paul's just gone through the reports and had the investigating officers testify. He's got Doc on the stand now, talking about the wounds on all the victims. Quick Silver is just sitting there next to Tommy, looking like he just swallowed some of somebody else's vomit."

Wilder walked to the door of Toddman's inner office and glanced in. Berger was snoring peacefully. Wilder closed the door quietly and said, "If I ever live to be that old, I hope I've got the balls that old dude has."

"Did you see Mary Ellen or Patricia out there?"

Wilder shook his head. Murphy muttered a weary curse and slipped behind Toddman's secretary's desk, which was empty. She was down in the courtroom watching her boss do his stuff. Murphy punched nine to get out, then called his former home in Mount Airy.

"Hello," Mary Ellen said.

"Are you coming or not?" Murphy demanded. "Patricia said she wanted to see this."

"She's fiddling with her hair, Frank," Mary Ellen told him. "I've got the car running out in the driveway."

"Do me a favor, Mary Ellen? Would you go up there and light a fire under her? If that kid wants to see Berger testify, she's going to have to get her butt in gear."

"I'll see what I can do," Mary Ellen said. "I just hope

the wagon holds up on the way down. It's been acting funny lately."

"I've got my own problems there," Murphy told her. "I'm driving a rented Ford Escort. I'm going to have to buy something to replace the Toronado when I get a chance. I promise you, it won't be a Ford Escort. What a piece of shit that thing is."

"I could use a new car, too," Mary Ellen told him. "The wagon has about had it."

"Really?" Murphy said, immediately feeling pressure in the neighborhood of his wallet. "Well, that's just terrific timing on that one, Mary Ellen."

"Sorry, but it's true. Half the time it won't even start anymore."

"Talk to me about it another time," Murphy said, visibly annoyed.

"How's the head?" Mary Ellen said. "Still hurt?"

"Not bad," Murphy said, glancing up at Wilder. "Jimmy got hurt worse than I did. When he heard the shotgun go off in the cottage, he was way the hell out in the woods. He started to run back to the place and ran smack into a tree limb. His eye looks like it has a goiter."

Wilder gave Murphy the finger.

Mary Ellen said, "How about . . . the rest of it? Are you all right?"

"Fine," he lied to her. Then, to change the subject, he said, "I'm in better shape than my neighbor, anyway. You know, Mrs. Fronczek? She's probably at the bottom of the river right now, chained to an old cigarette machine. Toddman's talking about trying Tommy for murder two on that one after he gets this case out of the way."

"Even without a corpse?" Mary Ellen asked. "Isn't that pretty difficult?"

"It's been done a couple of times during the past thirty years or so, ever since some prosecutor got a guy in California for killing his wife and they couldn't find anything but her dentures. Toddman really wants Lucelli bad. He'd like to get him on four life terms instead of just three. He can be a vindictive bastard when he's got a real bad guy he's dealing with. Listen, can you get her moving? I promise you she's going to miss this."

"Patricia! " Mary Ellen called out. "Let's move it! Now!"

"That ought to do it," Murphy said, switching ears with the phone and rubbing the one that had just been numbed.

"You know, Frank," Mary Ellen said over the phone, "if I'd met her, I probably could have told you she was a phony right from the start."

Murphy said nothing. Mary Ellen listened to his silence, knowing that he could say nothing because of Wilder's presence, knowing, too, what his silence meant. It told her that Frank Murphy loved her above all else, that without her his capacity for making a fool of himself with other women was virtually unlimited. Of course, she had known all that already.

Just as she knew he would end up buying her the new car.

"I've got to go now," Murphy said hoarsely.

"We'll get there as soon as we can."

"Fine," Murphy said, and hung up. "They're going to miss it," he told Wilder. "I knew they couldn't get here on time."

"What time is it?" Wilder asked.

Murphy glanced at his watch. "Eleven thirty-four. Toddman better—"

The door from the hallway opened. A fuzzy-cheeked assistant district attorney stuck his head in. "Mr. Toddman's ready for you now. We'll take the witness in through the judge's chambers."

Wilder stood. "I'll get him."

He went into Toddman's inner office and gently shook Irving Berger. The old man's eyes flickered open.

"Wh-what?" he said.

"It's time, Irving," Wilder said.

Berger looked up blankly at the detective for a moment. Then full wakefulness came to him. "Yes," he said. "Good."

Wilder helped the old man to his feet. Berger was dressed in a blue, double-breasted suit with wide lapels and thick cuffs on the trousers.

"I didn't notice that suit when you put it on this morning," Wilder said. "Sharp looking."

Berger looked down at himself, smoothed the lapels with liver-spotted hands. "It's old," he said softly. "I wore this suit when I married Sophie. It still fits. I thought it was a good suit to wear on this day." Irving Berger looked up at Wilder. Then he stood up straight in his forty-year-old suit. "So," he said. "So take me to where I can be a *tzaddik*."

Wilder took the old man's arm.

"The suit looks great on you, Irving," he said.

THE ULTIMATE IN SPINE-TINGLING TERROR
FROM ZEBRA BOOKS!

TOY CEMETERY (2228, $3.95)
by William W. Johnstone

A young man is the inheritor of a magnificent doll collection. But an ancient, unspeakable evil lurks behind the vacant eyes and painted-on smiles of his deadly toys!

SMOKE (2255, $3.95)
by Ruby Jean Jensen

Seven-year-old Ellen was sure it was Aladdin's lamp that she had found at the local garage sale. And no power on earth would be able to stop the hideous terror unleashed when she rubbed the magic lamp to make the genie appear!

WITCH CHILD (2230, $3.95)
by Elizabeth Lloyd

The gruesome spectacle of Goody Glover's witch trial and hanging haunted the dreams of young Rachel Gray. But the dawn brought Rachel no relief when the terrified girl discovered that her innocent soul had been taken over by the malevolent sorceress' vengeful spirit!

HORROR MANSION (2210, $3.95)
by J.N. Williamson

It was a deadly roller coaster ride through a carnival of terror when a group of unsuspecting souls crossed the threshold into the old Minnifield place. For all those who entered its grisly chamber of horrors would never again be allowed to leave—not even in death!

NIGHT WHISPER (2092, $3.95)
by Patricia Wallace

Twenty-six years have passed since Paige Brown lost her parents in the bizarre Tranquility Murders. Now Paige has returned to her home town to discover that the bloody nightmare is far from over . . . it has only just begun!

SLEEP TIGHT (2121, $3.95)
by Matthew J. Costello

A rash of mysterious disappearances terrorized the citizens of Harley, New York. But the worst was yet to come. For the Tall Man had entered young Noah's dreams—to steal the little boy's soul and feed on his innocence!